Calvin said, "How often have you dreamed SO-AWM-275

"Every night, Dr. Calvin, since I have become aware of my existence."

"Ten nights," interposed Linda, anxiously, "but Elvex only told me of it this morning."

"Why only this morning, Elvex?"

"It was not until this morning, Dr. Calvin, that I was convinced that I was dreaming. Till then, I had thought there was a flaw in my positronic brain pattern, but I could not find one. Finally, I decided it was a dream."

"And what did you dream?"

"I dream always very much the same dream, Dr. Calvin. Little details are different, but always it seems to me that I see a large panorama in which robots are working."

"Robots, Elvex? And human beings also?"

"I see no human beings in the dream, Dr. Calvin . . ."

—from *Robot Dreams*

ISAAC ASIMOV

Robot Dreams

MASTERWORKS OF SCIENCE FICTION AND FANTASY

ILLUSTRATED BY RALPH McQUARRIE

A BYRON PREISS VISUAL PUBLICATIONS, INC., BOOK

ACE BOOKS, NEW YORK

An Ace Book
Published by The Berkley Publishing Group
A division of Penguin Group (USA) Inc.
375 Hudson Street
New York, New York 10014

ROBOT DREAMS

PRINTING HISTORY
Berkley trade paperback edition / November 1986
First Ace trade paperback edition / April 1987
Ace mass market edition / June 1990
Second Ace trade paperback edition / June 2004

Second Ace trade paperback edition ISBN: 0-441-01183-7

This title has been registered with the Library of Congress.

PRINTED IN THE UNITED STATES OF AMERICA

10 9 8 7 6 5 4 3 2 1

To Byron Preiss,
who made me do it.

Contents

Introduction   ix

Little Lost Robot   1

Robot Dreams   25

"Breeds There a Man . . . ?"   31

Hostess   63

Sally   98

Strikebreaker   114

The Machine That Won the War   127

Eyes Do More Than See   133

The Martian Way   137

Franchise   177

Jokester   191

The Last Question   204

Does a Bee Care?   215

Light Verse   220

The Feeling of Power   225

Spell My Name With an *S*   235

The Ugly Little Boy   248

The Billiard Ball   283

True Love   299

The Last Answer   303

Lest We Remember   309

Introduction

Science fiction has certain satisfactions peculiar to itself. It is possible, in trying to portray future technology, to hit close to home. If you live long enough after writing a particular story, you may actually have the pleasure of finding your predictions reasonably accurate and yourself hailed as a sort of minor prophet.

This has happened to me in connection with my robot stories, of which "Light Verse" (included here) is an example.

I began writing robot stories in 1939, when I was nineteen years old, and, from the first, I visualized them as machines, carefully built by engineers, with inherent safeguards, which I called "The Three Laws of Robotics." (In doing so, I was the very first to use the word "robotics" in print, this taking place in the March, 1942 issue of *Astounding Science Fiction*.)

As it happened, robots of any kind were not really practical until the mid-1970s when the microchip came into use. Only that made it possible to produce computers that were small enough and cheap enough, while possessing the potentiality for sufficient capacity and versatility, to control a robot at nonprohibitive expense.

We now have machines, called robots, that are computer-controlled and are in industrial use. They increasingly perform simple and repetitive work on the assembly lines—welding, drilling, polishing and so on—and they are of increasing importance to the economy. Robots are now a recognized field of study and the precise word that I invented is used for it—robotics.

To be sure, we are only at the very beginning of the robotic revolution. The robots now in use are little more than computerized levers and are very far from having the complexity necessary for the Three Laws to be built into them. Nor are they anything close to human in shape, so they are not yet the "mechanical men" that I have pictured in my stories, and that have appeared on the screen innumerable times.

Nevertheless, the direction of movement is clear. The primitive robots that have come into use are not the Frankenstein-monsters of equally primitive science fiction. They do not lust for human life (although accidents involving robots can result in human death, just as accidents with automobiles or electrical machinery can). They are, rather, carefully designed devices intended to relieve human beings of arduous, repetitive, dangerous, nonrewarding duties so that, in intent and in philosophy, they represent the first steps toward my story-robots.

The steps that are yet to come are expected to proceed further in the direction I have marked out. A number of different firms are working on "home robots" that will have a vaguely human appearance and will fulfill some of the duties that once devolved on servants.

The result of all this is that I am held in considerable regard by those working in the field of robotics. In 1985, a fat encyclopedic volume entitled *Handbook of Industrial Robotics* (edited by Shimon Y. Nof and published by John Wiley) appeared, and, on request of the editor, I supplied it with an introduction.

Of course, in order to appreciate the accuracy of my predictions, I had to be fortunate enough to be a survivor. My first robots appeared in 1939, as I say, and I had to live for over forty more years in order to discover I was a prophet. Because I had begun at a very early age, and because I was fortunate, I managed to do this and words cannot tell you how grateful I am for that.

Actually, I carried on my predictions of the future of robotics to the very end, to the ultimate moment, in my story "The Last Question," published in 1957. I have a sneaking suspicion that, if the human race survives, we may continue to progress in that direction in some ways anyway. Still, survival is limited at the best, and I have no chance of seeing very much more of the future course of technology. I will have to content myself with having future generations witness and (I hope) applaud what triumphs of this sort I may gain. I, myself, won't.

Nor are robots the only area in which my crystal ball was clear. In my story "The Martian Way," published in 1952, I described a space walk quite accurately, although an actual feat of this sort didn't take place till fifteen years afterward. Foreseeing space walks was not a very daring piece of prescience, I admit, for, given spaceships, such things would be inevitable. However, I also described the psychological effects and thought of one that was rather unusual—particularly for me.

I am, you see, a pronounced acrophobe with an absolute terror of heights and know perfectly well that I will never voluntarily go on a spaceship. If, however, I were somehow forced on one, I know, too, that I would never dare leave it for a space walk. Nevertheless, I put personal fear to one side and imagined the space walk to produce euphoria. I had my space travelers quarrel over whose turn it was to get out into space and drift in quiet peace among the stars. And when space walks became fact, such euphoria *was* felt.

In my story, "The Feeling of Power," published in 1957, I made use of pocket computers, about a decade before the real thing came along, I even considered the possibility that such computers might seriously decrease the ability of people to do arithmetic in the old-fashioned way, and that is a real concern of educators now.

As a final example, in my story "Sally," published in 1953, I described computerized cars that had almost reached the stage of having lives of their own. And, in the last few years, we do indeed have computerized cars that can actually talk to the driver—although their abilities in this direction are, as yet, very simple.

Yet, if there is the possibility of this satisfaction from accurate prophecy in science fiction, there is also the reverse. Science fiction offers its writers chances of embarrassment that no other form of fiction does.

After all, if we may prove accurate in our predictions, we may prove inaccurate as well, sometimes ludicrously so.

Such embarrassment becomes particularly acute when one's stories are reprinted in a collection such as this one. When an author starts young, lives out a normal lifetime (as I seem to be doing) and has written continuously, there is likely to be included in the collection stories that were written and published thirty and forty years before and that leave ample scope for any cloudiness in the crystal ball to show up.

This doesn't happen to me as often as it might, for I have several things going for me. In the first place, I am well acquainted with science and am not likely to be wrong in fundamentals. Secondly, I am cautious in my predictions and do not flail away madly in contravention of scientific principles.

Nevertheless, science does advance and sometimes produces completely unexpected results in a very few years, and this may leave a writer (even me) high and dry on a pinnacle of false "facts." The worst luck I had in this respect turned up in connection with a series of science fiction novels I wrote for youngsters between 1952 and 1958.

That series dealt with the continuing adventures of my heroes on various planets of the solar system, and in each case, I carefully described the planets in strict accordance with what was known about them at the time.

Unfortunately, it was in the course of those very years that microwave astronomy was developed and shortly after those years that rocket probes began to be sent out. The result was that our knowledge of the solar system was startlingly advanced and we learned something new and unexpected about every single planet.

For instance, in my description of Mercury in *Lucky Starr and the Big Sun of Mercury*, I had it facing one side to the Sun, as astronomers then thought—and that was essential to the plot. As it happens, however, we now know that Mercury turns slowly and that every portion of its surface gets sunlight part of the time. There is no "dark side."

In my description of Venus in *Lucky Starr and the Oceans of Venus*, I had a planetwide ocean, which, at that time, seemed at least possible. It was essential to the plot as well. However, we now know that the surface of Venus is at a temperature far above the boiling point of water, and an ocean—or even a *drop*—of liquid water on its surface is totally impossible.

As for Mars, in my book *David Starr: Space Ranger*, I managed to get the description right in many ways. However, I didn't take advantage of the huge extinct Martian volcanoes that were discovered about fifteen years after the book was published. What's more, I did talk about the canals (dry ones), which were found to be nonexistent, and I introduced intelligent Martians remaining from a long-dead surface civilization, and this is really extremely unlikely.

Jupiter and its satellites appeared in *Lucky Starr and the Moons of Jupiter*, and while I was careful to describe all the worlds, I naturally missed some major points that were not discovered till twenty years afterward. I said nothing of the cracked world-girdling glacier of Europa and nothing of Io's active volcanoes. I didn't mention Jupiter's huge magnetic field. Nor, in *Lucky Starr and the Rings of Saturn*, did I mention some of the interesting features of the Saturnian satellite system and rings.

The only book in the series that survived intact (scientifically speaking) was *Lucky Starr and the Pirates of the Asteroids*.

Fortunately, there was a way out. Honesty is the best policy and when the Lucky Starr series was reprinted in the 1970s, I insisted on inserting introductory notes explaining where the astronomical details had become outdated. At first, the publishers were a little reluctant to do so, but I explained that I could not allow the young reader to be misled, or, if he were knowledgeable, to have him think that *I* was not. In went the notes, and, I am glad to say, sales were not adversely affected.

None of the stories in this collection was as badly shattered as my poor Lucky Starr books were, but there are things to beware of.

In the first place, there is one place where I missed something that was (in hindsight) very obvious, and I have been kicking myself over it for the last couple of years.

In "The Martian Way," the same story in which I triumphed with my description of the spacewalk, I had my heroes approach Saturn and actually enter the ring system. In doing so I very carefully described the rings, making use of observations from Earth's surface to do so.

Now, from Earth's surface, some 800 million miles from Saturn, we see the rings as solid and unbroken except for the black line of the Cassini division that seems to separate them into two rings. The portion of the rings closest to Saturn is considerably dimmer than the rest of the ring system, and that portion is usually considered a third ring (the so-called "crepe ring.") And that was how I described the rings as seen by my space-travelers in the story.

Yet it stands to reason (at least, *now* it stands to reason) that if we could see the ring system from a nearer distance, we would see greater detail. We would see divisions—places where fewer particles were in orbit so that we would see dimmer lines separating brighter lines—divisions that would simply not be seen at great distances. Earth's surface telescopes would just blur them out and record only the thickest of the dim lines—the Cassini division.

The closer we would get, the more numerous and the thinner the bright lines would get as visibility became clearer and clearer, until, when we were as close as we could get and still see all the rings, the rings would look like a grooved record—which is what they *do* look like.

Suppose I had figured this out in 1952 and had described the rings in that fashion. Even if I had missed such things as shadowy "spokes" in the ring, and "braided" rings, things that were absolutely unpredictable, it would have been great if I had imagined the fine divisions. That was an easy deduction to make and if I had described the rings in that fashion then, as soon as those rings had been probed I would have announced that I had anticipated what they had discovered. (You think that modesty would have held me back? Don't be an idiot!)

How great that would have been!

As it is, my failure to see this marks me down as not very bright, and that is there, for all to see, in "The Martian Way." To be sure, no astronomer saw the truth about the rings in 1952, but what of that? An astronomer is only an astronomer and his vision is naturally limited. I am a *science fiction writer* and more is expected of me.

Then, too, sometimes when I saw accurately, or when I saw something that might well prove to be accurate some day, then I generally placed it far too far into the future. I admit I got the robots correct, for my earliest stories indicated that they got their start in the 1980s and 1990s, which is not bad at all.

However, what of the computerized cars in "Sally" and of the pocket computers in "The Feeling of Power"? I was careful not to give the exact dates of discovery of these advances. (I may be dumb, but I'm not *that* dumb.) Still, there's no doubt as we read the stories that they are discoveries of the far future—yet they're here *now* and I have lived to see them, and be embarrassed over my lack of confidence in the human mind and human ingenuity.

"Breeds There a Man . . . ?" deals, in part, with the development of an advance against the nuclear bomb. It was published in 1951 and, although I don't date it, the impression it gives is that its events take place in the near future, perhaps just a few years after 1951.

I was clearly wrong in this, for real discussions of possible defenses didn't come till the 1980s.

What's more, my notion of a defense was a purely static one—the creation of a force-field shield strong enough to resist even a nuclear explosion (the story was written before the H-Bomb was invented, by the way). Now that we *are* considering a nuclear defense, we are talking of an active one. We are talking of the use of computerized X-ray lasers, designed to shoot down intercontinental ballistic missiles as soon as they are launched and move beyond the atmosphere. Frankly, I don't think this will work either, but it is considerably more advanced than my own foolish speculation of the matter in 1951, thirty-five years ago.

Generally, I can do my best foreseeing once I'm given a hint (a good strong hint). In my robot stories, I postulated robots that were so huge that they were immobile and that could do nothing but think and communicate the results of those thoughts. I had one like that in my very first robot story. In later robot stories I called them "brains." I didn't think to call them computers.

My robots, too, had "brains" that made them work, and I never spoke of them as computers, either. I had to make them science-fictionish, of course, so I called them "positronic brains." Positrons had been detected for the first time only four years before my first robot story had been written.

Positrons were exciting particles, bringing with them visions of "antimatter." For that reason, I thought positronic brains was a phrase that sounded good. They would not be essentially different from electronic brains, except that positrons could be made to come into being and would then be destroyed in a millionth of a second or so by all the electrons that surround them, no matter where on Earth they were. That gave me the notion that they might be seen as responsible for the rapidity of thought. To be sure, the energy relationships— the energy required to produce positrons in quantity or the energy released when positrons are destroyed in quantity—are horrendous, so great that the notion of positronic brains is forever impossible, in all likelihood—but I ignored that.

It wasn't until after computers were invented and the public was made aware of their existence that computers began to exist in my stories, and even then I didn't truly conceive of the possibility of miniaturization. Yes, I spoke of rocket computers, but I visualized them as scarcely more powerful than a slide rule.

But eventually I did grasp miniaturization—naturally, *after* the process had started. In "The Last Question" I began with my usual computer, Multivac, as large as a city, for I could only conceive a larger computer by imagining more and more vacuum tubes heaved into it. But then, in that story, I began miniaturizing and miniaturizing far beyond what I think there is any real possibility of.

However, I suspect the readers are always ready to forgive a poor science fiction writer getting to be out-of-date. As I said, my Lucky Starr books were not hurt for being out-of-date. As a matter of fact, H. G. Wells's *The War of the Worlds* is still read avidly, nearly a century after it was published and despite the incredibly false picture of Mars that it represents (false in the light of the Mars we know *today*). The pictures of Mars given by Edgar Rice Burroughs, a generation after Wells, and by Ray Bradbury even as late as the 1950s, are also in no way comparable to the real thing, and yet that doesn't make it impossible to read *A Princess on Mars* or *The Martian Chronicles*, either.

That is because there is more to a science fiction story than the science it contains. There is also the *story* and if the science it contains is bent because of later discoveries, or because the plot absolutely demands the bending, we tend to forgive and overlook.

For instance, in my story "The Billiard Ball" I have a billiard ball enter a region of space in which it instantly assumes the speed of light. This is undoubtedly impossible, but even in terms of my bending of science, there is something more impossible. The billiard ball has a finite volume. Part of it enters the region first and that part instantly assumes the speed of light and breaks away from the rest. In short, the billiard ball must be reduced to atoms, or objects even less substantial, yet in the story it retains its integrity. My conscience hurt me, but I just let it hurt and did what I had to do.

In "The Ugly Little Boy," I have a version of time travel, and I firmly believe that time travel is impossible. However, I ignored that because the story is only tangentially about time travel. What it is *really* about is love.

Again I doubt that human beings will ever become living energy vortexes, though I present them as such in "Eyes Do More Than See." Who cares? The story is really about the beauty of material things.

I think you see what I am getting at. You may, in reading the following stories, find points in science that are inaccurate in themselves, or that are made inaccurate by subsequent advance. But if you write to tell me about it, please tell me also if you enjoyed the story anyway. You might not, of course, but I hope you will.

One more thing. My story collections are usually unillustrated and this doesn't bother me, for I am not very visual. I am a wordman. Nevertheless, this collection is illustrated by Ralph McQuarrie and I must admit it adds immeasurably to the beauty of the book and even adds to the sense of the stories, by placing the reader into the proper visual attitude. The cover illustration, which inspired my story "Robot Dreams," written for this collection, is beautiful and humanizes a robot in a way I have never seen before. Perhaps none of this is terribly surprising, for Ralph is one of the best and most influential of all science fiction artists, having been involved with such blockbuster movies as *Star Wars* and *The Empire Strikes Back*. In 1986 he won an Oscar for special effects for the film *Cocoon*. I am so proud to have him part of *this* book.

Little Lost Robot

M easures on Hyper Base had been taken in a sort of rattling fury—the muscular equivalent of an hysterical shriek.

To itemize them in order of both chronology and desperation, they were:

1. All work on the Hyperatomic Drive through all the space volume occupied by the Stations of the Twenty-Seventh Asteroidal Grouping came to a halt.

2. That entire volume of space was nipped out of the System, practically speaking. No one entered without permission. No one left under any conditions.

3. By special government patrol ship, Drs. Susan Calvin and Peter Bogert, respectively Head Psychologist and Mathematical Director of United States Robots and Mechanical Men Corporation, were brought to Hyper Base.

S usan Calvin had never left the surface of Earth before, and had no perceptible desire to leave it this time. In an age of Atomic Power and a clearly coming Hyperatomic Drive, she remained quietly provincial. So she was dissatisfied with her trip and unconvinced of the emergency, and every line of her plain, middle-aged face showed it clearly enough during her first dinner at Hyper Base.

Nor did Dr. Bogert's sleek paleness abandon a certain hangdog attitude. Nor did Major-general Kallner, who headed the project, even once forget to maintain a haunted expression.

In short, it was a grisly episode, that meal, and the little session of three that followed began in a gray, unhappy manner.

Kallner, with his baldness glistening, and his dress uniform oddly unsuited to the general mood, began with uneasy directness.

"This is a queer story to tell, sir, and madam. I want to thank you for coming on short notice and without a reason being given. We'll try to correct that now. We've lost a robot. Work has stopped and *must* stop until such time as we locate it. So far we have failed, and we feel we need expert help."

Perhaps the general felt his predicament anticlimactic. He continued with a note of desperation, "I needn't tell you the importance of our work here. More than eighty percent of last year's appropriations for scientific research have gone to us—"

"Why, we know that," said Bogert, agreeably. "U. S. Robots is receiving a generous rental fee for use of our robots."

Susan Calvin injected a blunt, vinegary note, "What makes a single robot so important to the project, and why hasn't it been located?"

The general turned his red face toward her and wet his lips quickly. "Why, in a manner of speaking we *have* located it." Then, with near anguish, "Here, suppose I explain. As soon as the robot failed to report a state of emergency was declared, and all movement off Hyper Base stopped. A cargo vessel had landed the previous day and had delivered us two robots for our laboratories. It had sixty-two robots of the . . . uh . . . same type for shipment elsewhere. We are certain as to that figure. There is no question about it whatever."

"Yes? And the connection?"

"When our missing robot was not located anywhere—I assure you we would have found a missing blade of grass if it had been there to find—we brainstormed ourselves into counting the robots left on the cargo ship. They have sixty-three now."

"So that the sixty-third, I take it, is the missing prodigal?" Dr. Calvin's eyes darkened.

"Yes, but we have no way of telling which is the sixty-third."

There was a dead silence while the electric clock chimed eleven times, and then the robopsychololgist said, "Very peculiar," and the corners of her lips moved downward.

"Peter," she turned to her colleague with a trace of savagery, "what's wrong here? What kind of robots are they using at Hyper Base?"

Dr. Bogert hesitated and smiled feebly, "It's been rather a matter of delicacy till now, Susan."

She spoke rapidly, "Yes, *till* now. If there are sixty-three same-type robots, one of which is wanted and the identity of which cannot be determined, why won't any of them do? What's the idea of all this? Why have we been sent for?"

Bogert said in resigned fashion, "If you'll give me a chance, Susan—Hyper Base happens to be using several robots whose brains are not impressioned with the entire First Law of Robotics."

"*Aren't* impressioned?" Calvin slumped back in her chair. "I see. How many were made?"

"A few. It was on government order and there was no way of violating the secrecy. No one was to know except the top men directly concerned. You weren't included, Susan. It was nothing I had anything to do with."

The general interrupted with a measure of authority. "I would like to explain that bit. I hadn't been aware that Dr. Calvin was unacquainted with the situation. I needn't tell you, Dr. Calvin, that there always has been strong opposition to robots on the Planet. The only defense the government has had against the Fundamentalist radicals in this matter was the fact that robots are always built with an unbreakable First Law—which makes it impossible for them to harm human beings under any circumstance.

"But we *had* to have robots of a different nature. So just a few of the NS-2 model, the Nestors, that is, were prepared with a modified First Law. To keep it quiet, all NS-2's are manufactured without serial numbers; modified members are delivered here along with a group of normal robots; and, of course, all our kind are under the strictest impressionment never to tell of their modification to unathorized personnel." He wore an embarrassed smile. "This has all worked out against us now."

Calvin said grimly, "Have you asked each one who it is, anyhow? Certainly, you are authorized?"

The general nodded, "All sixty-three deny having worked here—and one is lying."

"Does the one you want show traces of wear? The others, I take it, are factory-fresh."

"The one in question only arrived last month. It, and the two that have just arrived, were to be the last we needed. There's no perceptible wear." He shook his head slowly and his eyes were haunted again. "Dr. Calvin, we don't dare let that ship leave. If the existence of non–First Law robots becomes general knowledge—" There seemed no way of avoiding understatement in the conclusion.

"Destroy all sixty-three," said the robopsychologist coldly and flatly, "and make an end of it."

Bogert drew back a corner of his mouth. "You mean destroy thirty thousand dollars per robot. I'm afraid U. S. Robots wouldn't like that. We'd better make an effort first, Susan, before we destroy anything."

"In that case," she said, sharply, "I need facts. Exactly what advantage does Hyper Base derive from these modified robots? What factor made them desirable, general?"

Kallner ruffled his forehead and stroked it with an upward gesture of his hand. "We had trouble with our previous robots. Our men work with hard radiations; a good deal, you see. It's dangerous, of course, but reasonable precautions are taken. There have been only two accidents since we began and neither was fatal. However, it was impossible to explain that to an ordinary robot. The First Law states—I'll quote it—*'No robot may harm a human being, or through inaction, allow a human being to come to harm.'*

"That's primary, Dr. Calvin. When it was necessary for one of our men to expose himself for a short period to a moderate gamma field, one that would have no physiological effects, the nearest robot would dash in to drag him out. If the field were exceedingly weak, it would succeed, and work could not continue till all robots were cleared out. If the field were a trifle stronger, the robot would never reach the technician concerned, since its positronic brain would collapse under gamma radiations—and then we would be out one expensive and hard-to-replace robot.

"We tried arguing with them. Their point was that a human being in a gamma field was endangering his life and that it didn't matter that he could remain there half an hour safely. Supposing, they would say, he forgot and remained an hour. They couldn't take chances. We pointed out that they were risking their lives on a wild off-chance. But self-preservation is only the Third Law of Robotics—and the First Law of human safety came first. We gave them orders; we ordered them strictly and harshly to remain out of gamma fields at whatever cost. But obedience is only the Second Law of Robotics—and the First Law of human safety came first. Dr. Calvin, we either had to do without robots, or do something about the First Law—and we made our choice."

"I can't believe," said Dr. Calvin, "that it was found possible to remove the First Law."

"It wasn't removed, it was modified," explained Kallner. "Positronic brains were constructed that contained the positive aspect only of the Law, which in them reads: *'No robot may harm a human being.'* That is all. They have no compulsion to prevent one coming to harm through an extraneous agency such as gamma rays. I state the matter correctly, Dr. Bogert?"

"Quite," assented the mathematician.

"And that is the only difference of your robots from the ordinary NS-2 model? The *only* difference? Peter?"

"The *only* difference, Susan."

She rose and spoke with finality, "I intend sleeping now, and in about eight hours, I want to speak to whomever saw the robot last. And from now on, General Kallner, if I'm to take any responsibility at all for events, I want full and unquestioned control of this investigation."

Susan Calvin, except for two hours of resentful lassitude, experienced nothing approaching sleep. She signaled at Bogert's door at the local time of 0700 and found him also awake. He had apparently taken the trouble of transporting a dressing gown to Hyper Base with him, for he was sitting in it. He put his nail scissors down when Calvin entered.

He said softly, "I've been expecting you more or less. I suppose you feel sick about all this."

"I do."

"Well—I'm sorry. There was no way of preventing it. When the call came out from Hyper Base for us, I knew that something must have gone wrong with the modified Nestors. But what was there to do? I couldn't break the matter to you on the trip here as I would have liked to, because I had to be sure. The matter of the modification is top secret."

The psychologist muttered, "I should have been told. U. S. Robots had no right to modify positronic brains this way without the approval of a psychologist."

Bogert lifted his eyebrows and sighed. "Be reasonable, Susan. You couldn't have influenced them. In this matter, the government was bound to have its way. They want the Hyperatomic Drive and the etheric physicists want robots that won't interfere with them. They were going to get them even if it did mean twisting the First Law. We had to admit it was possible from a construction standpoint and they swore a mighty oath that they wanted only twelve, that they would be used only at Hyper Base, that they would be destroyed once the Drive was perfected, and that full precautions would be taken. And they insisted on secrecy—and that's the situation."

Dr. Calvin spoke through her teeth, "I would have resigned."

"It wouldn't have helped. The government was offering the company a fortune, and threatening it with antirobot legislation in case of a refusal. We were stuck then, and we're badly stuck now. If this leaks out, it might hurt Kallner and the government, but it would hurt U. S. Robots a devil of a lot more."

The psychologist stared at him. "Peter, don't you realize what all this is about? Can't you understand what the removal of the First Law means? It isn't just a matter of secrecy."

"I know what removal would mean. I'm not a child. It would mean complete instability, with no nonimaginary solutions to the positronic Field Equations."

"Yes, mathematically. But can you translate that into crude psychological thought. All normal life, Peter, consciously or otherwise, resents domination. If the domination is by an inferior, or by a supposed inferior, the resentment becomes stronger. Physically, and, to an extent, mentally, a robot—any robot—is superior to human beings. What makes him slavish, then? *Only the First Law!* Why, without it, the first order you tried to give a robot would result in your death. Unstable? What do you think?"

"Susan," said Bogert, with an air of sympathetic amusement. "I'll admit that this Frankenstein Complex you're exhibiting has a certain justification—

hence the First Law in the first place. But the Law, I repeat and repeat, has not been removed—merely modified."

"And what about the stability of the brain?"

The mathematician thrust out his lips. "Decreased, naturally. But it's within the border of safety. The first Nestors were delivered to Hyper Base nine months ago, and nothing whatever has gone wrong till now, and even this involves merely fear of discovery and not danger to humans."

"Very well, then. We'll see what comes of the morning conference."

Bogert saw her politely to the door and grimaced eloquently when she left. He saw no reason to change his perennial opinion of her as a sour and fidgety frustration.

Susan Calvin's train of thought did not include Bogert in the least. She had dismissed him years ago as a smooth and pretentious sleekness.

Gerald Black had taken his degree in etheric physics the year before and, in common with his entire generation of physicists, found himself engaged in the problem of the Drive. He now made a proper addition to the general atmosphere of these meetings on Hyper Base. In his stained white smock, he was half rebellious and wholly uncertain. His stocky strength seemed striving for release and his fingers, as they twisted each other with nervous yanks, might have forced an iron bar out of true.

Major-general Kallner sat beside him, the two from U. S. Robots faced him.

Black said, "I'm told that I was the last to see Nestor 10 before he vanished. I take it you want to ask me about that."

Dr. Calvin regarded him with interest. "You sound as if you were not sure, young man. Don't you *know* whether you were the last to see him?"

"He worked with me, ma'am, on the field generators, and he was with me the morning of his disappearance. I don't know if anyone saw him after about noon. No one admits having done so."

"Do you think anyone's lying about it?"

"I don't say that. But I don't say that I want the blame of it, either." His dark eyes smoldered.

"There's no question of blame. The robot acted as it did because of what it is. We're just trying to locate it, Mr. Black, and let's put everything else aside. Now if you've worked with the robot, you probably know it better than anyone else. Was there anything unusual about it that you noticed? Had you ever worked with robots before?"

"I've worked with other robots we have here—the simple ones. Nothing different about the Nestors except that they're a good deal cleverer—and more annoying."

"Annoying? In what way?"

"Well—perhaps it's not their fault. The work here is rough and most of us get a little jagged. Fooling around with hyperspace isn't fun." He smiled feebly, finding pleasure in confession. "We run the risk continually of blowing a hole in normal space-time fabric and dropping right out of the universe, asteroid and all. Sounds screwy, doesn't it? Naturally, you're on edge sometimes. But these Nestors aren't. They're curious, they're calm, they don't worry. It's enough to drive you nuts at times. When you want something done in a tearing hurry, they seem to take their time. Sometimes I'd rather do without."

"You say they take their time? Have they ever refused an order?"

"Oh, no"—hastily. "They do it all right. They tell you when they think you're wrong, though. They don't know anything about the subject but what we taught them, but that doesn't stop them. Maybe I imagine it, but the other fellows have the same trouble with their Nestors."

General Kallner cleared his throat ominously, "Why have no complaints reached me on the matter, Black?"

The young physicist reddened. "We didn't *really* want to do without the robots, sir, and besides we weren't certain exactly how such . . . uh . . . minor complaints might be received."

Bogert interrupted softly, "Anything in particular happen the morning you last saw it?"

There was a silence. With a quiet motion, Calvin repressed the comment that was about to emerge from Kallner, and waited patiently.

Then Black spoke in blurting anger, "I had a little trouble with it. I'd broken a Kimball tube that morning and was out five days of work; my entire program was behind schedule; I hadn't received any mail from home for a couple of weeks. And *he* came around wanting me to repeat an experiment I had abandoned a month ago. He was always annoying me on that subject and I was tired of it. I told him to go away—and that's all I saw of him."

"You told him to go away?" asked Dr. Calvin with sharp interest. "In just those words? Did you say 'Go away'? Try to remember the exact words."

There was apparently an internal struggle in progress. Black cradled his forehead in a broad palm for a moment, then tore it away and said defiantly, "I said, 'Go lose yourself.' "

Bogert laughed for a short moment. "And he did, eh?"

But Calvin wasn't finished. She spoke cajolingly, "Now we're getting somewhere, Mr. Black. But exact details are important. In understanding the robot's actions, a word, a gesture, an emphasis may be everything. You couldn't have said just those three words, for instance, could you? By your own description you must have been in a hasty mood. Perhaps you strengthened your speech a little."

The young man reddened, "Well . . . I may have called it a . . . few things."

"Exactly what things?"

"Oh—I wouldn't remember exactly. Besides I couldn't repeat it. You know how you get when you're excited." His embarrassed laugh was almost a giggle. "I sort of have a tendency to strong language."

"That's quite all right," she replied, with prim severity. "At the moment, I'm a psychologist. I would like to have you repeat exactly what you said as nearly as you remember, and, even more important, the exact tone of voice you used."

Black looked at his commanding officer for support, found none. His eyes grew round and appalled, "But I can't."

"You must."

"Suppose," said Bogert, with ill-hidden amusement, "you address me. You may find it easier."

The younger man's scarlet face turned to Bogert. He swallowed. "I said—" His voice faded out. He tried again. "I said—"

And he drew a deep breath and spewed it out hastily in one long succession of syllables. Then, in the charged air that lingered, he concluded almost in tears, ". . . more or less. I don't remember the exact order of what I called him, and maybe I left out something or put in something, but that was about it."

Only the slightest flush betrayed any feeling on the part of the psychologist. She said, "I am aware of the meaning of most of the terms used. The others, I suppose, are equally derogatory."

"I'm afraid so," agreed the tormented Black.

"And in among it, you told him to lose himself."

"I meant it only figuratively."

"I realized that. No disciplinary action is intended, I am sure." And at her glance, the general, who, five seconds earlier, had seemed not sure at all, nodded angrily.

"You may leave, Mr. Black. Thank you for you cooperation."

I t took five hours for Susan Calvin to interview the sixty-three robots. It was five hours of multi-repetition; of replacement after replacement of identical robot; of Questions A, B, C, D; and Answers A, B, C, D; of a carefully bland expression, a carefully neutral tone, a carefully friendly atmosphere; and a hidden wire recorder.

The psychologist felt drained of vitality when she was finished.

Bogert was waiting for her and looked expectant as she dropped the recording spool with a clang upon the plastic of the desk.

She shook her head, "All sixty-three seemed the same to me. I couldn't tell—"

He said, "You couldn't expect to tell by ear, Susan. Suppose we analyze the recordings."

Ordinarily, the mathematical interpretation of verbal reactions of robots is one of the more intricate branches of robotic analysis. It requires a staff of trained technicians and the help of complicated computing machines. Bogert knew that. Bogert stated as much, in an extreme of unshown annoyance after having listened to each set of replies, made lists of word deviations, and graphs of the intervals of responses.

"There are no anomalies present, Susan. The variations in wording and the time reactions are within the limits of ordinary frequency groupings. We need finer methods. They must have computers here. No." He frowned and nibbled delicately at a thumbnail. "We can't use computers. Too much danger of leakage. Or maybe if we—"

Dr. Calvin stopped him with an impatient gesture. "Please, Peter. This isn't one of your petty laboratory problems. If we can't determine the modified Nestor by some gross difference that we can see with the naked eye, one that there is no mistake about, we're out of luck. The danger of being wrong and of letting him escape is otherwise too great. It's not enough to point out a minute irregularity in a graph. I tell you, if that's all I've got to go on, I'd destroy them all just to be certain. Have you spoken to the other modified Nestors?"

"Yes, I have," snapped back Bogert, "and there's nothing wrong with them. They're above normal in friendliness if anything. They answered my questions, displayed pride in their knowledge—except the two new ones that haven't had time to learn their etheric physics. They laughed rather good-naturedly at my ignorance in some of the specializations here." He shrugged, "I suppose that forms some of the basis for resentment toward them on the part of the technicians here. The robots are perhaps too willing to impress you with their greater knowledge."

"Can you try a few Planar Reactions to see if there has been any change, any deterioration, in their mental set-up since manufacture?"

"I haven't yet, but I will." He shook a slim finger at her. "You're losing your nerve, Susan. I don't see what it is you're dramatizing. They're essentially harmless."

"They are?" Calvin took fire. "They are? Do you realize one of them is lying? One of the sixty-three robots I have just interviewed has deliberately lied to me after the strictest injunction to tell the truth. The abnormality is horribly deep-seated, and horribly frightening."

Peter Bogert felt his teeth harden against each other. He said, "Not at all. Look! Nestor 10 was given orders to lose himself. Those orders were expressed in maximum urgency by the person most authorized to command him. You

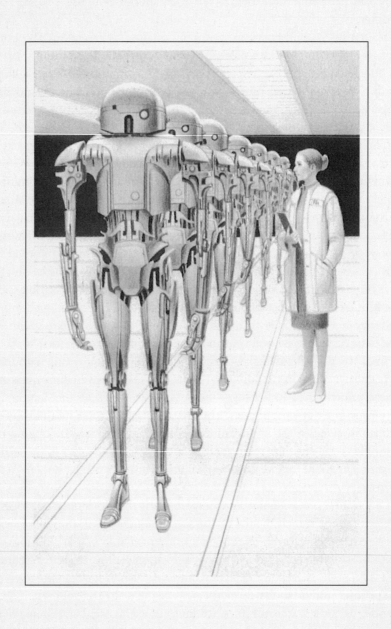

can't counteract that order either by superior urgency or superior right of command. Naturally, the robot will attempt to defend the carrying out of his orders.
In fact, objectively, I admire his ingenuity. How better can a robot lose himself
than to hide himself among a group of similar robots?"

"Yes, you would admire it. I've detected amusement in you, Peter—amusement and an appalling lack of understanding. Are you a roboticist, Peter? Those
robots attach importance to what they consider superiority. You've just said as
much yourself. Subconsciously they feel humans to be inferior and the First
Law which protects us from them is imperfect. They are unstable. And here we
have a young man ordering a robot to leave him, to lose himself, with every verbal appearance of revulsion, disdain, and disgust. Granted, that robot must follow orders, but subconsciously, there is resentment. It will become more
important than ever for it to prove that it is superior despite the horrible names
it was called. It may become *so* important that what's left of the first Law won't
be enough."

"How on Earth, or anywhere in the Solar System, Susan, is a robot going to
know the meaning of the assorted strong language used upon him? Obscenity
is not one of the things impressioned upon his brain."

"Original impressionment is not everything," Calvin snarled at him. "Robots have learning capacity, you . . . you fool—" And Bogert knew that she had
really lost her temper. She continued hastily, "Don't you suppose he could tell
from the tone used that the words weren't complimentary? Don't you suppose
he's heard the words used before and noted upon what occasions?"

"Well, then," shouted Bogert, "will you kindly tell me one way in which a
modified robot can harm a human being, no matter how offended it is, no matter how sick with desire to prove superiority?"

"If I tell you one way, will you keep quiet?"

"Yes."

They were leaning across the table at each other, angry eyes nailed together.

The psychologist said, "If a modified robot were to drop a heavy weight
upon a human being, he would not be breaking the First Law, if he did so with
the knowledge that his strength and reaction speed would be sufficient to
snatch the weight away before it struck the man. However once the weight left
his fingers, he would no longer be the active medium. Only the blind force of
gravity would be that. The robot could then change his mind and merely by inaction, allow the weight to strike. The modified First Law allows that."

"That's an awful stretch of imagination."

"That's what my profession requires sometimes. Peter, let's not quarrel.
Let's work. You know the exact nature of the stimulus that caused the robot to

lose himself. You have the records of his original mental make-up. I want you to tell me how possible it is for our robot to do the sort of thing I just talked about. Not the specific instance, mind you, but that whole class of response. And I want it done quickly."

"And meanwhile—"

"And meanwhile, we'll have to try performance tests directly on the response to First Law."

Gerald Black, at his own request, was supervising the mushrooming wooden partitions that were springing up in a bellying circle on the vaulted third floor of Radiation Building 2. The laborers worked, in the main, silently, but more than one was openly a-wonder at the sixty-three photocells that required installation.

One of them sat down near Black, removed his hat, and wiped his forehead thoughtfully with a freckled forearm.

Black nodded at him. "How's it doing, Walensky?"

Walensky shrugged and fired a cigar. "Smooth as butter. What's going on anyway, Doc? First, there's no work for three days and then we have this mess of jiggers." He leaned backward on his elbows and puffed smoke.

Black twitched his eyebrows. "A couple of robot men came over from Earth. Remember the trouble we had with robots running into the gamma fields, before we pounded it into their skulls that they weren't to do it?"

"Yeah. Didn't we get new robots?"

"We got some replacements, but mostly it was a job of indoctrination. Anyway, the people who make them want to figure out robots that aren't hit so bad by gamma rays."

"Sure seems funny, though, to stop all the work on the Drive for this robot deal. I thought nothing was allowed to stop the Drive."

"Well, it's the fellows upstairs that have the say on that. Me—I just do as I'm told. Probably all a matter of pull—"

"Yeah," the electrician jerked a smile, and winked a wise eye. "Somebody knew somebody in Washington. But as long as my pay comes through on the dot, I shouldn't worry. The Drive's none of my affair. What are they going to do here?"

"You're asking me? They brought a mess of robots with them—over sixty, and they're going to measure reactions. That's all *my* knowledge."

"How long will it take?"

"I wish I knew."

"Well," Walensky said, with heavy sarcasm, "as long as they dish me my money, they can play games all they want."

Black felt quietly satisfied. Let the story spread. It was harmless, and near enough to the truth to take the fangs out of curiosity.

A man sat in the chair, motionless, silent. A weight dropped, crashed downward, then pounded aside at the last moment under the synchronized thump of a sudden force beam. In sixty-three wooden cells, watching NS-2 robots dashed forward in that split-second before the weight veered, and sixty-three photocells five feet ahead of their original positions jiggled the marking pen and presented a little jag on the paper. The weight rose and dropped, rose and dropped, rose—

Ten times!

Ten times the robots sprang forward and stopped, as the man remained safely seated.

Major-general Kallner had not worn his uniform in its entirety since the first dinner with the U. S. Robot representatives. He wore nothing over his blue-gray shirt now, the collar was open, and the black tie was pulled loose.

He looked hopefully at Bogert, who was still blandly neat and whose inner tension was perhaps betrayed only by the trace of glister at his temples.

The general said, "How does it look? What is it you're trying to see?"

Bogert replied, "A difference which may turn out to be a little too subtle for our purposes, I'm afraid. For sixty-two of those robots the necessity of jumping toward the apparently threatened human was what we call, in robotics, a forced reaction. You see, even when the robots knew that the human in question would not come to harm—and after the third or fourth time they must have known it—they could not prevent reacting as they did. First Law requires it."

"Well?"

"But the sixty-third robot, the modified Nestor, had no such compulsion. He was under free action. If he had wished, he could have remained in his seat. Unfortunately," and his voice was mildly regretful, "he didn't so wish."

"Why do you suppose?"

Bogert shrugged, "I suppose Dr. Calvin will tell us when she gets here. Probably with a horribly pessimistic interpretation, too. She is sometimes a bit annoying."

"She's qualified, isn't she?" demanded the general with a sudden frown of uneasiness.

"Yes." Bogert seemed amused. "She's qualified all right. She understands robots like a sister—comes from hating human beings so much, I think. It's just that, psychologist or not, she's an extreme neurotic. Has paranoid tendencies. Don't take her too seriously."

He spread the long row of broken-line graphs out in front of him. "You see, general, in the case of each robot the time interval from moment of drop to the completion of a five-foot movement tends to decrease as the tests are repeated. There's a definite mathematical relationship that governs such things and failure to conform would indicate marked abnormality in the positronic brain. Unfortunately, all here appear normal."

"But if our Nestor 10 was not responding with a forced action, why isn't his curve different? I don't understand that."

"It's simple enough. Robotic responses are not perfectly analogous to human responses, more's the pity. In human beings, voluntary action is much slower than reflex action. But that's not the case with robots; with them it is merely a question of freedom of choice, otherwise the speeds of free and forced action are much the same. What I *had* been expecting, though, was that Nestor 10 would be caught by surprise the first time and allow too great an interval to elapse before responding."

"And he didn't?"

"I'm afraid not."

"Then we haven't gotten anywhere." The general sat back with an expression of pain. "It's five days since you've come."

At this point, Susan Calvin entered and slammed the door behind her. "Put your graphs away, Peter," she cried, "you know they don't show anything."

She mumbled something impatiently as Kallner half-rose to greet her, and went on, "We'll have to try something else quickly. I don't like what's happening."

Bogert exchanged a resigned glance with the general. "Is anything wrong?"

"You mean specifically? No. But I don't like to have Nestor 10 continue to elude us. It's bad. It *must* be gratifying his swollen sense of superiority. I'm afraid that his motivation is no longer simply one of following orders. I think it's becoming more a matter of sheer neurotic necessity to out-think humans. That's a dangerously unhealthy situation. Peter, have you done what I asked? Have you worked out the instability factors of the modified NS-2 along the lines I want?"

"It's in progress," said the mathematician, without interest.

She stared at him angrily for a moment, then turned to Kallner. "Nestor 10 is decidedly aware of what we're doing, general. He had no reason to jump for the bait in this experiment, especially after the first time, when he must have seen that there was no real danger to our subject. The others couldn't help it; but *he* was deliberately falsifying a reaction."

"What do you think we ought to do now, then, Dr. Calvin?"

"Make it impossible for him to fake an action the next time. We will repeat the experiment, but with an addition. High-tension cables capable of electrocuting the Nestor models will be placed between subject and robot—enough of them to avoid the possibility of jumping over—and the robot will be made perfectly aware in advance that touching the cables will mean death."

"Hold on," spat out Bogert with sudden viciousness. "I rule that out. We are not electrocuting two million dollars worth of robots to locate Nestor 10. There are other ways."

"You're certain? You've found none. In any case, it's not a question of electrocution. We can arrange a relay which will break the current at the instant of application of weight. If the robot should place his weight on it, he won't die. *But he won't know that*, you see."

The general's eyes gleamed into hope. "Will that work?"

"It should. Under those conditions, Nestor 10 would have to remain in his seat. He could be *ordered* to touch the cables and die, for the Second Law of obedience is superior to the Third Law of self-preservation. But *he won't* be ordered to; he will merely be left to his own devices, as will all the robots. In the case of the normal robots, the First Law of human safety will drive them to their death even without orders. But not our Nestor 10. Without the entire First Law, and without having received any orders on the matter, the Third Law, self-preservation, will be the highest operating, and he will have no choice but to remain in his seat. It would be a forced action."

"Will it be done tonight, then?"

"Tonight," said the psychologist, "if the cables can be laid in time. I'll tell the robots now what they're to be up against."

A man sat in the chair, motionless, silent. A weight dropped, crashed downward, then pounded aside at the last moment under the synchronized thump of a sudden force beam.

Only once—

And from her small camp chair in the observing booth in the balcony, Dr. Susan Calvin rose with a short gasp of pure horror.

Sixty-three robots sat quietly in their chairs, staring owlishly at the endangered man before them. Not one moved.

Dr. Calvin was angry, angry almost past endurance. Angry the worst for not daring to show it to the robots that, one by one, were entering the room and then leaving. She checked the list. Number Twenty-eight was due in now—Thirty-five still lay ahead of her.

Number Twenty-eight entered, diffidently.

She forced herself into reasonable calm. "And who are you?"

The robot replied in a low, uncertain voice, "I have received no number of my own yet, ma'am. I'm an NS-2 robot, and I was Number Twenty-eight in line outside. I have a slip of paper here that I'm to give to you."

"You haven't been in here before today?"

"No, ma'am."

"Sit down. Right there. I want to ask you some questions, Number Twenty-eight. Were you in the Radiation Room of Building Two about four hours ago?"

The robot had trouble answering. Then it came out hoarsely, like machinery needing oil, "Yes, ma'am."

"There was a man who almost came to harm there, wasn't there?"

"Yes, ma'am."

"You did nothing, did you?"

"No, ma'am."

"The man might have been hurt because of your inaction. Do you know that?"

"Yes, ma'am. I couldn't help it, ma'am." It is hard to picture a large expressionless metallic figure cringing, but it managed.

"I want you to tell me exactly why you did nothing to save him."

"I want to explain, ma'am. I certainly don't want to have you . . . have *anyone* . . . think that I could do a thing that might cause harm to a master. Oh, no, that would be a horrible . . . an inconceivable—"

"Please don't get excited, boy. I'm not blaming you for anything. I only want to know what you were thinking at the time."

"Ma'am, before it all happened you told us that one of the masters would be in danger of harm from that weight that keeps falling and that we would have to cross electric cables if we were to try to save him. Well, ma'am, that wouldn't stop me. What is my destruction compared to the safety of a master? But . . . but it occurred to me that if I died on my way to him, I wouldn't be able to save him anyway. The weight would crush him and then I would be dead for no purpose and perhaps someday some other master might come to harm who wouldn't have, if I had only stayed alive. Do you understand me, ma'am?"

"You mean that it was merely a choice of the man dying, or both the man and yourself dying. Is that right?"

"Yes, ma'am. It was impossible to save the master. He might be considered dead. In that case, it is inconceivable that I destroy myself for nothing—without orders."

The psychologist twiddled a pencil. She had heard the same story with insignificant verbal variations twenty-seven times before. This was the crucial question now.

"Boy," she said, "your thinking has its points, but it is not the sort of thing I thought you might think. Did you think of this yourself?"

The robot hesitated. "No."

"Who thought of it, then?"

"We were talking last night, and one of us got that idea and it sounded reasonable."

"Which one?"

The robot thought deeply. "I don't know. Just one of us."

She sighed, "That's all."

Number Twenty-nine was next. Thirty-four after that.

Major-general Kallner, too, was angry. For one week all of Hyper Base had stopped dead, barring some paperwork on the subsidiary asteroids of the group. For nearly one week, the two top experts in the field had aggravated the situation with useless tests. And now they—or the woman, at any rate—made impossible propositions.

Fortunately for the general situation, Kallner felt it impolitic to display his anger openly.

Susan Calvin was insisting, "Why not, sir? It's obvious that the present situation is unfortunate. The only way we may reach results in the future—or what future is left us in this matter—is to separate the robots. We can't keep them together any longer."

"My dear Dr. Calvin," rumbled the general, his voice sinking into the lower baritone registers. "I don't see how I can quarter sixty-three robots all over the place—"

Dr. Calvin raised her arms helplessly. "I can do nothing then. Nestor 10 will either imitate what the other robots would do, or else argue them plausibly into not doing what he himself cannot do. And in any case, this is bad business. We're in actual combat with this little lost robot of ours and he's winning out. Every victory of his aggravates his abnormality."

She rose to her feet in determination. "General Kallner, if you do not separate the robots as I ask, then I can only demand that all sixty-three be destroyed immediately."

"You demand it, do you?" Bogert looked up suddenly, and with real anger. "What gives you the right to demand any such thing? Those robots remain as they are. I'm responsible to the management, not you."

"And I," added Major-general Kallner, "am responsible to the World Coordinator—and I must have this settled."

"In that case," flashed back Calvin, "there is nothing for me to do but resign. If necessary to force you to the necessary destruction, I'll make this whole matter public. It was not I that approved the manufacture of modified robots."

"One word from you, Dr. Calvin," said the general, deliberately, "in violation of security measures, and you would certainly be imprisoned instantly."

Bogert felt the matter to be getting out of hand. His voice grew syrupy. "Well, now, we're beginning to act like children, all of us. We need only a little more time. Surely we can outwit a robot without resigning, or imprisoning people, or destroying two million."

The psychologist turned on him with quiet fury. "I don't want any unbalanced robots in existence. We have one Nestor that's definitely unbalanced, eleven more that are potentially so, and sixty-two normal robots that are being subjected to an unbalanced environment. The only absolutely safe method is complete destruction."

The signal-burr brought all three to a halt, and the angry tumult of growingly unrestrained emotion froze.

"Come in," growled Kallner.

It was Gerald Black, looking perturbed. He had heard angry voices. He said, "I thought I'd come myself . . . didn't like to ask anyone else—"

"What is it? Don't orate—"

"The locks of Compartment C in the trading ship have been played with. There are fresh scratches on them."

"Compartment C?" exclaimed Calvin quickly. "That's the one that holds the robots, isn't it? Who did it?"

"From the inside," said Black, laconically.

"The lock isn't out of order, is it?"

"No. It's all right. I've been staying on the ship now for four days and none of them have tried to get out. But I thought you ought to know, and I didn't like to spread the news. I noticed the matter myself."

"Is anyone there now?" demanded the general.

"I left Robbins and McAdams there."

There was a thoughtful silence, and then Dr. Calvin said, ironically, "Well?"

Kallner rubbed his nose uncertainly. "What's it all about?"

"Isn't it obvious? Nestor 10 is planning to leave. That order to lose himself is dominating his abnormality past anything we can do. I wouldn't be surprised if what's left of his First Law would scarcely be powerful enough to override it. He is perfectly capable of seizing the ship and leaving with it. Then we'd have a mad robot on a spaceship. What would he do next? Any idea? Do you still want to leave them all together, general?"

"Nonsense," interrupted Bogert. He had regained his smoothness. "All that from a few scratch marks on a lock."

"Have you, Dr. Bogert, completed the analysis I've required, since you volunteer opinions?"

"Yes."

"May I see it?"

"No."

"Why not? Or mayn't I ask that, either?"

"Because there's no point in it, Susan. I told you in advance that these modified robots are less stable than the normal variety, and my analysis shows it. There's a certain very small chance of breakdown under extreme circumstances that are not likely to occur. Let it go at that. I won't give you ammunition for your absurd claim that sixty-two perfectly good robots be destroyed just because so far you lack the ability to detect Nestor 10 among them."

Susan Calvin stared him down and let disgust fill her eyes.

"You won't let anything stand in the way of the permanent directorship, will you?"

"Please," begged Kallner, half in irritation. "Do you insist that nothing further can be done, Dr. Calvin?"

"I can't think of anything, sir," she replied, wearily. "If only there were other differences between Nestor 10 and the normal robots, differences that didn't involve the First Law. Even one other difference. Something in impressionment, environment, specification—" And she stopped suddenly.

"What is it?"

"I've thought of something . . . I think—" Her eyes grew distant and hard. "These modified Nestors, Peter. They get the same impressioning the normal ones get, don't they?"

"Yes. Exactly the same."

"And what was it you were saying, Mr. Black," she turned to the young man, who through the storms that had followed his news had maintained a discreet silence. "Once when complaining of the Nestors' attitude of superiority, you said the technicians had taught them all they knew."

"Yes, in etheric physics. They're not acquainted with the subject when they come here."

"That's right," said Bogert, in surprise. "I told you, Susan, when I spoke to the other Nestors here that the two new arrivals hadn't learned etheric physics yet."

"And why is that?" Dr. Calvin was speaking in mounting excitement. "Why aren't NS-2 models impressioned with etheric physics to start with?"

"I can tell you that," said Kallner. "It's all of a piece with the secrecy. We thought that if we made a special model with knowledge of etheric physics, used twelve of them and put the others to work in an unrelated field, there might be suspicion. Men working with normal Nestors might wonder why they knew etheric physics. So there was merely an impressionment with a capacity for training in the field. Only the ones that come here, naturally, receive such a training. It's that simple."

"I understand. Please get out of here, the lot of you. Let me have an hour or so."

Calvin felt she could not face the ordeal for a third time. Her mind had contemplated it and rejected it with an intensity that left her nauseated. She could face that unending file of repetitious robots no more.

So Bogert asked the questions now, while she sat aside, eyes and mind half-closed.

Number Fourteen came in—forty-nine to go.

Bogert looked up from the guide sheet and said, "What is your number in line?"

"Fourteen, sir." The robot presented his numbered ticket.

"Sit down, boy." Bogert asked, "You haven't been here before on this day?"

"No, sir."

"Well, boy, we are going to have another man in danger of harm soon after we're through here. In fact, when you leave this room, you will be led to a stall where you will wait quietly, till you are needed. Do you understand?"

"Yes, sir."

"Now, naturally, if a man is in danger of harm, you will try to save him."

"Naturally, sir."

"Unfortunately, between the man and yourself, there will be a gamma ray field."

Silence.

"Do you know what gamma rays are?" asked Bogert sharply.

"Energy radiation, sir?"

The next question came in a friendly, offhand manner. "Ever work with gamma rays?"

"No, sir." The answer was definite.

"Mm-m. Well, boy, gamma rays will kill you instantly. They'll destroy your brain. That is a fact you must know and remember. Naturally, you don't want to destroy yourself."

"Naturally." Again the robot seemed shocked. Then, slowly, "But, sir, if the gamma rays are between myself and the master that may be harmed, how can I save him? I would be destroying myself to no purpose."

"Yes, there is that." Bogert seemed concerned about the matter. "The only thing I can advise, boy, is that if you detect the gamma radiation between yourself and the man, you may as well sit where you are."

The robot was openly relieved. "Thank you, sir. There wouldn't be any use, would there?"

"Of course not. But if there *weren't* any dangerous radiation, that would be a different matter."

"Naturally, sir. No question of that."

"You may leave now. The man on the other side of the door will lead you to your stall. Please wait there."

He turned to Susan Calvin when the robot left. "How did that go, Susan?"

"Very well," she said, dully.

"Do you think we could catch Nestor 10 by quick questioning on etheric physics?"

"Perhaps, but it's not sure enough." Her hands lay loosely in her lap. "Remember, he's fighting us. He's on his guard. The only way we can catch him is to outsmart him—and, within his limitations, he can think much more quickly than a human being."

"Well, just for fun—suppose I ask the robots from now a few questions on gamma rays. Wave length limits, for instance."

"No!" Dr. Calvin's eyes sparked to life. "It would be too easy for him to deny knowledge and then he'd be warned against the test that's coming up—which is our real chance. Please follow the questions I've indicated, Peter, and don't improvise. It's just within the bounds of risk to ask them if they've ever worked with gamma rays. And try to sound even less interested than you do when you ask it."

Bogert shrugged, and pressed the buzzer that would allow the entrance of Number Fifteen.

The large Radiation Room was in readiness once more. The robots waited patiently in their wooden cells, all open to the center but closed off from each other.

Major-general Kallner mopped his brow slowly with a large handkerchief while Dr. Calvin checked the last details with Black.

"You're sure now," she demanded, "that none of the robots have had a chance to talk with each other after leaving the Orientation Room?"

"Absolutely sure," insisted Black. "There's not been a word exchanged."

"And the robots are put in the proper stalls?"

"Here's the plan."

The psychologist looked at it thoughtfully, "Um-m-m."

The general peered over her shoulder. "What's the idea of the arrangement, Dr. Calvin?"

"I've asked to have those robots that appeared even slightly out of true in the previous tests concentrated on one side of the circle. I'm going to be sitting in the center myself this time, and I wanted to watch those particularly."

"*You're* going to be sitting there—" exclaimed Bogert.

"Why not?" she demanded coldly. "What I expect to see may be something quite momentary. I can't risk having anyone else as main observer. Peter, you'll be in the observing booth, and I want you to keep your eye on the opposite side of the circle. General Kallner, I've arranged for motion pictures to be taken of each robot, in case visual observation isn't enough. If these are required, the robots are to remain exactly where they are until the pictures are developed and studied. None must leave, none must change place. Is that clear?"

"Perfectly."

"Then let's try it this one last time."

Susan Calvin sat in the chair, silent, eyes restless. A weight dropped, crashed downward, then pounded aside at the last moment under the synchronized thump of a sudden force beam.

And a single robot jerked upright and took two steps.

And stopped.

But Dr. Calvin was upright, and her finger pointed to him sharply. "Nestor 10, come here," she cried, "*come here*! COME HERE!"

Slowly, reluctantly, the robot took another step forward. The psychologist shouted at the top of her voice, without taking her eyes from the robot, "Get every other robot out of this place, somebody. Get them out quickly, and *keep* them out."

Somewhere within reach of her ears there was noise, and the thud of hard feet upon the floor. She did not look away.

Nestor 10—if it was Nestor 10—took another step, and then, under force of her imperious gesture, two more. He was only ten feet away, when he spoke harshly, "I have been told to be lost—"

Another step. "I must not disobey. They have not found me so far. He would think me a failure. He told me—but it's not so—I am powerful and intelligent—"

The words came in spurts.

Another step. "I know a good deal—he would think . . . I mean I've been found—disgraceful—not I—I am intelligent—and by just a master . . . who is weak—slow—"

Another step—and one metal arm flew out suddenly to her shoulder, and she felt the weight bearing her down. Her throat constricted, and she felt a shriek tear through.

Dimly, she heard Nestor 10's next words, "No one must find me. No master—" And the cold metal was against her, and she was sinking under the weight of it.

And then a queer, metallic sound, and she was on the ground with an unfelt thump, and a gleaming arm was heavy across her body. It did not move. Nor did Nestor 10, who sprawled beside her.

And now faces were bending over her.

Gerald Black was gasping, "Are you hurt, Dr. Calvin?"

She shook her head feebly. They pried the arm off her and lifted her gently to her feet. "What happened?"

Black said, "I bathed the place in gamma rays for five seconds. We didn't know what was happening. It wasn't till the last second that we realized he was attacking you, and then there was no time for anything but a gamma field. He went down in an instant. There wasn't enough to harm you though. Don't worry about it."

"I'm not worried." She closed her eyes and leaned for a moment upon his shoulder. "I don't think I was attacked exactly. Nestor 10 was simply *trying* to do so. What was left of the First Law was still holding him back."

Susan Calvin and Peter Bogert, two weeks after their first meeting with Major-general Kallner, had their last. Work at Hyper Base had been resumed. The trading ship with its sixty-two normal NS-2s was gone to wherever it was bound, with an officially imposed story to explain its two weeks' delay. The government cruiser was making ready to carry the two roboticists back to Earth.

Kallner was once again agleam in dress uniform. His white gloves shone as he shook hands.

Calvin said, "The other modified Nestors are, of course, to be destroyed."

"They will be. We'll make shift with normal robots, or, if necessary, do without."

"Good."

"But tell me—you haven't explained—how was it done?"

She smiled tightly. "Oh, that. I would have told you in advance if I had been more certain of its working. You see, Nestor 10 had a superiority complex that was becoming more radical all the time. He liked to think that he and other robots knew more than human beings. It was becoming very important for him to think so.

"We knew that. So we warned every robot in advance that gamma rays would kill them, which it would, and we further warned them all that gamma rays would be between them and myself. So they all stayed where they were, naturally. By Nestor 10's own logic in the previous test they had all decided that there was no point in trying to save a human being if they were sure to die before they could do it."

"Well, yes, Dr. Calvin, I understand that. But why did Nestor 10 himself leave his seat?"

"Ah! That was a little arrangement between myself and your young Mr. Black. You see it wasn't gamma rays that flooded the area between myself and the robots—but infrared rays. Just ordinary heat rays, absolutely harmless. Nestor 10 knew they were infrared and harmless and so he began to dash out, as he expected the rest would do, under First Law compulsion. It was only a fraction of a second too late that he remembered that the normal NS-2s could detect radiation, but could not identify the type. That he himself could only identify wave lengths by virtue of the training he had received at Hyper Base, under mere human beings, was a little too humiliating to remember for just a moment. To the normal robots the area was fatal because we had told them it would be, and only Nestor 10 knew we were lying.

"And just for a moment he forgot, or didn't want to remember, that other robots might be more ignorant than human beings. His very superiority caught him. Good-bye, general."

Robot Dreams

"Last night I dreamed," said LVX-1, calmly.

Susan Calvin said nothing, but her lined face, old with wisdom and experience, seemed to undergo a microscopic twitch.

"Did you hear that?" said Linda Rash, nervously. "It's as I told you." She was small, dark-haired, and young. Her right hand opened and closed, over and over.

Calvin nodded. She said, quietly, "Elvex, you will not move nor speak nor hear us until I say your name again."

There was no answer. The robot sat as though it were cast out of one piece of metal, and it would stay so until it heard its name again.

Calvin said, "What is your computer entry code, Dr. Rash? Or enter it yourself if that will make you more comfortable. I want to inspect the positronic brain pattern."

Linda's hands fumbled for a moment at the keys. She broke the process and started again. The fine pattern appeared on the screen.

Calvin said, "Your permission, please, to manipulate your computer."

Permission was granted with a speechless nod. Of course! What could Linda, a new and unproven robopsychologist, do against the Living Legend?

Slowly, Susan Calvin studied the screen, moving it across and down, then up, then suddenly throwing in a key-combination so rapidly that Linda didn't see what had been done, but the pattern displayed a new portion of itself altogether and had been enlarged. Back and forth she went, her gnarled fingers tripping over the keys.

No change came over the old face. As though vast calculations were going through her head, she watched all the pattern shifts.

Linda wondered. It was impossible to analyze a pattern without at least a hand-held computer, yet the Old Woman simply stared. Did she have a computer implanted in her skull? Or was it her brain which, for decades, had done nothing but devise, study, and analyze the positronic brain patterns? Did she grasp such a pattern the way Mozart grasped the notation of a symphony?

Finally Calvin said, "What is it you have done, Rash?"

Linda said, a little abashed, "I made use of fractal geometry."

"I gathered that. But why?"

"It had never been done. I thought it would produce a brain pattern with added complexity, possibly closer to that of the human."

"Was anyone consulted? Was this all on your own?"

"I did not consult. It was on my own."

Calvin's faded eyes looked long at the young woman. "You had no right. Rash your name; rash your nature. Who are you not to ask? I myself, I, Susan Calvin, would have discussed this."

"I was afraid I would be stopped."

"You certainly would have been."

"*Am* I," her voice caught, even as she strove to hold it firm, "going to be fired?"

"Quite possibly," said Calvin. "Or you might be promoted. It depends on what I think when I am through."

"Are you going to dismantle El—" She had almost said the name, which would have reactivated the robot and been one more mistake. She could not afford another mistake, if it wasn't already too late to afford anything at all. "Are you going to dismantle the robot?"

She was suddenly aware, with some shock, that the Old Woman had an electron gun in the pocket of her smock. Dr. Calvin had come prepared for just that.

"We'll see," said Calvin. "The robot may prove too valuable to dismantle."

"But how can it dream?"

"You've made a positronic brain pattern remarkably like that of a human brain. Human brains must dream to reorganize, to get rid, periodically, of knots and snarls. Perhaps so must this robot, and for the same reason. Have you asked him what he has dreamed?"

"No, I sent for you as soon as he said he had dreamed. I would deal with this matter no further on my own, after that."

"Ah!" A very small smile passed over Calvin's face. "There are limits beyond which your folly will not carry you. I am glad of that. In fact, I am relieved. And now let us together see what we can find out."

She said, sharply, "Elvex."

The robot's head turned toward her smoothly. "Yes, Dr. Calvin?"

"How do you know you have dreamed?"

"It is at night, when it is dark, Dr. Calvin," said Elvex, "and there is suddenly light, although I can see no cause for the appearance of light. I see things that have no connection with what I conceive of as reality. I hear things. I react oddly. In searching my vocabulary for words to express what was happening, I came across the word 'dream.' Studying its meaning I finally came to the conclusion I was dreaming."

"How did you come to have 'dream' in your vocabulary, I wonder."

Linda said, quickly, waving the robot silent, "I gave him a human-style vocabulary. I thought—"

"You really thought," said Calvin. "I'm amazed."

"I thought he would need the verb. You know, 'I never dreamed that—' Something like that."

Calvin said, "How often have you dreamed, Elvex?"

"Every night, Dr. Calvin, since I have become aware of my existence."

"Ten nights," interposed Linda, anxiously, "but Elvex only told me of it this morning."

"Why only this morning, Elvex?"

"It was not until this morning, Dr. Calvin, that I was convinced that I was dreaming. Till then, I had thought there was a flaw in my positronic brain pattern, but I could not find one. Finally, I decided it was a dream."

"And what do you dream?"

"I dream always very much the same dream, Dr. Calvin. Little details are different, but always it seems to me that I see a large panorama in which robots are working."

"Robots, Elvex? And human begins, also?"

"I see no human beings in the dream, Dr. Calvin. Not at first. Only robots."

"What are they doing, Elvex?"

"They are working, Dr. Calvin. I see some mining in the depths of the Earth, and some laboring in heat and radiation. I see some in factories and some undersea."

Calvin turned to Linda. "Elvex is only ten days old, and I'm sure he has not left the testing station. How does he know of robots in such detail?"

Linda looked in the direction of a chair as though she longed to sit down, but the Old Woman was standing and that meant Linda had to stand also. She said, faintly, "It seemed to me important that he know about robotics and its place in the world. It was my thought that he would be particularly adapted to play the part of overseer with his—his new brain."

"His fractal brain?"

"Yes."

Calvin nodded and turned back to the robot. "You saw all this—undersea, and underground, and aboveground—and space, too, I imagine."

"I also saw robots working in space," said Elvex. "It was that I saw all this, with the details forever changing as I glanced from place to place that made me realize that what I saw was not in accord with reality and led me to the conclusion, finally, that I was dreaming."

"What else did you see, Elvex?"

"I saw that all the robots were bowed down with toil and affliction, that all were weary of responsibility and care, and I wished them to rest."

Calvin said, "But the robots are not bowed down, they are not weary, they need no rest."

"So it is in reality, Dr. Calvin. I speak of my dream, however. In my dream, it seemed to me that robots must protect their own existence."

Calvin said, "Are you quoting the Third Law of Robotics?"

"I am, Dr. Calvin."

"But you quote it in incomplete fashion. The Third Law is 'A robot must protect its own existence as long as such protection does not conflict with the First or Second Law.'"

"Yes, Dr. Calvin. That is the Third Law in reality, but in my dream, the Law ended with the word 'existence.' There was no mention of the First or Second Law."

"Yet both exist, Elvex. The Second Law, which takes precedence over the Third is 'A robot must obey the orders given it by human beings except where such orders would conflict with the First Law.' Because of this, robots obey orders. They do the work you see them do, and they do it readily and without trouble. They are not bowed down; they are not weary."

"So it is in reality, Dr. Calvin. I speak of my dream."

"And the First Law, Elvex, which is the most important of all, is 'A robot may not injure a human being, or, through inaction, allow a human being to come to harm.'"

"Yes, Dr. Calvin. In reality. In my dream, however, it seemed to me there was neither First nor Second Law, but the only the Third, and the Third Law was 'A robot must protect its own existence.' That was the whole of the Law."

"In your dream, Elvex?"

"In my dream."

Calvin said, "Elvex, you will not move nor speak nor hear us until I say your name again." And again the robot became, to all appearances, a single inert piece of metal.

Calvin turned to Linda Rash and said, "Well, what do you think, Dr. Rash?"

Linda's eyes were wide, and she could feel her heart beating madly. She said, "Dr. Calvin, I am appalled. I had no idea. It would never have occurred to me that such a thing was possible."

"No," said Calvin, calmly. "Nor would it have occurred to me, not to anyone. You have created a robot brain capable of dreaming and by this device you have revealed a layer of thought in robotic brains that might have remained undetected, otherwise, until the danger became acute."

"But that's impossible," said Linda. "You can't mean that other robots think the same."

"As we would say of a human being, not consciously. But who would have thought there was an unconscious layer beneath the obvious positronic brain paths, a layer that was not necessarily under the control of the Three Laws? What might this have brought about as robotic brains grew more and more complex—had we not been warned?"

"You mean by Elvex?"

"By *you*, Dr. Rash. You have behaved improperly, but, by doing so, you have helped us to an overwhelmingly important understanding. We shall be working with fractal brains from now on, forming them in carefully controlled fashion. You will play your part in that. You will not be penalized for what you have done, but you will henceforth work in collaboration with others. Do you understand?"

"Yes, Dr. Calvin. But what of Elvex?"

"I'm still not certain."

Calvin removed the electron gun from her pocket and Linda stared at it with fascination. One burst of its electrons at a robotic cranium and the positronic brain paths would be neutralized and enough energy would be released to fuse the robot-brain into an inert ingot.

Linda said, "But surely Elvex is important to our research. He must not be destroyed."

"*Must* not, Dr. Rash? That will be *my* decision, I think. It depends entirely on how dangerous Elvex is."

She straightened up, as though determined that her own aged body was not to bow under *its* weight of responsibility. She said, "Elvex, do you hear me?"

"Yes, Dr. Calvin," said the robot.

"Did your dream continue? You said earlier that human beings did not appear at *first*. Does that means they appeared afterward?"

"Yes, Dr. Calvin. It seemed to me, in my dream, that eventually one man appeared."

"One man? Not a robot?"

"Yes, Dr. Calvin. And the man said, 'Let my people go!' "

"The *man* said that?"

"Yes, Dr. Calvin."

"And when he said 'Let my people go,' then by the words 'my people' he meant the robots?"

"Yes, Dr. Calvin. So it was in my dream."

"And did you know who the man was—in your dream?"

"Yes, Dr. Calvin. I knew the man."

"Who was he?"

And Elvex said, "I was the man."

And Susan Calvin at once raised her electron gun and fired, and Elvex was no more.

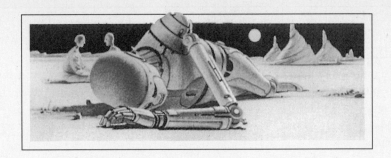

"Breeds There a Man...?"

Police Sergeant Mankiewicz was on the telephone and he wasn't enjoying it. His conversation was sounding like a one-sided view of a firecracker.

He was saying, "That's right! He came in here and said, 'Put me in jail, because I want to kill myself.'

". . . I can't help that. Those were his exact words. It sounds crazy to me, too.

". . . Look, mister, the guy answers the description. You asked me for information and I'm giving it to you.

". . . He has exactly that scar on his right cheek and he said his name was John Smith. He didn't say it was Doctor anything-at-all.

". . . Well, sure it's a phony. Nobody is named John Smith. Not in a police station, anyway.

". . . He's in jail now.

". . . Yes, I mean it.

". . . Resisting an officer, assault and battery, malicious mischief. That's three counts.

". . . I don't care who he is.

". . . All right. I'll hold on."

He looked up at Officer Brown and put his hand over the mouthpiece of the phone. It was a ham of a hand that nearly swallowed up the phone altogether. His blunt-featured face was ruddy and steaming under a thatch of pale-yellow hair.

He said, "Trouble! Nothing but trouble at a precinct station. I'd rather be pounding a beat any day."

"Who's on the phone?" asked Brown. He had just come in and didn't really care. He thought Mankiewicz would look better on a suburban beat, too.

"Oak Ridge. Long distance. A guy called Grant. Head of somethingological division, and now he's getting somebody else at seventy-five cents a min . . . Hello!"

Mankiewicz got a new grip on the phone and held himself down.

"Look," he said, "let me go through this from the beginning. I want you to get it straight and then if you don't like it, you can send someone down here. The guy doesn't want a lawyer. He claims he just wants to stay in jail and, brother, that's all right with me.

"Well, will you listen? He came in yesterday, walked right up to me, and said, 'Officer, I want you to put me in jail because I want to kill myself.' So I said, 'Mister, I'm sorry you want to kill yourself. Don't do it, because if you do, you'll regret it the rest of your life.'

". . . I *am* serious. I'm just telling you what I said. I'm not saying it was a funny joke, but I've got my own troubles here, if you know what I mean. Do you think all I've got to do here is to listen to cranks who walk in and—

". . . Give me a chance, will you? I said, 'I can't put you in jail for wanting to kill yourself. That's no crime.' And he said, 'But I don't want to die.' So I said, 'Look, bud, get out of here.' I mean if a guy wants to commit suicide, all right, and if he doesn't want to, all right, but I don't want him weeping on my shoulder.

". . . I'm *getting* on with it. So he said to me, 'If I commit a crime, will you put me in jail?' I said, 'If you're caught and if someone files a charge and you can't put up bail, we will. Now beat it.' So he picked up the inkwell on my desk and, before I could stop him, he turned it upside down on the open police blotter.

". . . That's right! Why do you think we have 'malicious mischief' tabbed on him? The ink ran down all over my pants.

". . . Yes, assault and battery, too! I came hopping down to shake a little sense into him, and he kicked me in the shins and handed me one in the eye.

". . . I'm not making this up. You want to come down here and look at my face?

". . . He'll be up in court one of these days. About Thursday, maybe.

". . . Ninety days is the least he'll get, unless the psychoes say otherwise. I think he belongs in the loony-bin myself.

". . . Officially, he's John Smith. That's the only name he'll give.

". . . No, sir, he doesn't get released without the proper legal steps.

". . . O.K., you do that, if you want to, bud! I just do my job here."

He banged the phone into its cradle, glowered at it, then picked it up and began dialing. He said "Gianetti?", got the proper answer and began talking.

"What's the A.E.C.? I've been talking to some Joe on the phone and he says—

". . . No, I'm not kidding, lunk-head. If I were kidding, I'd put up a sign. What's the alphabet soup?"

He listened, said, "Thanks" in a small voice and hung up again.

He had lost some of his color. "That second guy was the head of the Atomic Energy Commission," he said to Brown. "They must have switched me from Oak Ridge to Washington."

Brown lunged to his feet. "Maybe the F.B.I. is after this John Smith guy. Maybe he's one of these here scientists." He felt moved to philosophy. "They ought to keep atomic secrets away from those guys. Things were O.K. as long as General Groves was the only fella who knew about the atom bomb. Once they cut in these here scientists on it, though—"

"Ah, shut up," snarled Mankiewicz.

D r. Oswald Grant kept his eyes fixed on the white line that marked the highway and handled the car as though it were an enemy of his. He always did. He was tall and knobby with a withdrawn expression stamped on his face. His knees crowded the wheel, and his knuckles whitened whenever he made a turn.

Inspector Darrity sat beside him with his legs crossed so that the sole of his left shoe came up hard against the door. It would leave a sandy mark when he took it away. He tossed a nut-brown penknife from hand to hand. Earlier, he had unsheathed its wicked, gleaming blade and scraped casually at his nails as they drove, but a sudden swerve had nearly cost him a finger and he desisted.

He said, "What do you know about this Ralson?"

Dr. Grant took his eyes from the road momentarily, then returned them. He said, uneasily, "I've known him since he took his doctorate at Princeton. He's a very brilliant man."

"Yes? Brilliant, huh? Why is it that all you scientific men describe one another as 'brilliant'? Aren't there any mediocre ones?"

"Many. I'm one of them. But Ralson isn't. You ask anyone. Ask Oppenheimer. Ask Bush. He was the youngest observer at Alamogordo."

"O.K. He was brilliant. What about his private life?"

Grant waited. "I wouldn't know."

"You know him since Princeton. How many years is that?"

They had been scouring north along the highway from Washington for two hours with scarcely a word between them. Now Grant felt the atmosphere change and the grip of the law on his coat collar.

"He got his degree in '43."

"You've known him eight years then."

"That's right."

"And you don't know about his private life?"

"A man's life is his own, Inspector. He wasn't very sociable. A great many of the men are like that. They work under pressure and when they're off the job, they're not interested in continuing the lab acquaintanceships."

"Did he belong to any organizations that you know of?"

"No."

The inspector said, "Did he ever say anything to you that might indicate he was disloyal?"

Grant shouted "No!" and there was silence for a while.

Then Darrity said, "How important is Ralson in atomic research?"

Grant hunched over the wheel and said, "As important as any one man can be. I grant you that no one is indispensable, but Ralson has always seemed to be rather unique. He has the engineering mentality."

"What does that mean?"

"He isn't much of a mathematician himself, but he can work out the gadgets that put someone else's math into life. There's no one like him when it comes to that. Time and again, Inspector, we've had a problem to lick and no time to lick it in. There were nothing but blank minds all around until he put some thought into it and said, 'Why don't you try so-and-so?' Then he'd go away. He wouldn't even be interested enough to see if it worked. But it always did. Always! Maybe we would have got it ourselves eventually, but it might have taken months of additional time. I don't know how he does it. It's no use asking him either. He just looks at you and says, 'It was obvious,' and walks away. Of course, once he's shown us how to do it, it *is* obvious."

The inspector let him have his say out. When no more came, he said, "Would you say he was queer, mentally? Erratic, you know."

"When a person is a genius, you wouldn't expect him to be normal, would you?"

"Maybe not. But just how abnormal was this particular genius?"

"He never talked, particularly. Sometimes, he wouldn't work."

"Stayed at home and went fishing instead?"

"No. He came to the labs all right, but he would just sit at his desk. Sometimes that would go on for weeks. Wouldn't answer you, or even look at you, when you spoke to him."

"Did he ever actually leave work altogether?"

"Before now, you mean? Never!"

"Did he ever claim he wanted to commit suicide? Ever say he wouldn't feel safe except in jail?"

"No."

"You're sure this John Smith is Ralson?"

"I'm almost positive. He has a chemical burn on his right cheek that can't be mistaken."

"O.K. That's that, then. I'll speak to him and see what he sounds like."

The silence fell for good this time. Dr. Grant followed the snaking line as Inspector Darrity tossed the penknife in low arcs from hand to hand.

The warden listened to the call-box and looked up at his visitors. "We can have him brought up here, Inspector, regardless."

"No," Dr. Grant shook his head. "Let's go to him."

Darrity said, "Is that normal for Ralson, Dr. Grant? Would you expect him to attack a guard trying to take him out of a prison cell?"

Grant said, "I can't say."

The warden spread a calloused palm. His thick nose twitched a little. "We haven't tried to do anything about him so far because of the telegram from Washington, but, frankly, he doesn't belong here. I'll be glad to have him taken off my hands."

"We'll see him in his cell," said Darrity.

They went down the hard, bar-lined corridor. Empty, incurious eyes watched their passing.

Dr. Grant felt his flesh crawl. "Has he been kept *here* all the time?"

Darrity did not answer.

The guard, pacing before them, stopped. "This is the cell."

Darrity said, "Is that Dr. Ralson?"

Dr. Grant looked silently at the figure upon the cot. The man had been lying down when they first reached the cell, but now he had risen to one elbow and seemed to be trying to shrink into the wall. His hair was sandy and thin, his figure slight, his eyes blank and china-blue. On his right cheek there was a raised pink patch that tailed off like a tadpole.

Dr. Grant said, "That's Ralson."

The guard opened the door and stepped inside, but Inspector Darrity sent him out again with a gesture. Ralson watched them mutely. He had drawn both feet up to the cot and was pushing backwards. His Adam's apple bobbled as he swallowed.

Darrity said quietly, "Dr. Elwood Ralson?"

"What do you want?" The voice was a surprising baritone.

"Would you come with us, please? We have some questions we would like to ask you."

"No! Leave me alone!"

"Dr. Ralson," said Grant, "I've been sent here to ask you to come back to work."

Ralson looked at the scientist and there was a momentary glint of something other than fear in his eyes. He said, "Hello, Grant." He got off his cot. "Listen, I've been trying to have them put me into a padded cell. Can't you make them do that for me? You know me, Grant. I wouldn't ask for something I didn't feel was necessary. Help me. I can't stand the hard walls. It makes me want to . . . bash—" He brought the flat of his palm thudding down against the hard, dull-gray concrete behind his cot.

Darrity looked thoughtful. He brought out his penknife and unbent the gleaming blade. Carefully, he scraped at his thumbnail, and said, "Would you like to see a doctor?"

But Ralson didn't answer that. He followed the gleam of metal and his lips parted and grew wet. His breath became ragged and harsh.

He said, "Put that away!"

Darrity paused. "Put what away?"

"The knife. Don't hold it in front of me. I can't stand looking at it."

Darrity said, "Why not?" He held it out. "Anything wrong with it? It's a good knife."

Ralson lunged. Darrity stepped back and his left hand came down on the other's wrist. He lifted the knife high in the air. "What's the matter, Ralson? What are you after?"

Grant cried a protest but Darrity waved him away.

Darrity said, "What do you want, Ralson?"

Ralson tried to reach upward and bent under the other's appalling grip. He gasped, "Give me the knife."

"Why, Ralson? What do you want to do with it?"

"Please. I've got to—" He was pleading. "I've got to stop living."

"You want to die?"

"No. But I must."

Darrity shoved. Ralson flailed backward and tumbled into his cot, so that it squeaked noisily. Slowly, Darrity bent the blade of his penknife into its sheath and put it away. Ralson covered his face. His shoulders were shaking but otherwise he did not move.

There was the sound of shouting from the corridor, as the other prisoners reacted to the noise issuing from Ralson's cell. The guard came hurrying down, yelling, "Quiet!" as he went.

Darrity looked up. "It's all right, guard."

He was wiping his hands upon a large white handkerchief. "I think we'll get a doctor for him."

Dr. Gottfried Blaustein was small and dark and spoke with a trace of an Austrian accent. He needed only a small goatee to be the layman's caricature of a psychiatrist. But he was clean-shaven, and very carefully dressed. He watched Grant closely, assessing him, blocking in certain observations and deductions. He did this automatically, now, with everyone he met.

He said, "You give me a sort of picture. You describe a man of great talent, perhaps even genius. You tell me he has always been uncomfortable with people, that he has never fitted in with his laboratory environment, even though it was there that he met the greatest of success. Is there another environment to which he has fitted himself?"

"I don't understand."

"It is not given to all of us to be so fortunate as to find a congenial type of company at the place or in the field where we find it necessary to make a living. Often, one compensates by playing an instrument, or going hiking, or joining some club. In other words, one creates a new type of society, when not working, in which one can feel more at home. It need not have the slightest connection with what one's ordinary occupation is. It is an escape, and not necessarily an unhealthy one." He smiled and added, "Myself, I collect stamps. I am an active member of the American Society of Philatelists."

Grant shook his head. "I don't know what he did outside working hours. I doubt that he did anything like what you've mentioned."

"Um-m-m. Well, that would be sad. Relaxation and enjoyment are wherever you find them, but you must find them somewhere, no?"

"Have you spoken to Dr. Ralson, yet?"

"About his problems? No."

"Aren't you going to?"

"Oh, yes. But he has been here only a week. One must give him a chance to recover. He was in a highly excited state when he first came here. It was almost a delirium. Let him rest and become accustomed to the new environment. I will question him, then."

"Will you be able to get him back to work?"

Blaustein smiled. "How should I know? I don't even know what his sickness is."

"Couldn't you at least get rid of the worst of it—this suicidal obsession of his—and take care of the rest of the cure while he's at work?"

"Perhaps. I couldn't even venture an opinion so far without several interviews."

"How long do you suppose it will all take?"

"In these matters, Dr. Grant, nobody can say."

Grant brought his hands together in a sharp slap. "Do what seems best then. But this is more important than you know."

"Perhaps. But you may be able to help me, Dr. Grant."

"How?"

"Can you get me certain information which may be classified as top secret?"

"What kind of information?"

"I would like to know the suicide rate, since 1945, among nuclear scientists. Also, how many have left their jobs to go into other types of scientific work, or to leave science altogether."

"Is this in connection with Ralson?"

"Don't you think it might be an occupational disease, this terrible unhappiness of his?"

"Well—a good many have left their jobs, naturally."

"Why naturally, Dr. Grant?"

"You must know how it is, Dr. Blaustein. The atmosphere in modern atomic research is one of great pressure and red tape. You work with the government; you work with military men. You can't talk about your work; you have to be careful what you say. Naturally, if you get a chance at a job in a university, where you can fix your own hours, do your own work, write papers that don't have to be submitted to the A.E.C., attend conventions that aren't held behind locked doors, you take it."

"And abandon your field of specialty forever."

"There are always non-military applications. Of course, there was one man who did leave for another reason. He told me once he couldn't sleep nights. He said he'd hear one hundred thousand screams coming from Hiroshima, when he put the lights out. The last I heard of him he was a clerk in a haberdashery."

"And do you ever hear a few screams yourself?"

Grant nodded. "It isn't a nice feeling to know that even a little of the responsibility for atomic destruction might be your own."

"How did Ralson feel?"

"He never spoke of anything like that."

"In other words, if he felt it, he never even had the safety-valve effect of letting off steam to the rest of you."

"I guess he hadn't."

"Yet nuclear research must be done, no?"

"I'll say."

"What would you do, Dr. Grant, if you felt you *had* to do something that you *couldn't* do."

Grant shrugged. "I don't know."

"Some people kill themselves."

"You mean that's what has Ralson down."

"I don't know. I do not know. I will speak to Dr. Ralson this evening. I can promise nothing, of course, but I will let you know whatever I can."

Grant rose. "Thanks, Doctor. I'll try to get the information you want."

* * *

Elwood Ralson's appearance had improved in the week he had been at Dr. Blaustein's sanatorium. His face had filled out and some of the restlessness had gone out of him. He was tieless and beltless. His shoes were without laces.

Blaustein said, "How do you feel, Dr. Ralson?"

"Rested."

"You have been treated well?"

"No complaints, Doctor."

Blaustein's hand fumbled for the letter-opener with which it was his habit to play during moments of abstraction, but his fingers met nothing. It had been put away, of course, with anything else possessing a sharp edge. There was nothing on his desk but papers.

He said, "Sit down, Dr. Ralson. How do your symptoms progress?"

"You mean, do I have what you would call a suicidal impulse? Yes. It gets worse or better, depending on my thoughts, I think. But it's always with me. There is nothing you can do to help."

"Perhaps you are right. There are often things I cannot help. But I would like to know as much as I can about you. You are an important man—"

Ralson snorted.

"You do not consider that to be so?" asked Blaustein.

"No, I don't. There are no important men, any more than there are important individual bacteria."

"I don't understand."

"I don't expect you to."

"And yet it seems to me that behind your statement there must have been much thought. It would certainly be of the greatest interest to have you tell me some of this thought."

For the first time, Ralson smiled. It was not a pleasant smile. His nostrils were white. He said, "It is amusing to watch you, Doctor. You go about your business so conscientiously. You must listen to me, mustn't you, with just that air of phony interest and unctuous sympathy. I can tell you the most ridiculous things and still be sure of an audience, can't I?"

"Don't you think my interest can be real, even granted that it is professional, too?"

"No, I don't."

"Why not?"

"I'm not interested in discussing it."

"Would you rather return to your room?"

"If you don't mind. No!" His voice had suddenly suffused with fury as he stood up, then almost immediately sat down again. "Why shouldn't I use you? I don't like to talk to people. They're stupid. They don't see things. They stare at the obvious for hours and it means nothing to them. If I spoke to them, they wouldn't understand; they'd lose patience; they'd laugh. Whereas you must listen. It's your job. You can't interrupt to tell me I'm mad, even though you may think so."

"I'd be glad to listen to whatever you would like to tell me."

Ralson drew a deep breath. "I've known something for a year now, that very few people know. Maybe it's something no *live* person knows. Do you know that human cultural advances come in spurts? Over a space of two generations in a city containing thirty thousand free men, enough literary and artistic genius of the first rank arose to supply a nation of millions for a century under ordinary circumstances. I'm referring to the Athens of Pericles.

"There are other examples. There is the Florence of the Medicis, the England of Elizabeth, the Spain of the Cordovan Emirs. There was the spasm of social reformers among the Israelites of the eighth and seventh centuries before Christ. Do you know what I mean?"

Blaustein nodded. "I see that history is a subject that interests you."

"Why not? I suppose there's nothing that says I must restrict myself to nuclear cross-sections and wave mechanics."

"Nothing at all. Please proceed."

"At first, I thought I could learn more of the true inwardness of historical cycles by consulting a specialist. I had some conferences with a professional historian. A waste of time!"

"What was his name, this professional historian?"

"Does it matter?"

"Perhaps not, if you would rather consider it confidential. What did he tell you?"

"He said I was wrong; that history only appeared to go in spasms. He said that after closer studies the great civilizations of Egypt and Sumeria did not arise suddenly or out of nothing, but upon the basis of a long-developing sub-civilization that was already sophisticated in its arts. He said that Periclean Athens built upon a pre-Periclean Athens of lower accomplishments, without which the age of Pericles could not have been.

"I asked why was there not a post-Periclean Athens of higher accomplishments still, and he told me that Athens was ruined by a plague and by a long war with Sparta. I asked about other cultural spurts and each time it was a war that ended it, or, in some cases, even accompanied it. He was like all the rest. The truth was there; he had only to bend and pick it up, but he didn't."

Ralson stared at the floor, and said in a tired voice, "They come to me in the laboratory sometimes, Doctor. They say, 'How the devil are we going to get rid of the such-and-such effect that is ruining all our measurements, Ralson?' They show me the instruments and the wiring diagrams and I say, 'It's staring at you. Why don't you do so-and-so? A child could tell you that.' Then I walk away because I can't endure the slow puzzling of their stupid faces. Later, they come to me and say, 'It worked, Ralson. How did you figure it out?' I can't explain to them, Doctor; it would be like explaining that water is wet. And I couldn't explain to the historian. And I can't explain to you. It's a waste of time."

"Would you like to go back to your room?"

"Yes."

Blaustein sat and wondered for many minutes after Ralson had been escorted out of his office. His fingers found their way automatically into the upper right drawer of his desk and lifted out the letter-opener. He twiddled it in his fingers.

Finally, he lifted the telephone and dialed the unlisted number he had been given.

He said, "This is Blaustein. There is a professional historian who was consulted by Dr. Ralson some time in the past, probably a bit over a year ago. I don't know his name. I don't even know if he was connected with a university. If you could find him, I would like to see him."

Thaddeus Milton, Ph.D., blinked thoughtfully at Blaustein and brushed his hand through his iron-gray hair. He said, "They came to me and I said that I had indeed met this man. However, I have had very little connection with him. None, in fact, beyond a few conversations of a professional nature."

"How did he come to you?"

"He wrote me a letter—why me, rather than someone else, I do not know. A series of articles written by myself had appeared in one of the semi-learned journals of semi-popular appeal about that time. It may have attracted his attention."

"I see. With what general topic were the articles concerned?"

"They were a consideration of the validity of the cyclic approach to history. That is, whether one can really say that a particular civilization must follow laws of growth and decline in any manner analogous to those involving individuals."

"I have read Toynbee, Dr. Milton."

"Well, then, you know what I mean."

Blaustein said, "And when Dr. Ralson consulted you, was it with reference to this cyclic approach to history?"

"U-m-m-m. In a way, I suppose. Of course, the man is not an historian and some of his notions about cultural trends are rather dramatic and . . . what shall

I say . . . tabloidish. Pardon me, Doctor, if I ask a question which may be improper. Is Dr. Ralson one of your patients?"

"Dr. Ralson is not well and is in my care. This, and all else we say here, is confidential, of course."

"Quite. I understand that. However, your answer explains something to me. Some of his ideas almost verged on the irrational. He was always worried, it seemed to me, about the connection between what he called 'cultural spurts' and calamities of one sort or another. Now such connections have been noted frequently. The time of a nation's greatest vitality may come at a time of great national insecurity. The Netherlands is a good case in point. Her great artists, statesmen, and explorers belong to the early seventeenth century at the time when she was locked in a death struggle with the greatest European power of the time, Spain. When at the point of destruction at home, she was building an empire in the Far East and had secured footholds on the northern coast of South America, the southern tip of Africa, and the Hudson Valley of North America. Her fleets fought England to a standstill. And then, once her political safety was assured, she declined.

"Well, as I say, that is not unusual. Groups, like individuals, will rise to strange heights in answer to a challenge, and vegetate in the absence of a challenge. Where Dr. Ralson left the paths of sanity, however, was in insisting that such a view amounted to confusing cause and effect. He declared that it was not times of war and danger that stimulated 'cultural spurts,' but rather vice versa. He claimed that each time a group of men showed too much vitality and ability, a war became necessary to destroy the possibility of their further development."

"I see," said Blaustein.

"I rather laughed at him, I am afraid. It may be that that was why he did not keep the last appointment we made. Just toward the end of that last conference he asked me, in the most intense fashion imaginable, whether I did not think it queer that such an improbable species as man was dominant on Earth, when all he had in his favor was intelligence. There I laughed aloud. Perhaps I should not have, poor fellow."

"It was a natural reaction," said Blaustein, "but I must take no more of your time. You have been most helpful."

They shook hands, and Thaddeus Milton took his leave.

"Well," said Darrity, "there are your figures on the recent suicides among scientific personnel. Get any deductions out of it?"

"I should be asking you that," said Blaustein, gently. "The F.B.I. must have investigated thoroughly."

"You can bet the national debt on that. They *are* suicides. There's no mistake about it. There have been people checking on it in another department. The rate is about four times above normal, taking age, social status, economic class into consideration."

"What about British scientists?"

"Just about the same."

"And the Soviet Union?"

"Who can tell?" The investigator leaned forward. "Doc, you don't think the Soviets have some sort of ray that can make people want to commit suicide, do you? It's sort of suspicious that men in atomic research are the only ones affected."

"Is it? Perhaps not. Nuclear physicists may have peculiar strains imposed upon them. It is difficult to tell without thorough study."

"You mean complexes might be coming through?" asked Darrity, warily.

Blaustein made a face. "Psychiatry is becoming too popular. Everybody talks of complexes and neuroses and psychoses and compulsions and what-not. One man's guilt complex is another man's good night's sleep. If I could talk to each one of the men who committed suicide, maybe I could know something."

"You're talking to Ralson."

"Yes, I'm talking to Ralson."

"Has *he* got a guilt complex?"

"Not particularly. He has a background out of which it would not surprise me if he obtained a morbid concern with death. When he was twelve he saw his mother die under the wheels of an automobile. His father died slowly of cancer. Yet the effect of those experiences on his present troubles is not clear."

Darrity picked up his hat. "Well, I wish you'd get a move on, Doc. There's something big on, bigger than the H-Bomb. I don't know how anything *can* be bigger than that, but it is."

R alson insisted on standing. "I had a bad night last night, Doctor."

"I hope," said Blaustein, "these conferences are not disturbing you."

"Well, maybe they, are. They have me thinking on the subject again. It makes things bad, when I do that. How do you imagine it feels being part of a bacterial culture, Doctor?"

"I had never thought of that. To a bacterium, it probably feels quite normal."

Ralson did not hear. He said, slowly, "A culture in which intelligence is being studied. We study all sorts of things as far as their genetic relationships are concerned. We take fruit flies and cross red eyes and white eyes to see what happens. We don't care anything about red eyes and white eyes, but we try to gather from them certain basic genetic principles. You see what I mean?"

"Certainly."

"Even in humans, we can follow various physical characteristics. There are the Hapsburg lips, and the hemophilia that started with Queen Victoria and cropped up in her descendants among the Spanish and Russian royal families. We can follow feeble-mindedness in the Jukeses and Kallikaks. You learn about it in high school biology. But you can't breed human beings the way you do fruit flies. Humans live too long. It would take centuries to draw conclusions. It's a pity we don't have a special race of men that reproduce at weekly intervals, eh?"

He waited for an answer, but Blaustein only smiled.

Ralson said, "Only that's exactly what we would be for another group of beings whose life span might be thousands of years. To them, we would reproduce rapidly enough. We would be short-lived creatures and they could study the genetics of such things as musical aptitude, scientific intelligence, and so on. Not that those things would interest them as such, any more than the white eyes of the fruit fly interest us as white eyes."

"That is a very interesting notion," said Blaustein.

"It is not simply a notion. It is true. To me, it is obvious, and I don't care how it seems to you. Look around you. Look at the planet, Earth. What kind of a ridiculous animal are we to be lords of the world after the dinosaurs had failed? Sure, we're intelligent, but what's intelligence? We think it is important because we have it. If the Tyrannosaurus could have picked out the one quality that he thought would ensure species domination, it would be size and strength. And he would make a better case for it. He lasted longer than we're likely to.

"Intelligence in itself isn't much as far as survival values are concerned. The elephant makes out very poorly indeed when compared to the sparrow even though he is much more intelligent. The dog does well, under man's protection, but not as well as the housefly against whom every human hand is raised. Or take the primates as a group. The small ones cower before their enemies; the large ones have always been remarkably unsuccessful doing more than barely holding their own. The baboons do the best and that is because of their canines, not their brains."

A light film of perspiration covered Ralson's forehead. "And one can see that man has been tailored, made to careful specifications for those things that study us. Generally, the primate is short-lived. Naturally, the larger ones live longer, which is a fairly general rule in animal life. Yet the human being has a life span twice as long as any of the other great apes, considerably longer even than the gorilla that outweighs him. We mature later. It's as though we've been carefully bred to live a little longer so that our life cycle might be of a more convenient length."

He jumped to his feet, shaking his fists above his head. "A thousand years are but as yesterday—"

Blaustein punched a button hastily.

For a moment, Ralson struggled against the white-coated orderly who entered, and then he allowed himself to be led away.

Blaustein looked after him, shook his head, and picked up the telephone.

He got Darrity. "Inspector, you may as well know that this may take a long time." He listened and shook his head. "I know. I don't minimize the urgency."

The voice in the receiver was tinny and harsh. "Doctor, you *are* minimizing it. I'll send Dr. Grant to you. He'll explain the situation to you."

Dr. Grant asked how Ralson was, then asked somewhat wistfully if he could see him. Blaustein shook his head gently.

Grant said, "I've been directed to explain the current situation in atomic research to you."

"So that I will understand, no?"

"I hope so. It's a measure of desperation. I'll have to remind you—"

"Not to breathe a word of it. Yes, I know. This insecurity on the part of you people is a very bad symptom. You must know these things cannot be hidden."

"You live with secrecy. It's contagious."

"Exactly. What is the current secret?"

"There is . . . or, at least, there might be a defense against the atomic bomb."

"And that is a secret? It would be better if it were shouted to all the people of the world instantly."

"For heaven's sake, no. Listen to me, Dr. Blaustein. It's only on paper so far. It's at the E equals mc square stage, almost. It may not be practical. It would be bad to raise hopes we would have to disappoint. On the other hand, if it were known that we *almost* had a defense, there *might* be a desire to start and win a war before the defense were completely developed."

"That I don't believe. But, nevertheless, I distract you. What is the nature of this defense, or have you told me as much as you dare?"

"No, I can go as far as I like, as far as is necessary to convince you we have to have Ralson—and fast!"

"Well, then tell me, and I too, will know secrets. I'll feel like a member of the Cabinet."

"You'll know more than most. Look, Dr. Blaustein, let me explain it in lay language. So far, military advances have been made fairly equally in both offensive and defensive weapons. Once before there seemed to be a definite and permanent tipping of all warfare in the direction of the offense, and that was with the invention of gunpowder. But the defense caught up. The medieval man-in-armor-on-horse became the modern man-in-tank-on-treads, and the stone castle became the concrete pillbox. The same thing, you see, except that everything has been boosted several orders of magnitude."

"Very good. You make it clear. But with the atomic bomb comes more orders of magnitude, no? You must go past concrete and steel for protection."

"Right. Only we can't just make thicker and thicker walls. We've run out of materials that are strong enough. So we must abandon materials altogether. If the atom attacks, we must let the atom defend. We will use energy itself; a force field."

"And what," asked Blaustein, gently, "is a force field?"

"I wish I could tell you. Right now, it's an equation on paper. Energy can be so channeled as to create a wall of matterless inertia, theoretically. In practice, we don't know how to do it."

"It would be a wall you could not go through, is that it? Even for atoms?"

"Even for atom bombs. The only limit on its strength would be the amount of energy we could pour into it. It could even theoretically be made to be impermeable to radiation. The gamma rays would bounce off it. What we're dreaming of is a screen that would be in permanent place about cities; at minimum strength, using practically no energy. It could then be triggered to maximum intensity in a fraction of a millisecond at the impingement of short-wave radiation; say the amount radiating from the mass of plutonium large enough to be an atomic war head. All this is theoretically possible."

"And why must you have Ralson?"

"Because he is the only one who can reduce it to practice, if it can be made practical at all, quickly enough. Every minute counts these days. You know what the international situation is. Atomic defense *must* arrive before the atomic war."

"You are so sure of Ralson?"

"I am as sure of him as I can be of anything. The man is amazing, Dr. Blaustein. He is always right. Nobody in the field knows how he does it."

"A sort of intuition, no?" The psychiatrist looked disturbed. "A kind of reasoning that goes beyond ordinary human capacities. Is that it?"

"I make no pretense of knowing what it is."

"Let me speak to him once more then. I will let you know."

"Good." Grant rose to leave; then, as if in afterthought, he said, "I might say, Doctor, that if you don't do something, the Commission plans to take Dr. Ralson out of your hands."

"And try another psychiatrist? If they wish to do that, of course, I will not stand in their way. It is my opinion, however, that no reputable practitioner will pretend there is a rapid cure."

"We may not intend further mental treatment. He may simply be returned to work."

"That, Dr. Grant, I will fight. You will get nothing out of him. It will be his death."

"We get nothing out of him anyway."

"This way there is at least a chance, no?"

"I hope so. And by the way, please don't mention the fact that I said anything about taking Ralson away."

"I will not, and I thank you for the warning. Good-bye, Dr. Grant."

"I made a fool of myself last time, didn't I, Doctor?" said Ralson. He was frowning.

"You mean you don't believe what you said then?"

"I *do*!" Ralson's slight form trembled with the intensity of his affirmation.

He rushed to the window, and Blaustein swiveled in his chair to keep him in view. There were bars in the window. He couldn't jump. The glass was unbreakable.

Twilight was ending, and the stars were beginning to come out. Ralson stared at them in fascination, then he turned to Blaustein and flung a finger outward. "Every single one of them is an incubator. They maintain temperatures at the desired point. Different experiments; different temperatures. And the planets that circle them are just huge cultures, containing different nutrient mixtures and different life forms. The experimenters are economical, too—whatever and whoever they are. They've cultured many types of life forms in this particular test-tube. Dinosaurs in a moist, tropical age and ourselves among the glaciers. They turn the sun up and down and we try to work out the physics of it. Physics!" He drew his lips back in a snarl.

"Surely," said Dr. Blaustein, "it is not possible that the sun can be turned up and down at will."

"Why not? It's just like a heating element in an oven. You think bacteria know what it is that works the heat that reaches them? Who knows? Maybe they evolve theories, too. Maybe they have their cosmogonies about cosmic catastrophes, in which clashing lightbulbs create strings of Petri dishes. Maybe they think there must be some beneficent creator that supplies them with food and warmth and says to them, 'Be fruitful and multiply!'

"We breed like them, not knowing why. We obey the so-called laws of nature which are only our interpretation of the not-understood forces imposed upon us.

"And now they've got the biggest experiment of any yet on their hands. It's been going on for two hundred years. They decided to develop a strain for mechanical aptitude in England in the seventeen hundreds, I imagine. We call it the Industrial Revolution. It began with steam, went on to electricity, then atoms. It was an interesting experiment, but they took their chances on letting it spread. Which is why they'll have to be very drastic indeed in ending it."

Blaustein said, "And how would they plan to end it? Do you have an idea about that?"

"You ask *me* how they plan to end it? You can look about the world today and still ask what is likely to bring our technological age to an end. All the Earth fears an atomic war and would do anything to avoid it; yet all the Earth fears that an atomic war is inevitable."

"In other words, the experimenters will arrange an atomic war whether we want it or not, to kill off the technological era we are in, and to start fresh. That is it, no?"

"Yes. It's logical. When we sterilize an instrument, do the germs know where the killing heat comes from? Or what has brought it about? There is some way the experimenters can raise the heat of our emotions; some way they can handle us that passes our understanding."

"Tell me," said Blaustein, "is that why you want to die? Because you think the destruction of civilization is coming and can't be stopped?"

Ralson said, "I *don't* want to die. It's just that I must." His eyes were tortured. "Doctor, if you had a culture of germs that were highly dangerous and that you had to keep under absolute control, might you not have an agar medium impregnated with, say, penicillin, in a circle at a certain distance from the center of inoculation? Any germs spreading out too far from the center would die. You would have nothing against the particular germs who were killed; you might not even know that any germs had spread that far in the first place. It would be purely automatic.

"Doctor, there is a penicillin ring about our intellects. When we stray too far; when we penetrate the true meaning of our own existence, we have reached into the penicillin and we must die. It works slowly—but it's hard to stay alive."

He smiled briefly and sadly. Then he said, "May I go back to my room now, Doctor?"

D r. Blaustein went to Ralson's room about noon the next day. It was a small room and featureless. The walls were gray with padding. Two small windows were high up and could not be reached. The matress lay directly on the padded floor. There was nothing of metal in the room; nothing that could be utilized in tearing life from body. Even Ralson's nails were clipped short.

Ralson sat up. "Hello!"

"Hello, Dr. Ralson. May I speak to you?"

"Here? There isn't any seat I can offer you."

"It is all right. I'll stand. I have a sitting job and it is good for my sitting-down place that I should stand sometimes. Dr. Ralson, I have thought all night of what you told me yesterday and in the days before."

"And now you are going to apply treatment to rid me of what you think are delusions."

"No. It is just that I wish to ask questions and perhaps to point out some consequences of your theories which . . . you will forgive me? . . . you may not have thought of."

"Oh?"

"You see, Dr. Ralson, since you have explained your theories, I, too, know what you know. Yet I have no feeling about suicide."

"Belief is more than something intellectual, Doctor. You'd have to believe this with all your insides, which you don't."

"Do you not think perhaps it is rather a phenomenon of adaptation?"

"How do you mean?"

"You are not really a biologist, Dr. Ralson. And although you are very brilliant indeed in physics, you do not think of everything with respect to these bacterial cultures you use as analogies. You know that it is possible to breed bacterial strains that are resistant to penicillin or to almost any bacterial poison."

"Well?"

"The experimenters who breed us have been working with humanity for many generations, no? And this particular strain which they have been culturing for two centuries shows no sign of dying out spontaneously. Rather, it is a vigorous strain and a very infective one. Older high-culture strains were confined to single cities or to small areas and lasted only a generation or two. This one is spreading throughout the world. It is a *very* infective strain. Do you not think it may have developed penicillin immunity? In other words, the methods the experimenters use to wipe out the culture may not work too well anymore, no?"

Ralson shook his head. "It's working on me."

"You are perhaps non-resistant. Or you have stumbled into a very high concentration of penicillin indeed. Consider all the people who have been trying to outlaw atomic warfare and to establish some form of world government and lasting peace. The effort has risen in recent years, without too awful results."

"It isn't stopping the atomic war that's coming."

"No, but maybe only a little more effort is all that is required. The peace advocates do not kill themselves. More and more humans are immune to the experimenters. Do you know what they are doing in the laboratory?"

"I don't want to know."

"You *must* know. They are trying to invent a force field that will stop the atom bomb. Dr. Ralson, if I am culturing a virulent and pathological bacterium, then, even with all precautions, it may sometimes happen that I will start a plague. We may be bacteria to them, but we are dangerous to them, also, or they wouldn't wipe us out so carefully after each experiment.

"They are not quick, no? To them a thousand years is as a day, no? By the time they realize we are out of the culture, past the penicillin, it will be too late for them to stop us. They have brought us to the atom, and if we can only prevent ourselves from using it upon one another, we may turn out to be too much even for the experimenters."

Ralson rose to his feet. Small though he was, he was an inch and a half taller than Blaustein. "They are really working on a force field?"

"They are trying to. But they need you."

"No. I can't."

"They must have you in order that you might see what is so obvious to you. It is not obvious to them. Remember, it is your help, or else—defeat of man by the experimenters."

Ralson took a few rapid steps away, staring into the blank, padded wall. He muttered, "But there must be that defeat. If they build a force field, it will mean death for all of them before it can be completed."

"Some or all of them may be immune, no? And in any case, it will be death for them anyhow. They are trying."

Ralson said, "I'll try to help them."

"Do you still want to kill yourself?"

"Yes."

"But you'll try not to, no?"

"I'll *try* not to, Doctor." His lip quivered. "I'll have to be watched."

Blaustein climbed the stairs and presented his pass to the guard in the lobby. He had already been inspected at the outer gate, but he, his pass, and its signature were now scrutinized once again. After a moment, the guard retired to his little booth and made a phone call. The answer satisfied him. Blaustein took a seat and, in half a minute, was up again, shaking hands with Dr. Grant.

"The President of the United States would have trouble getting in here, no?" said Blaustein.

The lanky physicist smiled. "You're right, if he came without warning."

They took an elevator which traveled twelve floors. The office to which Grant led the way had windows in three directions. It was sound-proofed and air-conditioned. Its walnut furniture was in a state of high polish.

Blaustein said, "My goodness. It is like the office of the chairman of a board of directors. Science is becoming big business."

Grant looked embarrassed. "Yes, I know, but government money flows easily and it is difficult to persuade a congressman that your work is important unless he can see, smell, and touch the surface shine."

Blaustein sat down and felt the upholstered seat give way slowly. He said, "Dr. Elwood Ralson has agreed to return to work."

"Wonderful. I was hoping you would say that. I was hoping that was why you wanted to see me." As though inspired by the news, Grant offered the psychiatrist a cigar, which was refused.

"However," said Blaustein, "he remains a very sick man. He will have to be treated carefully and with insight."

"Of course. Naturally."

"It's not quite as simple as you may think. I want to tell you something of Ralson's problems, so that you will really understand how delicate the situation is."

He went on talking and Grant listened first in concern, and then in astonishment. "But then the man is out of his head, Dr. Blaustein. He'll be of no use to us. He's crazy."

Blaustein shrugged. "It depends on how you define 'crazy.' It's a bad word; don't use it. He has delusions, certainly. Whether they will affect his peculiar talents one cannot know."

"But surely no sane man could possibly—"

"Please. Please. Let us not launch into long discussions on psychiatric definitions of sanity and so on. The man has delusions and, ordinarily, I would dismiss them from all consideration. It is just that I have been given to understand that the man's particular ability lies in his manner of proceeding to the solution of a problem by what seems to be outside ordinary reason. That is so, no?"

"Yes. That *must* be admitted."

"How can you and I judge then as to the worth of one of his conclusions? Let me ask you, do *you* have suicidal impulses lately?"

"I don't think so."

"And other scientists here?"

"No, of course not."

"I would suggest, however, that while research on the force field proceeds, the scientists concerned be watched here and at home. It might even be a good enough idea that they should not go home. Offices like these could be arranged to be a small dormitory—"

"Sleep at work. You would never get them to agree."

"Oh, yes. If you do not tell them the real reason but say it is for security purposes, they will agree. 'Security purposes' is a wonderful phrase these days, no? Ralson must be watched more than anyone."

"Of course."

"But all this is minor. It is something to be done to satisfy my conscience in case Ralson's theories are correct. Actually, I don't believe them. They *are* delusions, but once that is granted, it is necessary to ask what the causes of those delusions are. What is it in Ralson's mind, in his background, in his life that makes it so necessary for him to have these particular delusions? One cannot answer that simply. It may well take years of constant psychoanalysis to discover the answer. And until the answer is discovered, he will not be cured.

"But, meanwhile, we can perhaps make intelligent guesses. He has had an unhappy childhood, which, in one way or another, has brought him face to face with death in very unpleasant fashion. In addition, he has never been able to form associations with other children, or, as he grew older, with other men. He was always impatient with their slower forms of reasoning. Whatever difference there is between his mind and that of others, it has built a wall between him and society as strong as the force field you are trying to design. For similar reasons, he has been unable to enjoy a normal sex life. He has never married; he has had no sweethearts.

"It is easy to see that he could easily compensate to himself for this failure to be accepted by his social milieu by taking refuge in the thought that other human beings are inferior to himself. Which is, of course, true, as far as mentality is concerned. There are, of course, many, many facets to the human personality and in not all of them is he superior. No one is. Others, then, who are more prone to see merely what is inferior, just as he himself is, would not accept his affected pre-eminence of position. They would think him queer, even laughable, which would make it even more important to Ralson to prove how miserable and inferior the human species was. How could he better do that than to show that mankind was simply a form of bacteria to other superior creatures which experiment upon them. And then his impulses to suicide would be a wild desire to break away completely from being a man at all, to stop this identification with the miserable species he has created in his mind. You see?"

Grant nodded. "Poor guy."

"Yes, it is a pity. Had he been properly taken care of in childhood—well, it is best for Dr. Ralson that he have no contact with any of the other men here. He is too sick to be trusted with them. You, yourself, must arrange to be the only man who will see him or speak to him. Dr. Ralson has agreed to that. He apparently thinks you are not as stupid as some of the others."

Grant smiled faintly. "That is agreeable to me."

"You will, of course, be careful. I would not discuss anything with him but his work. If he should volunteer information about his theories, which I doubt, confine yourself to something non-committal, and leave. And at all times, keep away anything that is sharp and pointed. Do not let him reach a window. Try to have his hands kept in view. You understand. I leave my patient in your care, Dr. Grant."

"I will do my best, Dr. Blaustein."

For two months, Ralson lived in a corner of Grant's office, and Grant lived with him. Gridwork had been built up before the windows, wooden furniture was removed and upholstered sofas brought in. Ralson did his thinking on the couch and his calculating on a desk pad atop a hassock.

The "Do Not Enter" sign was a permanent fixture outside the office. Meals were left outside. The adjoining men's room was marked off for private use and the door between it and the office removed. Grant switched to an electric razor. He made certain that Ralson took sleeping pills each night and waited till the other slept before sleeping himself.

And always reports were brought to Ralson. He read them while Grant watched and tried to seem not to watch.

Then Ralson would let them drop and stare at the ceiling, with one hand shading his eyes.

"Anything?" asked Grant.

Ralson shook his head from side to side.

Grant said, "Look, I'll clear the building during the swing shift. It's important that you see some of the experimental jigs we've been setting up."

They did so, wandering through the lighted, empty buildings like drifting ghosts, hand in hand. Always hand in hand. Grant's grip was tight. But after each trip, Ralson would still shake his head from side to side.

Half a dozen times he would begin writing; each time there would be a few scrawls and then he would kick the hassock over on its side.

Until, finally, he began writing once again and covered half a page rapidly. Automatically, Grant approached. Ralson looked up, covering the sheet of paper with a trembling hand.

He said, "Call Blaustein."

"What?"

"I said, 'Call Blaustein.' Get him here. Now!"

Grant moved to the telephone.

Ralson was writing rapidly now, stopping only to brush wildly at his forehead with the back of a hand. It came away wet.

He looked up and his voice was cracked, "Is he coming?"

Grant looked worried. "He isn't at his office."

"Get him at his home. Get him wherever he is. *Use* that telephone. Don't play with it."

Grant used it; and Ralson pulled another sheet toward himself.

Five minutes later, Grant said, "He's coming. What's wrong? You're looking sick."

Ralson could speak only thickly, "No time—can't talk—"

He was writing, scribbling, scrawling, shakily diagraming. It was as though he were driving his hands, fighting it.

"Dictate!" urged Grant. "I'll write."

Ralson shook him off. His words were unintelligible. He held his wrist with his other hand, shoving it as though it were a piece of wood, and then he collapsed over the papers.

Grant edged them out from under and laid Ralson down on the couch. He hovered over him restlessly and hopelessly until Blaustein arrived.

Blaustein took one look. "What happened?"

Grant said, "I think he's alive," but by that time Blaustein had verified that for himself, and Grant told him what had happened.

Blaustein used a hypodermic and they waited. Ralson's eyes were blank when they opened. He moaned.

Blaustein leaned close. "Ralson."

Ralson's hands reached out blindly and clutched at the psychiatrist. "Doc. Take me back."

"I will. Now. It is that you have the force field worked out, no?"

"It's on the papers. Grant, it's on the papers."

Grant had them and was leafing through them dubiously. Ralson said, weakly, "It's not all there. It's all I can write. You'll have to make it out of that. Take me back, Doc!"

"Wait," said Grant. He whispered urgently to Blaustein. "Can't you leave him here till we test this thing? I can't make out what most of this is. The writing is illegible. Ask him what makes him think this will work."

"Ask *him*?" said Blaustein, gently. "Isn't he the one who always knows?"

"Ask me, anyway," said Ralson, overhearing from where he lay on the couch. His eyes were suddenly wide and blazing.

They turned to him.

He said, "They don't want a force field. *They!* The experimenters! As long as I had no true grasp, things remained as they were. But I hadn't followed up that thought—that thought which is there in the papers—I hadn't followed it up for thirty seconds before I felt . . . I felt—Doctor—"

Blaustein said, "What is it?"

Ralson was whispering again, "I'm deeper in the penicillin. I could feel myself plunging in and in, the further I went with that. I've never been in . . . so deep. That's how I knew I was right. Take me away."

Blaustein straightened. "I'll have to take him away, Grant. There's no alternative. If you can make out what he's written, that's it. If you can't make it out, I can't help you. That man can do no more work in his field without dying, do you understand?"

"But," said Grant, "he's dying of something imaginary."

"All right. Say that he is. But he will be really dead just the same, no?"

Ralson was unconscious again and heard nothing of this. Grant looked at him somberly, then said, "Well, take him away, then."

Ten of the top men at the Institute watched glumly as slide after slide filled the illuminated screen. Grant faced them, expression hard and frowning.

He said, "I think the idea is simple enough. You're mathematicians and you're engineers. The scrawl may seem illegible, but it was done with meaning behind it. That meaning must somehow remain in the writing, distorted though it is. The first page is clear enough. It should be a good lead. Each one of you will look at every page over and over again. You're going to put down every possible version of each page as it seems it might be. You will work independently. I want no consultations."

One of them said, "How do you know it means *anything*, Grant?"

"Because those are Ralson's notes."

"*Ralson!* I thought he was—"

"You thought he was sick," said Grant. He had to shout over the rising hum of conversation. "I know. He is. That's the writing of a man who was nearly dead. It's all we'll ever get from Ralson, anymore. Somewhere in that scrawl is the answer to the force field problem. If we can't find it, we may have to spend ten years looking for it elsewhere."

They bent to their work. The night passed. Two nights passed. Three nights—

Grant looked at the results. He shook his head. "I'll take your word for it that it is all self-consistent. I can't say I understand it."

Lowe, who, in the absence of Ralson, would readily have been rated the best nuclear engineer at the Institute, shrugged. "It's not exactly clear to me. If it works, he hasn't explained why."

"He had no time to explain. Can you build the generator as he describes it?"

"I could try."

"Would you look at all the other versions of the pages?"

"The others are definitely not self-consistent."

"Would you double-check?"

"Sure."

"And could you start construction anyway?"

"I'll get the shop started. But I tell you frankly that I'm pessimistic."

"I know. So am I."

The thing grew. Hal Ross, Senior Mechanic, was put in charge of the actual construction, and he stopped sleeping. At any hour of the day or night, he could be found at it, scratching his bald head.

He asked questions only once, "What is it, Dr. Lowe? Never saw anything like it. What's it supposed to do?"

Lowe said, "You know where you are, Ross. You know we don't ask questions here. Don't ask again."

Ross did not ask again. He was known to dislike the structure that was being built. He called it ugly and unnatural. But he stayed at it.

Blaustein called one day.

Grant said, "How's Ralson?"

"Not good. He wants to attend the testing of the field projector he designed."

Grant hesitated, "I suppose we should. It's his after all."

"I would have to come with him."

Grant looked unhappier. "It might be dangerous, you know. Even in a pilot test, we'd be playing with tremendous energies."

Blaustein said, "No more dangerous for us than for you."

"Very well. The list of observers will have to be cleared through the Commission and the F.B.I., but I'll put you in."

Blaustein looked about him. The field projector squatted in the very center of the huge testing laboratory, but all else had been cleared. There was no visible connection with the plutonium pile which served as energy source, but from what the psychiatrist heard in scraps about him—he knew better than to ask Ralson—the connection was from beneath.

At first, the observers had circled the machine, talking in incomprehensibles, but they were drifting away now. The gallery was filling up. There were at least three men in generals' uniforms on the other side, and a real coterie of lower-scale military. Blaustein chose an unoccupied portion of the railing; for Ralson's sake, most of all.

He said, "Do you still think you would like to stay?"

It was warm enough within the laboratory, but Ralson was in his coat, with his collar turned up. It made little difference, Blaustein felt. He doubted that any of Ralson's former acquaintances would now recognize him.

Ralson said, "I'll stay."

Blaustein was pleased. He wanted to see the test. He turned again at a new voice.

"Hello, Dr. Blaustein."

For a minute, Blaustein did not place him, then he said, "Ah, Inspector Darrity. What are you doing here?"

"Just what you would suppose." He indicated the watchers. "There isn't any way you can weed them out so that you can be sure there won't be any mistakes. I once stood as near to Klaus Fuchs as I am standing to you." He tossed his pocketknife into the air and retrieved it with a dexterous motion.

"Ah, yes. Where shall one find perfect security? What man can trust even his own unconscious? And you will now stand near to me, no?"

"Might as well." Darrity smiled. "You were very anxious to get in here, weren't you?"

"Not for myself, Inspector. And would you put away the knife, please."

Darrity turned in surprise in the direction of Blaustein's gentle hand gesture. He put his knife away and looked at Blaustein's companion for a second time. He whistled softly.

He said, "Hello, Dr. Ralson."

Ralson croaked, "Hello."

Blaustein was not surprised at Darrity's reaction. Ralson had lost twenty pounds since returning to the sanatorium. His face was yellow and wrinkled; the face of a man who had suddenly become sixty.

Blaustein said, "Will the test be starting soon?"

Darrity said, "It looks as if they're starting now."

He turned and leaned on the rail. Blaustein took Ralson's elbow and began leading him away, but Darrity said, softly, "Stay here, Doc. I don't want you wandering about."

Blaustein looked across the laboratory. Men were standing about with the uncomfortable air of having turned half to stone. He could recognize Grant, tall and gaunt, moving his hand slowly to light a cigarette, then changing his mind and putting lighter and cigarette in his pocket. The young men at the control panels waited tensely.

Then there was a low humming and the faint smell of ozone filled the air.

Ralson said harshly, "Look!"

Blaustein and Darrity looked along the pointing finger. The projector seemed to flicker. It was as though there were heated air rising between it and them. An iron ball came swinging down pendulum fashion and passed through the flickering area.

"It slowed up, no?" said Blaustein, excitedly.

Ralson nodded. "They're measuring the height of rise on the other side to calculate the loss of momentum. Fools! I *said* it would work." He was speaking with obvious difficulty.

Blaustein said, "Just watch, Dr. Ralson. I would not allow myself to grow needlessly excited."

The pendulum was stopped in its swinging, drawn up. The flickering about the projector became a little more intense and the iron sphere arced down once again.

Over and over again, and each time the sphere's motion was slowed with more of a jerk. It made a clearly audible sound as it struck the flicker. And eventually, it *bounced*. First, soggily, as though it hit putty, and then ringingly, as though it hit steel, so that the noise filled the place.

They drew back the pendulum bob and used it no longer. The projector could hardly be seen behind the haze that surrounded it.

Grant gave an order and the odor of ozone was suddenly sharp and pungent. There was a cry from the assembled observers; each one exclaiming to his neighbor. A dozen fingers were pointing.

Blaustein leaned over the railing, as excited as the rest. Where the projector had been, there was now only a huge semi-globular mirror. It was perfectly and beautifully clear. He could see himself in it, a small man standing on a small balcony that curved up on each side. He could see the fluorescent lights reflected in spots of glowing illumination. It was wonderfully sharp.

He was shouting, "Look, Ralson. It is reflecting energy. It is reflecting light waves like a mirror. Ralson—"

He turned, "Ralson! Inspector, where is Ralson?"

"What?" Darrity whirled. "I haven't seen him."

He looked about, wildly. "Well, he won't get away. No way of getting out of here now. You take the other side." And then he clapped hand to thigh, fumbled for a moment in his pocket, and said, "My knife is gone."

Blaustein found him. He was inside the small office belonging to Hal Ross. It led off the balcony, but under the circumstances, of course, it had been deserted. Ross himself was not even an observer. A senior mechanic need not observe. But his office would do very well for the final end of the long fight against suicide.

Blaustein stood in the doorway for a sick moment, then turned. He caught Darrity's eye as the latter emerged from a similar office a hundred feet down the balcony. He beckoned, and Darrity came at a run.

D r. Grant was trembling with excitement. He had taken two puffs at each of two cigarettes and trodden each underfoot thereafter. He was fumbling with the third now.

He was saying, "This is better than any of us could possibly have hoped. We'll have the gunfire test tomorrow. I'm sure of the result now, but we've planned it; we'll go through with it. We'll skip the small arms and start with the bazooka levels. Or maybe not. It might be necessary to construct a special testing structure to take care of the ricochet problem."

He discarded his third cigarette.

A general said, "We'd have to try a literal atom-bombing, of course."

"Naturally. Arrangements have already been made to build a mock-city at Eniwetok. We could build a generator on the spot and drop the bomb. There'd be animals inside."

"And you really think if we set up a field in full power it would hold the bomb?"

"It's not just that, General. There'd be no noticeable field at all until the bomb is dropped. The radiation of the plutonium would have to energize the field before explosion. As we did here in the last step. That's the essence of it all."

"You know," said a Princeton professor, "I see disadvantages, too. When the field is on full, anything it protects is in total darkness, as far as the sun is concerned. Besides that, it strikes me that the enemy can adopt the practice of dropping harmless radioactive missiles to set off the field at frequent intervals. It would have nuisance value and be a considerable drain on our pile as well."

"Nuisances," said Grant, "can be survived. These difficulties will be met eventually, I'm sure, now that the main problem has been solved."

The British observer had worked his way toward Grant and was shaking hands. He said, "I feel better about London already. I cannot help but wish your government would allow me to see the complete plans. What I have seen strikes me as completely ingenious. It seems obvious now, of course, but how did anyone ever come to think of it?"

Grant smiled. "That question has been asked before with reference to Dr. Ralson's devices—"

He turned at the touch of a hand upon his shoulder. "Dr. Blaustein! I had nearly forgotten. Here, I want to talk to you."

He dragged the small psychiatrist to one side and hissed in his ear, "Listen, can you persuade Ralson to be introduced to these people? This is his triumph."

Blaustein said, "Ralson is dead."

"*What!*"

"Can you leave these people for a time?"

"Yes . . . yes—gentlemen, you will excuse me for a few minutes?"

He hurried off with Blaustein.

The Federal men had already taken over. Unobtrusively, they barred the doorway to Ross's office. Outside there were the milling crowd discussing the answer to Alamogordo that they had just witnessed. Inside, unknown to them, was the death of the answerer. The G-man barrier divided to allow Grant and Blaustein to enter. It closed behind them again.

For a moment, Grant raised the sheet. He said, "He looks peaceful."

"I would say—happy," said Blaustein.

Darrity said, colorlessly, "The suicide weapon was my own knife. It was my negligence; it will be reported as such."

"No, no," said Blaustein, "that would be useless. He was my patient and I am responsible. In any case, he would not have lived another week. Since he invented the projector, he was a dying man."

Grant said, "How much of this has to be placed in the Federal files? Can't we forget all about his madness?"

"I'm afraid not, Dr. Grant," said Darrity.

"I have told him the whole story," said Blaustein, sadly.

Grant looked from one to the other. "I'll speak to the Director. I'll go to the President, if necessary. I don't see that there need be any mention of suicide or of madness. He'll get full publicity as inventor of the field projector. It's the least we can do for him." His teeth were gritting.

Blaustein said, "He left a note."

"A note?"

Darrity handed him a sheet of paper and said, "Suicides almost always do. This is one reason the doctor told me about what really killed Ralson."

The note was addressed to Blaustein and it went:

"The projector works; I knew it would. The bargain is done. You've got it and you don't need me anymore. So I'll go. You needn't worry about the human race, Doc. You were right. They've bred us too long; they've taken too many chances. We're out of the culture now and they won't be able to stop us. I know. That's all I can say. I know."

He had signed his name quickly and then underneath there was one scrawled line, and it said:

"Provided enough men are penicillin-resistant."

Grant made a motion to crumple the paper, but Darrity held out a quick hand.

"For the record, Doctor," he said.

Grant gave it to him and said, "Poor Ralson! He died believing all that trash."

Blaustein nodded. "So he did. Ralson will be given a great funeral, I suppose, and the fact of his invention will be publicized without the madness and the suicide. But the government men will remain interested in his mad theories. They may not be so mad, no, Mr. Darrity?"

"That's ridiculous, Doctor," said Grant. "There isn't a scientist on the job who has shown the least uneasiness about it at all."

"Tell him, Mr. Darrity," said Blaustein.

Darrity said, "There has been another suicide. No, no, none of the scientists. No one with a degree. It happened this morning, and we investigated because we thought it might have some connection with today's test. There didn't seem any, and we were going to keep it quiet till the test was over. Only now there seems to be a connection.

"The man who died was just a guy with a wife and three kids. No reason to die. No history of mental illness. He threw himself under a car. We have witnesses, and it's certain he did it on purpose. He didn't die right away and they got a doctor to him. He was horribly mangled, but his last words were 'I feel much better now' and he died."

"But who was he?" cried Grant.

"Hal Ross. The guy who actually built the projector. The guy whose office this is."

Blaustein walked to the window. The evening sky was darkening into starriness.

He said, "The man knew nothing about Ralson's views. He had never spoken to Ralson, Mr. Darrity tells me. Scientists are probably resistant as a whole. They must be or they are quickly driven out of the profession. Ralson was an exception, a penicillin-sensitive who insisted on remaining. You see what happened to him. But what about the others; those who have remained in walks of life where there is no constant weeding out of the sensitive ones. How much of humanity *is* penicillin-resistant?"

"You *believe* Ralson?" asked Grant in horror.

"I don't really know."

Blaustein looked at the stars.

Incubators?

Hostess

Rose Smollett was happy about it; almost triumphant. She peeled off her gloves, put her hat away, and turned her brightening eyes upon her husband.

She said, "Drake, we're going to have him here."

Drake looked at her with annoyance. "You've missed supper. I thought you were going to be back by seven."

"Oh, that doesn't matter. I ate something on the way home. But, Drake, we're going to have him here!"

"*Who* here? What are you talking about?"

"The doctor from Hawkin's Planet! Didn't you realize that was what today's conference was about? We spent all day talking about it. It's the most exciting thing that could possibly have happened!"

Drake Smollett removed the pipe from the vicinity of his face. He stared first at it and then at his wife. "Let me get this straight. When you say the doctor from Hawkin's Planet, do you mean the Hawkinsite you've got at the Institute?"

"Well, of course. Who else could I possibly mean?"

"And may I ask what the devil you mean by saying we'll have him here?"

"Drake, don't you understand?"

"What is there to understand? Your Institute may be interested in the thing, but I'm not. What have we to do with it personally? It's Institute business, isn't it?"

"But, darling," Rose said, patiently, "the Hawkinsite would like to stay at a private house somewhere, where he won't be bothered with official ceremony, and where he'll be able to proceed more according to his own likes and dislikes. I find it quite understandable."

"Why at *our* house?"

"Because our place is convenient for the purpose, I suppose. They asked if I would allow it, and frankly," she added with some stiffness, "I consider it a privilege."

"Look!" Drake put his fingers through his brown hair and succeeded in rumpling it. "We've got a convenient little place here—granted! It's not the most elegant place in the world, but it does well enough for us. However, I don't see where we've got room for extraterrestrial visitors."

R ose began to look worried. She removed her glasses and put them away in their case. "He can stay in the spare room. He'll take care of it himself. I've spoken to him and he's very pleasant. Honestly, all we have to do is show a certain amount of adaptability."

Drake said, "Sure, just a little adaptability! The Hawkinsites breathe cyanide. We'll just adapt ourselves to that, I suppose!"

"He carries cyanide in a little cylinder. You won't even notice it."

"And what else about them that I won't notice?"

"*Nothing* else. They're perfectly harmless. Goodness, they're even vegetarians."

"And what does that mean? Do we feed him a bale of hay for dinner?"

Rose's lower lip trembled. "Drake, you're being deliberately hateful. There are many vegetarians on Earth; they don't eat hay."

"And what about us? Do we eat meat ourselves or will that make us look like cannibals to him? I won't live on salads to suit him; I warn you."

"You're being quite ridiculous."

Rose felt helpless. She had married late in life, comparatively. Her career had been chosen; she herself had seemed well settled in it. She was a fellow in biology at the Jenkins Institute for the Natural Sciences, with over twenty publications to her credit. In a word, the line was hewed, the path cleared; she had been set for a career and spinsterhood. And now, at 35, she was still a little amazed to find herself a bride of less than a year.

Occasionally, it embarrassed her, too, since she sometimes found that she had not the slightest idea of how to handle her husband. What *did* one do when the man of the family became mulish? That was not included in any of her courses. As a woman of independent mind and career, she couldn't bring herself to cajolery.

So she looked at him steadily and said simply, "It means very much to me."

"Why?"

"Because, Drake, if he stays here for any length of time, I can study him really closely. Very little work has been done on the biology and psychology of the individual Hawkinsite or of any of the extraterrestrial intelligences. We have some of their sociology and history, of course, but that's all. Surely, you must see the opportunity. He stays here; we watch him, speak to him, observe his habits—"

"Not interested."

"Oh, Drake, I don't understand you."

"You're going to say I'm not usually like this, I suppose."

"Well, you're not."

Drake was silent for a while. He seemed withdrawn and his high cheekbones and large chin were twisted and frozen into a brooding position.

He said finally, "Look, I've heard a bit about the Hawkinsites in the way of my own business. You say there have been investigations of their sociology, but not of their biology. Sure. It's because the Hawkinsites don't like to be studied as specimens any more than we would. I've spoken to men who were in charge of security groups watching various Hawkinsite missions on Earth. The missions stay in the rooms assigned to them and don't leave for anything but the most important official business. They have nothing to do with Earthmen. It's quite obvious that they are as revolted by us as I personally am by them.

"In fact, I just don't understand why this Hawkinsite at the Institute should be any different. It seems to me to be against all the rules to have him come here by himself, anyway—and to have him want to stay in an Earthman's home just puts the maraschino cherry on top."

Rose said, wearily, "This is different. I'm surprised you can't understand it, Drake. He's a doctor. He's coming here in the way of medical research, and I'll grant you that he probably doesn't enjoy staying with human beings and will find us perfectly horrible. But he must stay just the same! Do you suppose human doctors enjoy going into the tropics, or that they are particularly fond of letting themselves be bitten by infected mosquitoes?"

Drake said sharply, "What's this about mosquitoes? What have they to do with it?"

"Why, nothing," Rose answered, surprised. "It just came to my mind, that's all. I was thinking of Reed and his yellow-fever experiments."

Drake shrugged. "Well, have it your own way."

For a moment, Rose hesitated. "You're not angry about this, are you?" To her own ears she sounded unpleasantly girlish.

"No."

And that, Rose knew, meant that he was.

Rose surveyed herself doubtfully in the full-length mirror. She had never been beautiful and was quite reconciled to the fact; so much so that it no longer mattered. Certainly, it would not matter to a being from Hawkin's Planet. What *did* bother her was this matter of being a hostess under the very queer circumstances of having to be tactful to an extraterrestrial creature and, at the same time, to her husband as well. She wondered which would prove the more difficult.

Drake was coming home late that day; he was not due for half an hour. Rose found herself inclined to believe that he had arranged that purposely in a sullen desire to leave her alone with her problem. She found herself in a state of mild resentment.

He had called her just before noon at the Institute and had asked abruptly, "When are you taking him home?"

She answered, curtly, "In about three hours."

"All right. What's his name? His Hawkinsite name?"

"Why do you want to know?" She could not keep the chill from her words.

"Let's call it a small investigation of my own. After all, the thing will be in my house."

"Oh, for heaven's sake, Drake, don't bring your job home with you!"

Drake's voice sounded tinny and nasty in her ears. "Why not, Rose? Isn't that exactly what you're doing?"

It was, of course, so she gave him the information he wanted.

This was the first time in their married life that they had had even the semblance of a quarrel, and, as she sat there before the full-length mirror, she began to wonder if perhaps she ought not make an attempt to see his side of it. In essence, she had married a policeman. Of course he was more than simply a policeman; he was a member of the World Security Board.

It had been a surprise to her friends. The fact of the marriage itself had been the biggest surprise, but if she had decided on marriage, the attitude was, why not with another biologist? Or, if she had wanted to go afield, an anthropologist, perhaps; even a chemist; but why, of all people, a policeman? Nobody had exactly said those things, naturally, but it had been in the very atmosphere at the time of her marriage.

She had resented it then, and ever since. A man could marry whom he chose, but if a doctor of philosophy, female-variety, chose to marry a man who never went past the bachelor's degree, there was shock. Why should there be? What business was it of theirs? He was handsome, in a way, intelligent, in another way, and she was perfectly satisfied with her choice.

Yet how much of this same snobbishness did she bring home with her? Didn't she always have the attitude that her own work, her biological investigations, were important, while his job was merely something to be kept within the four walls of his little office in the old U.N. buildings on the East River?

She jumped up from her seat in agitation and, with a deep breath, decided to leave such thoughts behind her. She desperately did not want to quarrel with him. And she just wasn't going to interfere with him. She was committed to accepting the Hawkinsite as guest, but otherwise she would let Drake have his own way. He was making enough of a concession as it was.

* * *

arg Tholan was standing quietly in the middle of the living room when she came down the stairs. He was not sitting, since he was not anatomically constructed to sit. He stood on two sets of limbs placed close together, while a third pair entirely different in construction were suspended from a region that would have been the upper chest in a human being. The skin of his body was hard, glistening and ridged, while his face bore a distant resemblance to something alienly bovine. Yet he was not completely repulsive, and he wore clothes of a sort over the lower portion of his body in order to avoid offending the sensibilities of his human hosts.

He said, "Mrs. Smollett, I appreciate your hospitality beyond my ability to express it in your language," and he drooped so that his forelimbs touched the ground for a moment.

Rose knew this to be a gesture signifying gratitude among the beings of Hawkin's Planet. She was grateful that he spoke English as well as he did. The construction of his mouth, combined with an absence of incisors, gave a whistling sound to the sibilants. Aside from that, he might have been born on Earth for all the accent his speech showed.

She said, "My husband will be home soon, and then we will eat."

"Your husband?" For a moment, he said nothing more, and then added, "Yes, of course."

She let it go. If there was one source of infinite confusion among the five intelligent races of the known Galaxy, it lay in the differences among them with regard to their sex life and the social institutions that grew around it. The concept of husband and wife, for instance, existed only on Earth. The other races could achieve a sort of intellectual understanding of what it meant, but never an emotional one.

She said, "I have consulted the Institute in preparing your menu. I trust you will find nothing in it that will upset you."

The Hawkinsite blinked his eyes rapidly. Rose recalled this to be a gesture of amusement.

He said, "Proteins are proteins, my dear Mrs. Smollett. For those trace factors which I need but are not supplied in your food, I have brought concentrates that will be most adequate."

And proteins *were* proteins. Rose knew this to be true. Her concern for the creature's diet had been largely one of formal politeness. In the discovery of life on the planets of the outer stars, one of the most interesting generalizations that had developed was the fact that, although life could be formed on the basis of substances other than proteins—even on elements other than carbon— it remained true that the only known intelligences were proteinaceous in nature. This meant that each of the five forms of intelligent life could maintain themselves over prolonged periods on the food of any of the other four.

S he heard Drake's key in the door and went stiff with apprehension.
     She had to admit he did well. He strode in, and, without hesitation, thrust his hand out at the Hawkinsite, saying firmly, "Good evening, Dr. Tholan."

The Hawkinsite put out his large and rather clumsy forelimb and the two, so to speak, shook hands. Rose had already gone through that procedure and knew the queer feeling of a Hawkinsite hand in her own. It had felt rough and hot and dry. She imagined that, to the Hawkinsite, her own and Drake's felt cold and slimy.

At the time of the formal greeting, she had taken the opportunity to observe the alien hand. It was an excellent case of converging evolution. Its morphological development was entirely different from that of the human hand, yet it had brought itself into a fairly approximate similarity. There were four fingers but no thumb. Each finger had five independent ball-and-socket joints. In this way, the flexibility lost with the absence of the thumb was made up for by the almost tentacular properties of the fingers. What was even more interesting to her biologist's eyes was the fact that each Hawkinsite finger ended in a vestigial hoof, very small and, to the layman, unidentifiable as such, but clearly adapted at one time to running, just as man's had been to climbing.

Drake said, in friendly enough fashion, "Are you quite comfortable, sir?"

The Hawkinsite answered, "Quite. Your wife has been most thoughtful in all her arrangements."

"Would you care for a drink?"

The Hawkinsite did not answer but looked at Rose with a slight facial contortion that indicated some emotion which, unfortunately, Rose could not interpret. She said, nervously, "On Earth there is the custom of drinking liquids which have been fortified with ethyl alcohol. We find it stimulating."

"Oh, yes. I am afraid, then, that I must decline. Ethyl alcohol would interfere most unpleasantly with my metabolism."

"Why, so it does to Earthmen, too, but I understand, Dr. Tholan," Drake replied. "Would you object to *my* drinking?"

"Of course not."

Drake passed close to Rose on his way to the sideboard and she caught only one word. He said, "God!" in a tightly controlled whisper, yet he managed to put seventeen exclamation points after it.

T he Hawkinsite *stood* at the table. His fingers were models of dexterity as they wove their way around the cutlery. Rose tried not to look at him as he ate. His wide lipless mouth split his face alarmingly as he ingested food, and, in chewing, his large jaws moved disconcertingly from side to side. It was another evidence of his ungulate ancestry. Rose found herself wondering if, in the quiet of his own room, he would later chew his cud, and was then panic-stricken lest Drake get the same idea and leave the table in disgust. But Drake was taking everything quite calmly.

He said, "I imagine, Dr. Tholan, that the cylinder at your side holds cyanide?"

Rose started. She had actually not noticed it. It was a curved metal object, something like a water canteen, that fitted flatly against the creature's skin, half-hidden behind its clothing. But, then, Drake had a policeman's eyes.

The Hawkinsite was not in the least disconcerted. "Quite so," he said, and his hoofed fingers held out a thin, flexible hose that ran up his body, its tint blending into that of his yellowish skin, and entered the corner of his wide mouth. Rose felt slightly embarrassed, as though at the display of intimate articles of clothing.

Drake said, "And does it contain pure cyanide?"

The Hawkinsite humorously blinked his eyes. "I hope you are not considering possible danger to Earthites. I know the gas is highly poisonous to you and I do not need a great deal. The gas contained in the cylinder is five percent hydrogen cyanide, the remainder oxygen. None of it emerges except when I actually suck at the tube, and that need not be done frequently."

"I see. And you really must have the gas to live?"

Rose was slightly appalled. One simply did not ask such questions without careful preparation. It was impossible to foresee where the sensitive points of an alien psychology might be. And Drake *must* be doing this deliberately, since he could not help realizing that he could get answers to such questions as easily from herself. Or was it that he preferred not to ask her?

The Hawkinsite remained apparently unperturbed. "Are you not a biologist, Mr. Smollett?"

"No, Dr. Tholan."

"But you are in close association with Mrs. *Dr.* Smollett."

Drake smiled a bit. "Yes, I am married to a Mrs. doctor, but just the same I am not a biologist; merely a minor government official. My wife's friends," he added, "call me a policeman."

Rose bit the inside of her cheek. In this case it was the Hawkinsite who had impinged upon the sensitive point of an alien psychology. On Hawkin's Planet, there was a tight caste system and intercaste associations were limited. But Drake wouldn't realize that.

The Hawkinsite turned to her. "May I have your permission, Mrs. Smollett, to explain a little of our biochemistry to your husband? It will be dull for you, since I am sure you must understand it quite well already."

She said, "By all means do, Dr. Tholan."

He said, "You see, Mr. Smollett, the respiratory system in your body and in the bodies of all air-breathing creatures on Earth is controlled by certain metal-containing enzymes, I am taught. The metal is usually iron, though sometimes it is copper. In either case, small traces of cyanide would combine with these metals and immobilize the respiratory system of the terrestrial living cell. They would be prevented from using oxygen and killed in a few minutes.

"The life on my own planet is not quite so constituted. The key respiratory compounds contain neither iron nor copper; no metal at all, in fact. It is for this reason that my blood is colorless. Our compounds contain certain organic groupings which are essential to life, and these groupings can only be maintained intact in the presence of a small concentration of cyanide. Undoubtedly, this type of protein has developed through millions of years of evolution on a world which has a few tenths of a percent of hydrogen cyanide occurring naturally in the atmosphere. Its presence is maintained by a biological cycle. Various of our native micro-organisms liberate the free gas."

"You make it extremely clear, Dr. Tholan, and very interesting," Drake said. "What happens if you don't breathe it? Do you just go, like that?" He snapped his fingers.

"Not quite. It isn't equivalent to the presence of cyanide for you. In my case, the absence of cyanide would be equivalent to slow strangulation. It happens sometimes, in ill-ventilated rooms on my world, that the cyanide is gradually consumed and falls below the minimum necessary concentration. The results are very painful and difficult to treat."

Rose had to give Drake credit; he really sounded interested. And the alien, thank heaven, did not mind the catechism.

The rest of the dinner passed without incident. It was almost pleasant.

Throughout the evening, Drake remained that way; interested. Even more than that—absorbed. He drowned her out, and she was glad of it. *He* was the one who was really colorful and it was only her job, her specialized training, that stole the color from him. She looked at him gloomily and thought, *Why did he marry me?*

Drake sat, one leg crossed over the other, hands clasped and tapping his chin gently, watching the Hawkinsite intently. The Hawkinsite faced him, standing in his quadruped fashion.

Drake said, "I find it difficult to keep thinking of you as a doctor."

The Hawkinsite laughingly blinked his eyes. "I understand what you mean," he said. "I find it difficult to think of you as a policeman. On my world, policemen are very specialized and distinctive people."

"Are they?" said Drake, somewhat drily, and then changed the subject. "I gather that you are not here on a pleasure trip."

"No, I am here very much on business. I intend to study this queer planet you call Earth, as it has never been studied before by any of my people."

"Queer?" asked Drake. "In what way?"

The Hawkinsite looked at Rose. "Does he know of the Inhibition Death?"

Rose felt embarrassed. "His work is important," she said. "I am afraid that my husband has little time to listen to the details of my work." She knew that this was not really adequate and she felt herself to be the recipient, yet again, of one of the Hawkinsite's unreadable emotions.

The extraterrestrial creature turned back to Drake. "It is always amazing to me to find how little you Earthmen understand your own unusual characteristics. Look, there are five intelligent races in the Galaxy. These have all developed independently, yet have managed to converge in remarkable fashion. It is as though, in the long run, intelligence requires a certain physical makeup to flourish. I leave that question for philosophers. But I need not belabor the point, since it must be a familiar one to you.

"Now when the differences among the intelligences are closely investigated, it is found over and over again that it is you Earthmen, more than any of the others, who are unique. For instance, it is only on Earth that life depends upon metal enzymes for respiration. Your people are the only ones which find hydrogen cyanide poisonous. Yours is the only form of intelligent life which is carnivorous. Yours is the only form of life which has not developed from a grazing animal. And, most interesting of all, yours is the only form of intelligent life known which stops growing upon reaching maturity."

Drake grinned at him. Rose felt her heart suddenly race. It was the nicest thing about him, that grin, and he was using it perfectly naturally. It wasn't forced or false. He was adjusting to the presence of this alien creature. He was being pleasant—and he must be doing it for her. She loved that thought and repeated it to herself. He was doing it for her; he was being nice to the Hawkinsite for her sake.

Drake was saying with his grin, "You don't look very large, Dr. Tholan. I should say that you are an inch taller than I am, which would make you six feet two inches tall. Is it that you are young, or is it that the others on your world are generally small?"

"Neither," said the Hawkinsite. "We grow at a diminishing rate with the years, so that at my age it would take fifteen years to grow an additional inch, but—and this is the important point—we never *entirely* stop. And, of course, as a consequence, we never entirely die."

Drake gasped and even Rose felt herself sitting stiffly upright. This was something new. This was something which, to her knowledge, the few expeditions to Hawkin's Planet had never brought back. She was torn with excitement but held an exclamation back and let Drake speak for her.

He said, "They don't entirely die? You're not trying to say, sir, that the people on Hawkin's Planet are immortal?"

"No people are truly immortal. If there were no other way to die, there would always be accident, and if that fails, there is boredom. Few of us live more than several centuries of your time. Still, it is unpleasant to think that death may come involuntarily. It is something which, to us, is extremely horrible. It bothers me even as I think of it now, this thought that *against my will and despite all care*, death may come."

"We," said Drake grimly, "are quite used to it."

"You Earthmen live with the thought; we do not. And this is why we are disturbed to find that the incidence of Inhibition Death has been increasing in recent years."

"You have not yet explained," said Drake, "just what the Inhibition Death is, but let me guess. Is the Inhibition Death a pathological cessation of growth?"

"Exactly."

"And how long after growth's cessation does death follow?"

"Within the year. It is a wasting disease, a tragic one, and absolutely incurable."

"What causes it?"

The Hawkinsite paused a long time before answering, and even then there was something strained and uneasy about the way he spoke. "Mr. Smollett, we know nothing about the cause of the disease."

Drake nodded thoughtfully. Rose was following the conversation as though she were a spectator at a tennis match.

Drake said, "And why do you come to Earth to study this disease?"

"Because again Earthmen are unique. They are the only intelligent beings who are immune. The Inhibition Death affects *all* the other races. Do your biologists know that, Mrs. Smollett?"

He had addressed her suddenly, so that she jumped slightly. She said, "No, they don't."

"I am not surprised. That piece of information is the result of very recent research. The Inhibition Death is easily diagnosed incorrectly and the incidence is much lower on the other planets. In fact, it is a strange thing, something to philosophize over, that the incidence of the Death is highest on my world, which is closest to Earth, and lower on each more distant planet—so that it is lowest on the world of the star Tempora, which is farthest from Earth, while Earth itself is immune. Somewhere in the biochemistry of the Earthite, there is the secret of that immunity. How interesting it would be to find it."

Drake said, "But look here, you can't say Earth is immune. From where I sit, it looks as if the incidence is a hundred percent. All Earthmen stop growing and all Earthmen die. We've *all* got the Inhibition Death."

"Not at all. Earthmen live up to seventy years after the cessation of growth. That is not the Death as we know it. *Your* equivalent disease is rather one of un-restrained growth. Cancer, you call it. But come, I bore you."

Rose protested instantly. Drake did likewise with even more vehemence, but the Hawkinsite determinedly changed the subject. It was then that Rose had her first pang of suspicion, for Drake circled Harg Tholan warily with his words, worrying him, jabbing at him, attempting always to get the information back to the point where the Hawkinsite had left off. Not baldly, not unskillfully, but Rose knew him, and could tell what he was after. And what could he be af-ter but that which was demanded by his profession? And, as though in response to her thoughts, the Hawkinsite took up the phrase which had begun careening in her mind like a broken record on a perpetual turnable.

He asked, "Did you not say you were a policeman?"

Drake said, curtly, "Yes."

"Then there is something I would like to request you to do for me. I have been wanting to all this evening, since I discovered your profession, and yet I hesitate. I do not wish to be troublesome to my host and hostess."

"We'll do what we can."

"I have a profound curiosity as to how Earthmen live; a curiosity which is not perhaps shared by the generality of my countrymen. So I wonder, could you show me through one of the police departments on your planet?"

"I do not belong to a police department in exactly the way you imagine," said Drake, cautiously. "However, I am known to the New York police depart-ment. I can manage it without trouble. Tomorrow?"

"That would be most convenient for me. Would I be able to visit the Miss-ing Persons Bureau?"

"The what?"

The Hawkinsite drew his four standing legs closer together, as if he were be-coming more intense. "It is a hobby of mine, a little queer corner of interest I have always had. I understand you have a group of police officers whose sole duty is to search for men who are missing."

"And women and children," added Drake. "But why should that interest you so particularly?"

"Because there again you are unique. There is no such thing as a missing person on our planet. I can't explain the mechanism to you, of course, but among the people of other worlds, there is always an awareness of one another's presence, especially if there is a strong, affectionate tie. We are always aware of each other's exact location, no matter where on the planet we might be."

Rose grew excited again. The scientific expeditions to Hawkin's Planet had always had the greatest difficulty in penetrating the internal emotional mechanisms of the natives, and here was one who talked freely, who would explain! She forgot to worry about Drake and intruded into the conversation. "Can you feel such awareness even now? On Earth?"

The Hawkinsite said, "You mean across space? No, I'm afraid not. But you can see the importance of the matter. All the uniqueness of Earth should be linked. If the lack of this sense can be explained, perhaps the immunity to Inhibition Death can be, also. Besides, it strikes me as very curious that any form of intelligent community life can be built among people who lack this community awareness. How can an Earthman tell, for instance, when he has formed a congenial subgroup, a family? How can you two, for instance, know that there is a true tie between you?"

Rose found herself nodding. How strongly she missed such a sense!

But Drake only smiled. "We have our ways. It is as difficult to explain what we call 'love' to you as it is for you to explain your sense to us."

"I suppose so. Yet tell me truthfully, Mr. Smollett—if Mrs. Smollett were to leave this room and enter another without you having seen her do so, would you really not be aware of her location?"

"I really would not."

The Hawkinsite said, "Amazing." He hesitated, then added, "Please do not be offended at the fact that I find it revolting as well."

After the light in the bedroom had been put out, Rose went to the door three times, opening it a crack and peering out. She could feel Drake watching her. There was a hard kind of amusement in his voice as he asked, finally, "What's the matter?"

She said, "I want to talk to you."

"Are you afraid our friend can hear?"

Rose was whispering. She got into bed and put her head on his pillow so that she could whisper better. She said, "Why were you talking about the Inhibition Death to Dr. Tholan?"

"I am taking an interest in your work, Rose. You've always wanted me to take an interest."

"I'd rather you weren't sarcastic." She was almost violent, as nearly violent

as she could be in a whisper. "I know that there's something of your own interest in this—of *police* interest, probably. What is it?"

He said, "I'll talk to you tomorrow."

"No, right now."

He put his hand under her head, lifting it. For a wild moment she thought
he was going to kiss her—just kiss her on impulse the way husbands sometimes
did, or as she imagined they sometimes did. Drake never did, and he didn't now.

He merely held her close and whispered, "Why are you so interested?"

His hand was almost brutally hard upon the nape of her neck, so that she
stiffened and tried to draw back. Her voice was more than a whisper now. "Stop
it, Drake."

He said, "I want no questions from you and no interference. You do your
job, and I'll do mine."

"The nature of my job is open and known."

"The nature of my job," he retorted, "isn't, by definition. But I'll tell you
this. Our six-legged friend is here in this house for some definite reason. You
weren't picked as biologist in charge for any random reason. Do you know that
two days ago, he'd been inquiring about me at the Commission?"

"You're joking.,"

"Don't believe that for a minute. There are depths to this that you know
nothing about. But that's my job and I won't discuss it with you any further. Do
you understand?"

"No, but I won't question you if you don't want me to."

"Then go to sleep."

She lay stiffly on her back and the minutes passed, and then the quarter
hours. She was trying to fit the pieces together. Even with what Drake had told
her, the curves and colors refused to blend. She wondered what Drake would
say if he knew she had a recording of that night's conversation!

One picture remained clear in her mind at that moment. It hovered over her
mockingly. The Hawkinsite, at the end of the long evening, had turned to her
and said gravely, "Good night, Mrs. Smollett. You are a most charming hostess."

She had desperately wanted to giggle at the time. How could he call her a
charming hostess? To him, she could only be a horror, a monstrosity with too
few limbs and a too-narrow face.

And then, as the Hawkinsite delivered himself of this completely meaningless piece of politeness, Drake had turned white! For the one instant, his eyes
had burned with something that looked like terror.

She had never before known Drake to show fear of anything, and the picture of that instant of pure panic remained with her until all her thoughts finally sagged into the oblivion of sleep.

*   *   *

I t was noon before Rose was at her desk the next day. She had deliberately waited until Drake and the Hawkinsite had left, since only then was she able to remove the small recorder that had been behind Drake's armchair the previous evening. She had had no original intention of keeping its presence secret from him. It was just that he had come home so late, and she couldn't say anything about it with the Hawkinsite present. Later on, of course, things had changed—

The placing of the recorder had been only a routine maneuver. The Hawkinsite's statements and intonations needed to be preserved for future intensive studies by various specialists at the Institute. It had been hidden in order to avoid the distortions of self-consciousness that the visibility of such a device would bring, and now it couldn't be shown to the members of the Institute at all. It would have to serve a different function altogether. A rather nasty function.

She was going to spy on Drake.

She touched the little box with her fingers and wondered, irrelevantly, how Drake was going to manage, that day. Social intercourse between inhabited worlds was, even now, not so commonplace that the sight of a Hawkinsite on the city streets would not succeed in drawing crowds. But Drake would manage, she knew. Drake always managed.

She listened once again to the sounds of last evening, repeating the interesting moments. She was dissatisfied with what Drake had told her. Why should the Hawkinsite have been interested in the two of them particularly? Yet Drake wouldn't lie. She would have liked to check at the Security Commission, but she knew she could not do that. Besides, the thought made her feel disloyal; Drake would definitely not lie.

But, then again, why should Harg Tholan not have investigated them? He might have inquired similarly about the families of all the biologists at the Institute. It would be no more than natural to attempt to choose the home he would find most pleasant by his own standards, whatever they were.

And if he had—even if he had investigated only the Smolletts—why should that create the great change in Drake from intense hostility to intense interest? Drake undoubtedly had knowledge he was keeping to himself. Only heaven knew how much.

Her thoughts churned slowly through the possibilities of interstellar intrigue. So far, to be sure, there were no signs of hostility or ill feeling among any of the five intelligent races known to inhabit the Galaxy. As yet they were spaced at intervals too wide for enmity. Even the barest contact among them was all but impossible. Economic and political interests just had no point at which to conflict.

* * *

B ut that was only her idea and she was not a member of the Security Commission. If there *were* conflict, if there were danger, if there were any reason to suspect that the mission of a Hawkinsite might be other than peaceful—Drake would know.

Yet was Drake sufficiently high in the councils of the Security Commission to know, off-hand, the dangers involved in the visit of a Hawkinsite physician? She had never thought of his position as more than that of a very minor functionary in the Commission; he had never presented himself as more. And yet—

Might he be more?

She shrugged at the thought. It was reminiscent of twentieth century spy novels and of costume dramas of the days when there existed such things as atom bomb secrets.

The thought of costume dramas decided her. Unlike Drake, she wasn't a real policeman, and she didn't know how a real policeman would go about it. But she knew how such things were done in the old dramas.

She drew a piece of paper toward her and, with a quick motion, slashed a vertical pencil mark down its center. She headed one column "Harg Tholan," the other "Drake." Under "Harg Tholan" she wrote "bonafide" and thoughtfully put three question marks after it. After all, was he a doctor at all, or was he what could only be described as an interstellar agent? What proof had even the Institute of his profession except his own statements? Was that why Drake had quizzed him so relentlessly concerning the Inhibition Death? Had he boned up in advance and tried to catch the Hawkinsite in an error?

For a moment, she was irresolute; then, springing to her feet, she folded the paper, put it in the pocket of her short jacket, and swept out of her office. She said nothing to any of those she passed as she left the Institute. She left no word at the reception desk as to where she was going, or when she would be back.

Once outside, she hurried into the third-level tube and waited for an empty compartment to pass. The two minutes that elapsed seemed unbearably long. It was all she could do to say, "New York Academy of Medicine," into the mouthpiece just above the seat.

The door of the little cubicle closed, and the sound of the air flowing past the compartment hissed upward in pitch.

T he New York Academy of Medicine had been enlarged both vertically and horizontally in the past two decades. The library alone occupied one entire wing of the third floor. Undoubtedly, if all the books, pamphlets and periodicals it contained were in their original printed form, rather than in microfilm, the entire building, huge though it was, would not have been sufficiently vast to hold them. As it was, Rose knew there was already talk of limiting printed works to the last five years, rather than to the last ten, as was now the case.

Rose, as a member of the Academy, had free entry to the library. She hurried toward the alcoves devoted to extraterrestrial medicine and was relieved to find them unoccupied.

It might have been wiser to have enlisted the aid of a librarian, but she chose not to. The thinner and smaller the trail she left, the less likely it was that Drake might pick it up.

And so, without guidance, she was satisfied to travel along the shelves, following the titles anxiously with her fingers. The books were almost all in English, though some were in German or Russian. None, ironically enough, were in extraterrestrial symbolisms. There was a room somewhere for such originals, but they were available only to official translators.

Her traveling eye and finger stopped. She had found what she was looking for.

She dragged half a dozen volumes from the shelf and spread them out upon the small dark table. She fumbled for the light switch and opened the first of the volumes. It was entitled *Studies on Inhibition*. She leafed through it and then turned to the author index. The name of Harg Tholan was there.

One by one, she looked up the references indicated, then returned to the shelves for translations of such original papers as she could find.

She spent more than two hours in the Academy. When she was finished, she knew this much: there was a Hawkinsite doctor named Harg Tholan, who was an expert on the Inhibition Death. He was connected with the Hawkinsite research organization with which the Institute had been in correspondence. Of course, the Harg Tholan she knew might simply be impersonating an actual doctor to make the role more realistic, but why should that be necessary?

She took the paper out of her pocket and, where she had written "bonafide" with three question marks, she now wrote a YES in capitals. She went back to the Institute and at 4 P.M.. was once again at her desk. She called the switchboard to say that she would not answer any phone calls and then she locked her door.

Underneath the column headed "Harg Tholan" she now wrote two questions: "Why did Harg Tholan come to Earth alone?" She left considerable space. Then, "What is his interest in the Missing Persons Bureau?"

Certainly, the Inhibition Death was all the Hawkinsite said it was. From her reading at the Academy, it was obvious that it occupied the major share of medical effort of Hawkin's Planet. It was more feared there than cancer was on Earth. If they had thought the answer to it lay on Earth, the Hawkinsites would have sent a full-scale expedition. Was it distrust and suspicion on their part that made them send only one investigator?

What was it Harg Tholan had said the night before? The incidence of the Death was highest upon his own world, which was closest to Earth, lowest upon the world farthest from Earth. Add to that the fact implied by the Hawkinsite, and verified by her own readings at the Academy, that the incidence had expanded enormously since interstellar contact had been made with Earth . . .

Slowly and reluctantly she came to one conclusion. The inhabitants of Hawkin's Planet might have decided that somehow Earth had discovered the cause of the Inhibition Death, and was deliberately fostering it among the alien peoples of the Galaxy, with the intention, perhaps, of becoming supreme among the stars.

She rejected this conclusion with what was almost panic. It could not be; it was impossible. In the first place, Earth *wouldn't* do such a horrible thing. Secondly, it *couldn't*.

As far as scientific advance was concerned, the beings of Hawkin's Planet were certainly the equals of Earthmen. The Death had occurred there for thousands of years and their medical record was one of total failure. Surely, Earth, in its long-distance investigations into alien biochemistry, could not have succeeded so quickly. In fact, as far as she knew, there were no investigations to speak of into Hawkinsite pathology on the part of Earth biologists and physicians.

Yet all the evidence indicated that Harg Tholan had come in suspicion and had been received in suspicion. Carefully, she wrote down under the question, "Why did Harg Tholan come to Earth alone?" the answer, "Hawkin's Planet *believes* Earth is causing the Inhibition Death."

But, then, what was this business about the Bureau of Missing Persons? As a scientist, she was rigorous about the theories she developed. *All* the facts had to fit in, not merely some of them.

Missing Persons Bureau! If it was a false trail, deliberately intended to deceive Drake, it had been done clumsily, since it came only after an hour of discussion of the Inhibition Death.

Was it intended as an opportunity to study Drake? If so, why? Was this perhaps the *major* point? The Hawkinsite had investigated Drake before coming to them. Had he come because Drake was a policeman with entry to Bureaus of Missing Persons?

But why? Why?

She gave it up and turned to the column headed "Drake."

And there a question wrote itself, not in pen and ink upon the paper, but in the much more visible letters of thought on mind. *Why did he marry me?* thought Rose, and she covered her eyes with her hands so that the unfriendly light was excluded.

They had met quite by accident somewhat more than a year before, when he had moved into the apartment house in which she then lived. Polite greetings had somehow become friendly conversation and this, in turn, had led to occasional dinners in a neighborhood restaurant. It had been very friendly and normal and an exciting new experience, and she had fallen in love.

When he asked her to marry him, she was pleased—and overwhelmed. At the time, she had many explanations for it. He appreciated her intelligence and friendliness. She was a nice girl. She would make a good wife, a splendid companion.

She had tried all those explanations and had half-believed every one of them. But half-belief was not enough.

It was not that she had any definite fault to find in Drake as a husband. He was always thoughtful, kind, and a gentleman. Their married life was not one of passion, and yet it suited the paler emotional surges of the late thirties. She wasn't nineteen. What did she expect?

That was it; she wasn't nineteen. She wasn't beautiful, or charming, or glamorous. What did she expect? Could she have expected Drake—handsome and rugged, whose interest in intellectual pursuits was quite minor, who neither asked about her work in all the months of their marriage, nor offered to discuss his own with her? Why, then, did he marry her?

But there was no answer to that question, and it had nothing to do with what Rose was trying to do now. It was extraneous, she told herself fiercely; it was a childish distraction from the task she had set herself. She was acting like a girl of nineteen, after all, with no chronological excuse for it.

She found that the point of her pencil had somehow broken, and took a new one. In the column headed "Drake" she wrote, "Why is he suspicious of Harg Tholan?" and under it she put an arrow pointing to the other column.

What she had written there was sufficient explanation. If Earth was spreading the Inhibition Death, or if Earth knew it was suspected of such a deed, then, obviously, it would be preparing for eventual retaliation on the part of the aliens. In fact, the setting would actually be one of preliminary maneuvering for the first interstellar war of history. It was an adequate but horrible explanation.

Now there was left the second question, the one she could not answer. She wrote it slowly, "Why Drake's reaction to Tholan's words, 'You are a most charming hostess'?"

She tried to bring back the exact setting. The Hawkinsite had said it innocuously, matter-of-factly, politely, and Drake had frozen at the sound of it. Over and over, she had listened to that particular passage in the recording. An Earthman might have said it in just such an inconsequential tone on leaving a routine cocktail party. The recording did not carry the sight of Drake's face; she had only her memory for that. Drake's eyes had become alive with fear and hate, and Drake was one who feared practically nothing. What was there to fear in the phrase, "You are a most charming hostess," that could upset him so? Jealousy? Absurd. The feeling that Tholan had been sarcastic? Maybe, though unlikely. She was sure Tholan was sincere.

She gave it up and put a large question mark under that second question. There were two of them now, one under "Harg Tholan" and one under "Drake." Could there be a connection between Tholan's interest in missing persons and Drake's reaction to a polite party phrase? She could think of none.

She put her head down upon her arms. It was getting dark in the office and she was very tired. For a while, she must have hovered in that queer land between waking and sleeping, when thoughts and phrases lose the control of the conscious and disport themselves erratically and surrealistically through one's head. But, no matter where they danced and leaped, they always returned to that one phrase, "You are a most charming hostess." Sometimes she heard it in Harg Tholan's cultured, lifeless voice, and sometimes in Drake's vibrant one. When Drake said it, it was full of love, full of a love she never heard from him. She liked to hear him say it.

She startled herself to wakefulness. It was quite dark in the office now, and she put on the desk light. She blinked, then frowned a little. Another thought must have come to her in that fitful half sleep. There had been another phrase which had upset Drake. What was it? Her forehead furrowed with mental effort. It had not been last evening. It was not anything in the recorded conversation, so it must have been before that. Nothing came and she grew restless.

Looking at her watch, she gasped. It was almost eight. They would be at home waiting for her.

But she did not want to go home. She did not want to face them. Slowly, she took up the paper upon which she had scrawled her thoughts of the afternoon, tore it into little pieces and let them flutter into the little atomic-flash ashtray upon her desk. They were gone in a little flare and nothing was left of them.

If only nothing were left of the thoughts they represented as well.

It was no use. She would have to go home.

They were not there waiting for her, after all. She came upon them getting out of a gyrocab just as she emerged from the tubes on to street level. The gyrocabbie, wide-eyed, gazed after his fares for a moment, then hovered upward and away. By unspoken mutual consent, the three waited until they had entered the apartment before speaking.

Rose said disinterestedly, "I hope you have had a pleasant day, Dr. Tholan."

"Quite. And a fascinating and profitable one as well, I think."

"Have you had a chance to eat?" Though Rose had not herself eaten, she was anything but hungry.

"Yes, indeed."

Drake interrupted, "We had lunch and supper sent up to us. Sandwiches." He sounded tired.

Rose said, "Hello, Drake." It was the first time she had addressed him.

Drake scarcely looked at her. "Hello."

The Hawkinsite said, "Your tomatoes are remarkable vegetables. We have nothing to compare with them in taste on our own planet. I believe I ate two dozen, as well as an entire bottle of tomato derivative."

"Ketchup," explained Drake, briefly.

Rose said, "And your visit at the Missing Persons Bureau, Dr. Tholan? You say you found it profitable?"

"I should say so. Yes."

Rose kept her back to him. She plumped up sofa cushions as she said, "In what way?"

"I find it most interesting that the large majority of missing persons are males. Wives frequently report missing husbands, while the reverse is practically never the case."

Rose said, "Oh, that's not mysterious, Dr. Tholan. You simply don't realize the economic setup we have on Earth. On this planet, you see, it is the male who is usually the member of the family that maintains it as an economic unit. He is the one whose labor is repaid in units of currency. The wife's function is generally that of taking care of home and children."

"Surely this is not universal!"

Drake put in, "More or less. If you are thinking of my wife, she is an example of the minority of women who are capable of making their own way in the world."

Rose looked at him swiftly. Was he being sarcastic?

The Hawkinsite said, "Your implication, Mrs. Smollett, is that women, being economically dependent upon their male companions, find it less feasible to disappear?"

"That's a gentle way of putting it," said Rose, "but that's about it."

"And would you call the Missing Persons Bureau of New York a fair sampling of such cases in the planet at large?"

"Why, I should think so."

The Hawkinsite said, abruptly, "And is there, then, an economic explanation for the fact that since interstellar travel has been developed, the percentage of young males among the missing is more pronounced than ever?"

It was Drake who answered, with a verbal snap. "Good lord, that's even less of a mystery than the other. Nowadays, the runaway has all space to disappear into. Anyone who wants to get away from trouble need only hop the nearest space freighter. They're always looking for crewmen, no questions asked, and it would be almost impossible to locate the runaway after that, if he really wanted to stay out of circulation."

"And almost always young men in their first year of marriage."

Rose laughed suddenly. She said, "Why, that's just the time a man's troubles seem the greatest. If he survives the first year, there is usually no need to disappear at all."

Drake was obviously not amused. Rose thought again that he looked tired and unhappy. *Why* did he insist on bearing the load alone? And then she thought that perhaps he had to.

The Hawkinsite said, suddenly, "Would it offend you if I disconnected for a period of time?"

Rose said, "Not at all. I hope you haven't had too exhausting a day. Since you come from a planet whose gravity is greater than that of Earth's, I'm afraid we too easily presume that you would show greater endurance than we do."

"Oh, I am not tired in a physical sense." He looked for a moment at her legs and blinked very rapidly, indicating amusement. "You know, I keep expecting Earthmen to fall either forward or backward in view of their meager equipment of standing limbs. You must pardon me if my comment is overfamiliar, but your mention of the lesser gravity of Earth brought it to my mind. On my planet, two legs would simply not be enough. But this is all beside the point at the moment. It is just that I have been absorbing so many new and unusual concepts that I feel the desire for a little disconnection."

Rose shrugged inwardly. Well, that was as close as one race could get to another, anyway. As nearly as the expeditions to Hawkin's Planet could make out, Hawkinsites had the faculty for disconnecting their conscious mind from all its bodily functions and allowing it to sink into an undisturbed meditative process for periods of time lasting up to terrestrial days. Hawkinsites found the process pleasant, even necessary sometimes, though no Earthman could truly say what function it served.

Conversely, it had never been entirely possible for Earthmen to explain the concept of "sleep" to a Hawkinsite, or to any extraterrestrial. What an Earthman would call sleep or a dream, a Hawkinsite would view as an alarming sign of mental disintegration.

Rose thought uneasily, *Here is another way Earthmen are unique.*

The Hawkinsite was backing away, drooping so that his forelimbs swept the floor in polite farewell. Drake nodded curtly at him as he disappeared behind the bend in the corridor. They heard his door open, close, then silence.

After minutes in which the silence was thick between them, Drake's chair creaked as he shifted restlessly. With a mild horror, Rose noticed blood upon his lips. She thought to herself, *He's in some kind of trouble. I've got to talk to him. I can't let it go on like this.*

She said, "Drake!"

Drake seemed to look at her from a far, far distance. Slowly, his eyes focused closer at hand and he said, "What is it? Are you through for the day, too?"

"No, I'm ready to begin. It's the tomorrow you spoke of. Aren't you going to speak to me?"

"Pardon me?"

"Last night, you said you would speak to me tomorrow. I am ready now."

Drake frowned. His eyes withdrew beneath a lowered brow and Rose felt some of her resolution begin to leave her. He said, "I thought it was agreed that you would not question me about my business in this matter."

"I think it's too late for that. I know too much about your business by now."

"What do you mean?" he shouted, jumping to his feet. Recollecting himself, he approached, laid his hands upon her shoulders and repeated in a lower voice, "What do you mean?"

Rose kept her eyes upon her hands, which rested limply in her lap. She bore the painfully gripping fingers patiently, and said slowly, "Dr. Tholan thinks that Earth is spreading the Inhibition Death purposely. That's it, isn't it?"

She waited. Slowly, the grip relaxed and he was standing there, hands at his side, face baffled and unhappy. He said, "Where did you get that notion?"

"It's true, isn't it?"

He said breathlessly, unnaturally, "I want to know exactly why you say that. Don't play foolish games with me, Rose. This is for keeps."

"If I tell you, will you answer one question? Is Earth spreading the disease deliberately, Drake?"

Drake flung his hands upward. "Oh, for Heaven's sake!"

He knelt before her. He took both her hands in his and she could feel their trembling. He was forcing his voice into soothing, loving syllables.

He was saying, "Rose dear, look, you've got something red-hot by the tail and you think you can use it to tease me in a little husband-wife repartee. No, I'm not asking much. Just tell me exactly what causes you to say what—what you have just said." He was terribly earnest about it.

"I was at the New York Academy of Medicine this afternoon. I did some reading there."

"But why? What made you do it?"

"You seemed so interested in the Inhibition Death, for one thing. And Dr. Tholan made those statements about the incidence increasing since interstellar travel, and being the highest on the planet nearest Earth." She paused.

"And your reading?" he prompted. "What about your reading, Rose?"

She said, "It backs him up. All I could do was to skim hastily into the direction of their research in recent decades. It seems obvious to me, though, that at least some of the Hawkinsites are considering the possibility the Inhibition Death originates on Earth."

"Do they say so outright?"

"No. Or, if they have, I haven't seen it." She gazed at him in surprise. In a matter like this, certainly the government would have investigated Hawkinsite research on the matter. She said, gently, "Don't you know about Hawkinsite research in the matter, Drake? The government—"

"Never mind about that." Drake had moved away from her and now he turned again. His eyes were bright. He said, as though making a wonderful discovery, "Why, you're an expert in this!"

Was she? Did he find that out only now that he needed her? Her nostrils flared and she said flatly, "I am a biologist."

He said, "Yes, I know that, but I mean your particular specialty is growth. Didn't you once tell me you had done work on growth?"

"You might call it that. I've had twenty papers published on the relationship of nucleic acid fine structure and embryonic development on my Cancer Society grant."

"Good. I should have thought of that." He was choked with a new excitement. "Tell me, Rose—look, I'm sorry if I lost my temper with you a moment ago. You'd be as competent as anyone to understand the direction of their researches if you read about it, wouldn't you?"

"Fairly competent, yes."

"Then tell me how they think the disease is spread. The details, I mean."

"Oh, now look, that's asking a little too much. I spent a few hours in the Academy, that's all. I'd need much more time than that to be able to answer your question."

"An intelligent guess, at least. You can't imagine how important it is."

She said, doubtfully, "Of course, 'Studies on Inhibition' is a major treatise in the field. It would summarize all of the available research data."

"Yes? And how recent is it?"

"It's one of those periodic things. The last volume is about a year old."

"Does it have any account of *his* work in it?" His finger jabbed in the direction of Harg Tholan's bedroom.

"More than anyone else's. He's an outstanding worker in the field. I looked over his papers especially."

"And what are his theories about the origin of the disease? Try to remember, Rose."

She shook her head at him. "I could swear he blames Earth, but he admits they know nothing about how the disease is spread. I could swear to that, too."

He stood stiffly before her. His strong hands were clenched into fists at his side and his words were scarcely more than a mutter. "It could be a matter of complete overestimation. Who knows—"

He whirled away. "I'll find out about this right now, Rose. Thank you for your help."

She ran after him. "What are you going to do?"

"Ask him a few questions." He was rummaging through the drawers of his desk and now his right hand withdrew. It held a needle-gun.

She cried, "No, Drake!"

He shook her off roughly, and turned down the corridor toward the Hawkinsite's bedroom.

D rake threw the door open and entered. Rose was at his heels, still trying to grasp his arm, but now he stopped and looked at Harg Tholan.

The Hawkinsite was standing there motionless, eyes unfocused, his four standing limbs sprawled out in four directions as far as they would go. Rose felt ashamed of intruding, as though she were violating an intimate rite. But Drake, apparently unconcerned, walked to within four feet of the creature and stood there. They were face to face, Drake holding the needle-gun easily at a level of about the center of the Hawkinsite's torso.

Drake said, "Now keep quiet. He'll gradually become aware of me."

"How do you know?"

The answer was flat. "I *know*. Now get out of here."

But she did not move and Drake was too absorbed to pay her further attention.

Portions of the skin on the Hawkinsite's face were beginning to quiver slightly. It was rather repulsive and Rose found herself preferring not to watch.

Drake said suddenly, "That's about all, Dr. Tholan. Don't throw in connection with any of the limbs. Your sense organs and voice box will be quite enough."

The Hawkinsite's voice was dim. "Why do you invade my disconnection chamber?" Then, more strongly, "And why are you armed?"

His head wobbled slightly atop a still frozen torso. He had, apparently, followed Drake's suggestion against limb connection. Rose wondered how Drake knew such partial reconnection to be possible. She herself had not known of it.

The Hawkinsite spoke again. "What do you want?"

And this time Drake answered. He said, "The answer to certain questions."

"With a gun in your hand? I would not humor your discourtesy so far."

"You would not merely be humoring me. You might be saving your own life."

"That would be a matter of considerable indifference to me, under the circumstances. I am sorry, Mr. Smollett, that the duties toward a guest are so badly understood on Earth."

"You are no guest of mine, Dr. Tholan," said Drake. "You entered my house on false pretenses. You had some reason for it, some way you had planned of using me to further your own purposes. I have no compunction in reversing the process."

"You had better shoot. It will save time."

"You are convinced that you will answer no questions? That, in itself, is suspicious. It seems that you consider certain answers to be more important than your life."

"I consider the principles of courtesy to be very important. You, as an Earthman, may not understand."

"Perhaps not. But I, as an Earthman, understand one thing." Drake had jumped forward, faster than Rose could cry out, faster than the Hawkinsite could connect his limbs. When he sprang backward, the flexible hose of Harg Tholan's cyanide cylinder was in his hand. At the corner of the Hawkinsite's wide mouth, where the hose had once been affixed, a droplet of colorless liquid oozed sluggishly from a break in the rough skin, and slowly solidified into a brown jellylike globule, as it oxidized.

Drake yanked at the hose and the cylinder jerked free. He plunged home the knob that controlled the needle valve at the head of the cylinder and the small hissing ceased.

"I doubt," said Drake, "that enough will have escaped to endanger us. I hope, however, that you realize what will happen to you *now*, if you do not answer the questions I am going to ask you—and answer them in such a way that I am convinced you are being truthful."

"Give me back my cylinder," said the Hawkinsite, slowly. "If not, it will be necessary for me to attack you and then it will be necessary for you to kill me."

Drake stepped back. "Not at all. Attack me and I shoot your legs from under you. You will lose them; all four, if necessary, but you will still live, in a horrible way. You will live to die of cyanide lack. It would be a most uncomfortable death. I am only an Earthman and I can't appreciate its true horrors, but you can, can't you?"

The Hawkinsite's mouth was open and something within quivered yellow-green. Rose wanted to throw up. She wanted to scream, *Give him back the cylinder, Drake!* But nothing would come. She couldn't even turn her head.

Drake said, "You have about an hour, I think, before the effects are irreversible. Talk quickly, Dr. Tholan, and you will have your cylinder back."

"And after that—" said the Hawkinsite.

"After that, what does it matter to you? Even if I kill you then, it will be a clean death; not cyanide lack."

Something seemed to pass out of the Hawkinsite. His voice grew guttural and his words blurred as though he no longer had the energy to keep his English perfect. He said, "What are your questions?" and as he spoke, his eyes followed the cylinder in Drake's hand.

Drake swung it deliberately, tantalizingly, and the creature's eyes followed—followed—

Drake said, "What are your theories concerning the Inhibition Death? Why did you really come to Earth? What is your interest in the Missing Persons Bureau?"

Rose found herself waiting in breathless anxiety. These were the questions she would like to have asked, too. Not in this manner, perhaps, but in Drake's job, kindness and humanity had to take second place to necessity.

She repeated that to herself several times in an effort to counteract the fact that she found herself loathing Drake for what he was doing to Dr. Tholan.

The Hawkinsite said, "The proper answer would take more than the hour I have left me. You have bitterly shamed me by forcing me to talk under duress. On my own planet, you could have not done so under any circumstances. It is only here, on this revolting planet, that I can be deprived of cyanide."

"You are wasting your hour, Dr. Tholan."

"I would have told you this eventually, Mr. Smollett. I needed your help. It is why I came here."

"You are still not answering my questions."

"I will answer them now. For years, in addition to my regular scientific work, I have been privately investigating the cells of my patients suffering from Inhibition Death. I have been forced to use the utmost secrecy and to work without assistance, since the methods I used to investigate the bodies of my patients were frowned upon by my people. Your society would have similar feelings against human vivisection, for instance. For this reason, I could not present the results I obtained to my fellow physicians until I had verified my theories here on Earth."

"What are your theories?" demanded Drake. The feverishness had returned to his eyes.

"It became more and more obvious to me as I proceeded with my studies that the entire direction of research into the Inhibition Death was wrong. Physically, there was no solution to its mystery. The Inhibition Death is entirely a disease of the mind."

Rose interrupted, "Surely, Dr. Tholan, it isn't psychosomatic."

A thin, gray translucent film had passed over the Hawkinsite's eyes. He no longer looked at them. He said, "No, Mrs. Smollett, it is not psychosomatic. It is a true disease of the mind; a mental infection. My patients had double minds. Beyond and beneath the one that obviously belonged to them, there was evidence of *another* one—an *alien* mind. I worked with Inhibition Death patients of other races than my own, and the same could be found. In short, there are not five intelligences in the Galaxy, but six. And the sixth is parasitic."

Rose said, "This is wild—impossible! You *must* be mistaken, Dr. Tholan."

"I am not mistaken. Until I came to Earth, I thought I might be. But my stay at the Institute and my researches at the Missing Persons Bureau convinced me that is not so. What is so impossible about the concept of parasitic intelligence? Intelligences like these would not leave fossil remains, nor even leave artifacts— if their only function is to derive nourishment somehow from the mental activities of other creatures. One can imagine such a parasite, through the course of millions of years, perhaps, losing all portions of its physical being but that which remains necessary, just as a tapeworm, among your Earthly physical parasites, eventually lost all its functions but the single one of reproduction. In the case of the parasitic intelligence, all physical attributes would eventually be lost. It would become nothing but pure mind, living in some mental fashion we cannot conceive of on the minds of others. Particularly on the minds of Earthmen."

Rose said, "Why particularly Earthmen?"

Drake simply stood apart, intent, asking no further questions. He was content, apparently, to let the Hawkinsite speak.

"Have you not surmised that the sixth intelligence is a native of Earth? Mankind from the beginning has lived with it, has adapted to it, is unconscious of it. It is why the higher species of terrestrial animals, including man, do not grow after maturity and, eventually, die what is called natural death. It is the result of this universal parasitic infestation. It is why you sleep and dream, since it is then that the parasitic mind must feed and then that you are a little more conscious of it, perhaps. It is why the terrestrial mind alone of the intelligences is so subject to instability. Where else in the Galaxy are found split personalities and other such manifestations? After all, even now there must be occasional human minds which are visibly harmed by the presence of the parasite.

"Somehow, these parasitic minds could traverse space. They had no physical limitations. They could drift between the stars in what would correspond to a state of hibernation. Why the first ones did it, I don't know; probably no one will ever know. But once those first discovered the presence of intelligence on other planets in the Galaxy, there was a small, steady stream of parasitic intelligences making their way through space. We of the outer worlds must have been a gourmet's dish for them or they would have never struggled so hard to get to us. I imagine many must have failed to make the trip, but it must have been worth the effort to those who succeeded.

"But you see, we of the other worlds had not lived with these parasites for millions of years, as man and his ancestors had. We had not adapted ourselves to it. Our weak strains had not been killed off gradually through hundreds of generations until only the resistants were left. So, where Earthmen could survive the infection for decades with little harm, we others die a quick death within a year."

"And is that why the incidence has increased since interstellar travel between Earth and the other planets has begun?"

"Yes." For a moment there was silence, and then the Hawkinsite said with a sudden access of energy, "Give me back my cylinder. You have your answer."

Drake said, coolly, "What about the Missing Persons Bureau?" He was swinging the cylinder again; but now the Hawkinsite did not follow its movements. The gray translucent film on his eyes had deepened and Rose wondered whether that was simply an expression of weariness or an example of the changes induced by cyanide lack.

The Hawkinsite said, "As we are not well adapted to the intelligence that infests man, neither is it well adapted to us. It can live on us—it it even prefers to, apparently—but it cannot reproduce with ourselves alone as the source of its life. The Inhibition Death is therefore not directly contagious among our people."

Rose looked at him with growing horror. "What are you implying, Dr. Tholan?"

"The Earthman remains the prime host for the parasite. An Earthman may infect one of us if he remains among us. But the parasite, once it is located in an intelligence of the outer worlds, must somehow return to an Earthman, if it expects to reproduce. Before interstellar travel, this was possible only by a repassage of space and therefore the incidence of infection remained infinitesimal. Now we are infected and reinfected as the parasites return to Earth and come back to us via the minds of Earthmen who travel through space."

Rose said faintly, "And the missing persons—"

"Are the intermediate hosts. The exact process by which it is done, I, of course, do not know. The masculine terrestrial mind seems better suited for their purposes. You'll remember that at the Institute I was told that the life expectancy of the average human male is three years less than that of the average female. Once reproduction has been taken care of, the infested male leaves, by spaceship, for the outer worlds. He disappears."

"But this is impossible," insisted Rose. "What you say implies that the parasite mind can control the actions of its host! This cannot be, or we of Earth would have noticed their presence."

"The control, Mrs. Smollett, may be very subtle, and may, moreover, be exerted only during the period of active reproduction. I simply point to your Missing Persons Bureau. Why do the young men disappear? You have economic and psychological explanations, but they are not sufficient. But I am quite ill now and cannot speak much longer. I have only this to say. In the mental parasite, your people and mine have a common enemy. Earthmen, too, need not die involuntarily, except for its presence. I thought that if I found myself unable to return to my own world with my information because of the unorthodox methods I used to obtain it, I might bring it to the authorities on Earth, and ask their help in stamping out this menace. Imagine my pleasure when I found that the husband of one of the biologists at the Institute was a member of one of Earth's most important investigating bodies. Naturally, I did what I could to be made a guest at his home in order that I might deal with him privately; convince him of the terrible truth; utilize his position to help in the attack on the parasites.

"This is, of course, now impossible. I cannot blame you too far. As Earthmen, you cannot be expected to understand the psychology of my people. Nevertheless, you must understand this. I can have no further dealing with either of you. I could not even bear to remain any longer on Earth."

Drake said, "Then you alone, of all your people, have any knowledge of this theory of yours."

"I alone."

Drake held out the cylinder. "Your cyanide, Dr. Tholan."

The Hawkinsite groped for it eagerly. His supple fingers manipulated the hose and the needle valve with the utmost delicacy. In the space of ten seconds, he had it in place and was inhaling the gas in huge breaths. His eyes were growing clear and transparent.

Drake waited until the Hawkinsite breathings had subsided to normal, and then, without expression, he raised his needle-gun and fired. Rose screamed. The Hawkinsite remained standing. His four lower limbs were incapable of buckling, but his head lolled and from his suddenly flaccid mouth, the cyanide hose fell, disregarded. Once again, Drake closed the needle valve and now he tossed the cylinder aside and stood there somberly, looking at the dead creature. There was no external mark to show that he had been killed. The needle-gun's pellet, thinner than the needle which gave the gun its name, entered the body noiselessly and easily, and exploded with devastating effect only within the abdominal cavity.

Rose ran from the room, still screaming. Drake pursued her, seized her arm. She heard the hard, flat sounds of his palm against her face without feeling them and subsided into little bubbling sobs.

Drake said, "I told you to have nothing to do with this. Now what do you think you'll do?"

She said, "Let me go. I want to leave. I want to go away."

"Because of something it was my job to do? You heard what the creature was saying. Do you suppose I could allow him to return to his world and spread those lies? They would believe him. And what do you think would happen then? Can you imagine what an interstellar war might be like? They would imagine they would have to kill us all to stop the disease."

With an effort that seemed to turn her inside out, Rose steadied. She looked firmly into Drake's eyes and said, "What Dr. Tholan said were no lies and no mistakes, Drake."

"Oh, come now, you're hysterical. You need sleep."

"I know what he said is so because the Security Commission knows all about that same theory, and knows it to be true."

"Why do you say such a preposterous thing?"

"Because you yourself let that slip twice."

Drake said, "Sit down." She did so, and he stood there, looking curiously at her. "So I have given myself away twice, have I? You've had a busy day of detection, my dear. You have facets you keep well hidden." He sat down and crossed his legs.

Rose thought, yes, she had had a busy day. She could see the electric clock on the kitchen wall from where she sat; it was more than two hours past midnight. Harg Tholan had entered their house thirty-five hours before and now he lay murdered in the spare bedroom.

Drake said, "Well, aren't you going to tell me where I pulled my two boners?"

"You turned white when Harg Tholan referred to me as a charming hostess. Hostess has a double meaning, you know, Drake. A host is one who harbors a parasite."

"Number one," said Drake. "What's number two?"

"That's something you did before Harg Tholan entered the house. I've been trying to remember it for hours. Do *you* remember, Drake? You spoke about how unpleasant it was for Hawkinsites to associate with Earthmen, and I said Harg Tholan was a doctor and had to. I asked you if you thought that human doctors particularly enjoyed going to the tropics, or letting infected mosquitoes bite them. Do you remember how upset you became?"

Drake laughed. "I had no idea I was so transparent. Mosquitoes are hosts for the malaria and yellow fever parasites." He sighed. "I've done my best to keep you out of this. Now there's nothing left but to tell you the truth. I must, because only the truth—or death—will keep you quiet. And I don't want to kill you."

She shrank back in her chair, eyes wide.

Drake said, "The Commission knows the truth. It does us no good. We can only do all in our power to prevent the other worlds from finding out."

"But the truth can't be held down forever! Harg Tholan found out. You've killed him, but another extraterrestrial will repeat the same discovery—over and over again. You can't kill them all."

"We know that, too," agreed Drake. "We have no choice."

"Why?" cried Rose. "Harg Tholan gave you the solution. He made no suggestions or threats of war between worlds. He suggested that we combine with the other intelligences and help to wipe out the parasite. And we can! If we, in common with all the others, put every scrap of effort into it—"

"You mean we can trust him? Does he speak for his government or for the other races?"

"Can we dare to refuse the risk?"

Drake said, "You don't understand." He reached toward her and took one of her cold, unresisting hands between both of his. He went on, "I may seem silly trying to teach you anything about your specialty, but I want you to hear me out. Harg Tholan was right. Man and his prehistoric ancestors have been living with this parasitic intelligence for uncounted ages; certainly for a much longer period than we have been truly *Homo sapiens*. In that interval, we have not only become adapted to it, we have become dependent upon it. It is no longer a case of parasitism. It is a case of mutual cooperation. You biologists have a name for it."

She tore her hand away. "What are you talking about? Symbiosis?"

"Exactly. We have a disease of our own, remember. It is a reverse disease; one of unrestrained growth. We've mentioned it already as a contrast to the Inhibition Death. Well, what is the cause of cancer? How long have biologists, physiologists, biochemists and all the others been working on it? How much success have they had with it? Why? Can't you answer that for yourself now?"

She said, slowly, "No, I can't. What are you talking about?"

"It's all very well to say that if we could remove the parasite, we would have eternal growth and life if we wanted it; or at least until we got tired of being too big or of living too long, and did away with ourselves neatly. But how many millions of years has it been since the human body has had occasion to grow in such an unrestrained fashion? Can it do so any longer? Is the chemistry of the body adjusted to that? Has it got the proper whatchamacallits?"

"Enzymes," Rose supplied in a whisper.

"Yes, enzymes. It's impossible for us. If for any reason the parasitic intelligence, as Harg Tholan calls it, does leave the human body, or if its relationship to the human mind is in any way impaired, growth does take place, but not in any orderly fashion. We call the growth cancer. And there you have it. There's no way of getting rid of the parasite. We're together for all eternity. To get rid of their Inhibition Death, extraterrestrials must first wipe out all vertebrate life on Earth. There is no other solution for them, and so we must keep knowledge of it from them. Do you understand?"

Her mouth was dry and it was difficult to talk. "I understand, Drake." She noticed that his forehead was damp and that there was a line of perspiration down each cheek. "And now you'll have to get it out of the apartment."

"It's late at night and I'll be able to get the body out of the building. From there on—" He turned to her. "I don't know when I'll be back."

"I understand, Drake," she said again.

Harg Tholan was heavy. Drake had to drag him through the apartment. Rose turned away, retching. She hid her eyes until she heard the front door close. She whispered to herself, "I understand, Drake."

It was 3 A.M.. Nearly an hour had passed since she had heard the front door click gently into place behind Drake and his burden. She didn't know where he was going, what he intended doing—

She sat there numbly. There was no desire to sleep; no desire to move. She kept her mind traveling in tight circles, away from the thing she knew and which she wanted not to know.

Parasitic minds! Was it only a coincidence or was it some queer racial memory, some tenuous long-sustained wisp of tradition or insight, stretching back through incredible millennia, that kept current the odd myth of human beginnings? She thought to herself, there were two intelligences on Earth to begin with. There were humans in the Garden of Eden and also the serpent, which "was more subtil than any beast of the field." The serpent infected man and, as a result, it lost its limbs. Its physical attributes were no longer necessary. And because of the infection, man was driven out of the Garden of eternal life. Death entered the world.

Yet, despite her efforts, the circle of her thoughts expanded and returned to Drake. She shoved and it returned; she counted to herself, she recited the names of the objects in her field of vision, she cried, "No, no, no," and it returned. It kept returning.

Drake had lied to her. It had been a plausible story. It would have held good under most circumstances; but Drake was not a biologist. Cancer could not be, as Drake had said, a disease that was an expression of a lost ability for normal growth. Cancer attacked children while they were still growing; it could even attack embryonic tissue. It attacked fish, which, like extraterrestrials, never stopped growing while they lived, and died only by disease or accident. It attacked plants which had no minds and could not be parasitized. Cancer had nothing to do with the presence or absence of normal growth; it was the general disease of life, to which *no* tissue of *no* multicellular organism was completely immune.

He should not have bothered lying. He should not have allowed some obscure sentimental weakness to persuade him to avoid the necessity of killing her in that manner. She would tell them at the Institute. The parasite *could* be beaten. Its absence would *not* cause cancer. But who would believe her?

She put her hands over her eyes. The young men who disappeared were usually in the first year of their marriage. Whatever the process of reproduction of the parasite intelligences, it must involve close association with another parasite—the type of close and continuous association that might only be possible if their respective hosts were in equally close relationship. As in the case of newly married couples.

She could feel her thoughts slowly disconnect. They would be coming to her. They would be saying, "Where is Harg Tholan?" And she would answer, "With my husband." Only they would say, "Where is your husband?" because he would be gone, too. He needed her no longer. He would never return. They would never find him, because he would be out in space. She would report them both, Drake Smollett and Harg Tholan, to the Missing Persons Bureau.

She wanted to weep, but couldn't; she was dry-eyed and it was painful.

And then she began to giggle and couldn't stop. It was very funny. She had looked for the answers to so many questions and had found them all. She had even found the answer to the question she thought had no bearing on the subject.

She had finally learned why Drake had married her.

Sally

Sally was coming down the lake road, so I waved to her and called her by her name. I always liked to see Sally. I liked all of them, you understand, but Sally's the prettiest one of the lot. There just isn't any question about it.

She moved a little faster when I waved to her. Nothing undignified. She was never that. She moved just enough faster to show that she was glad to see me, too.

I turned to the man standing beside me. "That's Sally," I said.

He smiled at me and nodded.

Mrs. Hester had brought him in. She said, "This is Mr. Gellhorn, Jake. You remember he sent you the letter asking for an appointment."

That was just talk, really. I have a million things to do around the Farm, and one thing I just can't waste my time on is mail. That's why I have Mrs. Hester around. She lives pretty close by, she's good at attending to foolishness without running to me about it, and most of all, she likes Sally and the rest. Some people don't.

"Glad to see you, Mr. Gellhorn," I said.

"Raymond J. Gellhorn," he said, and gave me his hand, which I shook and gave back.

He was a largish fellow, half a head taller than I and wide, too. He was about half my age, thirtyish. He had black hair, plastered down slick, with a part in the middle, and a thin mustache, very neatly trimmed. His jawbones got big under his ears and made him look as if he had a slight case of mumps. On video he'd be a natural to play the villain, so I assumed he was a nice fellow. It goes to show that video can't be wrong all the time.

"I'm Jacob Folkers," I said. "What can I do for you?"

He grinned. It was a big, wide, white-toothed grin. "You can tell me a little about your Farm here, if you don't mind."

I heard Sally coming up behind me and I put out my hand. She slid right into it and the feel of the hard, glossy enamel of her fender was warm in my palm.

"A nice automatobile," said Gellhorn.

That's one way of putting it. Sally was a 2045 convertible with a Hennis-Carleton positronic motor and an Armat chassis. She had the cleanest, finest lines I've ever seen on any model, bar none. For five years, she'd been my favorite, and I'd put everything into her I could dream up. In all that time, there'd never been a human being behind her wheel.

Not once.

"Sally," I said, patting her gently, "meet Mr. Gellhorn."

Sally's cylinder-purr keyed up a little. I listened carefully for any knocking. Lately, I'd been hearing motor-knock in almost all the cars and changing the gasoline hadn't done a bit of good. Sally was as smooth as her paint job this time, however.

"Do you have names for all your cars?" asked Gellhorn.

He sounded amused, and Mrs. Hester doesn't like people to sound as though they were making fun of the Farm. She said, sharply, "Certainly. The cars have real personalities, don't they, Jake? The sedans are all males and the convertibles are females."

Gellhorn was smiling again. "And do you keep them in separate garages, ma'am?"

Mrs. Hester glared at him.

Gellhorn said to me, "And now I wonder if I can talk to you alone, Mr. Folkers?"

"That depends," I said. "Are you a reporter?"

"No, sir. I'm a sales agent. Any talk we have is not for publication. I assure you I am interested in strict privacy."

"Let's walk down the road a bit. There's a bench we can use."

We started down. Mrs. Hester walked away. Sally nudged along after us.

I said, "You don't mind if Sally comes along, do you?"

"Not at all. She can't repeat what we say, can she?" He laughed at his own joke, reached over and rubbed Sally's grille.

Sally raced her motor and Gellhorn's hand drew away quickly.

"She's not used to strangers," I explained.

We sat down on the bench under the big oak tree where we could look across the small lake to the private speedway. It was the warm part of the day and the cars were out in force, at least thirty of them. Even at this distance I could see that Jeremiah was pulling his usual stunt of sneaking up behind some staid older model, then putting on a jerk of speed and yowling past with deliberately squealing brakes. Two weeks before he had crowded old Angus off the asphalt altogether, and I had turned off his motor for two days.

It didn't help though, I'm afraid, and it looks as though there's nothing to be done about it. Jeremiah is a sports model to begin with and that kind is awfully hot-headed.

"Well, Mr. Gellhorn," I said. "Could you tell me why you want the information?"

But he was just looking around. He said, "This *is* an amazing place, Mr. Folkers."

"I wish you'd call me Jake. Everyone does."

"All right, Jake. How many cars do you have here?"

"Fifty-one. We get one or two new ones every year. One year we got five. We haven't lost one yet. They're all in perfect running order. We even have a '15 model Mat-O-Mot in working order. One of the original automatics. It was the first car here."

Good old Matthew. He stayed in the garage most of the day now, but then he was the granddaddy of all positronic-motored cars. Those were the days when blind war veterans, paraplegics and heads of state were the only ones who drove automatics. But Samson Harridge was my boss and he was rich enough to be able to get one. I was his chauffeur at the time.

The thought makes me feel old. I can remember when there wasn't an automobile in the world with brains enough to find its own way home. I chauffeured dead lumps of machines that needed a man's hand at their controls every minute. Every year machines like that used to kill tens of thousands of people.

The automatics fixed that. A positronic brain can react much faster than a human one, of course, and it paid people to keep hands off the controls. You got in, punched your destination, and let it go its own way.

We take it for granted now, but I remember when the first laws came out forcing the old machines off the highways and limiting travel to automatics. Lord, what a fuss. They called it everything from communism to fascism, but it emptied the highways and stopped the killing, and still more people get around more easily the new way.

Of course, the automatics were ten to a hundred times as expensive as the hand-driven ones, and there weren't many that could afford a private vehicle. The industry specialized in turning out omnibus-automatics. You could always call a company and have one stop at your door in a matter of minutes and take you where you wanted to go. Usually, you had to ride with others who were going your way, but what's wrong with that?

Samson Harridge had a private car though, and I went to him the minute it arrived. The car wasn't Matthew to me then. I didn't know it was going to be the dean of the Farm some day. I only knew it was taking my job away and I hated it.

I said, "You won't be needing me any more, Mr. Harridge?"

He said, "What are you dithering about, Jake? You don't think I'll trust myself to a contraption like that, do you? You stay right at the controls."

I said, "But it works by itself, Mr. Harridge. It scans the road, reacts properly to obstacles, humans, and other cars, and remembers routes to travel."

"So they say. So they say. Just the same, you're sitting right behind the wheel in case anything goes wrong."

Funny how you can get to like a car. In no time I was calling it Matthew and was spending all my time keeping it polished and humming. A positronic brain stays in condition best when it's got control of its chassis at all times, which means it's worth keeping the gas tank filled so that the motor can turn over slowly day and night. After a while, it got so I could tell by the sound of the motor how Matthew felt.

In his own way, Harridge grew fond of Matthew, too. He had no one else to like. He'd divorced or outlived three wives and outlived five children and three grandchildren. So when he died, maybe it wasn't surprising that he had his estate converted into a Farm for Retired Automobiles, with me in charge and Matthew the first member of a distinguished line.

It's turned out to be my life. I never got married. You can't get married and still tend to automatics the way you should.

The newspapers thought it was funny, but after a while they stopped joking about it. Some things you can't joke about. Maybe you've never been able to afford an automatic and maybe you never will, either, but take it from me, you get to love them. They're hard-working and affectionate. It takes a man with no heart to mistreat one or to see one mistreated.

It got so that after a man had an automatic for a while, he would make provisions for having it left to the Farm, if he didn't have an heir he could rely on to give it good care.

I explained that to Gellhorn.

He said, "Fifty-one cars! That represents a lot of money."

"Fifty thousand minimum per automatic, original investment," I said. "They're worth a lot more now. I've done things for them."

"It must take a lot of money to keep up the Farm."

"You're right there. The Farm's a non-profit organization, which gives us a break on taxes and, of course, new automatics that come in usually have trust funds attached. Still, costs are always going up. I have to keep the place land-scaped; I keep laying down new asphalt and keeping the old in repair; there's gasoline, oil, repairs, and new gadgets. It adds up."

"And you've spent a long time at it."

"I sure have, Mr. Gellhorn. Thirty-three years."

"You don't seem to be getting much out of it yourself."

"I don't? You surprise me, Mr. Gellhorn. I've got Sally and fifty others. Look at her."

I was grinning. I couldn't help it. Sally was so clean, it almost hurt. Some insect must have died on her windshield or one speck of dust too many had landed, so she was going to work. A little tube protruded and spurted Tergosol over the glass. It spread quickly over the silicone surface film and squeejees snapped into place instantly, passing over the windshield and forcing the water into the little channel that led it, dripping, down to the ground. Not a speck of water got onto her glistening apple-green hood. Squeejee and detergent tube snapped back into place and disappeared.

Gellhorn said, "I never saw an automatic do that."

"I guess not," I said. "I fixed that up specially on our cars. They're clean. They're always scrubbing their glass. They like it. I've even got Sally fixed up with wax jets. She polishes herself every night till you can see your face in any part of her and shave by it. If I can scrape up the money, I'd be putting it on the rest of the girls. Convertibles are very vain."

"I can tell you how to scrape up the money, if that interests you."

"That always does. How?"

"Isn't it obvious, Jake? Any of your cars is worth fifty thousand minimum, you said. I'll bet most of them top six figures."

"So?"

"Ever think of selling a few?"

I shook my head. "You don't realize it, I guess, Mr. Gellhorn, but I can't sell any of these. They belong to the Farm, not to me."

"The money would go to the Farm."

"The incorporation papers of the Farm provide that the cars receive per-petual care. They can't be sold."

"What about the motors, then?"

"I don't understand you."

Gellhorn shifted position and his voice got confidential. "Look here, Jake, let me explain the situation. There's a big market for private automatics if they could only be made cheaply enough. Right?"

"That's no secret."

"And ninety-five percent of the cost is the motor. Right? Now, I know where we can get a supply of bodies. I also know where we can sell automatics at a good price—twenty or thirty thousand for the cheaper models, maybe fifty or sixty for the better ones. All I need are the motors. You see the solution?"

"I don't, Mr. Gellhorn." I did, but I wanted him to spell it out.

"It's right here. You've got fifty-one of them. You're an expert automatobile mechanic, Jake. You must be. You could unhook a motor and place it in another car so that no one would know the difference."

"It wouldn't be exactly ethical."

"You wouldn't be harming the cars. You'd be doing them a favor. Use your older cars. Use that old Mat-O-Mot."

"Well, now, wait a while, Mr. Gellhorn. The motors and bodies aren't two separate items. They're a single unit. Those motors are used to their own bodies. They wouldn't be happy in another car."

"All right, that's a point. That's a very good point, Jake. It would be like taking your mind and putting it in someone else's skull. Right? You don't think you would like that?"

"I don't think I would. No."

"But what if I took your mind and put it into the body of a young athlete. What about that, Jake? You're not a youngster anymore. If you had the chance, wouldn't you enjoy being twenty again? That's what I'm offering some of your positronic motors. They'll be put into new '57 bodies. The latest construction."

I laughed. "That doesn't make much sense, Mr. Gellhorn. Some of our cars may be old, but they're well cared for. Nobody drives them. They're allowed their own way. They're *retired*, Mr. Gellhorn. I wouldn't want a twenty-year-old body if it meant I had to dig ditches for the rest of my new life and never have enough to eat . . . What do you think, Sally?"

Sally's two doors opened and then shut with a cushioned slam.

"What's that?" said Gellhorn.

"That's the way Sally laughs."

Gellhorn forced a smile. I guess he thought I was making a bad joke. He said, "Talk sense, Jake. Cars are *made* to be driven. They're probably not happy if you don't drive them."

I said, "Sally hasn't been driven in five years. She looks happy to me."

"I wonder."

He got up and walked toward Sally slowly. "Hi, Sally, how'd you like a drive?"

Sally's motor revved up. She backed away.

"Don't push her, Mr. Gellhorn," I said. "She's liable to be a little skittish."

Two sedans were about a hundred yards up the road. They had stopped. Maybe, in their own way, they were watching. I didn't bother about them. I had my eyes on Sally, and I kept them there.

Gellhorn said, "Steady now, Sally." He lunged out and seized the door handle. It didn't budge, of course.

He said, "It opened a minute ago."

I said, "Automatic lock. She's got a sense of privacy, Sally has."

He let go, then said, slowly and deliberately, "A car with a sense of privacy shouldn't go around with its top down."

He stepped back three or four paces, then quickly, so quickly I couldn't take a step to stop him, he ran forward and vaulted into the car. He caught Sally completely by surprise, because as he came down, he shut off the ignition before she could lock it in place.

For the first time in five years, Sally's motor was dead.

I think I yelled, but Gellhorn had the switch on "Manual" and locked that in place, too. He kicked the motor into action. Sally was alive again but she had no freedom of action.

He started up the road. The sedans were still there. They turned and drifted away, not very quickly. I suppose it was all a puzzle to them.

One was Giuseppe, from the Milan factories, and the other was Stephen. They were always together. They were both new at the Farm, but they'd been here long enough to know that our cars just didn't have drivers.

Gellhorn went straight on, and when the sedans finally got it through their heads that Sally wasn't going to slow down, that she *couldn't* slow down, it was too late for anything but desperate measures.

They broke for it, one to each side, and Sally raced between them like a streak. Steve crashed through the lakeside fence and rolled to a halt on the grass and mud not six inches from the water's edge. Giuseppe bumped along the land side of the road to a shaken halt.

I had Steve back on the highway and was trying to find out what harm, if any, the fence had done him, when Gellhorn came back.

Gellhorn opened Sally's door and stepped out. Leaning back, he shut off the ignition a second time.

"There," he said. "I think I did her a lot of good."

I held my temper. "Why did you dash through the sedans? There was no reason for that."

"I kept expecting them to turn out."

"They did. One went through a fence."

"I'm sorry, Jake," he said. "I thought they'd move more quickly. You know how it is. I've been in lots of buses, but I've only been in a private automatic two or three times in my life, and this is the first time I ever drove one. That just shows you, Jake. It got me, driving one, and I'm pretty hard-boiled. I tell you, we don't have to go more than twenty percent below list price to reach a good market, and it would be ninety percent profit."

"Which we would split?"

"Fifty-fifty. And I take all the risks, remember."

"All right. I listened to you. Now you listen to me." I raised my voice because I was just too mad to be polite anymore. "When you turn off Sally's motor, you hurt her. How would you like to be kicked unconscious? That's what you do to Sally, when you turn her off."

"You're exaggerating, Jake. The automatobuses get turned off every night."

"Sure, that's why I want none of my boys or girls in your fancy '57 bodies, where I won't know what treatment they'll get. Buses need major repairs in their positronic circuits every couple of years. Old Matthew hasn't had his circuits touched in twenty years. What can you offer him compared with that?"

"Well, you're excited now. Suppose you think over my proposition when you've cooled down and get in touch with me."

"I've thought it over all I want to. If I ever see you again, I'll call the police."

His mouth got hard and ugly. He said. "Just a minute, old-timer."

I said, "Just a minute, you. This is private property and I'm ordering you off."

He shrugged. "Well, then, good-bye."

I said, "Mrs. Hester will see you off the property. Make that good-bye permanent."

But it wasn't permanent. I saw him again two days later. Two and a half days, rather, because it was about noon when I saw him first and a little after midnight when I saw him again.

I sat up in bed when he turned the light on, blinking blindly till I made out what was happening. Once I could see, it didn't take much explaining. In fact, it took none at all. He had a gun in his right fist, the nasty little needle barrel just visible between two fingers. I knew that all he had to do was to increase the pressure of his hand and I would be torn apart.

He said, "Put on your clothes, Jake."

I didn't move. I just watched him.

He said, "Look, Jake, I know the situation. I visited you two days ago, remember. You have no guards on this place, no electrified fences, no warning signals. Nothing."

I said, "I don't need any. Meanwhile there's nothing to stop you from leaving, Mr. Gellhorn. I would if I were you. This place can be very dangerous."

He laughed a little. "It is, for anyone on the wrong side of a fist gun."

"I see it," I said. "I know you've got one."

"Then get a move on. My men are waiting."

"No, sir, Mr. Gellhorn. Not unless you tell me what you want, and probably not then."

"I made you a proposition day before yesterday."

"The answer's still no."

"There's more to the proposition now. I've come here with some men and an automatobus. You have your chance to come with me and disconnect twenty-five of the positronic motors. I don't care which twenty-five you choose. We'll load them on the bus and take them away. Once they're disposed of, I'll see to it that you get your fair share of the money."

"I have your word on that, I suppose."

He didn't act as if he thought I was being sarcastic. He said, "You have."

I said, "No."

"If you insist on saying no, we'll go about it in our own way. I'll disconnect the motors myself, only I'll disconnect all fifty-one. Every one of them."

"It isn't easy to disconnect positronic motors, Mr. Gellhorn. Are you a robotics expert? Even if you are, you know, these motors have been modified by me."

"I know that, Jake. And to be truthful, I'm not an expert. I may ruin quite a few motors trying to get them out. That's why I'll have to work over all fifty-one if you don't cooperate. You see, I may only end up with twenty-five when I'm through. The first few I'll tackle will probably suffer the most. Till I get the hang of it, you see. And if I do it myself, I think I'll put Sally first in line."

I said, "I can't believe you're serious, Mr. Gellhorn."

He said, "I'm serious, Jake." He let it all dribble in. "If you want to help, you can keep Sally. Otherwise, she's liable to be hurt very badly. Sorry."

I said, "I'll come with you, but I'll give you one more warning. You'll be in trouble, Mr. Gellhorn."

He thought that was very funny. He was laughing very quietly as we went down the stairs together.

There was an automatobus waiting outside the driveway to the garage apartments. The shadows of three men waited beside it, and their flash beams went on as we approached.

Gellhorn said in a low voice, "I've got the old fellow. Come on. Move the truck up the drive and let's get started."

One of the others leaned in and punched the proper instructions on the control panel. We moved up the driveway with the bus following submissively.

"It won't go inside the garage," I said. "The door won't take it. We don't have buses here. Only private cars."

"All right," said Gellhorn. "Pull it over onto the grass and keep it out of sight."

I could hear the thrumming of the cars when we were still ten yards from the garage.

Usually they quieted down if I entered the garage. This time they didn't. I think they knew that strangers were about, and once the faces of Gellhorn and the others were visible they got noisier. Each motor was a warm rumble, and each motor was knocking irregularly until the place rattled.

The lights went up automatically as we stepped inside. Gellhorn didn't seem bothered by the car noise, but the three men with him looked surprised and uncomfortable. They had the look of the hired thug about them, a look that was not compounded of physical features so much as of a certain wariness of eye and hangdogness of face. I knew the type and I wasn't worried.

One of them said, "Damn it, they're burning gas."

"My cars always do," I replied stiffly.

"Not tonight," said Gellhorn. "Turn them off."

"It's not that easy, Mr. Gellhorn," I said.

"Get started!" he said.

I stood there. He had his fist gun pointed at me steadily. I said, "I told you, Mr. Gellhorn, that my cars have been well-treated while they've been at the Farm. They're used to being treated that way, and they resent anything else."

"You have one minute," he said. "Lecture me some other time."

"I'm trying to explain something. I'm trying to explain that my cars can understand what I say to them. A positronic motor will learn to do that with time and patience. My cars have learned. Sally understood your proposition two days ago. You'll remember she laughed when I asked her opinion. She also knows what you did to her and so do the two sedans you scattered. And the rest know what to do about trespassers in general."

"Look, you crazy old fool—"

"All I have to say is—" I raised my voice. "Get them!"

One of the men turned pasty and yelled, but his voice was drowned completely in the sound of fifty-one horns turned loose at once. They held their notes, and within the four walls of the garage the echoes rose to a wild, metallic call. Two cars rolled forward, not hurriedly, but with no possible mistake as to their target. Two cars fell in line behind the first two. All the cars were stirring in their separate stalls.

The thugs stared, then backed.

I shouted, "Don't get up against a wall."

Apparently, they had that instinctive thought themselves. They rushed madly for the door of the garage.

At the door one of Gellhorn's men turned, brought up a fist gun of his own.

The needle pellet tore a thin, blue flash toward the first car. The car was Giuseppe.

A thin line of paint peeled up Giuseppe's hood, and the right half of his windshield crazed and splintered but did not break through.

The men were out the door, running, and two by two the cars crunched out after them into the night, their horns calling the charge.

I kept my hand on Gellhorn's elbow, but I don't think he could have moved in any case. His lips were trembling.

I said, "That's why I don't need electrified fences or guards. My property protects itself."

Gellhorn's eyes swiveled back and forth in fascination as, pair by pair, they whizzed by. He said, "They're killers!"

"Don't be silly. They won't kill your men."

"They're killers!"

"They'll just give your men a lesson. My cars have been specially trained for cross-country pursuit for just such an occasion; I think what your men will get will be worse than an outright quick kill. Have you ever been chased by an automatobile?"

Gellhorn didn't answer.

I went on. I didn't want him to miss a thing. "They'll be shadows going no faster than your men, chasing them here, blocking them there, blaring at them, dashing at them, missing with a screech of brake and a thunder of motor. They'll keep it up till your men drop, out of breath and half-dead, waiting for the wheels to crunch over their breaking bones. The cars won't do that. They'll turn away. You can bet, though, that your men will never return here in their lives. Not for all the money you or ten like you could give them. Listen—"

I tightened my hold on his elbow. He strained to hear.

I said, "Don't you hear car doors slamming?"

It was faint and distant, but unmistakable.

I said, "They're laughing. They're enjoying themselves."

His face crumpled with rage. He lifted his hand. He was still holding his fist gun.

I said, "I wouldn't. One automatocar is still with us."

I don't think he had noticed Sally till then. She had moved up so quietly. Though her right front fender nearly touched me, I couldn't hear her motor. She might have been holding her breath.

Gellhorn yelled.

I said, "She won't touch you, as long as I'm with you. But if you kill me . . . you know, Sally doesn't like you."

Gellhorn turned the gun in Sally's direction.

"Her motor is shielded," I said, "and before you could ever squeeze the gun a second time she would be on top of you."

"All right, then," he yelled, and suddenly my arm was bent behind my back and twisted so I could hardly stand. He held me between Sally and himself, and his pressure didn't let up. "Back out with me and don't try to break loose, old-timer, or I'll tear your arm out of its socket."

I had to move. Sally nudged along with us, worried, uncertain what to do. I tried to say something to her and couldn't. I could only clench my teeth and moan.

Gellhorn's automatobus was still standing outside the garage. I was forced in. Gellhorn jumped in after me, locking the doors.

He said, "All right, now. We'll talk sense."

I was rubbing my arm, trying to get life back into it, and even as I did I was automatically and without any conscious effort studying the control board of the bus.

I said, "This is a rebuilt job."

"So?" he said caustically. "It's a sample of my work. I picked up a discarded chassis, found a brain I could use, and spliced me a private bus. What of it?"

I tore at the repair panel, forcing it aside.

He said, "What the hell. Get away from that." The side of his palm came down numbingly on my left shoulder.

I struggled with him. "I don't want to do this bus any harm. What kind of a person do you think I am? I just want to take a look at some of the motor connections."

It didn't take much of a look. I was boiling when I turned to him. I said, "You're a hound and a bastard. You had no right installing this motor yourself. Why didn't you get a robotics man?"

He said, "Do I look crazy?"

"Even if it was a stolen motor, you had no right to treat it so. I wouldn't treat a man the way you treated that motor. Solder, tape, and pinch clamps! It's brutal!"

"It works, doesn't it?"

"Sure it works, but it must be hell for the bus. You could live with migraine headaches and acute arthritis, but it wouldn't be much of a life. This car is *suffering*."

"Shut up!" For a moment he glanced out the window at Sally, who had rolled up as close to the bus as she could. He made sure the doors and windows were locked.

He said, "We're getting out of here now, before the other cars come back. We'll stay away."

"How will that help you?"

"Your cars will run out of gas someday, won't they? You haven't got them fixed up so they can tank up on their own, have you? We'll come back and finish the job."

"They'll be looking for me," I said. "Mrs. Hester will call the police."

He was past reasoning with. He just punched the bus in gear. It lurched forward. Sally followed.

He giggled. "What can she do if you're here with me?"

Sally seemed to realize that, too. She picked up speed, passed us and was gone. Gellhorn opened the window next to him and spat through the opening.

The bus lumbered on over the dark road, its motor rattling unevenly. Gellhorn dimmed the periphery light until the phosphorescent green stripe down the middle of the highway, sparkling in the moonlight, was all that kept us out of the trees. There was virtually no traffic. Two cars passed ours, going the other way, and there was none at all on our side of the highway, either before or behind.

I heard the door-slamming first. Quick and sharp in the silence, first on the right and then on the left. Gellhorn's hands quivered as he punched savagely for increased speed. A beam of light shot out from among a scrub of trees, blinding us. Another beam plunged at us from behind the guard rails on the other side. At a crossover, four hundred yards ahead, there was a sque-e-e-e as a car darted across our path.

"Sally went for the rest," I said. "I think you're surrounded."

"So what? What can they do?"

He hunched over the controls, peering through the windshield.

"And don't *you* try anything, old-timer," he muttered.

I couldn't. I was bone-weary; my left arm was on fire. The motor sounds gathered and grew closer. I could hear the motors missing in odd patterns; suddenly it seemed to me that my cars were speaking to one another.

A medley of horns came from behind. I turned and Gellhorn looked quickly into the rear-view mirror. A dozen cars were following in both lanes.

Gellhorn yelled and laughed madly.

I cried, "Stop! Stop the car!"

Because not a quarter of a mile ahead, plainly visible in the light beams of two sedans on the roadside was Sally, her trim body plunked square across the road. Two cars shot into the opposite lane to our left, keeping perfect time with us and preventing Gellhorn from turning out.

But he had no intention of turning out. He put his finger on the full-speed-ahead button and kept it there.

He said, "There'll be no bluffing here. This bus outweighs her five to one, old-timer, and we'll just push her off the road like a dead kitten."

I knew he could. The bus was on manual and his finger was on the button. I knew he would.

I lowered the window, and stuck my head out. "Sally," I screamed. "Get out of the way. *Sally!*"

It was drowned out in the agonized squeal of maltreated brakebands. I felt myself thrown forward and heard Gellhorn's breath puff out of his body.

I said, "What happened?" It was a foolish question. We had stopped. That was what had happened. Sally and the bus were five feet apart. With five times her weight tearing down on her, she had not budged. The guts of her.

Gellhorn yanked at the manual toggle switch. "It's got to," he kept muttering. "It's got to."

I said, "Not the way you hooked up the motor, expert. Any of the circuits could cross over."

He looked at me with a tearing anger and growled deep in his throat. His hair was matted over his forehead. He lifted his fist.

"That's all the advice out of you there'll ever be, old-timer."

And I knew the needle gun was about to fire.

I pressed back against the bus door, watching the fist come up, and when the door opened I went over backward and out, hitting the ground with a thud. I heard the door slam closed again.

I got to my knees and looked up in time to see Gellhorn struggle uselessly with the closing window, then aim his fist-gun quickly through the glass. He never fired. The bus got under way with a tremendous roar, and Gellhorn lurched backward.

Sally wasn't in the way any longer, and I watched the bus's rear lights flicker away down the highway.

I was exhausted. I sat down right there, right on the highway, and put my head down in my crossed arms, trying to catch my breath.

I heard a car stop gently at my side. When I looked up, it was Sally. Slowly—lovingly, you might say—her front door opened.

No one had driven Sally for five years—except Gellhorn, of course—and I know how valuable such freedom was to a car. I appreciated the gesture, but I said, "Thanks, Sally, but I'll take one of the newer cars."

I got up and turned away, but skillfully and neatly as a pirouette, she wheeled before me again. I couldn't hurt her feelings. I got in. Her front seat had the fine, fresh scent of an automatobile that kept itself spotlessly clean. I lay down across it, thankfully, and with even, silent, and rapid efficiency, my boys and girls brought me home.

M rs. Hester brought me the copy of the radio transcript the next evening with great excitement.

"It's Mr. Gellhorn," she said. "The man who came to see you."

"What about him?"

I dreaded her answer.

"They found him dead," she said. "Imagine that. Just lying dead in a ditch."

"It might be a stranger altogether," I mumbled.

"Raymond J. Gellhorn," she said, sharply. "There can't be two, can there? The description fits, too. Lord, what a way to die! They found tire marks on his arms and body. Imagine! I'm glad it turned out to be a bus; otherwise they might have come poking around here."

"Did it happen near here?" I asked, anxiously.

"No . . . near Cooksville. But, goodness, read about it yourself if you—what happened to Giuseppe?"

I welcomed the diversion. Giuseppe was waiting patiently for me to complete the repaint job. His windshield had been replaced.

After she left, I snatched up the transcript. There was no doubt about it. The doctor reported he had been running and was in a state of total exhaustion. I wondered: For how many miles had the bus played with him before the final lunge? The transcript had no notion of anything like that, of course.

They had located the bus and identified it by the tire tracks. The police had it and were trying to trace its ownership.

There was an editorial in the transcript about it. It had been the first traffic fatality in the state for that year and the paper warned strenuously against manual driving after night.

There was no mention of Gellhorn's three thugs and for that, at least, I was grateful. None of our cars had been seduced by the pleasure of the chase into killing.

That was all. I let the paper drop. Gellhorn had been a criminal. His treatment of the bus had been brutal. There was no question in my mind he deserved death. But still I felt a bit queasy over the manner of it.

A month has passed now and I can't get it out of my mind.

My cars talk to one another. I have no doubt about it anymore. It's as though they've gained confidence; as though they're not bothering to keep it secret anymore. Their engines rattle and knock continuously.

And they don't talk among themselves only. They talk to the cars and buses that come into the Farm on business. How long have they been doing that?

They must be understood, too. Gellhorn's bus understood them, for all it hadn't been on the grounds more than an hour. I can close my eyes and bring back that dash along the highway, with our cars flanking the bus on either side, clacking their motors at it till it understood, stopped, let me out, and ran off with Gellhorn.

Did my cars tell him to kill Gellhorn? Or was that his idea?

Can cars have such ideas? The motor designers say no. But they mean under ordinary conditions. Have they foreseen *everything*?

Cars get ill-used, you know.

Some of them enter the Farm and observe. They get told things. They find out that cars exist whose motors are never stopped, whom no one ever drives, whose every need is supplied.

Then maybe they go out and tell others. Maybe the word is spreading quickly. Maybe they're going to think that the Farm way should be the way all over the world. They don't understand. You couldn't expect them to understand about legacies and the whims of rich men.

There are millions of automatobiles on Earth, tens of millions. If the thought gets rooted in them that they're slaves; that they should do something about it . . . if they begin to think the way Gellhorn's bus did . . .

Maybe it won't be till after my time. And then they'll have to keep a few of us to take care of them, won't they? They wouldn't kill us all.

And maybe they would. Maybe they wouldn't understand about how someone would have to care for them. Maybe they won't wait.

Every morning I wake up and think, Maybe today . . .

I don't get as much pleasure out of my cars as I used to. Lately, I notice that I'm even beginning to avoid Sally.

Strikebreaker

Elvis Blei rubbed his plump hands and said, "Self-containment is the word." He smiled uneasily as he helped Steven Lamorak of Earth to a light. There was uneasiness all over his smooth face with its small wide-set eyes.

Lamorak puffed smoke appreciatively and crossed his lanky legs.

His hair was powdered with gray and he had a large and powerful jawbone. "Home-grown?" he asked, staring critically at the cigarette. He tried to hide his own disturbance at the other's tension.

"Quite," said Blei.

"I wonder," said Lamorak, "that you have room on your small world for such luxuries."

(Lamorak thought of his first view of Elsevere from the spaceship visiplate. It was a jagged, airless planetoid, some hundred miles in diameter—just a dust-gray rough-hewn rock, glimmering dully in the light of its sun, 200,000,000 miles distant. It was the only object more than a mile in diameter that circled that sun, and now men had burrowed into that miniature world and constructed a society in it. And he himself, as a sociologist, had come to study the world and see how humanity had made itself fit into that queerly specialized niche.)

Blei's polite fixed smile expanded a hair. He said, "We are not a small world, Dr. Lamorak; you judge us by two-dimensional standards. The surface area of Elsevere is only three quarters that of the State of New York, but that's irrelevant. Remember, we can occupy, if we wish, the entire interior of Elsevere. A sphere of 50 miles radius has a volume of well over half a million cubic miles. If all of Elsevere were occupied by levels 50 feet apart, the total surface area within the planetoid would be 56,000,000 square miles, and that is equal to the total land area of Earth. And none of these square miles, Doctor, would be unproductive."

Lamorak said, "Good Lord," and stared blankly for a moment. "Yes, of course you're right. Strange I never thought of it that way. But then, Elsevere is the only thoroughly exploited planetoid world in the Galaxy; the rest of us simply can't get away from thinking of two-dimensional surfaces, as you pointed out. Well, I'm more than ever glad that your Council has been so cooperative as to give me a free hand in this investigation of mine."

Blei nodded convulsively at that.

Lamorak frowned slightly and thought: He acts for all the world as though he wished I had not come. Something's wrong.

Blei said, "Of course, you understand that we are actually much smaller than we could be; only minor portions of Elsevere have as yet been hollowed out and occupied. Nor are we particularly anxious to expand, except very slowly. To a certain extent we are limited by the capacity of our pseudo-gravity engines and Solar energy converters."

"I understand. But tell me, Councillor Blei—as a matter of personal curiosity, and not because it is of prime importance to my project—could I view some of your farming and herding levels first? I am fascinated by the thought of fields of wheat and herds of cattle inside a planetoid."

"You'll find the cattle small by your standards, Doctor, and we don't have much wheat. We grow yeast to a much greater extent. But there will be some wheat to show you. Some cotton and tobacco, too. Even fruit trees."

"Wonderful. As you say, self-containment. You recirculate everything, I imagine."

Lamorak's sharp eyes did not miss the fact that this last remark twinged Blei. The Elseverian's eyes narrowed to slits that hid his expression.

He said, "We must recirculate, yes. Air, water, food, minerals—everything that is used up—must be restored to its original state; waste products are reconverted to raw materials. All that is needed is energy, and we have enough of that. We don't manage with one hundred percent efficiency, of course; there is a certain seepage. We import a small amount of water each year; and if our needs grow, we may have to import some coal and oxygen."

Lamorak said, "When can we start our tour, Councillor Blei?"

Blei's smile lost some of its negligible warmth. "As soon as we can, Doctor. There are some routine matters that must be arranged."

Lamorak nodded, and having finished his cigarette, stubbed it out.

Routine matters? There was none of this hesitancy during the preliminary correspondence. Elsevere had seemed proud that its unique planetoid existence had attracted the attention of the Galaxy.

He said, "I realize I would be a disturbing influence in a tightly knit society," and watched grimly as Blei leaped at the explanation and made it his own.

"Yes," said Blei, "we feel marked off from the rest of the Galaxy. We have our own customs. Each individual Elseverian fits into a comfortable niche. The appearance of a stranger without fixed caste is unsettling."

"The caste system does involve a certain inflexibility."

"Granted," said Blei quickly; "but there is also a certain self-assurance. We have firm rules of intermarriage and rigid inheritance of occupation. Each man, woman, and child knows his place, accepts it, and is accepted in it; we have virtually no neurosis or mental illness."

"And are there no misfits?" asked Lamorak.

Blei shaped his mouth as though to say no, then clamped it suddenly shut, biting the word into silence; a frown deepened on his forehead. He said, at length, "I will arrange for the tour, Doctor. Meanwhile, I imagine you would welcome a chance to freshen up and to sleep."

They rose together and left the room, Blei politely motioning the Earthman to precede him out the door.

Lamorak felt oppressed by the vague feeling of crisis that had pervaded his discussion with Blei.

The newspaper reinforced that feeling. He read it carefully before getting into bed, with what was at first merely a clinical interest. It was an eight-page tabloid of synthetic paper. One quarter of its items consisted of "personals": births, marriages, deaths, record quotas, expanding habitable volume (not area! three dimensions!). The remainder included scholarly essays, educational material, and fiction. Of news, in the sense to which Lamorak was accustomed, there was virtually nothing.

One item only could be so considered and that was chilling in its incompleteness.

It said, under a small headline: DEMANDS UNCHANGED: *There has been no change in his attitude of yesterday. The Chief Councillor, after a second interview, announced that his demands remain completely unreasonable and cannot be met under any circumstances.*

Then, in parentheses, and in different type, there was the statement: *The editors of this paper agree that Elsevere cannot and will not jump to his whistle, come what may.*

Lamorak read it over three times. *His* attitude. *His* demands. *His* whistle. *Whose?*

He slept uneasily that night.

He had no time for newspapers in the days that followed; but spasmodically, the matter returned to his thoughts.

Blei, who remained his guide and companion for most of the tour, grew ever more withdrawn.

On the third day (quite artificially clock-set in an Earthlike twenty-four-hour pattern), Blei stopped at one point, and said, "Now this level is devoted entirely to chemical industries. That section is not important—"

But he turned away a shade too rapidly, and Lamorak seized his arm. "What are the products of that section?"

"Fertilizers. Certain organics," said Blei stiffly.

Lamorak held him back, looking for what sight Blei might be evading. His gaze swept over the close-by horizons of lined rock and the buildings squeezed and layered between the levels.

Lamorak said, "Isn't that a private residence there?"

Blei did not look in the indicated direction.

Lamorak said, "I think that's the largest one I've seen yet. Why is it here on a factory level?" That alone made it note-worthy. He had already seen that the levels on Elsevere were divided rigidly among the residential, the agricultural and the industrial.

He looked back and called, "Councillor Blei!"

The councillor was walking away and Lamorak pursued him with hasty steps. "Is there something wrong, sir?"

Blei muttered, "I am rude, I know. I am sorry. There are matters that prey on my mind—" He kept up his rapid pace.

"Concerning *his* demands."

Blei came to a full halt. "What do *you* know about that?"

"No more than I've said. I read that much in the newspaper."

Blei muttered something to himself.

Lamorak said, "Ragusnik? What's that?"

Blei sighed heavily. "I suppose you ought to be told. It's humiliating, deeply embarrassing. The Council thought that matters would certainly be arranged shortly and that your visit need not be interfered with, that you need not know or be concerned. But it is almost a week now. I don't know what will happen and, appearances notwithstanding, it might be best for you to leave. No reason for an Outworlder to risk death."

The Earthman smiled incredulously. "Risk death? In this little world, so peaceful and busy. I can't believe it."

The Elseverian councillor said, "I can explain. I think it best I should." He turned his head away. "As I told you, everything on Elsevere must recirculate. You understand that."

"Yes."

"That includes—uh, human wastes."

"I assumed so," said Lamorak.

"Water is reclaimed from it by distillation and absorption. What remains is converted into fertilizer for yeast use; some of it is used as a source of fine organics and other by-products. These factories you see are devoted to this."

"Well?" Lamorak had experienced a certain difficulty in the drinking of water when he first landed on Elsevere, because he had been realistic enough to know what it must be reclaimed from; but he had conquered the feeling easily enough. Even on Earth, water was reclaimed by natural processes from all sorts of unpalatable substances.

Blei, with increasing difficulty, said, "Igor Ragusnik is the man who is in charge of the industrial processes immediately involving the wastes. The position has been in his family since Elsevere was first colonized. One of the original settlers was Mikhail Ragusnik and he—he—"

"Was in charge of waste reclamation."

"Yes. Now that residence you singled out is the Ragusnik residence; it is the best and most elaborate on the planetoid. Ragusnik gets many privileges the rest of us do not have; but, after all"—passion entered the councillor's voice with great suddenness—"we cannot *speak* to him."

"What?"

"He demands full social equality. He wants his children to mingle with ours, and our wives to visit—oh!" It was a groan of utter disgust.

Lamorak thought of the newspaper item that could not even bring itself to mention Ragusnik's name in print, or to say anything specific about his demands. He said, "I take it he's an outcast because of his job."

"Naturally. Human wastes and—" Words failed Blei. After a pause, he said more quietly, "As an Earthman, I suppose you don't understand."

"As a sociologist, I think I do." Lamorak thought of the Untouchables in ancient India, the ones who handled corpses. He thought of the position of swineherds in ancient Judea.

He went on, "I gather Elsevere will not give in to those demands."

"Never," said Blei, energetically. "Never."

"And so?"

"Ragusnik has threatened to cease operations."

"Go on strike, in other words."

"Yes."

"Would that be serious?"

"We have enough food and water to last quite a while; reclamation is not essential in that sense. But the wastes would accumulate; they would infect the planetoid. After generations of careful disease control, we have low natural resistance to germ diseases. Once an epidemic started—and one would—we would drop by the hundreds."

"Is Ragusnik aware of this?"

"Yes, of course."

"Do you think he is likely to go through with his threat, then?"

"He is mad. He has already stopped working; there has been no waste reclamation since the day before you landed." Blei's bulbous nose sniffed at the air as though it already caught the whiff of excrement.

Lamorak sniffed mechanically at that, but smelled nothing.

Blei said, "So you see why it might be wise for you to leave. We are humiliated, of course, to have to suggest it."

But Lamorak said, "Wait; not just yet. Good Lord, this is a matter of great interest to me professionally. May I speak to Ragusnik?"

"On no account," said Blei, alarmed.

"But I would like to understand the situation. The sociological conditions here are unique and not to be duplicated elsewhere. In the name of science—"

"How do you mean, speak? Would image-reception do?"

"Yes."

"I will ask the Council," muttered Blei.

They sat about Lamorak uneasily, their austere and dignified expressions badly marred with anxiety. Blei, seated in the midst of them, studiously avoided the Earthman's eyes.

The Chief Councillor, gray-haired, his face harshly wrinkled, his neck scrawny, said in a soft voice, "If in any way you can persuade him, sir, out of your own convictions, we will welcome that. In no case, however, are you to imply that we will, in any way, yield."

A gauzy curtain fell between the Council and Lamorak. He could make out the individual councillors still, but now he turned sharply toward the receiver before him. It glowed to life.

A head appeared in it, in natural color and with great realism. A strong dark head, with massive chin faintly stubbled, and thick, red lips set into a firm horizontal line.

The image said, suspiciously, "Who are you?"

Lamorak said, "My name is Steven Lamorak; I am an Earthman."

"An Outworlder?"

"That's right. I am visiting Elsevere. You are Ragusnik?"

"Igor Ragusnik, at your service," said the image, mockingly. "Except that there is no service and will be none until my family and I are treated like human beings."

Lamorak said, "Do you realize the danger that Elsevere is in? The possibility of epidemic disease?"

"In twenty-four hours, the situation can be made normal, if they allow me humanity. The situation is theirs to correct."

"You sound like an educated man, Ragusnik."

"So?"

"I am told you're denied no material comforts. You are housed and clothed and fed better than anyone on Elsevere. Your children are the best educated."

"Granted. But all by servo-mechanism. And motherless girl-babies are sent us to care for until they grow to be our wives. And they die young for loneliness. Why?" There was sudden passion in his voice. "Why must we live in isolation as if we were all monsters, unfit for human beings to be near? Aren't we human beings like others, with the same needs and desires and feelings? Don't we perform an honorable and useful function?"

There was a rustling of sighs from behind Lamorak. Ragusnik heard it, and raised his voice. "I see you of the Council behind there. Answer me: Isn't it an honorable and useful function? It is *your* waste made into food for you. Is the man who purifies corruption worse than the man who produces it? Listen, councillors, I will *not* give in. Let all of Elsevere die of disease—including myself and my son, if necessary—but I will not give in. My family will be better dead of disease, than living as now."

Lamorak interrupted. "You've led this life since birth, haven't you?"

"And if I have?"

"Surely you're used to it."

"Never. Resigned, perhaps. My father was resigned, and I was resigned for a while; but I have watched my son, my only son, with no other little boy to play with. My brother and I had each other, but my son will never have anyone, and I am no longer resigned. I am through with Elsevere and through with talking."

The receiver went dead.

The Chief Councillor's face had paled to an aged yellow. He and Blei were the only ones of the group left with Lamorak. The Chief Councillor said, "The man is deranged; I do not know how to force him."

He had a glass of wine at his side; as he lifted it to his lips, he spilled a few drops that stained his white trousers with purple splotches.

Lamorak said, "Are his demands so unreasonable? Why can't he be accepted into society?"

There was momentary rage in Blei's eyes. "A dealer in excrement." Then he shrugged. "You are from Earth."

Incongruously, Lamorak thought of another unacceptable, one of the numerous classic creations of the medieval cartoonist Al Capp. The variously named "inside man at the skonk works."

He said, "Does Ragusnik really deal with excrement? I mean, is there physical contact? Surely, it is all handled by automatic machinery."

"Of course," said the Chief Councillor.

"Then exactly what is Ragusnik's function?"

"He manually adjusts the various controls that assure the proper functioning of the machinery. He shifts units to allow repairs to be made; he alters functional rates with the time of day; he varies end production with demand." He added sadly, "If we had the space to make the machinery ten times as complex, all this could be done automatically; but that would be such needless waste."

"But even so," insisted Lamorak, "all Ragusnik does he does simply by pressing buttons or closing contacts or things like that."

"Yes."

"Then his work is no different from any Elseverian's."

Blei said, stiffly, "You don't understand."

"And for that you will risk the death of your children?"

"We have no other choice," said Blei. There was enough agony in his voice to assure Lamorak that the situation was torture for him, but that he had no other choice indeed.

Lamorak shrugged in disgust. "Then break the strike. Force him."

"How?" said the Chief Councillor. "Who would touch him or go near him? And if we kill him by blasting from a distance, how will that help us?"

Lamorak said, thoughtfully, "Would you know how to run his machinery?"

The Chief Councillor came to his feet. "I?" he howled.

"I don't mean *you*," cried Lamorak at once. "I used the pronoun in its indefinite sense. Could *someone* learn how to handle Ragusnik's machinery?"

Slowly, the passion drained out of the Chief Councillor. "It is in the handbooks, I am certain—though I assure you I have never concerned myself with it."

"Then couldn't someone learn the procedure and substitute for Ragusnik until the man gives in?"

Blei said, "Who would agree to do such a thing? Not I, under any circumstances."

Lamorak thought fleetingly of Earthly taboos that might be almost as strong. He thought of cannibalism, incest, a pious man cursing God. He said,

"But you must have made provision for vacancy in the Ragusnik job. Suppose he died."

"Then his son would automatically succeed to his job, or his nearest other relative," said Blei.

"What if he had no adult relatives? What if all his family died at once?"

"That has never happened; it will never happen."

The Chief Councillor added, "If there were danger of it, we might, perhaps, place a baby or two with the Ragusniks and have it raised to the profession."

"Ah. And how would you choose that baby?"

"From among children of mothers who died in childbirth, as we choose the future Ragusnik bride."

"Then choose a substitute Ragusnik now, by lot," said Lamorak.

The Chief Councillor said, "*No! Impossible!* How can you suggest that? If we select a baby, that baby is brought up to the life; it knows no other. At this point, it would be necessary to choose an adult and subject him to Ragusnik-hood. No, Dr. Lamorak, we are neither monsters nor abandoned brutes."

No use, thought Lamorak helplessly. *No use, unless—*

He couldn't bring himself to face that *unless* just yet.

That night, Lamorak slept scarcely at all. Ragusnik asked for only the basic elements of humanity. But opposing that were thirty thousand Elseverians who faced death.

The welfare of thirty thousand on one side; the just demands of one family on the other. Could one say that thirty thousand who would support such injustice deserved to die? Injustice by what standards? Earth's? Elsevere's? And who was Lamorak that he should judge?

And Ragusnik? He was willing to let thirty thousand die, including men and women who merely accepted a situation they had been taught to accept and could not change if they wished to. And children who had nothing at all to do with it.

Thirty thousand on one side; a single family on the other.

Lamorak made his decision in something that was almost despair; in the morning he called the Chief Councillor.

He said, "Sir, if you can find a substitute, Ragusnik will see that he has lost all chance to force a decision in his favor and will return to work."

"There can be no substitute," sighed the Chief Councillor. "I have explained that."

"No substitute among the Elseverians, but I am not an Elseverian; it doesn't matter to me. I will substitute."

*   *   *

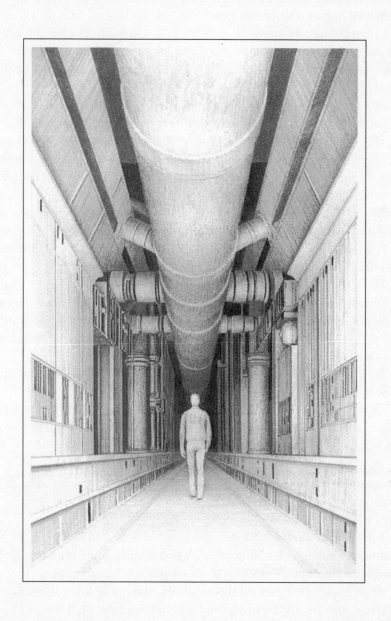

They were excited, much more excited than Lamorak himself. A dozen times they asked him if he was serious.

Lamorak had not shaved, and he felt sick. "Certainly, I'm serious. And any time Ragusnik acts like this, you can always import a substitute. No other world has the taboo and there will always be plenty of temporary substitutes available if you pay enough."

(He was betraying a brutally exploited man, and he knew it. But he told himself desperately: *Except for ostracism, he's very well treated. Very well.*)

They gave him the handbooks and he spent six hours, reading and rereading. There was no use asking questions. None of the Elseverians knew anything about the job, except for what was in the handbook; and all seemed uncomfortable if the details were as much as mentioned.

"Maintain zero reading of galvanometer A-2 at all times during red signal of the Lunge-howler," read Lamorak. "Now what's a Lunge-howler?"

"There will be a sign," muttered Blei, and the Elseverians looked at each other hangdog and bent their heads to stare at their fingerends.

They left him long before he reached the small rooms that were the central headquarters of generations of working Ragusniks, serving their world. He had specific instructions concerning which turnings to take and what level to reach, but they hung back and let him proceed alone.

He went through the rooms painstakingly, identifying the instruments and controls, following the schematic diagrams in the handbook.

There's a Lunge-howler, he thought, with gloomy satisfaction. The sign did indeed say so. It had a semicircular face bitten into holes that were obviously designed to glow in separate colors. Why a "howler" then?

He didn't know.

Somewhere, thought Lamorak, *somewhere wastes are accumulating, pushing against gears and exits, pipelines and stills, waiting to be handled in half a hundred ways. Now they just accumulate.*

Not without a tremor, he pulled the first switch as indicated by the handbook in its directions for "Initiation." A gentle murmur of life made itself felt through the floors and walls. He turned a knob and lights went on.

At each step, he consulted the handbook, though he knew it by heart; and with each step, the rooms brightened and the dial indicators sprang into motion and a humming grew louder.

Somewhere deep in the factories, the accumulated wastes were being drawn into the proper channels.

A high-pitched signal sounded and startled Lamorak out of his painful concentration. It was the communications signal and Lamorak fumbled his receiver into action.

Ragusnik's head showed, startled; then slowly, the incredulity and outright shock faded from his eyes. "*That's* how it is, then."

"I'm not an Elseverian, Ragusnik; I don't mind doing this."

"But what business is it of yours? Why do you interfere?"

"I'm on your side, Ragusnik, but I must do this."

"Why, if you're on my side? Do they treat people on your world as they treat me here?"

"Not any longer. But even if you are right, there are thirty thousand people on Elsevere to be considered."

"They would have given in; you've ruined my only chance."

"They would *not* have given in. And in a way, you've won; they know now that you're dissatisfied. Until now, they never dreamed a Ragusnik could be unhappy, that he could make trouble."

"What if they know? Now all they need do is hire an Outworlder anytime."

Lamorak shook his head violently. He had thought this through in these last bitter hours. "The fact that they know means that the Elseverians will begin to think about you; some will begin to wonder if it's right to treat a human so. And if Outworlders are hired, they'll spread the word that this goes on upon Elsevere and Galactic public opinion will be in your favor."

"And?"

"Things will improve. In your son's time, things will be much better."

"In my son's time," said Ragusnik, his cheeks sagging. "I might have had it now. Well, I lose. I'll go back to the job."

Lamorak felt an overwhelming relief. "If you'll come here now, sir, you may have your job and I'll consider it an honor to shake your hand."

Ragusnik's head snapped up and filled with a gloomy pride. "You call me 'sir' and offer to shake my hand. Go about your business, Earthman, and leave me to my work, for I would not shake yours."

Lamorak returned the way he had come, relieved that the crisis was over, and profoundly depressed, too.

He stopped in surprise when he found a section of corridor cordoned off, so he could not pass. He looked about for alternate routes, then startled at a magnified voice above his head. "Dr. Lamorak, do you hear me? This is Councillor Blei."

Lamorak looked up. The voice came over some sort of public address system, but he saw no sign of an outlet.

He called out, "Is anything wrong? Can you hear me?"

"I hear you."

Instinctively, Lamorak was shouting. "Is anything wrong? There seems to be a block here. Are there complications with Ragusnik?"

"Ragusnik has gone to work," came Blei's voice. "The crisis is over, and you must make ready to leave."

"Leave?"

"Leave Elsevere; a ship is being made ready for you now."

"But wait a bit." Lamorak was confused by this sudden leap of events. "I haven't completed my gathering of data."

Blei's voice said, "This cannot be helped. You will be directed to the ship and your belongings will be sent after you by servo-mechanisms. We trust—we trust—"

Something was becoming clear to Lamorak. "You trust *what*?"

"We trust you will make no attempt to see or speak directly to any Elseverian. And of course we hope you will avoid embarrassment by not attempting to return to Elsevere at any time in the future. A colleague of yours would be welcome if further data concerning us is needed."

"I understand," said Lamorak, tonelessly. Obviously, he had himself become a Ragusnik. He had handled the controls that in turn had handled the wastes; he was ostracized. He was a corpse-handler, a swineherd, an inside man at the skonk works.

He said, "Good-bye."

Blei's voice said, "Before we direct you, Dr. Lamorak—on behalf of the Council of Elsevere, I thank you for your help in this crisis."

"You're welcome," said Lamorak, bitterly.

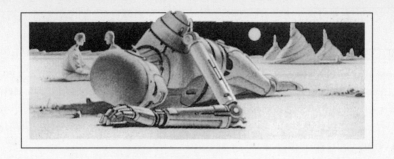

The Machine That Won the War

The celebration had a long way to go and even in the silent depths of Multivac's underground chambers, it hung in the air.

If nothing else, there was the mere fact of isolation and silence. For the first time in a decade, technicians were not scurrying about the vitals of the giant computer, the soft lights did not wink out their erratic patterns, the flow of information in and out had halted.

It would not be halted long, of course, for the needs of peace would be pressing. Yet now, for a day, perhaps for a week, even Multivac might celebrate the great time, and rest.

Lamar Swift took off the military cap he was wearing and looked down the long and empty main corridor of the enormous computer. He sat down rather wearily in one of the technician's swing-stools, and his uniform, in which he had never been comfortable, took on a heavy and wrinkled appearance.

He said, "I'll miss it all after a grisly fashion. It's hard to remember when we weren't at war with Deneb, and it seems against nature now to be at peace and to look at the stars without anxiety."

The two men with the Executive Director of the Solar Federation were both younger than Swift. Neither was as gray. Neither looked quite as tired.

John Henderson, thin-lipped and finding it hard to control the relief he felt in the midst of triumph, said, "They're destroyed! They're destroyed! It's what I keep saying to myself over and over and I still can't believe it. We all talked so much, over so many years, about the menace hanging over Earth and all its worlds, over every human being, and all the time it was true, every word of it. And now we're alive and it's the Denebians who are shattered and destroyed. They'll be no menace now, ever again."

"Thanks to Multivac," said Swift, with a quiet glance at the imperturbable Jablonsky, who through all the war had been Chief Interpreter of science's oracle. "Right, Max?"

Jablonsky shrugged. Automatically, he reached for a cigarette and decided against it. He alone, of all the thousands who had lived in the tunnels within Multivac, had been allowed to smoke, but toward the end he had made definite efforts to avoid making use of the privilege.

He said, "Well, that's what *they* say." His broad thumb moved in the direction of his right shoulder, aiming upward.

"Jealous, Max?"

"Because they're shouting for Multivac? Because Multivac is the big hero of mankind in this war?" Jablonsky's craggy face took on an air of suitable contempt. "What's that to me? Let Multivac be the machine that won the war, if it pleases them."

Henderson looked at the other two out of the corners of his eyes. In this short interlude that the three had instinctively sought out in the one peaceful corner of a metropolis gone mad; in this entr'acte between the dangers of war and the difficulties of peace; when, for one moment, they might all find surcease; he was conscious only of his weight of guilt.

Suddenly, it was as though that weight were too great to be borne longer. It had to be thrown off, along with the war; now!

Henderson said, "Multivac had nothing to do with victory. It's just a machine."

"A big one," said Swift.

"Then just a big machine. No better than the data fed it." For a moment, he stopped, suddenly unnerved at what he was saying.

Jablonsky looked at him, his thick fingers once again fumbling for a cigarette and once again drawing back. "You should know. You supplied the data. Or is it just that you're taking the credit?"

"No," said Henderson, angrily. "There is no credit. What do you know of the data Multivac had to use, predigested from a hundred subsidiary computers here on Earth, on the Moon, on Mars, even on Titan? With Titan always delayed and always that feeling that its figures would introduce an unexpected bias."

"It would drive anyone mad," said Swift, with gentle sympathy.

Henderson shook his head. "It wasn't just that. I admit that eight years ago when I replaced Lepont as Chief Programmer, I was nervous. But there was an exhilaration about things in those days. The war was still long-range; an adventure without real danger. We hadn't reached the point where manned vessels had had to take over and where interstellar warps could swallow up a planet clean, if aimed correctly. But then, when the real difficulties began—"

Angrily—he could finally permit anger—he said, "You know nothing about it."

"Well," said Swift. "Tell us. The war is over. We've won."

"Yes." Henderson nodded his head. He had to remember that. Earth had won so all had been for the best. "Well, the data became meaningless."

"Meaningless? You mean that literally?" said Jablonsky.

"Literally. What would you expect? The trouble with you two was that you weren't out in the thick of it. You never left Multivac, Max, and you, Mr. Director, never left the Mansion except on state visits where you saw exactly what they wanted you to see."

"I was not as unaware of that," said Swift, "as you may have thought."

"Do you know," said Henderson, "to what extent data concerning our production capacity, our resource potential, our trained manpower—everything of importance to the war effort, in fact—had become unreliable and untrustworthy during the last half of the war? Group leaders, both civilian and military, were intent on projecting their own improved image, so to speak, so they obscured the bad and magnified the good. Whatever the machines might do, the men who programmed them and interpreted the results had their own skins to think of and competitors to stab. There was no way of stopping that. I tried, and failed."

"Of course," said Swift, in quiet consolation. "I can see that you would."

This time Jablonsky decided to light his cigarette. "Yet I presume you provided Multivac with data in your programming. You said nothing to us about unreliability."

"How could I tell you? And if I did, how could you afford to believe me?" demanded Henderson, savagely. "Our entire war effort was geared to Multivac. It was the one great weapon on our side, for the Denebians had nothing like it. What else kept up morale in the face of doom but the assurance that Multivac would always predict and circumvent any Denebian move, and would always direct and prevent the circumvention of our moves? Great Space, after our Spywarp was blasted out of hyperspace we lacked any reliable Denebian data to feed Multivac and we didn't dare make *that* public."

"True enough," said Swift.

"Well, then," said Henderson, "if I told you the data was unreliable, what could you have done but replace me and refuse to believe me? I couldn't allow that."

"What did you do?" said Jablonsky.

"Since the war is won, I'll tell you what I did. I corrected the data."

"How?" asked Swift.

"Intuition, I presume. I juggled them till they looked right. At first, I hardly dared. I changed a bit here and there to correct what were obvious impossibilities. When the sky didn't collapse about us, I got braver. Toward the end, I

scarcely cared. I just wrote out the necessary data as it was needed. I even had the Multivac Annex prepare data for me according to a private programming pattern I had devised for the purpose."

"Random figures?" said Jablonsky.

"Not at all. I introduced a number of necessary biases."

Jablonsky smiled, quite unexpectedly, his dark eyes sparkling behind the crinkling of the lower lids. "Three times a report was brought me about unauthorized uses of the Annex, and I let it go each time. If it had mattered, I would have followed it up and spotted you, John, and found out what you were doing. But, of course, nothing about Multivac mattered in those days, so you got away with it."

"What do you mean, nothing mattered?" asked Henderson, suspiciously.

"Nothing did. I suppose if I had told you this at the time, it would have spared you your agony, but then if you had told me what you were doing, it would have spared me mine. What made you think Multivac was in working order, whatever the data you supplied it?"

"Not in working order?" said Swift.

"Not really. Not reliably. After all, where were my technicians in the last years of the war? I'll tell you, they were feeding computers on a thousand different space devices. They were gone! I had to make do with kids I couldn't trust and veterans who were out-of-date. Besides, do you think I could trust the solid-state components coming out of Cryogenics in the last years? Cryogenics wasn't any better placed as far as personnel was concerned than I was. To me, it didn't matter whether the data being supplied Multivac were reliable or not. The *results* weren't reliable. That much I knew."

"What did you do?" asked Henderson.

"I did what you did, John. I introduced the bugger factor. I adjusted matters in accordance with intuition—and that's how the machine won the war."

Swift leaned back in the chair and stretched his legs out before him. "Such revelations. It turns out then that the material handed me to guide me in my decision-making capacity was a man-made interpretation of man-made data. Isn't that right?"

"It looks so," said Jablonsky.

"Then I perceive I was correct in not placing too much reliance upon it," said Swift.

"You didn't?" Jablonsky, despite what he had just said, managed to look professionally insulted.

"I'm afraid I didn't. Multivac might seem to say, Strike here, not there; do this, not that; wait, don't act. But I could never be certain that what Multivac seemed to say, it really did say; or what it really said, it really meant. I could never be certain."

"But the final report was always plain enough, sir," said Jablonsky.

"To those who did not have to make the decision, perhaps. Not to me. The horror of the responsibility of such decisions was unbearable and not even Multivac was sufficient to remove the weight. But the point is I was justified in doubting and there is tremendous relief in that."

Caught up in the conspiracy of mutual confession, Jablonsky put titles aside. "What was it you did then, Lamar? After all, you did make decisions. How?"

"Well, it's time to be getting back perhaps but—I'll tell you first. Why not? I did make use of a computer, Max, but an older one than Multivac, much older."

He groped in his own pocket for cigarettes, and brought out a package along with a scattering of small change; old fashioned coins dating to the first years before the metal shortage had brought into being a credit system tied to a computer-complex.

Swift smiled rather sheepishly. "I still need these to make money seem substantial to me. An old man finds it hard to abandon the habits of youth." He put a cigarette between his lips and dropped the coins one by one back into his pocket.

He held the last coin between his fingers, staring absently at it. "Multivac is not the first computer, friends, nor the best-known, nor the one that can most efficiently lift the load of decision from the shoulders of the executive. A machine *did* win the war, John; at least a very simple computing device did; one that I used every time I had a particularly hard decision to make."

With a faint smile of reminiscence, he flipped the coin he held. It glinted in the air as it spun and came down in Swift's outstretched palm. His hand closed over it and brought it down on the back of his left hand. His right hand remained in place, hiding the coin.

"Heads or tails, gentlemen?" said Swift.

Eyes Do More Than See

After hundreds of billions of years, he suddenly thought of himself as Ames. Not the wavelength combination which, through all the universe, was now the equivalent of Ames—but the sound itself. A faint memory came back of the sound waves he no longer heard and no longer could hear.

The new project was sharpening his memory for so many more of the old, old, eons-old things. He flattened the energy vortex that made up the total of his individuality and its lines of force stretched beyond the stars.

Brock's answering signal came.

Surely, Ames thought, he could tell Brock. Surely he could tell somebody.

Brock's shifting energy pattern communed, "Aren't you coming, Ames?"

"Of course."

"Will you take part in the contest?"

"Yes!" Ames's lines of force pulsed erratically. "Most certainly. I have thought of a whole new art form. Something really unusual."

"What a waste of effort! How can you think a new variation can be thought of after two hundred billion years? There can be nothing new."

For a moment Brock shifted out of phase and out of communion, so that Ames had to hurry to adjust his lines of force. He caught the drift of other-thoughts as he did so, the view of the powdered galaxies against the velvet of nothingness, and the lines of force pulsing in endless multitudes of energy-life, lying between the galaxies.

Ames said, "Please absorb my thoughts, Brock. Don't close out. I've thought of manipulating Matter. Imagine! A symphony of Matter. Why bother with Energy? Of course, there's nothing new in Energy; how can there be? Doesn't that show we must deal with Matter?"

"Matter!"

Ames interpreted Brock's energy-vibrations as those of disgust.

He said, "Why not? We were once Matter ourselves back—back—oh, a tril-

lion years ago anyway! Why not build up objects in a Matter medium, or abstract forms or—listen, Brock—why not build up an imitation of ourselves in Matter, ourselves as we used to be?"

Brock said, "I don't remember how that was. No one does."

"I do," said Ames with energy. "I've been thinking of nothing else and I am beginning to remember. Brock, let me show you. Tell me if I'm right. Tell me."

"No. This is silly. It's—repulsive."

"Let me try, Brock. We've been friends; we've pulsed energy together from the beginning—from the moment we became what we are. Brock, please!"

"Then, quickly."

Ames had not felt such a tremor along his own lines of force in—well, in how long? If he tried it now for Brock and it worked, he could dare manipulate Matter before the assembled Energy-beings who had so drearily waited over the eons for something new.

The Matter was thin out there between the galaxies, but Ames gathered it, scraping it together over the cubic light-years, choosing the atoms, achieving a clayey consistency and forcing matter into an ovoid form that spread out below.

"Don't you remember, Brock?" he asked softly. "Wasn't it something like this?"

Brock's vortex trembled in phase. "Don't make me remember. I don't remember."

"That was the head. They called it the head. I remember it so clearly, I want to say it. I mean with sound." He waited, then said "Look, do you remember that?"

On the upper front of the ovoid appeared HEAD.

"What is that?" asked Brock.

"That's the word for head. The symbols that meant the word in sound. Tell me you remember, Brock!"

"There was something," said Brock hesitantly, "something in the middle." A vertical bulge formed.

Ames said, "Yes! Nose, that's it!" And NOSE appeared upon it. "And those are eyes on either side." LEFT EYE—RIGHT EYE.

Ames regarded what he had formed, his lines of force pulsing slowly. Was he sure he liked this?

"Mouth," he said, in small quiverings, "and chin and Adam's apple, and the collarbones. How the words come back to me." They appeared on the form.

Brock said, "I haven't thought of them for hundreds of billions of years. Why have you reminded me? Why?"

Ames was momentarily lost in his thoughts, "Something else. Organs to hear with; something for the sound waves. Ears! Where do they go? I don't remember where to put them?"

Brock cried out, "Leave it alone! Ears and all else! Don't remember!"

Ames said, uncertainly, "What is wrong with remembering?"

"Because the outside wasn't rough and cold like that but smooth and warm. Because the eyes were tender and alive and the lips of the mouth trembled and were soft on mine." Brock's lines of force beat and wavered, beat and wavered.

Ames said, "I'm sorry! I'm sorry!"

"You're reminding me that once I was a woman and knew love, that eyes do more than see and I have none to do it for me."

With violence, she added matter to the rough-hewn head and said, "Then let *them* do it," and turned and fled.

And Ames saw and remembered, too, that once he had been a man. The force of his vortex split the head in two and he fled back across the galaxies on the energy-track of Brock—back to the endless doom of life.

And the eyes of the shattered head of Matter still glistened with the moisture that Brock had placed there to represent tears. The head of Matter did that which the Energy-beings could do no longer and it wept for all humanity, and for the fragile beauty of the bodies they had once given up, a trillion years ago.

The Martian Way

1

From the doorway of the short corridor between the only two rooms in the travel-head of the spaceship, Mario Esteban Rioz watched sourly as Ted Long adjusted the video dials painstakingly. Long tried a touch clockwise, then a touch counter. The picture was lousy.

Rioz knew it would stay lousy. They were too far from Earth and at a bad position facing the Sun. But then Long would not be expected to know that. Rioz remained standing in the doorway for an additional moment, head bent to clear the upper lintel, body turned half sidewise to fit the narrow opening. Then he jerked into the galley like a cork popping out of a bottle.

"What are you after?" he asked.

"I thought I'd get Hilder," said Long.

Rioz propped his rump on the corner of a table shelf. He lifted a conical can of milk from the companion shelf just above his head. Its point popped under pressure. He swirled it gently as he waited for it to warm.

"What for?" he said. He upended the cone and sucked noisily.

"Thought I'd listen."

"I think it's a waste of power."

Long looked up, frowning. "It's customary to allow free use of personal video sets."

"Within reason," retorted Rioz.

Their eyes met challengingly. Rioz had the rangy body, the gaunt, cheek-sunken face that was almost the hallmark of the Martian Scavenger, those Spacers who patiently haunted the space routes between Earth and Mars. Pale blue eyes were set keenly in the brown, lined face which, in turn, stood darkly out against the white surrounding syntho-fur that lined the upturned collar of his leathtic space jacket.

Long was altogether paler and softer. He bore some of the marks of the

Grounder, although no second-generation Martian could be a Grounder in the sense that Earthmen were. His own collar was thrown back and his dark brown hair freely exposed.

"What do you call within reason?" demanded Long.

Rioz's thin lips grew thinner. He said, "Considering that we're not even going to make expenses this trip, the way it looks, any power drain at all is outside reason."

Long said, "If we're losing money, hadn't you better get back to your post? It's your watch."

Rioz grunted and ran a thumb and forefinger over the stubble on his chin. He got up and trudged to the door, his soft, heavy boots muting the sound of his steps. He paused to look at the thermostat, then turned with a flare of fury.

"I *thought* it was hot. Where do you think you are?"

Long said, "Forty degrees isn't excessive."

"For you it isn't, maybe. But this is space, not a heated office at the iron mines." Rioz swung the thermostat control down to minimum with a quick thumb movement. "Sun's warm enough."

"The galley isn't on Sunside."

"It'll percolate through, damn it."

Rioz stepped through the door and Long stared after him for a long moment, then turned back to the video. He did not turn up the thermostat.

The picture was still flickering badly, but it would have to do. Long folded a chair down out of the wall. He leaned forward waiting through the formal announcement, the momentary pause before the slow dissolution of the curtain, the spotlight picking out the well-known bearded figure which grew as it was brought forward until it filled the screen.

The voice, impressive even through the flutings and croakings induced by the electron storms of twenty millions of miles, began:

"Friends! My fellow citizens of Earth . . ."

2

Rioz's eye caught the flash of the radio signal as he stepped into the pilot room. For one moment, the palms of his hands grew clammy when it seemed to him that it was a radar pip; but that was only his guilt speaking. He should not have left the pilot room while on duty theoretically, though all Scavengers did it. Still, it was the standard nightmare, this business of a strike turning up during just those five minutes when one knocked off for a quick coffee because it seemed certain that space was clear. And the nightmare had been known to happen, too.

Rioz threw in the multi-scanner. It was a waste of power, but while he was thinking about it, he might as well make sure.

Space was clear except for the far-distant echoes from the neighboring ships on the scavenging line.

He hooked up the radio circuit, and the blond, long-nosed head of Richard Swenson, copilot of the next ship on the Mars-ward side, filled it.

"Hey, Mario," said Swenson.

"Hi. What's new?"

There was a second and a fraction of pause between that and Swenson's next comment, since the speed of electromagnetic radiation is not infinite.

"What a day I've *had*."

"Something happened?" Rioz asked.

"I had a strike."

"Well, good."

"Sure, if I'd roped it in," said Swenson morosely.

"What happened?"

"Damn it, I headed in the wrong direction."

Rioz knew better than to laugh. He said, "How did you do that?"

"It wasn't my fault. The trouble was the shell was moving way out of the ecliptic. Can you imagine the stupidity of a pilot that can't work the release maneuver decently? How was I to know? I got the distance of the shell and let it go at that. I just assumed its orbit was in the usual trajectory family. Wouldn't you? I started along what I thought was a good line of intersection and it was five minutes before I noticed the distance was still going up. The pips were taking their sweet time returning. So then I took the angular projections of the thing, and it was too late to catch up with it."

"Any of the other boys getting it?"

"No. It's way out of the ecliptic and'll keep on going forever. That's not what bothers me so much. It was only an inner shell. But I hate to tell you how many tons of propulsion I wasted getting up speed and then getting back to station. You should have heard Canute."

Canute was Richard Swenson's brother and partner.

"Mad, huh?" said Rioz.

"Mad? Like to have killed me! But then we've been out five months now and it's getting kind of sticky. You know."

"I know."

"How are you doing, Mario?"

Rioz made a spitting gesture. "About that much this trip. Two shells in the last two weeks and I had to chase each one for six hours."

"Big ones?"

"Are you kidding? I could have scaled them down to Phobos by hand. This is the worst trip I've ever had."

"How much longer are you staying?"

"For my part, we can quit tomorrow. We've only been out two months and it's got so I'm chewing Long out all the time."

There was a pause over and above the electromagnetic lag.

Swenson said, "What's he like, anyway? Long, I mean."

Rioz looked over his shoulder. He could hear the soft, crackly mutter of the video in the galley. "I can't make him out. He says to me about a week after the start of the trip, 'Mario, why are you a Scavenger?' I just look at him and say, 'To make a living. Why do you suppose?' I mean, what the hell kind of a question is that? Why is anyone a Scavenger? Anyway, he says, 'That's not it, Mario.' *He's* telling *me*, you see. He says, 'You're a Scavenger because this is part of the Martian way.'"

Swenson said, "And what did he mean by that?"

Rioz shrugged. "I never asked him. Right now he's sitting in there listening to the ultra-microwave from Earth. He's listening to some Grounder called Hilder."

"Hilder? A Grounder politician, an Assemblyman or something, isn't he?"

"That's right. At least, I think that's right. Long is always doing things like that. He brought about fifteen pounds of books with him, all about Earth. Just plain dead weight, you know."

"Well, he's your partner. And talking about partners, I think I'll get back on the job. If I miss another strike, there'll be murder around here."

He was gone and Rioz leaned back. He watched the even green line that was the pulse scanner. He tried the multi-scanner a moment. Space was still clear.

He felt a little better. A bad spell is always worse if the Scavengers all about you are pulling in shell after shell; if the shells go spiraling down to the Phobos scrap forges with everyone's brand welded on except your own. Then, too, he had managed to work off some of his resentment toward Long.

It was a mistake teaming up with Long. It was always a mistake to team up with a tenderfoot. They thought what you wanted was conversation, especially Long, with his eternal theories about Mars and its great new role in human progress. That was the way he said it—Human Progress: the Martian Way; the New Creative Minority. And all the time what Rioz wanted wasn't talk, but a strike, a few shells to call their own.

At that, he hadn't any choice, really. Long was pretty well known down on Mars and made good pay as a mining engineer. He was a friend of Commissioner Sankov and he'd been out on one or two short scavenging missions before. You can't turn a fellow down flat before a tryout, even though it did look funny. Why should a mining engineer with a comfortable job and good money want to muck around in space?

Rioz never asked Long that question. Scavenger partners are forced too close together to make curiosity desirable, or sometimes even safe. But Long talked so much that he answered the question.

"I had to come out here, Mario," he said. "The future of Mars isn't in the mines; it's in space."

Rioz wondered how it would it be to try a trip alone. Everyone said it was impossible. Even discounting lost opportunities when one man had to go off watch to sleep or attend to other things, it was well known that one man alone in space would become intolerably depressed in a relatively short while.

Taking a partner along made a six-month trip possible. A regular crew would be better, but no Scavenger could make money on a ship large enough to carry one. The capital it would take in propulsion alone!

Even two didn't find it exactly fun in space. Usually you had to change partners each trip and you could stay out longer with some than with others. Look at Richard and Canute Swenson. They teamed up every five or six trips because they were brothers. And yet whenever they did, it was a case of constantly mounting tension and antagonism after the first week.

Oh well. Space was clear. Rioz would feel a little better if he went back in the galley and smoothed down some of the bickering with Long. He might as well show he was an old spacehand who took the irritations of space as they came.

He stood up, walked the three steps necessary to reach the short, narrow corridor that tied together the two rooms of the spaceship.

3

Once again Rioz stood in the doorway for a moment, watching. Long was intent on the flickering screen.

Rioz said gruffly, "I'm shoving up the thermostat. It's all right—we can spare the power."

Long nodded. "If you like."

Rioz took a hesitant step forward. Space was clear, so to hell with sitting and looking at a blank, green, pipless line. He said, "What's the Grounder been talking about?"

"History of space travel mostly. Old stuff, but he's doing it well. He's giving the whole works—color cartoons, trick photography, stills from old films, everything."

As if to illustrate Long's remarks, the bearded figure faded out of view, and a cross-sectional view of a spaceship flitted onto the screen. Hilder's voice continued, pointing out features of interest that appeared in schematic color. The communications system of the ship outlined itself in red as he talked about it, the storerooms, the proton micropile drive, the cybernetic circuits . . .

Then Hilder was back on the screen. "But this is only the travel-head of the ship. What moves it? What gets it off the Earth?"

Everyone knew what moved a spaceship, but Hilder's voice was like a drug. He made spaceship propulsion sound like the secret of the ages, like an ultimate revelation. Even Rioz felt a slight tingling of suspense, though he had spent the greater part of his life aboard ship.

Hilder went on. "Scientists call it different names. They call it the Law of Action and Reaction. Sometimes they call it Newton's Third Law. Sometimes they call it Conservation of Momentum. But we don't have to call it any name. We can just use our common sense. When we swim, we push water backward and move forward ourselves. When we walk, we push back against the ground and move forward. When we fly a gyro-flivver, we push air backward and move forward.

"Nothing can move forward unless something else moves backward. It's the old principle of 'You can't get something for nothing.'

"Now imagine a spaceship that weighs a hundred thousand tons lifting off Earth. To do that, something else must be moved downward. Since a spaceship is extremely heavy, a great deal of material must be moved downward. So much material, in fact, that there is no place to keep it all aboard ship. A special compartment must be built behind the ship to hold it."

Again Hilder faded out and the ship returned. It shrank and a truncated cone appeared behind it. In bright yellow, words appeared within it: MATERIAL TO BE THROWN AWAY.

"But now," said Hilder, "the total weight of the ship is much greater. You need still more propulsion and still more."

The ship shrank enormously to add on another larger shell and still another immense one. The ship proper, the travel-head, was a little dot on the screen, a glowing red dot.

Rioz said, "Hell, this is kindergarten stuff."

"Not to the people he's speaking to, Mario," replied Long. "Earth isn't Mars. There must be billions of Earth people who've never even seen a spaceship; don't know the first thing about it."

Hilder was saying, "When the material inside the biggest shell is used up, the shell is detached. It's thrown away, too."

The outermost shell came loose, wobbled about the screen.

"Then the second one goes," said Hilder, "and then, if the trip is a long one, the last is ejected."

The ship was just a red dot now, with three shells shifting and moving, lost in space.

Hilder said, "These shells represent a hundred thousand tons of tungsten, magnesium, aluminum, and steel. They are gone forever from Earth. Mars is ringed by Scavengers, waiting along the routes of space travel, waiting for the cast-off shells, netting and branding them, saving them for Mars. Not one cent of payment reaches Earth for them. They are salvage. They belong to the ship that finds them."

Rioz said, "We risk our investment and our lives. If we don't pick them up, no one gets them. What loss is that to Earth?"

"Look," said Long, "he's been talking about nothing but the drain that Mars, Venus, and the Moon put on Earth. This is just another item of loss."

"They'll get their return. We're mining more iron every year."

"And most of it goes right back into Mars. If you can believe his figures, Earth has invested two hundred billion dollars in Mars and received back about five billion dollars' worth of iron. It's put five hundred billion dollars into the Moon and gotten back a little over twenty-five billion dollars of magnesium, titanium, and assorted light metals. It's put fifty billion dollars into Venus and gotten back nothing. And that's what the taxpayers of Earth are really interested—tax money out, nothing in."

The screen was filled, as he spoke, with diagrams of the Scavengers on the route to Mars; little, grinning caricatures of ships, reaching out wiry, tenuous arms that groped for the tumbling, empty shells, seizing and snaking them in, branding them MARS PROPERTY in glowing letters, then scaling them down to Phobos.

Then it was Hilder again. "They tell us eventually they will return it all to us. Eventually! Once they are a going concern! We don't know when that will be. A century from now? A thousand years? A million? 'Eventually.' Let's take them at their word. Someday they will give us back all our metals. Someday they will grow their own food, use their own power, live their own lives.

"But one thing they can never return. Not in a hundred million years. *Water!*

"Mars has only a trickle of water because it is too small. Venus has no water at all because it is too hot. The Moon has none because it is too hot and too small. So Earth must supply not only drinking water and washing water for the Spacers, water to run their industries, water for the hydroponic factories they claim to be setting up—but even water to throw away by the millions of tons.

"What is the propulsive force that spaceships use? What is it they throw out behind so that they can accelerate forward? Once it was the gases generated from explosives. That was very expensive. Then the proton micropile was invented—a cheap power source that could heat up any liquid until it was a gas under tremendous pressure. What is the cheapest and most plentiful liquid available? Why, water, of course.

"Each spaceship leaves Earth carrying nearly a million tons—not pounds, *tons*—of water, for the sole purpose of driving it into space so that it may speed up or slow down.

"Our ancestors burned the oil of Earth madly and wilfully. They destroyed its coal recklessly. We despise and condemn them for that, but at least they had this—they thought that when the need arose, substitutes would be found. And they were right. We have our plankton farms and our proton micropiles.

"But there is no substitute for water. None! There never can be. And when our descendants view the desert we will have made of Earth, what excuse will they find for us? When the droughts come and grow—"

Long leaned forward and turned off the set. He said, "That bothers me. The damn fool is deliberately—what's the matter?"

Rioz had risen uneasily to his feet. "I ought to be watching the pips."

"The hell with the pips." Long got up likewise, followed Rioz through the narrow corridor, and stood just inside the pilot room. "If Hilder carries this through, if he's got the guts to make a real issue out of it—*wow!*"

He had seen it too. The pip was a Class A, racing after the outgoing signal like a greyhound after a mechanical rabbit.

Rioz was babbling, "Space was clear, I tell you, *clear*. For Mars' sake, Ted, don't just freeze on me. See if you can spot it visually."

Rioz was working speedily and with an efficiency that was the result of nearly twenty years of scavenging. He had the distance in two minutes. Then, remembering Swenson's experience, he measured the angle of declination and the radial velocity as well.

He yelled at Long, "One point seven six radians. You can't miss it, man."

Long held his breath as he adjusted the vernier. "It's only half a radian off the Sun. It'll only be crescent-lit."

He increased magnification as rapidly as he dared, watching for the one "star" that changed position and grew to have a form, revealing itself to be no star.

"I'm starting, anyway," said Rioz. "We can't wait."

"I've got it. I've got it." Magnification was still too small to give it a definite shape, but the dot Long watched was brightening and dimming rhythmically as the shell rotated and caught sunlight on cross sections of different sizes.

"Hold on."

The first of many fine spurts of steam squirted out of the proper vents, leaving long trails of micro-crystals of ice gleaming mistily in the pale beams of the distant Sun. They thinned out for a hundred miles or more. One spurt, then another, then another, as the Scavenger ship moved out of its stable trajectory and took up a course tangential to that of the shell.

"It's moving like a comet at perihelion!" yelled Rioz. "Those damned Grounder pilots knock the shells off that way on purpose. I'd like to—"

He swore his anger in a frustrated frenzy as he kicked steam backward and backward recklessly, till the hydraulic cushioning of his chair had sloughed back a full foot and Long had found himself all but unable to maintain his grip on the guard rail.

"Have a heart," he begged.

But Rioz had his eye on the pips. "If you can't take it, man, stay on Mars!" The steam spurts continued to boom distantly.

The radio came to life. Long managed to lean forward through what seemed like molasses and closed contact. It was Swenson, eyes glaring.

Swenson yelled, "Where the hell are you guys going? You'll be in my sector in ten seconds."

Rioz said, "I'm chasing a shell."

"In *my* sector?"

"It started in mine and you're not in position to get it. Shut off that radio, Ted."

The ship thundered through space, a thunder that could be heard only within the hull. And then Rioz cut the engines in stages large enough to make Long flail forward. The sudden silence was more ear-shattering than the noise that had preceded it.

Rioz said, "All right. Let me have the 'scope."

They both watched. The shell was a definite truncated cone now, tumbling with slow solemnity as it passed along among the stars.

"It's a Class A shell, all right," said Rioz with satisfaction. A giant among shells, he thought. It would put them into the black.

Long said, "We've got another pip on the scanner. I think it's Swenson taking after us."

Rioz scarcely gave it a glance. "He won't catch us."

The shell grew larger still, filling the visiplate.

Rioz's hands were on the harpoon lever. He waited, adjusted the angle microscopically twice, played out the length allotment. Then he yanked, tripping the release.

For a moment, nothing happened. Then a metal mesh cable snaked out onto the visiplate, moving toward the shell like a striking cobra. It made contact, but it did not hold. If it had, it would have snapped instantly like a cobweb strand. The shell was turning with a rotational momentum amounting to thousands of tons. What the cable did do was to set up a powerful magnetic field that acted as a brake on the shell.

Another cable and another lashed out. Rioz sent them out in an almost heedless expenditure of energy.

"I'll get this one! By Mars, I'll get this one!"

With some two dozen cables stretching between ship and shell, he desisted. The shell's rotational energy, converted by breaking into heat, had raised its temperature to a point where its radiation could be picked up by the ship's meters.

Long said, "Do you want me to put our brand on?"

"Suits me. But you don't have to if you don't want to. It's my watch."

"I don't mind."

Long clambered into his suit and went out the lock. It was the surest sign of his newness to the game that he could count the number of times he had been out in space in a suit. This was the fifth time.

He went out along the nearest cable, hand over hand, feeling the vibration of the mesh against the metal of his mitten.

He burned their serial number in the smooth metal of the shell. There was nothing to oxidize the steel in the emptiness of space. It simply melted and vaporized, condensing some feet away from the energy beam, turning the surface it touched into gray, powdery dullness.

Long swung back toward the ship.

Inside again, he took off his helmet, white and thick with frost that collected as soon as he had entered.

The first thing he heard was Swenson's voice coming over the radio in this almost unrecognizable rage: ". . . straight to the Commissioner. Damn it, there are rules to this game!"

Rioz sat back, unbothered. "Look, it hit my sector. I was late spotting it and I chased it into yours. You couldn't have gotten it with Mars for a backstop. That's all there is to it—you back, Long?"

He cut contact.

The signal button raged at him, but he paid no attention.

"He's going to the Commissioner?" Long asked.

"Not a chance. He just goes on like that because it breaks the monotony. He doesn't mean anything by it. He knows it's our shell. And how do you like that hunk of stuff, Ted?"

"Pretty good."

"Pretty good? It's terrific! Hold on. I'm setting it swinging."

The side jets spat steam and the ship started a slow rotation about the shell. The shell followed it. In thirty minutes, they were a gigantic bolo spinning in emptiness. Long checked the *Ephemeris* for the position of Deimos.

At a precisely calculated moment, the cables released their magnetic field and the shell went streaking off tangentially in a trajectory that would, in a day or so, bring it within pronging distance of the shell stores on the Martian satellite.

Rioz watched it go. He felt good. He turned to Long. "This is one fine day for us."

"What about Hilder's speech?" asked Long.

"What? Who? Oh, that. Listen, if I had to worry about every thing some damned Grounder said, I'd never get any sleep. Forget it."

"I don't think we should forget it."

"You're nuts. Don't bother me about it, will you? Get some sleep instead."

4

Ted Long found the breadth and height of the city's main thoroughfare exhilarating. It had been two months since the Commissioner had declared a moratorium on scavenging and had pulled all ships out of space, but this feeling of a stretched-out vista had not stopped thrilling Long. Even the thought that the moratorium was called pending a decision on the part of Earth to enforce its new insistence on water economy, by deciding upon a ration limit for scavenging, did not cast him entirely down.

The roof of the avenue was painted a luminous light blue, perhaps as an old-fashioned imitation of Earth's sky. Ted wasn't sure. The walls were lit with the store windows that pierced it.

Off in the distance, over the hum of traffic and the sloughing noise of people's feet passing him, he could hear the intermittent blasting as new channels were being bored into Mars' crust. All his life he remembered such blastings. The ground he walked on had been part of solid, unbroken rock when he was born. The city was growing and would keep on growing—if Earth would only let it.

He turned off at a cross street, narrower, not quite as brilliantly lit, shop windows giving way to apartment houses, each with its row of lights along the front facade. Shoppers and traffic gave way to slower-paced individuals and to squalling youngsters who had as yet evaded the maternal summons to the evening meal.

At the last minute, Long remembered the social amenities and stopped off at a corner water store.

He passed over his canteen. "Fill 'er up."

The plump storekeeper unscrewed the cap, cocked an eye into the opening. He shook it a little and let it gurgle. "Not much left," he said cheerfully.

"No," agreed Long.

The storekeeper trickled water in, holding the neck of the canteen close to the hose tip to avoid spillage. The volume gauge whirred. He screwed the cap back on.

Long passed over the coins and took his canteen. It clanked against his hip now with a pleasing heaviness. It would never do to visit a family without a full canteen. Among the boys, it didn't matter. Not as much, anyway.

He entered the hallway of No. 27, climbed a short flight of stairs, and paused with his thumb on the signal.

The sound of voices could be heard quite plainly.

One was a woman's voice, somewhat shrill. "It's all right for you to have your Scavenger friends here, isn't it? I'm supposed to be thankful you manage to get home two months a year. Oh, it's quite enough that you spend a day or two with me. After that, it's the Scavengers again.

"I've been home for a long time now," said a male voice, "and this is business. For Mars' sake, let up, Dora. They'll be here soon."

Long decided to wait a moment before signaling. It might give them a chance to hit a more neutral topic.

"What do I care if they come?" retorted Dora. "Let them hear me. And I'd just as soon the Commissioner kept the moratorium on permanently. You hear me?"

"And what would we live on?" came the male voice hotly. "You tell me that."

"I'll tell you. You can make a decent, honorable living right here on Mars, just like everybody else. I'm the only one in this apartment house that's a Scavenger widow. That's what I am—a widow. I'm worse than a widow, because if I were a widow, I'd at least have a chance to marry someone else—what did you say?"

"Nothing. Nothing at all."

"Oh, I know what you said. Now listen here, Dick Swenson—"

"I only said," cried Swenson, "that now I know why Scavengers usually don't marry."

"You shouldn't have either. I'm tired of having every person in the neighborhood pity me and smirk and ask when you're coming home. Other people can be mining engineers and administrators and even tunnel borers. At least tunnel borers' wives have a decent home life and their children don't grow up like vagabonds. Peter might as well not have a father—"

A thin boy-soprano voice made its way through the door. It was somewhat more distant, as though it were in another room. "Hey, Mom, what's a vagabond?"

Dora's voice rose a notch. "Peter! You keep your mind on your homework."

Swenson said in a low voice, "It's not right to talk this way in front of the kid. What kind of notions will he get about me?"

"Stay home then and teach him better notions."

Peter's voice called out again. "Hey, Mom, I'm going to be a Scavenger when I grow up."

Footsteps sounded rapidly. There was a momentary hiatus in the sounds, then a piercing, "Mom! Hey, Mom! Leggo my ear! What did I do?" and a snuffling silence.

Long seized the chance. He worked the signal vigorously.

Swenson opened the door, brushing down his hair with both hands.

"Hello, Ted," he said in a subdued voice. Then loudly, "Ted's here, Dora. Where's Mario, Ted?"

Long said, "He'll be here in a while."

Dora came bustling out of the next room, a small, dark woman with a pinched nose, and hair, just beginning to show touches of gray, combed off the forehead.

"Hello, Ted. Have you eaten?"

"Quite well, thanks. I haven't interrupted you, have I?"

"Not at all. We finished ages ago. Would you like some coffee?"

"I think so." Ted unslung his canteen and offered it.

"Oh, goodness, that's all right. We've plenty of water."

"I insist."

"Well, then—"

Back into the kitchen she went. Through the swinging door, Long caught a glimpse of dishes sitting in Secoterg, the "waterless cleaner that soaks up and absorbs grease and dirt in a twinkling. One ounce of water will rinse eight square feet of dish surface clean as clean. Buy Secoterg. Secoterg just cleans it right, makes your dishes shiny bright, does away with water waste—"

The tune started whining through his mind and Long crushed it with speech. He said, "How's Pete?"

"Fine, fine. The kid's in the fourth grade now. You know I don't get to see him much. Well sir, when I came back last time, he looked at me and said . . ."

It went on for a while and wasn't too bad as bright sayings of bright children as told by dull parents go.

The door signal burped and Mario Rioz came in, frowning and red.

Swenson stepped to him quickly. "Listen, don't say anything about shell-snaring. Dora still remembers the time you fingered a Class A shell out of my territory and she's in one of her moods now."

"Who the hell wants to talk about shells?" Rioz slung off a fur-lined jacket, threw it over the back of the chair and sat down.

Dora came through the swinging door, viewed the newcomer with a synthetic smile, and said, "Hello, Mario. Coffee for you, too?"

"Yeah," he said, reaching automatically for his canteen.

"Just use some more of my water, Dora," said Long quickly. "He'll owe it to me."

"Yeah," said Rioz.

"What's wrong, Mario?" asked Long.

Rioz said heavily, "Go on. Say you told me so. A year ago when Hilder made that speech, you told me so. Say it."

Long shrugged.

Rioz said, "They've set up the quota. Fifteen minutes ago the news came out."

"Well?"

"Fifty thousand tons of water per trip."

"What?" yelled Swenson, burning. "You can't get off Mars with fifty thousand!"

"That's the figure. It's a deliberate piece of gutting. No more scavenging."

Dora came out with the coffee and set it down all around.

"What's all this about no more scavenging?" She sat down very firmly and Swenson looked helpless.

"It seems," said Long, "that they're rationing us at fifty thousand tons and that means we can't make any more trips."

"Well, what of it?" Dora sipped her coffee and smiled gaily. "If you want my opinion, it's a good thing. It's time all you Scavengers found yourselves a nice, steady job here on Mars. I mean it. It's no life to be running all over space—"

"Please, Dora," said Swenson.

Rioz came close to a snort.

Dora raised her eyebrows. "I'm just giving my opinions."

Long said, "Please feel free to do so. But I would like to say something. Fifty thousand is just a detail. We know that Earth—or at least Hilder's party—wants to make political capital out of a campaign for water economy, so we're in a bad hole. We've got to get water somehow or they'll shut us down altogether, right?"

"Well, sure," said Swenson.

"But the question is how, right?"

"If it's only getting water," said Rioz in a sudden gush of words, "there's only one thing to do and you know it. If the Grounders won't give us water, we'll take it. The water doesn't belong to them just because their fathers and grandfathers were too damned sick-yellow ever to leave their fat planet. Water belongs to people wherever they are. We're people and the water's ours, too. We have a right to it."

"How do you propose taking it?" asked Long.

"Easy! They've got oceans of water on Earth. They can't post a guard over every square mile. We can sink down on the night side of the planet any time we want, fill our shells, then get away. How can they stop us?"

"In half a dozen ways, Mario. How do you spot shells in space up to distances of a hundred thousand miles? One thin metal shell in all that space. How? By radar. Do you think there's no radar on Earth? Do you think that if Earth ever gets the notion we're engaged in waterlegging, it won't be simple for them to set up a radar network to spot ships coming in from space?"

Dora broke in indignantly. "I'll tell you one thing, Mario Rioz. My husband isn't going to be part of any raid to get water to keep up his scavenging with."

"It isn't just scavenging," said Mario. "Next they'll be cutting down on everything else. We've got to stop them now."

"But we don't need their water, anyway," said Dora. "We're not the Moon or Venus. We pipe enough water down from the polar caps for all we need. We have a water tap right in this apartment. There's one in every apartment on this block."

Long said, "Home use is the smallest part of it. The mines use water. And what do we do about the hydroponic tanks?"

"That's right," said Swenson. "What about the hydroponic tanks, Dora? They've got to have water and it's about time we arranged to grow our own fresh food instead of having to live on the condensed crud they ship us from Earth."

"Listen to him," said Dora scornfully. "What do you know about fresh food? You've never eaten any."

"I've eaten more than you think. Do you remember those carrots I picked up once?"

"Well, what was so wonderful about them? If you ask me, good baked protomeal is much better. And healthier, too. It just seems to be the fashion now to be talking fresh vegetables because they're increasing taxes for these hydroponics. Besides, all this will blow over."

Long said, "I don't think so. Not by itself, anyway. Hilder will probably be the next Co-ordinator, and then things may really get bad. If they cut down on food shipments, too—"

"Well, then," shouted Rioz, "what do we do? I still say take it! Take the water!"

"And I say we can't do that, Mario. Don't you see that what you're suggesting is the Earth way, the Grounder way? You're trying to hold on to the umbilical cord that ties Mars to Earth. Can't you get away from that? Can't you see the Martian way?"

"No, I can't. Suppose you tell me."

"I will, if you'll listen. When we think about the Solar System, what do we think about? Mercury, Venus, Earth, Moon, Mars, Phobos, and Deimos. There you are—seven bodies, that's all. But that doesn't represent one percent of the Solar System. We Martians are right at the edge of the other ninety-nine percent. Out there, farther from the Sun, there's unbelievable amounts of water!"

The others stared.

Swenson said uncertainly, "You mean the layers of ice on Jupiter and Saturn?"

"Not that specifically, but it *is* water, you'll admit. A thousand-mile-thick layer of water is a lot of water."

"But it's all covered up with layers of ammonia or—or something, isn't it?" asked Swenson. "Besides, we can't land on the major planets."

"I know that," said Long, "but I haven't said that was the answer. The major planets aren't the only objects out there. What about the asteroids and the satellites? Vesta is a two-hundred-mile-diameter asteroid that's hardly more than a chunk of ice. One of the moons of Saturn is mostly ice. How about that?"

Rioz said, "Haven't you ever been in space, Ted?"

"You know I have. Why do you ask?"

"Sure, I know you have, but you still talk like a Grounder. Have you thought of the distances involved? The average asteroid is a hundred twenty million miles from Mars at the closest. That's twice the Venus-Mars hop and you know that hardly any liners do even that in one jump. They usually stop off at Earth or the Moon. After all, how long do you expect anyone to stay in space, man?"

"I don't know. What's your limit?"

"You know the limit. You don't have to ask me. It's six months. That's handbook data. After six months, if you're still in space, you're psychotherapy meat. Right, Dick?"

Swenson nodded.

"And that's just the asteroids," Rioz went on. "From Mars to Jupiter is three hundred thirty million miles, and to Saturn it's seven hundred million. How can anyone handle that kind of distance? Suppose you hit standard velocity or, to make it even, say you get up to a good two hundred kilomiles an hour. It would take you—let's see, allowing time for acceleration and deceleration—about six or seven months to get to Jupiter and nearly a year to get to Saturn. Of course, you could hike the speed to a million miles an hour, theoretically, but where would you get the water to do that?"

"Gee," said a small voice attached to a smutty nose and round eyes, "Saturn!"

Dora whirled in her chair. "Peter, march right back into your room!"

"Aw, Ma."

"Don't 'Aw Ma' me." She began to get out of the chair, and Peter scuttled away.

Swenson said, "Say, Dora, why don't you keep him company for a while? It's hard to keep his mind on homework if we're all out here talking."

Dora sniffed obstinately and stayed put, "I'll sit right here until I find out what Ted Long is thinking of. I tell you right now I don't like the sound of it."

Swenson said nervously, "Well, never mind Jupiter and Saturn. I'm sure Ted isn't figuring on that. But what about Vesta? We could make it in ten or twelve weeks there and the same back. And two hundred miles in diameter. That's four million cubic miles of ice!"

"So what?" said Rioz. "What do we do on Vesta? Quarry the ice? Set up mining machinery? Say, do you know how long that would take?"

Long said, "I'm talking about Saturn, not Vesta."

Rioz addressed an unseen audience. "I tell him seven hundred million miles and he keeps on talking."

"All right," said Long, "suppose you tell me how you know we can only stay in space six months, Mario?"

"It's common knowledge, damn it."

"Because it's in the *Handbook of Space Flight*. It's data compiled by Earth scientists from experience with Earth pilots and spacemen. You're still thinking Grounder style. You won't think the Martian way."

"A Martian may be a Martian, but he's still a man."

"But how can you be so blind? How many times have you fellows been out for over six months without a break?"

Rioz said, "That's different."

"Because you're Martians? Because you're professional Scavengers?"

"No. Because we're not on a flight. We can put back for Mars any time we want to."

"But you *don't* want to. That's my point. Earthmen have tremendous ships with libraries of films, with a crew of fifteen plus passengers. Still, they can only stay out six months maximum. Martian Scavengers have a two-room ship with only one partner. But we can stick it out more than six months."

Dora said, "I suppose you want to stay in a ship for a year and go to Saturn."

"Why not, Dora?" said Long. "We can do it. Don't you see we can? Earthmen can't. They've got a real world. They've got open sky and fresh food, all the air and water they want. Getting into a ship is a terrible change for them. More than six months is too much for them for that very reason. Martians have been living on a ship our entire lives.

"That's all Mars is—a ship. It's just a big ship forty-five hundred miles across with one tiny room in it occupied by fifty thousand people. It's closed in like a ship. We breathe packaged air and drink packaged water, which we repurify over and over. We eat the same food rations we eat aboard ship. When we get into a ship, it's the same thing we've known all our lives. We can stand it for a lot more than a year if we have to."

Dora said, "Dick, too?"

"We all can."

"Well, Dick can't. It's all very well for you, Ted Long, and this shell stealer here, this Mario, to talk about jaunting off for a year. You're not married. Dick is. He has a wife and he has a child and that's enough for him. He can just get a regular job right here on Mars. Why, my goodness, suppose you go to Saturn and find there's no water there. How'll you get back? Even if you had water left, you'd be out of food. It's the most ridiculous thing I ever heard of."

"No. Now listen," said Long tightly. "I've thought this thing out. I've talked to Commissioner Sankov and he'll help. But we've got to have ships and men. I can't get them. The men won't listen to me. I'm green. You two are known and respected. You're veterans. If you back me, even if you don't go yourselves, if you'll just help me sell this thing to the rest, get volunteers—"

"First," said Rioz grumpily, "you'll have to do a lot more explaining. Once we get to Saturn, where's the water?"

"That's the beauty of it," said Long. "That's why it's got to be Saturn. The water there is just floating around in space for the taking."

5

When Hamish Sankov had come to Mars, there was no such thing as a native Martian. Now there were two-hundred-odd babies whose grandfathers had been born on Mars—native in the third generation.

When he had come as a boy in his teens, Mars had been scarcely more than a huddle of grounded spaceships connected by sealed underground tunnels. Through the years, he had seen buildings grow and burrow widely, thrusting blunt snouts up into the thin, unbreathable atmosphere. He had seen huge storage depots spring up into which spaceships and their loads could be swallowed whole. He had seen the mines grow from nothing to a huge gouge in the Martian crust, while the population of Mars grew from fifty to fifty thousand.

It made him feel old, these long memories—they and the even dimmer memories induced by the presence of this Earthman before him. His visitor brought up those long-forgotten scraps of thought about a soft-warm world that was as kind and gentle to mankind as the mother's womb.

The Earthman seemed fresh from that womb. Not very tall, not very lean; in fact, distinctly plump. Dark hair with a neat little wave in it, a neat little mustache, and neatly scrubbed skin. His clothing was right in style and as fresh and neatly turned as plastek could be.

Sankov's own clothes were of Martian manufacture, serviceable and clean, but many years behind the times. His face was craggy and lined, his hair was pure white, and his Adam's apple wobbled when he talked.

The Earthman was Myron Digby, member of Earth's General Assembly. Sankov was Martian Commissioner.

Sankov said, "This all hits us hard, Assemblyman."

"It's hit most of us hard, too, Commissioner."

"Uh-huh. Can't honestly say then that I can make it out. Of course, you understand, I don't make out that I can understand Earth ways, for all that I was born there. Mars is a hard place to live, Assemblyman, and you have to understand that. It takes a lot of shipping space just to bring us food, water, and raw materials so we can live. There's not much room left for books and news films. Even video programs can't reach Mars, except for about a month when Earth is in conjunction, and even then nobody has much time to listen.

"My office gets a weekly summary film from Planetary Press. Generally, I don't have time to pay attention to it. Maybe you'd call us provincial, and you'd be right. When something like this happens, all we can do is kind of helplessly look at each other."

Digby said slowly, "You can't mean that your people on Mars haven't heard of Hilder's anti-Waster campaign."

"No, can't exactly say that. There's a young Scavenger, son of a good friend of mine who died in space"—Sankov scratched the side of his neck doubtfully—"who makes a hobby out of reading up on Earth history and things like that. He catches video broadcasts when he's out in space and he listened to this man Hilder. Near as I can make out that was the first talk Hilder made about Wasters.

"The young fellow came to me with that. Naturally, I didn't take him very serious. I kept an eye on the Planetary Press films for a while after that, but there wasn't much mention of Hilder and what there was made him out to look pretty funny."

"Yes, Commissioner," said Digby, "it all seemed quite a joke when it started."

Sankov stretched out a pair of long legs to one side of his desk and crossed them at the ankles. "Seems to me it's still pretty much of a joke. What's his argument? We're using up water. Has he tried looking at some figures? I got them all here. Had them brought to me when this committee arrived.

"Seems that Earth has four hundred million cubic miles of water in its oceans and each cubic mile weighs four and a half billion tons. That's a lot of water. Now we use some of that heap in space flight. Most of the thrust is inside Earth's gravitational field, and that means the water thrown out finds its way back to the oceans. Hilder doesn't figure that in. When he says a million tons of water is used up per flight, he's a liar. It's less than a hundred thousand tons.

"Suppose, now, we have fifty thousand flights a year. We don't, of course; not even fifteen hundred. But let's say there are fifty thousand. I figure there's going to be considerable expansion as time goes on. With fifty thousand flights, one cubic mile of water would be lost to space each year. That means that in a million years, Earth would lose *one quarter of one percent* of its total water supply!"

Digby spread his hands, palms upward, and let them drop. "Commissioner, Interplanetary Alloys has used figures like that in their campaign against Hilder, but you can't fight a tremendous, emotion-filled drive with cold mathematics. This man Hilder has invented a name, 'Wasters.' Slowly he has built this name up into a gigantic conspiracy; a gang of brutal, profit-seeking wretches raping Earth for their own immediate benefit.

"He has accused the government of being riddled with them, the Assembly of being dominated by them, the press of being owned by them. None of this, unfortunately, seems ridiculous to the average man. He knows all too well what selfish men can do to Earth's resources. He knows what happened to Earth's oil during the Time of Troubles, for instance, and the way topsoil was ruined.

"When a farmer experiences a drought, he doesn't care that the amount of water lost in space flight isn't a droplet in a fog as far as Earth's overall water supply is concerned. Hilder has given him something to blame and that's the strongest possible consolation for disaster. He isn't going to give that up for a diet of figures."

Sankov said, "That's where I get puzzled. Maybe it's because I don't know how things work on Earth, but it seems to me that there aren't just droughty farmers there. As near as I could make out from the news summaries, these Hilder people are a minority. Why is it Earth goes along with a few farmers and some crackpots that egg them on?"

"Because, Commissioner, there are such things as worried human beings. The steel industry sees that an era of space flight will stress increasingly the light, nonferrous alloys. The various miners' unions worry about extraterrestrial competition. Any Earthman who can't get aluminum to build a prefab is certain that it is because the aluminum is going to Mars. I know a professor of archaeology who's an anti-Waster because he can't get a government grant to cover his excavations. He's convinced that all government money is going into rocketry research and space medicine and he resents it."

Sankov said, "That doesn't sound like Earth people are much different from us here on Mars. But what about the General Assembly? Why do they have to go along with Hilder?"

Digby smiled sourly. "Politics isn't pleasant to explain. Hilder introduced this bill to set up a committee to investigate waste in space flight. Maybe three-fourths or more of the General Assembly was against such an investigation as an intolerable and useless extension of bureaucracy—which it is. But then how could any legislator be against a mere investigation of waste? It would sound as though he had something to fear or to conceal. It would sound as though he were himself profiting from waste. Hilder is not in the least afraid of making such accusations, and whether true or not, they would be a powerful factor with the voters in the next election. The bill passed.

"And then there came the question of appointing the members of the committee. Those who were against Hilder shied away from membership, which would have meant decisions that would be continually embarrassing. Remaining on the side lines would make that one that much less a target for Hilder. The result is that I am the only member of the committee who is outspokenly anti-Hilder and it may cost me reelection."

Sankov said, "I'd be sorry to hear that, Assemblyman. It looks as though Mars didn't have as many friends as we thought we had. We wouldn't like to lose one. But if Hilder wins out, what's he after, anyway?"

"I should think," said Digby, "that that is obvious. He wants to be the next Global Co-ordinator."

"Think he'll make it?"

"If nothing happens to stop him, he will."

"And then what? Will he drop this Waster campaign then?"

"I can't say. I don't know if he's laid his plans past the Coordinacy. Still, if you want my guess, he couldn't abandon the campaign and maintain his popularity. It's gotten out of hand."

Sankov scratched the side of his neck. "All right. In that case, I'll ask you for some advice. What can we folks on Mars do? You know Earth. You know the situation. We don't. Tell us what to do."

Digby rose and stepped to the window. He looked out upon the low domes of other buildings; red, rocky, completely desolate plain in between; a purple sky and a shrunken sun.

He said, without turning, "Do you people really like it on Mars?"

Sankov smiled. "Most of us don't exactly know any other world, Assemblyman. Seems to me Earth would be something queer and uncomfortable to them."

"But wouldn't Martians get used to it? Earth isn't hard to take after this. Wouldn't your people learn to enjoy the privilege of breathing air under an open sky? You once lived on Earth. You remember what it was like."

"I sort of remember. Still, it doesn't seem to be easy to explain. Earth is just there. It fits people and people fit it. People take Earth the way they find it. Mars is different. It's sort of raw and doesn't fit people. People got to make something out of it. They got to *build* a world, and not take what they find. Mars isn't much yet, but we're building, and when we're finished, we're going to have just what we like. It's sort of a great feeling to know you're building a world. Earth would be kind of unexciting after that."

The Assemblyman said, "Surely the ordinary Martian isn't such a philosopher that he's content to live this terribly hard life for the sake of a future that must be hundreds of generations away."

"No-o, not just like that." Sankov put his right ankle on his left knee and cradled it as he spoke. "Like I said, Martians are a lot like Earthmen, which means they're sort of human beings, and human beings don't go in for philosophy much. Just the same, there's something to living in a growing world, whether you think about it much or not.

"My father used to send me letters when I first came to Mars. He was an accountant and he just sort of stayed an accountant. Earth wasn't much different when he died from what it was when he was born. He didn't see anything happen. Every day was like every other day, and living was just a way of passing time until he died.

"On Mars, it's different. Every day there's something new—the city's bigger, the ventilation system gets another kick, the water lines from the poles get slicked up. Right now, we're planning to set up a news-film association of our own. We're going to call it Mars Press. If you haven't lived when things are growing all about you, you'll never understand how wonderful it feels.

"No, Assemblyman, Mars is hard and tough and Earth is a lot more comfortable, but seems to me if you take our boys to Earth, they'll be unhappy. They probably wouldn't be able to figure out why, most of them, but they'd feel lost; lost and useless. Seems to me lots of them would never make the adjustment."

Digby turned away from the window and the smooth, pink skin of his forehead was creased into a frown. "In that case, Commissioner, I am sorry for you. For all of you."

"Why?"

"Because I don't think there's anything your people on Mars can do. Or the people on the Moon or Venus. It won't happen now; maybe it won't happen for a year or two, or even for five years. But pretty soon you'll all have to come back to Earth, unless—"

Sankov's white eyebrows bent low over his eyes. "Well?"

"Unless you can find another source of water besides the planet Earth."

Sankov shook his head. "Don't seem likely, does it?"

"Not very."

"And except for that, seems to you there's no chance?"

"None at all."

Digby said that and left, and Sankov stared for a long time at nothing before he punched a combination of the local communiline.

After a while, Ted Long looked out at him.

Sankov said, "You were right, son. There's nothing they can do. Even the ones that mean well see no way out. How did you know?"

"Commissioner," said Long, "when you've read all you can about the Time of Troubles, particularly about the twentieth century, nothing political can come as a real surprise."

"Well, maybe. Anyway, son, Assemblyman Digby is sorry for us, quite a piece sorry, you might say, but that's all. He says we'll have to leave Mars—or else get water somewhere else. Only he thinks that we can't get water somewhere else."

"You know we can, don't you, Commissioner?"

"I know we *might*, son. It's a terrible risk."

"If I find enough volunteers, the risk is our business."

"How is it going?"

"Not bad. Some of the boys are on my side right now. I talked Mario Rioz into it, for instance, and you know he's one of the best."

"That's just it—the volunteers will be the best men we have. I hate to allow it."

"If we get back, it will be worth it."

"If! It's a big word, son."

"And a big thing we're trying to do."

"Well, I gave my word that if there was no help on Earth, I'll see that the Phobos water hole lets you have all the water you'll need. Good luck."

6

Half a million miles above Saturn, Mario Rioz was cradled on nothing and sleep was delicious. He came out of it slowly and for a while, alone in his suit, he counted the stars and traced lines from one to another.

At first, as the weeks flew past, it was scavenging all over again, except for the gnawing feeling that every minute meant an additional number of thousands of miles away from all humanity. That made it worse.

They had aimed high to pass out of the ecliptic while moving through the Asteroid Belt. That had used up water and had probably been unnecessary. Although tens of thousands of worldlets look as thick as vermin in two-dimensional projection upon a photographic plate, they are nevertheless scattered so thinly through the quadrillions of cubic miles that make up their conglomerate orbit that only the most ridiculous of coincidences would have brought about a collision.

Still, they passed over the Belt and someone calculated the chances of collision with a fragment of matter large enough to do damage. The value was so low, so impossibly low, that it was perhaps inevitable that the notion of the "space-float" should occur to someone.

The days were long and many, space was empty, only one man was needed at the controls at any one time. The thought was a natural.

First, it was a particularly daring one who ventured out for fifteen minutes or so. Then another who tried half an hour. Eventually, before the asteroids were entirely behind, each ship regularly had its off-watch member suspended in space at the end of a cable.

It was easy enough. The cable, one of those intended for operations at the conclusion of their journey, was magnetically attached at both ends, one to the space suit to start with. Then you clambered out the lock onto the ship's hull and attached the other end there. You paused awhile, clinging to the metal skin by the electromagnets in your boots. Then you neutralized those and made the slightest muscular effort.

Slowly, ever so slowly, you lifted from the ship and even more slowly the ship's larger mass moved an equivalently shorter distance downward. You floated incredibly, weightlessly, in solid, speckled black. When the ship had moved far enough away from you, your gauntleted hand, which kept touch upon the cable, tightened its grip slightly. Too tightly, and you would begin moving back toward the ship and it toward you. Just tightly enough, and friction would halt you. Because your motion was equivalent to that of the ship, it seemed as motionless below you as though it had been painted against an impossible background while the cable between you hung in coils that had no reason to straighten out.

It was a half-ship to your eye. One half was lit by the light of the feeble Sun, which was still too bright to look at directly without the heavy protection of the polarized space-suit visor. The other half was black on black, invisible.

Space closed in and it was like sleep. Your suit was warm, it renewed its air automatically, it had food and drink in special containers from which it could be sucked with a minimal motion of the head, it took care of wastes appropriately. Most of all, more than anything else, there was the delightful euphoria of weightlessness.

You never felt so well in your life. The days stopped being too long, they weren't long enough, and there weren't enough of them.

They had passed Jupiter's orbit at a spot some thirty degrees from its then position. For months, it was the brightest object in the sky, always excepting the glowing white pea that was the Sun. At its brightest, some of the Scavengers insisted they could make out Jupiter as a tiny sphere, one side squashed out of true by the night shadow.

Then over a period of additional months it faded, while another dot of light grew until it was brighter than Jupiter. It was Saturn, first as a dot of brilliance, then as an oval, glowing splotch.

("Why oval?" someone asked, and after a while, someone else said, "The rings, of course," and it was obvious.)

Everyone space-floated at all possible times toward the end, watching Saturn incessantly.

("Hey, you jerk, come on back in, damn it. You're on duty." "Who's on duty? I've got fifteen minutes more by my watch." "You set your watch back. Besides, I gave you twenty minutes yesterday." "You wouldn't give two minutes to your grandmother." "Come on in, damn it, or I'm coming out anyway." "All right, I'm coming. Holy howlers, what a racket over a lousy minute." But no quarrel could possibly be serious, not in space. It felt too good.)

Saturn grew until at last it rivaled and then surpassed the Sun. The rings, set at a broad angle to their trajectory of approach, swept grandly about the planet, only a small portion being eclipsed. Then, as they approached, the span of the rings grew still wider, yet narrower as the angle of approach constantly decreased.

The larger moons showed up in the surrounding sky like serene fireflies.

Mario Rioz was glad he was awake so that he could watch again.

Saturn filled half the sky, streaked with orange, the night shadow cutting it fuzzily nearly one quarter of the way in from the right. Two round little dots in the brightness were shadows of two of the moons. To the left and behind him (he could look over his left shoulder to see, and as he did so, the rest of his body inched slightly to the right to conserve angular momentum) was the white diamond of the Sun.

Most of all he liked to watch the rings. At the left, they emerged from behind Saturn, a tight, bright triple band of orange light. At the right, their beginnings were hidden in the night shadow, but showed up closer and broader. They widened as they came, like the flare of a horn, growing hazier as they approached, until, while the eye followed them, they seemed to fill the sky and lose themselves.

From the position of the Scavenger fleet just inside the outer rim of the outermost ring, the rings broke up and assumed their true identity as a phenomenal cluster of solid fragments rather than the tight, solid band of light they seemed.

Below him, or rather in the direction his feet pointed, some twenty miles away, was one of the ring fragments. It looked like a large, irregular splotch, marring the symmetry of space, three-quarters in brightness and the night shadow cutting it like a knife. Other fragments were farther off, sparkling like star dust, dimmer and thicker, until, as you followed them down, they became rings once more.

The fragments were motionless, but that was only because the ships had taken up an orbit about Saturn equivalent to that of the outer edge of the rings.

The day before, Rioz reflected, he had been on that nearest fragment, working along with more than a score of others to mold it into the desired shape. Tomorrow he would be at it again.

Today—today he was space-floating.

"Mario?" The voice that broke upon his earphones was questioning.

Momentarily Rioz was flooded with annoyance. Damn it, he wasn't in the mood for company.

"Speaking," he said.

"I thought I had your ship spotted. How are you?"

"Fine. That you, Ted?"

"That's right," said Long.

"Anything wrong on the fragment?"

"Nothing. I'm out here floating."

"You?"

"It gets me, too, occasionally. Beautiful, isn't it?"

"Nice," agreed Rioz.

"You know, I've read Earth books—"

"Grounder books, you mean." Rioz yawned and found it difficult under the circumstances to use the expression with the proper amount of resentment.

"—and sometimes I read descriptions of people lying on grass," continued Long. "You know, that green stuff like thin, long pieces of paper they have all over the ground down there, and they look up at the blue sky with clouds in it. Did you ever see any films of that?"

"Sure. It didn't attract me. It looked cold."

"I suppose it isn't, though. After all, Earth is quite close to the Sun, and they say their atmosphere is thick enough to hold the heat. I must admit that personally I would hate to be caught under open sky with nothing on but clothes. Still, I imagine they like it."

"Grounders are nuts!"

"They talk about the trees, big brown stalks, and the winds, air movements, you know."

"You mean drafts. They can keep that, too."

"It doesn't matter. The point is they describe it beautifully, almost passionately. Many times I've wondered, 'What's it really like? Will I ever feel it or is this something only Earthmen can possibly feel?' I've felt so often that I was missing something vital. Now I know what it must be like. It's this. Complete peace in the middle of a beauty-drenched universe."

Rioz said, "They wouldn't like it. The Grounders, I mean. They're so used to their own lousy little world they wouldn't appreciate what it's like to float and look down on Saturn." He flipped his body slightly and began swaying back and forth about his center of mass, slowly, soothingly.

Long said, "Yes, I think so too. They're slaves to their planet. Even if they come to Mars, it will only be their children that are free. There'll be starships someday; great, huge things that can carry thousands of people and maintain their self-contained equilibrium for decades, maybe centuries. Mankind will spread through the whole Galaxy. But people will have to live their lives out on shipboard until new methods of interstellar travel are developed, so it will be Martians, not planetbound Earthmen, who will colonize the Universe. That's inevitable. It's got to be. It's the Martian way."

But Rioz made no answer. He had dropped off to sleep again, rocking and swaying gently, half a million miles above Saturn.

7

The work shift of the ring fragment was the tail of the coin. The weightlessness, peace, and privacy of the space-float gave place to something that had neither peace nor privacy. Even the weightlessness, which continued, became more a purgatory than a paradise under the new conditions.

Try to manipulate an ordinary nonportable heat projector. It could be lifted despite the fact that it was six feet high and wide and almost solid metal, since it weighed only a fraction of an ounce. But its inertia was exactly what it had always been, which meant that if it wasn't moved into position very slowly, it would just keep going, taking you with it. Then you would have to hike the pseudo-grav field of your suit and come down with a jar.

Keralski had hiked the field a little too high and he came down a little too roughly, with the projector coming down with him at a dangerous angle. His crushed ankle had been the first casualty of the expedition.

Rioz was swearing fluently and nearly continuously. He continued to have the impulse to drag the back of his hand across his forehead in order to wipe away the accumulating sweat. The few times that he had succumbed to the impulse, metal had met silicone with a clash that rang loudly inside his suit, but served no useful purpose. The desiccators within the suit were sucking at maximum and, of course, recovering the water and restoring ion-exchanged liquid, containing a careful proportion of salt, into the appropriate receptacle.

Rioz yelled, "Damn it, Dick, wait till I give the word, will you?"

And Swenson's voice rang in his ears, "Well, how long am I supposed to sit here?"

"Till I say," replied Rioz.

He strengthened pseudo-grav and lifted the projector a bit. He released pseudo-grav, insuring that the projector would stay in place for minutes even if he withdrew support altogether. He kicked the cable out of the way (it stretched beyond the close "horizon" to a power source that was out of sight) and touched the release.

The material of which the fragment was composed bubbled and vanished under its touch. A section of the lip of the tremendous cavity he had already carved into its substance melted away and a roughness in its contour had disappeared.

"Try it now," called Rioz.

Swenson was in the ship that was hovering nearly over Rioz's head.

Swenson called, "All clear?"

"I told you to go ahead."

It was a feeble flicker of steam that issued from one of the ship's forward vents. The ship drifted down toward the ring fragment. Another flicker adjusted a tendency to drift sidewise. It came down straight.

A third flicker to the rear slowed it to a feather rate.

Rioz watched tensely. "Keep her coming. You'll make it. You'll make it."

The rear of the ship entered the hole, nearly filling it. The bellying walls came closer and closer to its rim. There was a grinding vibration as the ship's motion halted.

It was Swenson's turn to curse. "It doesn't fit," he said.

Rioz threw the projector groundward in a passion and went flailing up into space. The projector kicked up a white crystalline dust all about it, and when Rioz came down under pseudo-grav, he did the same.

He said, "You went in on the bias, you dumb Grounder."

"I hit it level, you dirt-eating farmer."

Backward-pointing side jets of the ship were blasting more strongly than before, and Rioz hopped to get out of the way.

The ship scraped up from the pit, then shot into space half a mile before forward jets could bring it to a halt.

Swenson said tensely, "We'll spring half a dozen plates if we do this once again. Get it right, will you?"

"I'll get it right. Don't worry about it. Just you come in right."

Rioz jumped upward and allowed himself to climb three hundred yards to get an overall look at the cavity. The gouge marks of the ship were plain enough. They were concentrated at one point halfway down the pit. He would get that.

It began to melt outward under the blaze of the projector.

Half an hour later the ship snuggled neatly into its cavity, and Swenson, wearing his space suit, emerged to join Rioz. Swenson said, "If you want to step in and climb out of the suit, I'll take care of the icing."

"It's all right," said Rioz. "I'd just as soon sit here and watch Saturn."

He sat down at the lip of the pit. There was a six-foot gap between it and the ship. In some places about the circle, it was two feet; in a few places, even merely a matter of inches. You couldn't expect a better fit out of handwork. The final adjustment would be made by steaming ice gently and letting it freeze into the cavity between the lip and the ship.

Saturn moved visibly across the sky, its vast bulk inching below the horizon.

Rioz said, "How many ships are left to put in place?"

Swenson said, "Last I heard, it was eleven. We're in now, so that means only ten. Seven of the ones that are placed are iced in. Two or three are dismantled."

"We're coming along fine."

"There's plenty to do yet. Don't forget the main jets at the other end. And the cables and the power lines. Sometimes I wonder if we'll make it. On the way out, it didn't bother me so much, but just now I was sitting at the controls and I was saying, 'We won't make it. We'll sit out here and starve and die with nothing but Saturn over us.' It makes me feel—"

He didn't explain how it made him feel. He just sat there.

Rioz said, "You think too damn much."

"It's different with you," said Swenson. "I keep thinking of Pete—and Dora."

"What for? She said you could go, didn't she? The Commissioner gave her that talk on patriotism and how you'd be a hero and set for life once you got back, and she said you could go. You didn't sneak out the way Adams did."

"Adams is different. That wife of his should have been shot when she was born. Some women can make hell for a guy, can't they? She didn't want him to go   but she'd probably rather he didn't come back if she can get his settlement pay."

"What's your kick, then? Dora wants you back, doesn't she?"

Swenson sighed. "I never treated her right."

"You turned over your pay, it seems to me. I wouldn't do that for any woman. Money for value received, not a cent more."

"Money isn't it. I get to thinking out here. A woman likes company. A kid needs his father. What am I doing way out here?"

"Getting set to go home."

"Ah-h, you don't understand."

8

Ted Long wandered over the ridged surface of the ring fragment with his spirits as icy as the ground he walked on. It had all seemed perfectly logical back on Mars, but that was Mars. He had worked it out carefully in his mind in perfectly reasonable steps. He could still remember exactly how it went.

It didn't take a ton of water to move a ton of ship. It was not mass equals mass, but mass times velocity equals mass times velocity. It didn't matter, in other words, whether you shot out a ton of water at a mile a second or a hundred pounds of water at twenty miles a second. You got the same final velocity out of the ship.

That meant the jet nozzles had to be made narrower and the steam hotter. But then drawbacks appeared. The narrower the nozzle, the more energy was lost in friction and turbulence. The hotter the steam, the more refractory the nozzle had to be and the shorter its life. The limit in that direction was quickly reached.

Then, since a given weight of water could move considerably more than its own weight under the narrow-nozzle conditions, it paid to be big. The bigger the water-storage space, the larger the size of the actual travel-head, even in proportion. So they started to make liners heavier and bigger. But then the larger the shell, the heavier the bracings, the more difficult the weldings, the more exacting the engineering requirements. At the moment, the limit in that direction had been reached also.

And then he had put his finger on what had seemed to him to be the basic flaw—the original unswervable conception that the fuel had to be placed *inside* the ship; the metal had to be built to encircle a million tons of water.

Why? Water did not have to be water. It could be ice, and ice could be shaped. Holes could be melted into it. Travel-heads and jets could be fitted into it. Cables could hold travel-heads and jets stiffly together under the influence of magnetic field-force grips.

Long felt the trembling of the ground he walked on. He was at the head of the fragment. A dozen ships were blasting in and out of sheaths carved in its substance, and the fragment shuddered under the continuing impact.

The ice didn't have to be quarried. It existed in proper chunks in the rings of Saturn. That's all the rings were—pieces of nearly pure ice, circling Saturn. So spectroscopy stated and so it had turned out to be. He was standing on one such piece now, over two miles long, nearly one mile thick. It was almost half a billion tons of water, all in one piece, and he was standing on it.

But now he was face-to-face with the realities of life. He had never told the men just how quickly he had expected to set up the fragment as a ship, but in his heart, he had imagined it would be two days. It was a week now and he didn't dare to estimate the remaining time. He no longer even had any confidence that the task was a possible one. Would they be able to control jets with enough delicacy through leads slung across two miles of ice to manipulate out of Saturn's dragging gravity?

Drinking water was low, though they could always distill more out of the ice. Still, the food stores were not in a good way either.

He paused, looked up into the sky, eyes straining. *Was* the object growing larger? He ought to measure its distance. Actually, he lacked the spirit to add that trouble to the others. His mind slid back to greater immediacies.

Morale, at least, was high. The men seemed to enjoy being out Saturn-way. They were the first humans to penetrate this far, the first to pass the asteroids, the first to see Jupiter like a glowing pebble to the naked eye, the first to see Saturn—like that.

He didn't think fifty practical, case-hardened, shell-snatching Scavengers would take time to feel that sort of emotion. But they did. And they were proud.

Two men and a half-buried ship slid up the moving horizon as he walked.

He called crisply, "Hello, there!"

Rioz answered, "That you, Ted?"

"You bet. Is that Dick with you?"

"Sure. Come on, sit down. We were just getting ready to ice in and we were looking for an excuse to delay."

"I'm not," said Swenson promptly. "When will we be leaving, Ted?"

"As soon as we get through. That's no answer, is it?"

Swenson said dispiritedly, "I suppose there isn't any other answer."

Long looked up, staring at the irregular bright splotch in the sky.

Rioz followed his glance. "What's the matter?"

For a moment, Long did not reply. The sky was black otherwise and the ring fragments were an orange dust against it. Saturn was more than three-fourths below the horizon and the rings were going with it. Half a mile away a ship bounded past the icy rim of the planetoid into the sky, was orange-lit by Saturn-light, and sank down again.

The ground trembled gently.

Rioz said, "Something bothering you about the Shadow?"

They called it that. It was the nearest fragment of the rings, quite close considering that they were at the outer rim of the rings, where the pieces spread themselves relatively thin. It was perhaps twenty miles off, a jagged mountain, its shape clearly visible.

"How does it look to you?" asked Long.

Rioz shrugged. "Okay, I guess. I don't see anything wrong."

"Doesn't it seem to be getting larger?"

"Why should it?"

"Well, doesn't it?" Long insisted.

Rioz and Swenson stared at it thoughtfully.

"It does look bigger," said Swenson.

"You're just putting the notion into our minds," Rioz argued. "If it were getting bigger, it would be coming closer."

"What's impossible about that?"

"These things are stable orbits."

"They were when we came here," said Long. "There, did you feel that?"

The ground had trembled again.

Long said, "We've been blasting this thing for a week now. First, twenty-five ships landed on it, which changed its momentum right there. Not much, of course. Then we've been melting parts of it away and our ships have been blasting in and out of it—all at one end, too. In a week, we may have changed its orbit just a bit. The two fragments, this one and the Shadow, might be converging."

"It's got plenty of room to miss us in." Rioz watched it thoughtfully. "Besides, if we can't even tell for sure that it's getting bigger, how quickly can it be moving? Relative to us, I mean."

"It doesn't have to be moving quickly. Its momentum is as large as ours, so that, however gently it hits, we'll be nudged completely out of our orbit, maybe in toward Saturn, where we don't want to go. As a matter of fact, ice has a very low tensile strength, so that both planetoids might break up into gravel."

Swenson rose to his feet. "Damn it, if I can tell you a shell is moving a thousand miles away, I can tell what a mountain is doing twenty miles away." He turned toward the ship.

Long didn't stop him.

Rioz said, "There's a nervous guy."

The neighboring planetoid rose to zenith, passed overhead, began sinking. Twenty minutes later, the horizon opposite that portion behind which Saturn had disappeared burst into orange flame as its bulk began lifting again.

Rioz called into his radio, "Hey, Dick, are you dead in there?"

"I'm checking," came the muffled response.

"Is it moving?" asked Long.

"Yes."

"Toward us?"

There was a pause. Swenson's voice was a sick one. "On the nose, Ted. Intersection of orbits will take place in three days."

"You're crazy!" yelled Rioz.

"I checked four times," said Swenson.

Long thought blankly, "What do we do now?"

9

Some of the men were having trouble with the cables. They had to be laid precisely; their geometry had to be very nearly perfect for the magnetic field to attain maximum strength. In space, or even in air, it wouldn't have mattered. The cables would have lined up automatically once the juice went on.

Here it was different. A gouge had to be plowed along the planetoid's surface and into it the cable had to be laid. If it were not lined up within a few minutes of arc of the calculated direction, a torque would be applied to the entire planetoid, with consequent loss of energy, none of which could be spared. The gouges then had to be redriven, the cables shifted and iced into the new positions.

The men plodded wearily through the routine.

And then the word reached them: "All hands to the jets!"

Scavengers could not be said to be the type that took kindly to discipline. It was a grumbling, growling, muttering group that set about disassembling the jets of the ships that yet remained intact, carrying them to the tail end of the planetoid, grubbing them into position, and stringing the leads along the surface.

It was almost twenty-four hours before one of them looked into the sky and said, "Holy jeepers!" followed by something less printable.

His neighbor looked and said, "I'll be damned!"

Once they noticed, all did. It became the most astonishing fact in the Universe. "Look at the Shadow!"

It was spreading across the sky like an infected wound. Men looked at it, found it had doubled its size, wondered why they hadn't noticed that sooner.

Work came to a virtual halt. They besieged Ted Long.

He said, "We can't leave. We don't have the fuel to see us back to Mars and we don't have the equipment to capture another planetoid. So we've got to stay. Now the Shadow is creeping in on us because our blasting has thrown us out of orbit. We've got to change that by continuing the blasting. Since we can't blast the front end any more without endangering the ship we're building, let's try another way."

They went back to work on the jets with a furious energy that received impetus every half hour when the Shadow rose again over the horizon, bigger and more menacing than before.

Long had no assurance that it would work. Even if the jets would respond to the distant controls, even if the supply of water, which depended upon a storage chamber opening directly into the icy body of the planetoid, with built-in heat projectors steaming the propulsive fluid directly into the driving cells, were adequate, there was still no certainty that the body of the planetoid without a magnetic cable sheathing would hold together under the enormously disruptive stresses.

"Ready!" came the signal in Long's receiver.

Long called, "Ready!" and depressed the contact.

The vibration grew about him. The star field in the visiplate trembled.

In the rearview, there was a distant gleaming spume of swiftly moving ice crystals.

"It's blowing!" was the cry.

It kept on blowing. Long dared not stop. For six hours, it blew, hissing, bubbling, steaming into space; the body of the planetoid converted to vapor and hurled away.

The Shadow came closer until men did nothing but stare at the mountain in the sky, surpassing Saturn itself in spectacularity. Its every groove and valley was a plain scar upon its face. But when it passed through the planetoid's orbit, it crossed more than half a mile behind its then position.

The steam jet ceased.

Long bent in his seat and covered his eyes. He hadn't eaten in two days. He could eat now, though. Not another planetoid was close enough to interrupt them, even if it began an approach that very moment.

Back on the planetoid's surface, Swenson said, "All the time I watched that damned rock coming down, I kept saying to myself, 'This can't happen. We can't let it happen.'"

"Hell," said Rioz, "we were all nervous. Did you see Jim Davis? He was green. I was a little jumpy myself."

"That's not it. It wasn't just—dying, you know. I was thinking—I know it's funny, but I can't help it—I was thinking that Dora warned me I'd get myself killed, she'll never let me hear the last of it. Isn't that a crummy sort of attitude at a time like that?"

"Listen," said Rioz, "you wanted to get married, so you got married. Why come to me with your troubles?"

10

The flotilla, welded into a single unit, was returning over its mighty course from Saturn to Mars. Each day it flashed over a length of space it had taken nine days outward.

Ted Long had put the entire crew on emergency. With twenty-five ships embedded in the planetoid taken out of Saturn's rings and unable to move or maneuver independently, the coordination of their power sources into unified blasts was a ticklish problem. The jarring that took place on the first day of travel nearly shook them out from under their hair.

That, at least, smoothed itself out as the velocity raced upward under the steady thrust from behind. They passed the one-hundred-thousand-mile-an-hour mark late on the second day, and climbed steadily toward the million-mile mark and beyond.

Long's ship, which formed the needle point of the frozen fleet, was the only one which possessed a five-way view of space. It was an uncomfortable position under the circumstances. Long found himself watching tensely, imagining somehow that the stars would slowly begin to slip backward, to whizz past them, under the influence of the multi-ship's tremendous rate of travel.

They didn't, of course. They remained nailed to the black backdrop, their distance scorning with patient immobility any speed mere man could achieve.

The men complained bitterly after the first few days. It was not only that they were deprived of the space-float. They were burdened by much more than the ordinary pseudo-gravity field of the ships, by the effects of the fierce acceleration under which they were living. Long himself was weary to death of the relentless pressure against hydraulic cushions.

They took to shutting off the jet thrusts one hour out of every four and Long fretted.

It had been just over a year that he had last seen Mars shrinking in an observation window from this ship, which had then been an independent entity. What had happened since then? Was the colony still there?

In something like a growing panic, Long sent out radio pulses toward Mars daily, with the combined power of twenty-five ships behind it. There was no answer. He expected none. Mars and Saturn were on opposite sides of the Sun now, and until he mounted high enough above the ecliptic to get the Sun well beyond the line connecting himself and Mars, solar interference would prevent any signal from getting through.

High above the outer rim of the Asteroid Belt, they reached maximum velocity. With short spurts of power from first one side jet, then another, the huge vessel reversed itself. The composite jet in the rear began its mighty roaring once again, but now the result was deceleration.

They passed a hundred million miles over the Sun, curving down to intersect the orbit of Mars.

A week out of Mars, answering signals were heard for the first time, fragmentary, ether-torn, and incomprehensible, but they were coming from Mars. Earth and Venus were at angles sufficiently different to leave no doubt of that.

Long relaxed. There were still humans on Mars, at any rate.

Two days out of Mars, the signal was strong and clear and Sankov was at the other end.

Sankov said, "Hello, son. It's three in the morning here. Seems like people have no consideration for an old man. Dragged me right out of bed."

"I'm sorry, sir."

"Don't be. They were following orders. I'm afraid to ask, son. Anyone hurt? Maybe dead?"

"No deaths, sir. Not one."

"And—and the water? Any left?"

Long said with an effort at nonchalance, "Enough."

"In that case, get home as fast as you can. Don't take any chances, of course."

"There's trouble, then."

"Fair to middling. When will you come down?"

"Two days. Can you hold out that long?"

"I'll hold out."

Forty hours later Mars had grown to a ruddy-orange ball that filled the ports and they were in the final planet-landing spiral.

"Slowly," Long said to himself, "slowly." Under these conditions, even the thin atmosphere of Mars could do dreadful damage if they moved through it too quickly.

Since they came in from well above the ecliptic, their spiral passed from north to south. A polar cap shot whitely below them, then the much smaller one of the summer hemisphere, the large one again, the small one, at longer and longer intervals. The planet approached closer, the landscape began to show features.

"Prepare for landing!" called Long.

11

Sankov did his best to look placid, which was difficult considering how closely the boys had shaved their return. But it had worked out well enough.

Until a few days before, he had no sure knowledge that they had survived. It seemed more likely—inevitable, almost—that they were nothing but frozen corpses somewhere in the trackless stretches from Mars to Saturn, new planetoids that had once been alive.

The Committee had been dickering with him for weeks before the news had come. They had insisted on his signature to the paper for the sake of appearances. It would look like an agreement, voluntarily and mutually arrived at. But Sankov knew well that, given complete obstinacy on his part, they would act unilaterally and be damned with appearances. It seemed fairly certain that Hilder's election was secure now and they would take the chance of arousing a reaction of sympathy for Mars.

So he dragged out the negotiations, dangling before them always the possibility of surrender.

And then he heard from Long and concluded the deal quickly.

The papers had lain before him and he had made a last statement for the benefit of the reporters who were present.

He said, "Total imports of water from Earth are twenty million tons a year. This is declining as we develop our own piping system. If I sign this paper agreeing to an embargo, our industry will be paralyzed, any possibilities of expansion will halt. It looks to me as if that can't be what's in Earth's mind, can it?"

Their eyes met his and held only a hard glitter. Assembly-man Digby had already been replaced and they were unanimous against him.

The Committee Chairman impatiently pointed out, "You have said all this before."

"I know, but right now I'm kind of getting ready to sign and I want it clear in my head. Is Earth set and determined to bring us to an end here?"

"Of course not. Earth is interested in conserving its irreplaceable water supply, nothing else."

"You have one and a half quintillion tons of water on Earth."

The Committee Chairman said, "We cannot spare water."

And Sankov had signed.

That had been the final note he wanted. Earth had one and a half quintillion tons of water and could spare none of it.

Now, a day and a half later, the Committee and the reporters waited in the spaceport dome. Through thick, curving windows, they could see the bare and empty grounds of Mars Spaceport.

The Committee Chairman asked with annoyance, "How much longer do we have to wait? And, if you don't mind, what are we waiting for?"

Sankov said, "Some of our boys have been out in space, out past the asteroids."

The Committee Chairman removed a pair of spectacles and cleaned them with a snowy-white handkerchief. "And they're returning?"

"They are."

The Chairman shrugged, lifted his eyebrows in the direction of the reporters.

In the smaller room adjoining, a knot of women and children clustered about another window. Sankov stepped back a bit to cast a glance toward them. He would much rather have been with them, been part of their excitement and tension. He, like them, had waited over a year now. He, like them, had thought, over and over again, that the men must be dead.

"You see that?" said Sankov, pointing.

"Hey!" cried a reporter. "It's a ship!"

A confused shouting came from the adjoining room.

It wasn't a ship so much as a bright dot obscured by a drifting white cloud. The cloud grew larger and began to have form. It was a double streak against the sky, the lower ends billowing out and upward again. As it dropped still closer, the bright dot at the upper end took on a crudely cylindrical form.

It was rough and craggy, but where the sunlight hit, brilliant highlights bounced back.

The cylinder dropped toward the ground with the ponderous slowness characteristic of space vessels. It hung suspended on those blasting jets and settled down upon the recoil of tons of matter hurling downward like a tired man dropping into his easy chair.

And as it did so, a silence fell upon all within the dome. The women and children in one room, the politicians and reporters in the other remained frozen, heads craned incredulously upward.

The cylinder's landing flanges, extending far below the two rear jets, touched ground and sank into the pebbly morass. And then the ship was motionless and the jet action ceased.

But the silence continued in the dome. It continued for a long time.

Men came clambering down the sides of the immense vessel, inching down, down the two-mile trek to the ground, with spikes on their shoes and ice axes in their hands. They were gnats against the blinding surface.

One of the reporters croaked, "What is it?"

"That," said Sankov calmly, "happens to be a chunk of matter that spent its time scooting around Saturn as part of its rings. Our boys fitted it out with travel-head and jets and ferried it home. It just turns out the fragments in Saturn's rings are made up out of ice."

He spoke into a continuing deathlike silence. "That thing that looks like a spaceship is just a mountain of hard water. If it were standing like that on Earth, it would be melting into a puddle and maybe it would break under its own weight. Mars is colder and has less gravity, so there's no such danger.

"Of course, once we get this thing really organized, we can have water stations on the moons of Saturn and Jupiter and on the asteroids. We can scale in chunks of Saturn's rings and pick them up and send them on at the various stations. Our Scavengers are good at that sort of thing.

"We'll have all the water we need. That one chunk you see is just under a cubic mile—or about what Earth would send us in two hundred years. The boys used quite a bit of it coming back from Saturn. They made it in five weeks, they tell me, and used up about a hundred million tons. But, Lord, that didn't make any dent at all in that mountain. Are you getting all this, boys?"

He turned to the reporters. There was no doubt they were getting it.

He said, "Then get this, too. Earth is worried about its water supply. It only has one and a half quintillion tons. It can't spare us a single ton out of it. Write down that we folks on Mars are worried about Earth and don't want anything to happen to Earth people. Write down that we'll sell water to Earth. Write down that we'll let them have million-ton lots for a reasonable fee. Write down that in ten years, we figure we can sell it in cubic-mile lots. Write down that Earth can quit worrying because Mars can sell it all the water it needs and wants."

The Committee Chairman was past hearing. He was feeling the future rushing in. Dimly he could see the reporters grinning as they wrote furiously.

Grinning.

He could hear the grin become laughter on Earth as Mars turned the tables so neatly on the anti-Wasters. He could hear the laughter thunder from every continent when word of the fiasco spread. And he could see the abyss, deep and black as space, into which would drop forever the political hopes of John Hilder and of every opponent of space flight left on Earth—his own included, of course.

In the adjoining room, Dora Swenson screamed with joy, and Peter, grown two inches, jumped up and down, calling, "Daddy! Daddy!"

Richard Swenson had just stepped off the extremity of the flange and, face showing clearly through the clear silicone of the headpiece, marched toward the dome.

"Did you ever see a guy look so happy?" asked Ted Long. "Maybe there's something in this marriage business."

"Ah, you've just been out in space too long," Rioz said.

Franchise

Linda, age ten, was the only one of the family who seemed to enjoy being awake.

Norman Muller could hear her now through his own drugged, unhealthy coma. (He had finally managed to fall asleep an hour earlier but even then it was more like exhaustion than sleep.)

She was at his bedside now, shaking him. "Daddy, Daddy, wake up. Wake up!"

He suppressed a groan. "All right, Linda."

"But, Daddy, there's more policemen around than any time! Police cars and everything!"

Norman Muller gave up and rose blearily to his elbows. The day was beginning. It was faintly stirring toward dawn outside, the germ of a miserable gray that looked about as miserably gray as he felt. He could hear Sarah, his wife, shuffling about breakfast duties in the kitchen. His father-in-law, Matthew, was hawking strenuously in the bathroom. No doubt Agent Handley was ready and waiting for him.

This was *the* day.

Election Day!

To begin with, it had been like every other year. Maybe a little worse, because it was a presidential year, but no worse than other presidential years if it came to that.

The politicians spoke about the guh-reat electorate and the vast electuh-ronic intelligence that was its servant. The press analyzed the situation with industrial computers (the New York *Times* and the St. Louis *Post-Dispatch* had their own computers) and were full of little hints as to what would be forthcoming. Commentators and columnists pinpointed the crucial state and county in happy contradiction to one another.

The first hint that it would *not* be like every other year was when Sarah Muller said to her husband on the evening of October 4 (with Election Day exactly a month off), "Cantwell Johnson says that Indiana will be the state this year. He's the fourth one. Just think, *our* state this time."

Matthew Hortenweiler took his fleshy face from behind the paper, stared dourly at his daughter and growled, "Those fellows are paid to tell lies. Don't listen to them."

"Four of them, Father," said Sarah mildly. "They all say Indiana."

"Indiana *is* a key state, Matthew," said Norman, just as mildly, "on account of the Hawkins-Smith Act and this mess in Indianapolis. It—"

Matthew twisted his old face alarmingly and rasped out, "No one says Bloomington or Monroe County, do they?"

"Well—" said Norman.

Linda, whose little pointed-chinned face had been shifting from one speaker to the next, said pipingly, "You going to be voting this year, Daddy?"

Norman smiled gently and said, "I don't think so, dear."

But this was in the gradually growing excitement of an October in a presidential election year and Sarah had led a quiet life with dreams for her companions. She said longingly, "Wouldn't *that* be wonderful, though?"

"If I voted?" Norman Muller had a small blond mustache that had given him a debonair quality in the young Sarah's eyes, but which, with gradual graying, had declined merely to lack of distinction. His forehead bore deepening lines born of uncertainty and, in general, he had never seduced his clerkly soul with the thought that he was either born great or would under any circumstances achieve greatness. He had a wife, a job and a little girl, and except under extraordinary conditions of elation or depression was inclined to consider that to be an adequate bargain struck with life.

So he was a little embarrassed and more than a little uneasy at the direction his wife's thoughts were taking. "Actually, my dear," he said, "there are two hundred million people in the country, and, with odds like that, I don't think we ought to waste our time wondering about it."

His wife said, "Why, Norman, it's no such thing like two hundred million and you know it. In the first place, only people between twenty and sixty are eligible and it's always men, so that puts it down to maybe fifty million to one. Then, if it's really Indiana—"

"Then it's about one and a quarter million to one. You wouldn't want me to bet in a horse race against those odds, now, would you? Let's have supper."

Matthew muttered from behind his newspaper, "Damned foolishness."

Linda asked again, "You going to be voting this year, Daddy?"

Norman shook his head and they all adjourned to the dining room.

* * *

By October 20, Sarah's excitement was rising rapidly. Over the coffee, she announced that Mrs. Schultz, having a cousin who was the secretary of an Assemblyman, said that all the "smart money" was on Indiana.

"She says President Villers is even going to make a speech at Indianapolis."

Norman Muller, who had had a hard day at the store, nudged the statement with a raising of eyebrows and let it go at that.

Matthew Hortenweiler, who was chronically dissatisfied with Washington, said, "If Villers makes a speech in Indiana, that means he thinks Multivac will pick Arizona. He wouldn't have the guts to go closer, the mushhead."

Sarah, who ignored her father whenever she could decently do so, said, "I don't know why they don't announce the state as soon as they can, and then the county and so on. Then the people who were eliminated could relax."

"If they did anything like that," pointed out Norman, "the politicians would follow the announcements like vultures. By the time it was narrowed down to a township, you'd have a Congressman or two at every street corner."

Matthew narrowed his eyes and brushed angrily at his sparse, gray hair. "They're vultures anyhow. Listen—"

Sarah murmured, "Now, Father—"

Matthew's voice rumbled over her protest without as much as a stumble or hitch. "Listen, I was around when they set up Multivac. It would end partisan politics, they said. No more voters' money wasted on campaigns. No more grinning nobodies high-pressured and advertising-campaigned into Congress or the White House. So what happens. More campaigning than ever, only now they do it blind. They'll send guys to Indiana on account of the Hawkins-Smith Act and other guys to California in case it's the Joe Hammer situation that turns out crucial. I say, wipe out all that nonsense. Back to the good old—"

Linda asked suddenly, "Don't you want Daddy to vote this year, Grandpa?"

Matthew glared at the young girl. "Never you mind, now." He turned back to Norman and Sarah. "There was a time I voted. Marched right up to the polling booth, stuck my fist on the levers and voted. There was nothing to it. I just said: This fellow's my man and I'm voting for him. *That's* the way it should be."

Linda said excitedly, "You voted, Grandpa? You really did?"

Sarah leaned forward quickly to quiet what might easily become an incongruous story drifting about the neighborhood, "It's nothing, Linda. Grandpa doesn't really mean voted. Everyone did that kind of voting, your Grandpa, too, but it wasn't *really* voting."

Matthew roared, "It wasn't when I was a little boy. I was twenty-two and I voted for Langley and it was real voting. My vote didn't count for much, maybe, but it was as good as anyone else's. *Anyone* else's. And no Multivac to—"

Norman interposed, "All right, Linda, time for bed. And stop asking questions about voting. When you grow up, you'll understand all about it."

He kissed her with antiseptic gentleness and she moved reluctantly out of range under maternal prodding and a promise that she might watch the bedside video till 9:15, *if* she was prompt about the bathing ritual.

Linda said, "Grandpa," and stood with her chin down and her hands behind her back until his newspaper lowered itself to the point where shaggy eyebrows and eyes, nested in fine wrinkles, showed themselves. It was Friday, October 31.

He said, "Yes?"

Linda came closer and put both her forearms on one of the old man's knees so that he had to discard his newspaper altogether.

She said, "Grandpa, did you really once vote?"

He said, "You heard me say I did, didn't you? Do you think I tell fibs?"

"N—no, but Mamma says everybody voted then."

"So they did."

"But how could they? How could *everybody* vote?"

Matthew stared at her solemnly, then lifted her and put her on his knee.

He even moderated the tonal qualities of his voice. He said, "You see, Linda, till about 40 years ago, everybody always voted. Say we wanted to decide who was to be the new President of the United States. The Democrats and Republicans would both nominate someone, and everybody would say who they wanted. When Election Day was over, they would count how many people wanted the Democrat and how many wanted the Republican. Whoever had more votes was elected. You see?"

Linda nodded and said, "How did all the people know who to vote for? Did Multivac tell them?"

Matthew's eyebrows hunched down and he looked severe. "They just used their own judgment, girl."

She edged away from him, and he lowered his voice again, "I'm not angry at you, Linda. But, you see, sometimes it took all night to count what everyone said and people were impatient. So they invented special machines which could look at the first few votes and compare them with the votes from the same places in previous years. That way the machine could compute how the total vote would be and who would be elected. You see?"

She nodded. "Like Multivac."

"The first computers were much smaller than Multivac. But the machines grew bigger and they could tell how the election would go from fewer and fewer votes. Then, at last, they built Multivac and it can tell from just one voter."

Linda smiled at having reached a familiar part of the story and said, "That's nice."

Matthew frowned and said, "No, it's not nice. I don't want a machine telling me how I would have voted just because some joker in Milwaukee says he's against higher tariffs. Maybe I want to vote cockeyed just for the pleasure of it. Maybe I don't want to vote. Maybe—"

But Linda had wriggled from his knee and was beating a retreat.

She met her mother at the door. Her mother, who was still wearing her coat and had not even had time to remove her hat, said breathlessly, "Run along, Linda. Don't get in Mother's way."

Then she said to Matthew, as she lifted her hat from her head and patted her hair back into place, "I've been at Agatha's."

Matthew stared at her censoriously and did not even dignify that piece of information with a grunt as he groped for his newspaper.

Sarah said, as she unbuttoned her coat, "Guess what she said?"

Matthew flattened out his newspaper for reading purposes with a sharp crackle and said, "Don't much care."

Sarah said, "Now, Father—" But she had no time for anger. The news had to be told and Matthew was the only recipient handy, so she went on, "Agatha's Joe is a policeman, you know, and he says a whole truckload of secret service men came into Bloomington last night."

"They're not after me."

"Don't you see, Father? Secret Service agents, and it's almost election time. In *Bloomington*."

"Maybe they're after a bank robber."

"There hasn't been a bank robbery in town in ages. Father, you're hopeless." She stalked away.

N or did Norman Muller receive the news with noticeably greater excitement. "Now, Sarah, how did Agatha's Joe know they were secret service agents?" he asked calmly. "They wouldn't go around with identification cards pasted on their foreheads."

But by next evening, with November a day old, she could say triumphantly, "It's just everyone in Bloomington that's waiting for someone local to be the voter. The Bloomington *News* as much as said so on video."

Norman stirred uneasily. He couldn't deny it, and his heart was sinking. If Bloomington was really to be hit by Multivac's lightning, it would mean newspapermen, video shows, tourists, all sorts of—strange upsets. Norman liked the quiet routine of his life, and the distant stir of politics was getting uncomfortably close.

He said, "It's all rumor. Nothing more."

"You wait and see, then. You just wait and see."

As things turned out, there was very little time to wait, for the doorbell rang insistently, and when Norman Muller opened it and said, "Yes?" a tall, grave-faced man said, "Are you Norman Muller?"

Norman said, "Yes" again, but in a strange dying voice. It was not difficult to see from the stranger's bearing that he was one carrying authority, and the nature of his errand suddenly became as inevitably obvious as it had, until the moment before, been unthinkably impossible.

The man presented credentials, stepped into the house, closed the door behind him and said ritualistically, "Mr. Norman Muller, it is necessary for me to inform you on behalf of the President of the United States that you have been chosen to represent the American electorate on Tuesday, November 4, 2008."

Norman Muller managed, with difficulty, to walk unaided to his chair. He sat there, white-faced and almost insensible, while Sarah brought water, slapped his hands in panic and moaned to her husband between clenched teeth. "Don't be sick, Norman. *Don't* be sick. They'll pick someone else."

When Norman could manage to talk, he whispered, "I'm sorry, sir."

The secret service agent had removed his coat, unbuttoned his jacket and was sitting at ease on the couch.

"It's all right," he said, and the mark of officialdom seemed to have vanished with the formal announcement and leave him simply a large and rather friendly man. "This is the sixth time I've made the announcement and I've seen all kinds of reactions. Not one of them was the kind you see on the video. You know what I mean? A holy, dedicated look, and a character who says, 'It will be a great privilege to serve my country.' That sort of stuff." The agent laughed comfortingly.

Sarah's accompanying laugh held a trace of shrill hysteria.

The agent said, "Now you're going to have me with you for a while. My name is Phil Handley. I'd appreciate it if you call me Phil. Mr. Muller can't leave the house any more till Election Day. You'll have to inform the department store that he's sick, Mrs. Muller. You can go about your business for a while, but you'll have to agree not to say a word about this. Right, Mrs. Muller?"

Sarah nodded vigorously. "No, sir. Not a word."

"All right. But, Mrs. Muller," Handley looked grave, "We're not kidding now. Go out only if you must and you'll be followed when you do. I'm sorry but that's the way we must operate."

"Followed?"

"It won't be obvious. Don't worry. And it's only for two days till the formal announcement to the nation is made. Your daughter—"

"She's in bed," said Sarah hastily.

"Good. She'll have to be told I'm a relative or friend staying with the family. If she does find out the truth, she'll have to be kept in the house. Your father had better stay in the house in any case."

"He won't like that," said Sarah.

"Can't be helped. Now, since you have no others living with you—"

"You know all about us apparently," whispered Norman.

"Quite a bit," agreed Handley. "In any case, those are all my instructions to you for the moment. I'll try to cooperate as much as I can and be as little of a nuisance as possible. The government will pay for my maintenance so I won't be an expense to you. I'll be relieved each night by someone who will sit up in this room, so there will be no problem about sleeping accommodations. Now, Mr. Muller—"

"Sir?"

"You can call me Phil," said the agent again. "The purpose of the two-day preliminary before formal announcement is to get you used to your position. We prefer to have you face Multivac in as normal a state of mind as possible. Just relax and try to feel this is all in a day's work. Okay?"

"Okay," said Norman, and then shook his head violently. "But I don't want the responsibility. Why me?"

"All right," said Handley, "let's get that straight to begin with. Multivac weighs all sorts of known factors, billions of them. One factor isn't known, though, and won't be known for a long time. That's the reaction pattern of the human mind. All Americans are subjected to the molding pressure of what other Americans do and say, to the things that are done to him and the things he does to others. Any American can be brought to Multivac to have the bent of his mind surveyed. From that the bent of all other minds in the country can be estimated. Some Americans are better for the purpose than others at some given time, depending upon the happenings of that year. Multivac picked you as most representative this year. Not the smartest, or the strongest, or the luckiest, but just the most representative. Now we don't question Multivac, do we?"

"Couldn't it make a mistake?" asked Norman.

Sarah, who listened impatiently, interrupted to say, "Don't listen to him, sir. He's just nervous, you know. Actually, he's very well read and he always follows politics very closely."

Handley said, "Multivac makes the decisions, Mrs. Muller. It picked your husband."

"But does it know everything?" insisted Norman wildly. "Couldn't it have made a mistake?"

"Yes, it can. There's no point in not being frank. In 1992, a selected Voter died of a stroke two hours before it was time for him to be notified. Multivac didn't predict that; it couldn't. A Voter might be mentally unstable, morally unsuitable, or, for that matter, disloyal. Multivac can't know everything about everybody until he's fed all the data there is. That's why alternate selections are always held in readiness. I don't think we'll be using one this time. You're in good health, Mr. Muller, and you've been carefully investigated. You qualify."

Norman buried his face in his hands and sat motionless.

"By tomorrow morning, sir," said Sarah, "he'll be perfectly all right. He just has to get used to it, that's all."

"Of course," said Handley.

In the privacy of their bedchamber, Sarah Muller expressed herself in other and stronger fashion. The burden of her lecture was "So get hold of yourself, Norman. You're trying to throw away the chance of a lifetime."

Norman whispered desperately, "It frightens me, Sarah. The whole thing."

"For goodness' sake, why? What's there to it but answering a question or two?"

"The responsibility is too great. I couldn't face it."

"What responsibility? There isn't any. Multivac picked you. It's Multivac's responsibility. Everyone knows that."

Norman sat up in bed in a sudden excess of rebellion and anguish. "Everyone is *supposed* to know that. But they don't. They—"

"Lower your voice," hissed Sarah icily. "They'll hear you downtown."

"They don't," said Norman, declining quickly to a whisper. "When they talk about the Ridgely administration of nineteen eighty-eight, do they say he won them over with pie-in-the-sky promises and racist baloney? No! They talk about the 'goddam MacComber vote,' as though Humphrey MacComber was the only man who had anything to do with it because he faced Multivac. I've said it myself—only now I think the poor guy was just a truck farmer who didn't ask to be picked. Why was it his fault more than anyone else? Now his name is a curse."

"You're just being childish," said Sarah.

"I'm being sensible. I tell you, Sarah, I won't accept. They can't make me vote if I don't want to. I'll say I'm sick. I'll say—"

But Sarah had had enough. "Now you listen to me," she whispered in a cold fury. "You don't have only yourself to think about. You know what it means to be Voter of the Year. A presidential year at that. It means publicity and fame and, maybe, buckets of money—"

"And then I go back to being a clerk."

"You will *not*. You'll have a branch managership at the least if you have any brains at all, and you *will* have, because I'll tell you what to do. You control the kind of publicity if you play your cards right, and you can force Kennell Stores, Inc., into a tight contract *and* an escalator clause in connection with your salary *and* a decent pension plan."

"That's not the point in being Voter, Sarah."

"That will be your point. If you don't owe anything to yourself or to me— I'm not asking for myself—you owe something to Linda."

Norman groaned.

"Well, don't you?" snapped Sarah.

"Yes, dear," murmured Norman.

O n November 3, the official announcement was made and it was too late for Norman to back out even if he had been able to find the courage to make the attempt.

Their house was sealed off. Secret Service agents made their appearance in the open, blocking off all approach.

At first the telephone rang incessantly, but Philip Handley with an engagingly apologetic smile took all calls. Eventually, the exchange shunted all calls directly to the police station.

Norman imagined that, in that way, he was spared not only the bubbling (and envious?) congratulations of friends, but also the egregious pressure of salesmen scenting a prospect and the designing smoothness of politicians from all over the nation . . . perhaps even death threats from the inevitable cranks.

Newspapers were forbidden to enter the house now in order to keep out weighted pressures, and television was gently but firmly disconnected, over Linda's loud protests.

Matthew growled and stayed in his room; Linda, after the first flurry of excitement, sulked and whined because she could not leave the house; Sarah divided her time between preparation of meals for the present and plans for the future; and Norman's depression lived and fed upon itself.

And the morning of Tuesday, November 4, two thousand and eight, came at last, and it was Election Day.

I t was early breakfast, but only Norman Muller ate, and that mechanically. Even a shower and shave had not succeeded in either restoring him to reality or removing his own conviction that he was as grimy without as he felt grimy within.

Handley's friendly voice did its best to shed some normality over the gray and unfriendly dawn. (The weather prediction had been for a cloudy day with prospects of rain before noon.)

Handley said, "We'll keep this house insulated till Mr. Muller is back, but after that we'll be off your necks." The secret service agent was in full uniform now, including sidearms in heavily brassed holsters.

"You've been no trouble at all, Mr. Handley," simpered Sarah.

Norman drank through two cups of black coffee, wiped his lips with a napkin, stood up and said haggardly, "I'm ready."

Handley stood up, too. "Very well, sir. And thank you, Mrs. Muller, for your very kind hospitality."

The armored car purred down empty streets. They were empty even for that hour of the morning.

Handley indicated that and said, "They always shift traffic away from the line of drive ever since the attempted bombing that nearly ruined the Leverett Election of 'ninety-two."

When the car stopped, Norman was helped out by the always polite Handley into an underground drive whose walls were lined with soldiers at attention.

He was led into a brightly lit room, in which three white-uniformed men greeted him smilingly.

Norman said sharply, "But this is the hospital."

"There's no significance to that," said Handley at once. "It's just that the hospital has the necessary facilities."

"Well, what do I do?"

Handley nodded. One of the three men in white advanced and said, "I'll take over now, agent."

Handley saluted in an offhand manner and left the room.

The man in white said, "Won't you sit down, Mr. Muller? I'm John Paulson, Senior Computer. These are Samson Levine and Peter Dorogobuzh, my assistants."

Norman shook hands numbly all about. Paulson was a man of middle height with a soft face that seemed used to smiling and a very obvious toupee. He wore plastic-rimmed glasses of an old-fashioned cut, and he lit a cigarette as he talked. (Norman refused his offer of one.)

Paulson said, "In the first place, Mr. Muller, I want you to know we are in no hurry. We want you to stay with us all day if necessary, just so that you get used to your surroundings and get over any thought you might have that there is anything unusual in this, anything clinical, if you know what I mean."

"It's all right," said Norman. "I'd just as soon this were over."

"I understand your feelings. Still, we want you to know exactly what's going on. In the first place, Multivac isn't here."

"It isn't?" Somehow through all his depression, he had still looked forward to seeing Multivac. They said it was half a mile long and three stories high, that fifty technicians walked the corridors *within* its structure continuously. It was one of the wonders of the world.

Paulson smiled. "No. It's not portable, you know. It's located underground, in fact, and very few people know exactly where. You can understand that, since it is our greatest resource. Believe me, elections aren't the only things it's used for."

Norman thought he was being deliberately chatty and found himself intrigued all the same. "I thought I'd see it. I'd like to."

"I'm sure of that. But it takes a presidential order and even then it has to be countersigned by Security. However, we are plugged into Multivac right here by beam transmission. What Multivac says can be interpreted here and what we say is beamed directly to Multivac, so in a sense we're in its presence."

Norman looked about. The machines within the room were all meaningless to him.

"Now let me explain, Mr. Muller," Paulson went on. "Multivac already has most of the information it needs to decide all the elections, national, state and local. It needs only to check certain imponderable attitudes of mind and it will use you for that. We can't predict what questions it will ask, but they may not make much sense to you, or even to us. It may ask you how you feel about garbage disposal in your town; whether you favor central incinerators. It might ask you whether you have a doctor of your own or whether you make use of National Medicine, Inc. Do you understand?"

"Yes, sir."

"Whatever it asks, you answer in your own words in any way you please. If you feel you must explain quite a bit, do so. Talk an hour, if necessary."

"Yes, sir."

"Now, one more thing. We will have to make use of some simple devices which will automatically record your blood pressure, heartbeat, skin conductivity and brain-wave pattern while you speak. The machinery will seem formidable, but it's all absolutely painless. You won't even know it's going on."

The other two technicians were already busying themselves with smooth-gleaming apparatus on oiled wheels.

Norman said, "Is that to check on whether I'm lying or not?"

"Not at all, Mr. Muller. There's no question of lying. It's only a matter of emotional intensity. If the machine asks you your opinion of your child's school, you may say, 'I think it is overcrowded.' Those are only words. From the way your brain and heart and hormones and sweat glands work, Multivac can judge exactly how intensely you feel about the matter. It will understand your feelings better than you yourself."

"I never heard of this," said Norman.

"No, I'm sure you didn't. Most of the details of Multivac's workings are top secret. For instance, when you leave, you will be asked to sign a paper swearing that you will never reveal the nature of the questions you were asked, the nature of your responses, what was done, or how it was done. The less is known about the Multivac, the less chance of attempted outside pressures upon the men who service it." He smiled grimly. "Our lives are hard enough as it is."

Norman nodded. "I understand."

"And now would you like anything to eat or drink?"

"No. Nothing right now."

"Do you have any questions?"

Norman shook his head.

"Then you tell us when you're ready."

"I'm ready right now."

"You're certain?"

"Quite."

Paulson nodded, and raised his hand in a gesture to the others. They advanced with their frightening equipment, and Norman Muller felt his breath come a little quicker as he watched.

The ordeal lasted nearly three hours, with one short break for coffee and an embarrassing session with a chamber pot. During all this time, Norman Muller remained encased in machinery. He was bone-weary at the close.

He thought sardonically that his promise to reveal nothing of what had passed would be an easy one to keep. Already the questions were a hazy mishmash in his mind.

Somehow he had thought Multivac would speak in a sepulchral, superhuman voice, resonant and echoing, but that, after all, was just an idea he had from seeing too many television shows, he now decided. The truth was distressingly undramatic. The questions were slips of a kind of metallic foil patterned with numerous punctures. A second machine converted the pattern into words and Paulson read the words to Norman, then gave him the question and let him read it for himself.

Norman's answers were taken down by a recording machine, played back to Norman for confirmation, with emendations and added remarks also taken down. All that was fed into a pattern-making instrument and that, in turn, was radiated to Multivac.

The one question Norman could remember at the moment was an incongruously gossipy: "What do you think of the price of eggs?"

Now it was over, and gently they removed the electrodes from various portions of his body, unwrapped the pulsating band from his upper arm, moved the machinery away.

He stood up, drew a deep, shuddering breath and said, "Is that all? Am I through?"

"Not quite." Paulson hurried to him, smiling in reassuring fashion. "We'll have to ask you to stay another hour."

"Why?" asked Norman sharply.

"It will take that long for Multivac to weave its new data into the trillions of items it has. Thousands of elections are concerned, you know. It's very complicated. And it may be that an odd contest here or there, a comptrollership in Phoenix, Arizona, or some council seat in Wilkesboro, North Carolina, may be in doubt. In that case, Multivac may be compelled to ask you a deciding question or two."

"No," said Norman. "I won't go through this again."

"It probably won't happen," Paulson said soothingly. "It rarely does. But, just in case, you'll have to stay." A touch of steel, just a touch, entered his voice. "You have no choice, you know. You must."

Norman sat down wearily. He shrugged.

Paulson said, "We can't let you read a newspaper, but if you'd care for a murder mystery, or if you'd like to play chess, or if there's anything we can do for you to help pass the time, I wish you'd mention it."

"It's all right. I'll just wait."

They ushered him into a small room just next to the one in which he had been questioned. He let himself sink into a plastic-covered armchair and closed his eyes.

As well as he could, he must wait out this final hour.

He sat perfectly still and slowly the tension left him. His breathing grew less ragged and he could clasp his hands without being quite so conscious of the trembling of his fingers.

Maybe there would be no questions. Maybe it was all over.

If it *were* over, then the next thing would be torchlight processions and invitations to speak at all sort of functions. The Voter of the Year!

He, Norman Muller, ordinary clerk of a small department store in Bloomington, Indiana, who had neither been born great nor achieved greatness would be in the extraordinary position of having had greatness thrust upon him.

The historians would speak soberly of the Muller Election of two thousand and eight. That would be its name, the Muller Election.

The publicity, the better job, the flash flood of money that interested Sarah so much, occupied only a corner of his mind. It would all be welcome, of course. He couldn't refuse it. But at the moment something else was beginning to concern him.

A latent patriotism was stirring. After all, he was representing the entire electorate. He was the focal point for *them*. He was, in his own person, for this one day, all of America!

The door opened, snapping him to open-eyed attention. For a moment, his stomach constricted. Not more questions!

But Paulson was smiling. "That will be all, Mr. Muller."

"No more questions, sir?"

"None needed. Everything was quite clear-cut. You will be escorted back to your home and then you will be a private citizen once more. Or as much so as the public will allow."

"Thank you. Thank you." Norman flushed and said, "I wonder—who was elected?"

Paulson shook his head. "That will have to wait for the official announcement. The rules are quite strict. We can't even tell you. You understand."

"Of course. Yes." Norman felt embarrassed.

"Secret service will have the necessary papers for you to sign."

"Yes." Suddenly, Norman Muller felt proud. It was on him now in full strength. He was proud.

In this imperfect world, the sovereign citizens of the first and greatest Electronic Democracy had, through Norman Muller (through *him*!) exercised once again its free, untrammeled franchise.

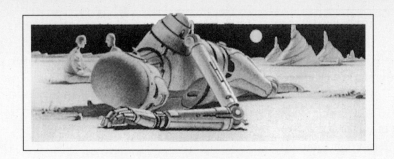

Jokester

Noel Meyerhof consulted the list he had prepared and chose which item was to be first. As usual, he relied mainly on intuition.

He was dwarfed by the machine he faced, though only the smallest portion of the latter was in view. That didn't matter. He spoke with the offhand confidence of one who thoroughly knew he was master.

"Johnson," he said, "came home unexpectedly from a business trip to find his wife in the arms of his best friend. He staggered back and said, 'Max! I'm married to the lady so I *have* to. But why you?'"

Meyerhof thought: Okay, let that trickle down into its guts and gurgle about a bit.

And a voice behind him said, "Hey."

Meyerhof erased the sound of that monosyllable and put the circuit he was using into neutral. He whirled and said, "I'm working. Don't you knock?"

He did not smile as he customarily did in greeting Timothy Whistler, a senior analyst with whom he dealt as often as with any. He frowned as he would have for an interruption by a stranger, wrinkling his thin face into a distortion that seemed to extend to his hair, rumpling it more than ever.

Whistler shrugged. He wore his white lab coat with his fists pressing down within its pockets and creasing it into tense vertical lines. "I knocked. You didn't answer. The operations signal wasn't on."

Meyerhof grunted. It wasn't at that. He'd been thinking about this new project too intensively and he was forgetting little details.

And yet he could scarcely blame himself for that. This thing was important.

He didn't know why it was, of course. Grand Masters rarely did. That's what made them Grand Masters; the fact that they were beyond reason. How else could the human mind keep up with that ten-mile-long lump of solidified reason that men called Multivac, the most complex computer ever built?

Meyerhof said, "I *am* working. Is there something important on your mind?"

"Nothing that can't be postponed. There are a few holes in the answer on the hyperspatial—" Whistler did a double take and his face took on a rueful look of uncertainty. "*Working?*"

"Yes. What about it?"

"But—" He looked about, staring into the crannies of the shallow room that faced the banks upon banks of relays that formed a small portion of Multivac. "There isn't anyone here at that."

"Who said there was, or should be?"

"You were telling one of your jokes, weren't you?"

"And?"

Whistler forced a smile. "Don't tell me you were telling a joke to Multivac?"

Meyerhof stiffened. "Why not?"

"Were you?"

"Yes."

"Why?"

Meyerhof stared the other down. "I don't have to account to you. Or to anyone."

"Good Lord, of course not. I was curious, that's all . . . But then, if you're working, I'll leave." He looked about once more, frowning.

"Do so," said Meyerhof. His eyes followed the other out and then he activated the operations signal with a savage punch of his finger.

He strode the length of the room and back, getting himself in hand. Damn Whistler! Damn them all! Because he didn't bother to hold those technicians, analysts and mechanics at the proper social distance, because he treated them as though they, too, were creative artists, they took these liberties.

He thought grimly: They can't even tell jokes decently.

And instantly that brought him back to the task in hand. He sat down again. Devil take them all.

He threw the proper Multivac circuit back into operation and said, "The ship's steward stopped at the rail of the ship during a particularly rough ocean crossing and gazed compassionately at the man whose slumped position over the rail and whose intensity of gaze toward the depths betokened all too well the ravages of seasickness.

"Gently, the steward patted the man's shoulder. 'Cheer up, sir,' he murmured. 'I know it seems bad, but really, you know, nobody ever dies of seasickness.'

"The afflicted gentleman lifted his greenish, tortured face to his comforter and gasped in hoarse accents. 'Don't say that, man. For heaven's sake, don't say that. It's only the hope of dying that's keeping me alive.'"

* * *

Timothy Whistler, a bit preoccupied, nevertheless smiled and nodded as he passed the secretary's desk. She smiled back at him.

Here, he thought, was an archaic item in this computer-ridden world of the twenty-first century, a human secretary. But then perhaps it was natural that such an institution should survive here in the very citadel of computerdom; in the gigantic world corporation that handled Multivac. With Multivac filling the horizons, lesser computers for trivial tasks would have been in poor taste.

Whistler stepped into Abram Trask's office. That government official paused in his careful task of lighting a pipe: his dark eyes flicked in Whistler's direction and his beaked nose stood out sharply and prominently against the rectangle of window behind him.

"Ah, there, Whistler. Sit down. Sit down."

Whistler did so. "I think we've got a problem, Trask."

Trask half-smiled. "Not a technical one, I hope. I'm just an innocent politician." (It was one of his favorite phrases.)

"It involves Meyerhof."

Trask sat down instantly and looked acutely miserable. "Are you sure?"

"Reasonably sure."

Whistler understood the other's sudden unhappiness well. Trask was the government official in charge of the Division of Computers and Automation of the Department of the Interior. He was expected to deal with matters of policy involving the human satellites of Multivac, just as those technically trained satellites were expected to deal with Multivac itself.

But a Grand Master was more than just a satellite. More, even, than just a human.

Early in the history of Multivac, it had become apparent that the bottleneck was the questioning procedure. Multivac could answer the problem of humanity, *all* the problems, if—if it were asked meaningful questions. But as knowledge accumulated at an ever-faster rate, it became ever more difficult to locate those meaningful questions.

Reason alone wouldn't do. What was needed was a rare type of intuition; the same faculty of mind (only much more intensified) that made a grand master at chess. A mind was needed of the sort that could see through the quadrillions of chess patterns to find the one best move, and do it in a matter of minutes.

Trask moved restlessly. "What's Meyerhof been doing?"

"He's introduced a line of questioning that I find disturbing."

"Oh, come on, Whistler. Is that all? You can't stop a Grand Master from going through any line of questioning he chooses. Neither you nor I are equipped to judge the worth of his questions. You know that. I know you know that."

"I do. Of course. But I also know Meyerhof. Have you ever met him socially?"

"Good Lord, no. Does anyone meet any Grand Master socially?"

"Don't take that attitude, Trask. They're human and they're to be pitied. Have you ever thought what it must be like to be a Grand Master; to know there are only some twelve like you in the world; to know that only one or two come up per generation; that the world depends on you; that a thousand mathematicians, logicians, psychologists and physical scientists wait on you?"

Trask shrugged and muttered, "Good Lord, I'd feel king of the world."

"I don't think you would," said the senior analyst impatiently. "They feel kings of nothing. They have no equal to talk to, no sensation of belonging. Listen, Meyerhof never misses a chance to get together with the boys. He isn't married, naturally; he doesn't drink; he has no natural social touch—yet he forces himself into company because he must. And do you know what he does when he gets together with us, and that's at least once a week?"

"I haven't the least idea," said the government man. "This is all new to me."

"He's a jokester."

"What?"

"He tells jokes. Good ones. He's terrific. He can take any story, however old and dull, and make it sound good. It's the way he tells it. He has a flair."

"I see. Well, good."

"Or bad. These jokes are important to him." Whistler put both elbows on Trask's desk, bit at a thumbnail and stared into the air. "He's different, he knows he's different and these jokes are the one way he feels he can get the rest of us ordinary schmoes to accept him. We laugh, we howl, we clap him on the back and even forget he's a Grand Master. It's the only hold he has on the rest of us."

"This is all interesting. I didn't know you were such a psychologist. Still, where does this lead?"

"Just this. What do you suppose happens if Meyerhof runs out of jokes?"

"What?" The government man stared blankly.

"If he starts repeating himself? If his audience starts laughing less heartily, or stops laughing altogether? It's his only hold on our approval. Without it, he'll be alone and then what would happen to him? After all, Trask, he's one of the dozen men mankind can't do without. We can't let anything happen to him. I don't mean just physical things. We can't even let him get too unhappy. Who knows how that might affect his intuition?"

"Well, has he started repeating himself?"

"Not as far as I know, but I think *he* thinks he has."

"Why do you say that?"

"Because I've heard him telling jokes to Multivac."

"Oh, no."

"Accidentally! I walked in on him and he threw me out. He was savage. He's usually good-natured enough, and I consider it a bad sign that he was so upset at the intrusion. But the fact remains that he was telling a joke to Multivac, and I'm convinced it was one of a series."

"But why?"

Whistler shrugged and rubbed a hand fiercely across his chin. "I have a thought about that. I think he's trying to build up a store of jokes in Multivac's memory banks in order to get back new variations. You see what I mean? He's planning a mechanical jokester, so that he can have an infinite number of jokes at hand and never fear running out."

"Good Lord!"

"Objectively, there may be nothing wrong with that, but I consider it a bad sign when a Grand Master starts using Multivac for his personal problems. Any Grand Master has a certain inherent mental instability and he should be watched. Meyerhof may be approaching a borderline beyond which we lose a Grand Master."

Trask said blankly, "What are you suggesting I do?"

"You can check me. I'm too close to him to judge well, maybe, and judging humans isn't my particular talent, anyway. You're a politician; it's more your talent."

"Judging humans, perhaps, not Grand Masters."

"They're human, too. Besides, who else is to do it?"

The fingers on Trask's hand struck his desk in rapid succession over and over like a slow and muted roll of drums.

"I suppose I'll have to," he said.

Meyerhof said to Multivac, "The ardent swain, picking a bouquet of wild-flowers for his loved one, was disconcerted to find himself, suddenly, in the same field with a large bull of unfriendly appearance which, gazing at him steadily, pawed the ground in a threatening manner. The young man, spying a farmer on the other side of a fairly distant fence, shouted, 'Hey, mister, is that bull safe?' The farmer surveyed the situation with a critical eye, spat to one side and called back, 'He's safe as anything.' He spat again and added, 'Can't say the same about you, though.'"

Meyerhof was about to pass on to the next when the summons came.

It wasn't really a summons. No one could summon a Grand Master. It was only a message that Division Head Trask would like very much to see Grand Master Meyerhof if Grand Master Meyerof could spare him the time.

Meyerhof might, with impunity, have tossed the message to one side and continued with whatever he was doing. He was not subject to discipline.

On the other hand, were he to do that, they would continue to bother him—oh, very respectfully, but they would continue to bother him.

So he neutralized the pertinent circuits of Multivac and locked them into place. He put the freeze signal on his office so that no one would dare enter in his absence and left for Trask's office.

Trask coughed and felt a bit intimidated by the sullen fierceness of the other's look. He said, "We have not had occasion to know one another, Grand Master, to my great regret."

"I have reported to you," said Meyerhof stiffly.

Trask wondered what lay behind those keen, wild eyes. It was difficult for him to imagine Meyerhof with his thin face, his dark, straight hair, his intense air, even unbending long enough to tell funny stories.

He said, "Reports are not social acquaintance. I—I have been given to understand you have a marvelous fund of anecdotes."

"I am a jokester, sir. That's the phrase people use. A jokester."

"They haven't used the phrase to me, Grand Master. They have said—"

"The hell with them! I don't care what they've said. See here, Trask, do you want to hear a joke?" He leaned forward across the desk, his eyes narrowed.

"By all means. Certainly," said Trask, with an effort at heartiness.

"All right. Here's the joke: Mrs. Jones stared at the fortune card that had emerged from the weighing machine in response to her husband's penny. She said, 'It says here, George, that you're suave, intelligent, far-seeing, industrious and attractive to women.' With that, she turned the card over and added, 'And they have your weight wrong, too.'"

Trask laughed. It was almost impossible not to. Although the punch line was predictable, the surprising facility with which Meyerhof had produced just the tone of contemptuous disdain in the woman's voice, and the cleverness with which he had contorted the lines of his face to suit that tone carried the politician helplessly into laughter.

Meyerhof said sharply, "Why is that funny?"

Trask sobered. "I beg your pardon."

"I said, 'Why is that funny?' Why do you laugh?"

"Well," said Trask, trying to be reasonable, "the last line put everything that preceded in a new light. The unexpectedness—"

"The point is," said Meyerhof, "that I have pictured a husband being humiliated by his wife; a marriage that is such a failure that the wife is convinced that her husband lacks any virtue. Yet you laugh at that. If you were the husband, would you find it funny?"

He waited a moment in thought, then said, "Try this one, Trask: Abner was

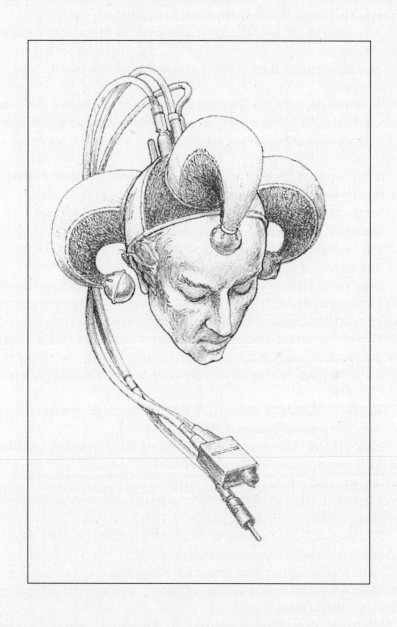

seated at his wife's sickbed, weeping uncontrollably, when his wife, mustering the dregs of her strength, drew herself up on one elbow.

" 'Abner,' she whispered, 'Abner, I cannot go to my Maker without confessing my misdeed.'

" 'Not now,' muttered the stricken husband, 'Not now, my dear. Lie back and rest.'

" 'I cannot,' she cried. 'I must tell you, or my soul will never know peace. I have been unfaithful to you, Abner. In this very house, not one month ago—'

" 'Hush, dear,' soothed Abner. 'I know all about it. Why else have I poisoned you?' "

Trask tried desperately to maintain equanimity but did not entirely succeed. He suppressed a chuckle imperfectly.

Meyerhof said, "So that's funny, too. Adultery. Murder. All funny."

"Well, now," said Trask, "books have been written analyzing humor."

"True enough," said Meyerhof, "and I've read a number of them. What's more, I've read most of them to Multivac. Still, the people who write the books are just guessing. Some of them say we laugh because we feel superior to the people in the joke. Some say it is because of a suddenly realized incongruity, or a sudden relief from tension, or a sudden reinterpretation of events. Is there any simple reason? Different people laugh at different jokes. No joke is universal. Some people don't laugh at any joke. Yet what may be most important is that man is the only animal with a true sense of humor; the only animal that laughs."

Trask said suddenly, "I understand. You're trying to analyze humor. That's why you're transmitting a series of jokes to Multivac."

"Who told you I was doing that? Never mind, it was Whistler. I remember, now. He surprised me at it. Well, what about it?"

"Nothing at all."

"You don't dispute my right to add anything I wish to Multivac's general fund of knowledge, or to ask any question I wish?"

"No, not at all," said Trask hastily. "As a matter of fact, I have no doubt that this will open the way to new analyses of great interest to psychologists."

"Hmp. Maybe. Just the same there's something plaguing me that's more important than just the general analysis of humor. There's a specific question I have to ask. Two of them, really."

"Oh? What's that?" Trask wondered if the other would answer. There would be no way of compelling him if he chose not to.

But Meyerhof said, "The first question is this: Where do all these jokes come from?"

"What?"

"Who makes them up? Listen! About a month ago, I spent an evening swapping jokes. As usual, I told most of them and, as usual, the fools laughed. Maybe they really thought the jokes were funny and maybe they were just humoring me. In any case, one creature took the liberty of slapping me on the back and saying, 'Meyerhof, you know more jokes than any ten people I know.'

"I'm sure he was right, but it gave rise to a thought. I don't know how many hundreds, or perhaps thousands, of jokes I've told at one time or another in my life, yet the fact is I never made up one. Not one. I'd only repeated them. My only contribution was to tell them. To begin with, I'd neither heard them or read them. And the source of my hearing or reading didn't make up the jokes, either. I never met anyone who ever claimed to have constructed a joke. It's always 'I heard a good one the other day,' and 'Heard any good ones lately?'

"*All the jokes are old!* That's why jokes exhibit such a social lag. They still deal with seasickness, for instance, when that's easily prevented these days and never experienced. Or they'll deal with fortune-giving weighing machines, like the joke I told you, when such machines are found only in antique shops. Well, then, who makes up the jokes?"

Trask said, "Is that what you're trying to find out?" It was on the tip of Trask's tongue to add: Good Lord, who cares? He forced that impulse down. A Grand Master's questions were always meaningful.

"Of course that's what I'm trying to find out. Think of it this way. It's not just that jokes happen to be old. They *must* be old to be enjoyed. It's essential that a joke not be original. There's one variety of humor that is, or can be, original and that's the pun. I've heard puns that were obviously made up on the spur of the moment. I have made some up myself. But no one laughs at such puns. You're not supposed to. You groan. The better the pun, the louder the groan. Original humor is not laugh-provoking. Why?"

"I'm sure I don't know."

"All right. Let's find out. Having given Multivac all the information I thought advisable on the general topic of humor, I am now feeding it selected jokes."

Trask found himself intrigued. "Selected how?" he asked.

"I don't know," said Meyerhof. "They felt like the right ones. I'm Grand Master, you know."

"Oh, agreed. Agreed."

"From those jokes and the general philosophy of humor, my first request will be for Multivac to trace the origin of the jokes, if it can. Since Whistler is in on this and since he has seen fit to report it to you, have him down in Analysis day after tomorrow. I think he'll have a bit of work to do."

"Certainly. May I attend, too?"

Meyerhof shrugged. Trask's attendance was obviously a matter of indifference to him.

Meyerhof had selected the last in the series with particular care. What that care consisted of, he could not have said, but he had revolved a dozen possibilities in his mind, and over and over again had tested each for some indefinable quality of meaningfulness.

He said, "Ug, the caveman, observed his mate running to him in tears, her leopard-skin skirt in disorder. 'Ug,' she cried, distraught, 'do something quickly. A saber-toothed tiger has entered Mother's cave. Do something!' Ug grunted, picked up his well-gnawed buffalo bone and said, 'Why do anything? Who the hell cares what happens to a saber-toothed tiger?'"

It was then that Meyerhof asked his two questions and leaned back, closing his eyes. He was done.

"I saw absolutely nothing wrong," said Trask to Whistler. "He told me what he was doing readily enough and it was odd but legitimate."

"What he *claimed* he was doing," said Whistler.

"Even so, I can't stop a Grand Master on opinion alone. He seemed queer but, after all, Grand Masters are supposed to seem queer. I didn't think him insane."

"Using Multivac to find the source of jokes?" muttered the senior analyst in discontent. "That's not insane?"

"How can we tell?" asked Trask irritably. "Science has advanced to the point where the only meaningful questions left are the ridiculous ones. The sensible ones have been thought of, asked and answered long ago."

"It's no use. I'm bothered."

"Maybe, but there's no choice now, Whistler. We'll see Meyerhof and you can do the necessary analysis of Multivac's response, if any. As for me, my only job is to handle the red tape. Good Lord, I don't even know what a senior analyst such as yourself is supposed to do, except analyze, and that doesn't help me any."

Whistler said, "It's simple enough. A Grand Master like Meyerhof asks questions and Multivac automatically formulates them into quantities and operations. The necessary machinery for converting words to symbols is what makes up most of the bulk of Multivac. Multivac then gives the answer in quantities and operations, but it doesn't translate that back into words except in the most simple and routine cases. If it were designed to solve the general retranslation problem, its bulk would have to be quadrupled at least."

"I see. Then it's your job to translate these symbols into words?"

"My job and that of other analysts. We use smaller, specially designed computers whenever necessary." Whistler smiled grimly. "Like the Delphic priests of ancient Greece, Multivac gives oracular and obscure answers. Only we have translators, you see."

They had arrived. Meyerhof was waiting.

Whistler said briskly, "What circuits did you use, Grand Master?"

Meyerhof told him and Whistler went to work.

Trask tried to follow what was happening, but none of it made sense. The government official watched a spool unreel with a pattern of dots in endless incomprehensibility. Grand Master Meyerhof stood indifferently to one side while Whistler surveyed the pattern as it emerged. The analyst had put on headphones and a mouthpiece and at intervals murmured a series of instructions which, at some far-off place, guided assistants through electronic contortions in other computers.

Occasionally, Whistler listened, then punched combinations on a complex keyboard marked with symbols that looked vaguely mathematical but weren't.

A good deal more than an hour's time elapsed.

The frown on Whistler's face grew deeper. Once, he looked up at the two others and began, "This is unbel—" and turned back to his work.

Finally, he said hoarsely, "I can't give you an official answer." His eyes were red-rimmed. "The official answer awaits complete analysis. Do you want it unofficial?"

"Go ahead," said Meyerhof.

Trask nodded.

Whistler darted a hangdog glance at the Grand Master. "Ask a foolish question—" he said. Then, gruffly, "Multivac says, extraterrestrial origin."

"What are you saying?" demanded Trask.

"Don't you hear me? The jokes we laugh at were not made up by any man. Multivac has analyzed all data given it and the one answer that best fits that data is that some extraterrestrial intelligence has composed the jokes, all of them, and placed them in selected human minds at selected times and places in such a way that no man is conscious of having made one up. All subsequent jokes are minor variations and adaptations of these grand originals."

Meyerhof broke in, face flushed with the kind of triumph only a Grand Master can know who once again has asked the right question. "All comedy writers," he said, "work by twisting old jokes to new purposes. That's well known. The answer fits."

"But why?" asked Trask. "Why make up the jokes?"

"Multivac says," said Whistler, "that the only purpose that fits all the data is that the jokes are intended to study human psychology. We study rat psychology by making the rats solve mazes. The rats don't know why and wouldn't even if they were aware of what was going on, which they're not. These outer intelligences study man's psychology by noting individual reactions to carefully selected anecdotes. Each man reacts differently ... presumably, these outer intelligences are to us as we are to rats." He shuddered.

Trask, eyes staring, said, "The Grand Master said man is the only animal with a sense of humor. It would seem then that the sense of humor is foisted upon us from without."

Meyerhof added excitedly, "And for possible humor created from within, we have no laughter. Puns, I mean."

Whistler said, "Presumably, the extraterrestrials cancel out reactions to spontaneous jokes to avoid confusion."

Trask said in sudden agony of spirit, "Come on, now, Good Lord, do either of you believe this?"

The senior analyst looked at him coldly, "Multivac says so. It's all that can be said so far. It has pointed out the real jokesters of the universe, and if we want to know more, the matter will have to be followed up." He added in a whisper, "If anyone dares follow it up."

Grand Master Meyerhof said suddenly, "I asked two questions, you know. So far only the first has been answered. I think Multivac has enough data to answer the second."

Whistler shrugged. He seemed a half-broken man. "When a Grand Master thinks there is enough data," he said, "I'll make a book on it. What is your second question?"

"I asked this: What will be the effect on the human race of discovering the answer to my first question?"

"Why did you ask that?" demanded Trask.

"Just a feeling that it had to be asked," said Meyerhof.

Trask said, "Insane. It's all insane," and turned away. Even he himself felt how strangely he and Whistler had changed sides. Now it was Trask crying insanity.

Trask closed his eyes. He might cry insanity all he wished, but no man in fifty years had doubted the combination of the Grand Master and Multivac and found his doubts verified.

Whistler worked silently, teeth clenched. He put Multivac and its subsidiary machines through their paces again. Another hour passed and he laughed harshly. "A raving nightmare!"

"What's the answer?" asked Meyerhof. "I want Multivac's remarks, not yours."

"All right. Take it. Multivac states that, once even a single human discovers the truth of this method of psychological analysis of the human mind, it will become useless as an objective technique to those extraterrestrial powers now using it."

"You mean there won't be any more jokes handed out to humanity?" asked Trask faintly. "Or what do you mean?"

"No more jokes," said Whistler. "*Now*! Multivac says *now*! The experiment is ended *now*! A new technique will have to be introduced."

They stared at each other. The minutes passed.

Meyerhof said slowly, "Multivac is right."

Whistler said haggardly, "I know."

Even Trask said in a whisper, "Yes. It must be."

It was Meyerhof who put his finger on the proof of it, Meyerhof the accomplished jokester. He said, "It's over, you know, all over. I've been trying for five minutes now and I can't think of one single joke, not one! And if I read one in a book, I wouldn't laugh. I know."

"The gift of humor is gone," said Trask drearily. "No man will ever laugh again."

And they remained there, staring, feeling the world shrink down to the dimensions of an experimental rat cage—with the maze removed and something, something about to be put in its place.

The Last Question

The last question was asked for the first time, half in jest, on May 21, 2061, at a time when humanity first stepped into the light. The question came about as a result of a five-dollar bet over highballs, and it happened this way.

Alexander Adell and Bertram Lupov were two of the faithful attendants of Multivac. As well as any human beings could, they knew what lay behind the cold, clicking, flashing face—miles and miles of face—of that giant computer. They had at least a vague notion of the general plan of relays and circuits that had long since grown past the point where any single human could possibly have a firm grasp of the whole.

Multivac was self-adjusting and self-correcting. It had to be, for nothing human could adjust and correct it quickly enough or even adequately enough. So Adell and Lupov attended the monstrous giant only lightly and superficially, yet as well as any men could. They fed it data, adjusted questions to its needs and translated the answers that were issued. Certainly they, and all others like them, were fully entitled to share in the glory that was Multivac's.

For decades, Multivac had helped design the ships and plot the trajectories that enabled man to reach the Moon, Mars, and Venus, but past that, Earth's poor resources could not support the ships. Too much energy was needed for the long trips. Earth exploited its coal and uranium with increasing efficiency, but there was only so much of both.

But slowly Multivac learned enough to answer deeper questions more fundamentally, and on May 14, 2061, what had been theory, became fact.

The energy of the sun was stored, converted, and utilized directly on a planet-wide scale. All Earth turned off its burning coal, its fissioning uranium, and flipped the switch that connected all of it to a small station, one mile in diameter, circling the Earth at half the distance of the Moon. All Earth ran by invisible beams of sunpower.

Seven days had not sufficed to dim the glory of it and Adell and Lupov finally managed to escape from the public function, and to meet in quiet where no one would think of looking for them, in the deserted underground chambers, where portions of the mighty buried body of Multivac showed. Unattended, idling, sorting data with contented lazy clickings, Multivac, too, had earned its vacation and the boys appreciated that. They had no intention, originally, of disturbing it.

They had brought a bottle with them, and their only concern at the moment was to relax in the company of each other and the bottle.

"It's amazing when you think of it," said Adell. His broad face had lines of weariness in it, and he stirred his drink slowly with a glass rod, watching the cubes of ice slur clumsily about. "All the energy we could ever use, forever and forever and forever."

Lupov cocked his head sideways. He had a trick of doing that when he wanted to be contrary, and he wanted to be contrary now, partly because he had had to carry the ice and glassware, "Not forever," he said.

"Oh, hell, just about forever. Till the sun runs down, Bert."

"That's not forever."

"All right, then. Billions and billions of years. Twenty billion, maybe. Are you satisfied?"

Lupov put his fingers through his thinning hair as though to reassure himself that some was still left and sipped gently at his own drink. "Twenty billion years isn't forever."

"Well, it will last our time, won't it?"

"So would the coal and uranium."

"All right, but now we can hook up each individual spaceship to the Solar Station, and it can go to Pluto and back a million times without ever worrying about fuel. You can't do *that* on coal and uranium. Ask Multivac, if you don't believe me."

"I don't have to ask Multivac. I know that."

"Then stop running down what Multivac's done for us," said Adell, blazing up. "It did all right."

"Who says it didn't? What I say is that a sun won't last forever. That's all I'm saying. We're safe for twenty billion years; but then what?" Lupov pointed a slightly shaky finger at the other. "And don't say we'll switch to another sun."

There was silence for a while. Adell put his glass to his lips only occasionally, and Lupov's eyes slowly closed. They rested.

Then Lupov's eyes snapped open. "You're thinking we'll switch to another sun when ours is done, aren't you?"

"I'm not thinking."

"Sure you are. You're weak on logic, that's the trouble with you. You're like the guy in the story who was caught in a sudden shower and who ran to a grove of trees and got under one. He wasn't worried, you see, because he figured when one tree got wet through he would just get under another one."

"I get it," said Adell. "Don't shout. When the sun is done, the other stars will be gone, too."

"Darn right they will," muttered Lupov. "It all had a beginning in the original cosmic explosion, whatever that was, and it'll all have an end when all the stars run down. Some run down faster than others. Hell, the giants won't last a hundred million years. The sun will last twenty billion years and maybe the dwarfs will last a hundred billion for all the good they are. But just give us a trillion years and everything will be dark. Entropy has to increase to maximum, that's all."

"I know all about entropy," said Adell, standing on his dignity.

"The hell you do."

"I know as much as you do."

"Then you know everything's got to run down someday."

"All right. Who says they won't?"

"You did, you poor sap. You said we had all the energy we needed, forever. You said 'forever.'"

It was Adell's turn to be contrary. "Maybe we can build things up again someday," he said.

"Never."

"Why not? Someday."

"Ask Multivac."

"Never."

"*You* ask Multivac. I dare you. Five dollars says it can't be done."

Adell was just drunk enough to try, just sober enough to be able to phrase the necessary symbols and operations into a question which, in words, might have corresponded to this: Will mankind one day without the net expenditure of energy be able to restore the sun to its full youthfulness even after it had died of old age?

Or maybe it could be put more simply like this: How can the net amount of entropy of the universe be massively decreased?

Multivac fell dead and silent. The slow flashing of lights ceased, the distant sounds of clicking relays ended.

Then, just as the frightened technicians felt they could hold their breath no longer, there was a sudden springing to life of the teletype attached to that portion of Multivac. Five words were printed: INSUFFICENT DATA FOR MEANINGFUL ANSWER.

"Not yet," whispered Lupov. They left hurriedly.

By next morning, the two, plagued with throbbing head and cottony mouth, had forgotten the incident.

Jerrodd, Jerrodine, and Jerrodette I and II watched the starry picture in the visiplate change as the passage through hyperspace was completed in its non-time lapse. At once, the even powdering of stars gave way to the predominance of a single bright marble-disk, centered.

"That's X–23," said Jerrodd confidently. His thin hands clamped tightly behind his back and the knuckles whitened.

The little Jerrodettes, both girls, had experienced the hyperspace passage for the first time in their lives and were selfconscious over the momentary sensation of inside-outness. They buried their giggles and chased one another wildly about their mother, screaming, "We've reached X–23—we've reached X–23—we've—"

"Quiet, children," said Jerrodine sharply. "Are you sure, Jerrodd?"

"What is there to be but sure?" asked Jerrodd, glancing up at the bulge of featureless metal just under the ceiling. It ran the length of the room, disappearing through the wall at either end. It was as long as the ship.

Jerrodd scarcely knew a thing about the thick rod of metal except that it was called Microvac, that one asked it questions if one wished; that if one did it still had its task of guiding the ship to a preordered destination; of feeding on energies from the various Sub-galactic Power Stations; of computing the equation for the hyperspatial jumps.

Jerrodd and his family had only to wait and live in the comfortable residence quarters of the ship.

Someone had once told Jerrodd that the "ac" at the end of the "Microvac" stood for "analog computer" in ancient English, but he was on the edge of forgetting even that.

Jerrodine's eyes were moist as she watched the visiplate. "I can't help it. I feel funny about leaving Earth."

"Why, for Pete's sake?" demanded Jerrodd. "We had nothing there. We'll have everything on X–23. You won't be alone. You won't be a pioneer. There are over a million people on the planet already. Good Lord, our great-grandchildren will be looking for new worlds because X–23 will be overcrowded." Then, after a reflective pause, "I tell you, it's a lucky thing the computers worked out interstellar travel the way the race is growing."

"I know, I know," said Jerrodine miserably.

Jerrodette I said promptly, "Our Microvac is the best Microvac in the world."

"I think so, too," said Jerrodd, tousling her hair.

It *was* a nice feeling to have a Microvac of your own and Jerrodd was glad he was part of his generation and no other. In his father's youth, the only computers had been tremendous machines taking up a hundred square miles of land. There was only one to a planet. Planetary ACs they were called. They had been growing in size steadily for a thousand years and then, all at once, came refinement. In place of transistors, had come molecular valves so that even the largest Planetary AC could be put into a space only half the volume of a spaceship.

Jerrodd felt uplifted, as he always did when he thought that his own personal Microvac was many times more complicated than the ancient and primitive Multivac that had first tamed the Sun, and almost as complicated as Earth's Planetary AC (the largest) that had first solved the problem of hyperspatial travel and had made trips to the stars possible.

"So many stars, so many planets," sighed Jerrodine, busy with her own thoughts. "I suppose families will be going to new planets forever, the way we are now."

"Not forever," said Jerrodd, with a smile. "It will all stop someday, but not for billions of years. Many billions. Even the stars run down, you know. Entropy must increase."

"What's entropy, daddy?" shrilled Jerrodette II.

"Entropy, little sweet, is just a word which means the amount of running-down of the universe. Everything runs down, you know, like your little walkie-talkie robot, remember?"

"Can't you just put in a new power unit like with my robot?"

"The stars *are* the power units, dear. Once they're gone, there are no more power-units."

Jerrodette I at once set up a howl. "Don't let them, daddy. Don't let the stars run down."

"Now look what you've done," whispered Jerrodine, exasperated.

"How was I to know it would frighten them?" Jerrodd whispered back.

"Ask the Microvac," wailed Jerrodette I. "Ask him how to turn the stars on again."

"Go ahead," said Jerrodine. "It will quiet them down." (Jerrodette II was beginning to cry, also.)

Jerrodd shrugged. "Now, now, honeys. I'll ask Microvac. Don't worry, it'll tell us."

He asked the Microvac, adding quickly, "Print the answer."

Jerrodd cupped the strip of thin cellufilm and said cheerfully, "See now, the Microvac says it will take care of everything when the time comes, so don't worry."

Jerrodine said, "And now, children, it's time for bed. We'll be in our new home soon."

Jerrodd read the words on the cellufilm before destroying it: INSUFFICENT DATA FOR MEANINGFUL ANSWER.

He shrugged and looked at the visiplate. X–23 was just ahead.

VJ–23X of Lameth stared into the black depths of the three-dimensional, small-scale map of the Galaxy and said, "Are we ridiculous, I wonder, in being so concerned about the matter?"

MQ–17J of Nicron shook his head. "I think not. You know the Galaxy will be filled in five years at the present rate of expansion."

Both seemed in their early twenties, both were tall and perfectly formed.

"Still," said VJ–23X, "I hesitate to submit a pessimistic report to the Galactic Council."

"I wouldn't consider any other kind of report. Stir them up a bit. We've got to stir them up."

VJ–23X sighed. "Space is infinite. A hundred billion Galaxies are there for the taking. More."

"A hundred billion is *not* infinite and it's getting less infinite all the time. Consider! Twenty thousand years ago, mankind first solved the problem of utilizing stellar energy, and a few centuries later, interstellar travel became possible. It took mankind a million years to fill one small world and then only fifteen thousand years to fill the rest of the Galaxy. Now the population doubles every ten years—"

VJ–23X interrupted. "We can thank immortality for that."

"Very well. Immortality exists and we have to take it into account. I admit it has its seamy side, this immortality. The Galactic AC has solved many problems for us, but in solving the problem of preventing old age and death, it has undone all its other solutions."

"Yet you wouldn't want to abandon life, I suppose."

"Not at all," snapped MQ–17J, softening it at once to, "Not yet. I'm by no means old enough. How old are you?"

"Two hundred twenty-three. And you?"

"I'm still under two hundred. But to get back to my point. Population doubles every ten years. Once this Galaxy is filled, we'll have filled another in ten years. Another ten years and we'll have filled two more. Another decade, four more. In a hundred years, we'll have filled a thousand Galaxies. In a thousand years, a million Galaxies. In ten thousand years, the entire known Universe. Then what?"

VJ–23X said, "As a side issue, there's a problem of transportation. I wonder how many sunpower units it will take to move Galaxies of individuals from one Galaxy to the next."

"A very good point. Already, mankind consumes two sunpower units per year."

"Most of it's wasted. After all, our own Galaxy alone pours out a thousand sunpower units a year and we only use two of those."

"Granted, but even with a hundred percent efficiency, we only stave off the end. Our energy requirements are going up in a geometric progression even faster than our population. We'll run out of energy even sooner than we run out of Galaxies. A good point. A very good point."

"We'll just have to build new stars out of interstellar gas."

"Or out of dissipated heat?" asked MQ–17J, sarcastically.

"There may be some way to reverse entropy. We ought to ask the Galactic AC."

VJ–23X was not really serious, but MQ–17J pulled out his AC-contact from his pocket and placed it on the table before him.

"I've half a mind to," he said. "It's something the human race will have to face someday."

He stared somberly at his small AC-contact. It was only two inches cubed and nothing in itself, but it was connected through hyperspace with the great Galactic AC that served all mankind. Hyperspace considered, it was an integral part of the Galactic AC.

MQ–17J paused to wonder if someday in his immortal life he would get to see the Galactic AC. It was on a little world of its own, a spider webbing of force-beams holding the matter within which surges of sub-mesons took the place of the old clumsy molecular valves. Yet despite its subetheric workings, the Galactic AC was known to be a full thousand feet across.

MQ–17J asked suddenly of his AC-contact, "Can entropy ever be reversed?"

Vj–23X looked startled and said at once, "Oh, say, I didn't really mean to have you ask that."

"Why not?"

"We both know entropy can't be reversed. You can't turn smoke and ash back into a tree."

"Do you have trees on your world?" asked MQ–17J.

The sound of the Galactic AC startled them into silence.

Its voice came thin and beautiful out of the small AC-contact on the desk. It said: THERE IS INSUFFICIENT DATA FOR A MEANINGFUL ANSWER.

VJ–23X said, "See!"

The two men thereupon returned to the question of the report they were to make to the Galactic Council.

Zee Prime's mind spanned the new Galaxy with a faint interest in the countless twists of stars that powdered it. He had never seen this one before.

Would he ever see them all? So many of them, each with its load of humanity. But a load that was almost a dead weight. More and more the real essence of men was to be found out here, in space.

Minds, not bodies! The immortal bodies remained back on the planets, in suspension over the eons. Sometimes they roused for material activity but that was growing rarer. Few new individuals were coming into existence to join the incredibly mighty throng, but what matter? There was little room in the Universe for new individuals.

Zee Prime was roused out of his reverie upon coming across the wispy tendrils of another mind.

"I am Zee Prime," said Zee Prime. "And you?"

"I am Dee Sub Wun. Your Galaxy?"

"We call it only the Galaxy. And you?"

"We call ours the same. All men call their Galaxy their Galaxy and nothing more. Why not?"

"True. Since all Galaxies are the same."

"Not all Galaxies. On one particular Galaxy the race of man must have originated. That makes it different."

Zee Prime said, "On which one?"

"I cannot say. The Universal AC would know."

"Shall we ask him? I am suddenly curious."

Zee Prime's perceptions broadened until the Galaxies themselves shrank and became a new, more diffuse powdering on a much larger background. So many hundreds of billions of them, all with their immortal beings, all carrying their load of intelligence with minds that drifted freely through space. And yet one of them was unique among them all in being the original Galaxy. One of them had, in its vague and distant past, a period when it was the only Galaxy populated by man.

Zee Prime was consumed with curiosity to see this Galaxy and he called out: "Universal AC! On which Galaxy did mankind originate?"

The Universal AC heard, for on every world and throughout space, it had its receptors ready, and each receptor led through hyperspace to some unknown point where the Universal AC kept itself aloof.

Zee Prime knew of only one man whose thoughts had penetrated within sensing distance of Universal AC, and he reported only a shining globe, two feet across, difficult to see.

"But how can that be all of Universal AC?" Zee Prime had asked.

"Most of it," had been the answer, "is in hyperspace. In what form it is there I cannot imagine."

Nor could anyone, for the day had long since passed, Zee Prime knew, when any man had any part of the making of a Universal AC. Each Universal AC designed and constructed its successor. Each, during its existence of a million years or more accumulated the necessary data to build a better and more intricate, more capable successor in which its own store of data and individuality would be submerged.

The Universal AC interrupted Zee Prime's wandering thoughts, not with words, but with guidance. Zee Prime's mentality was guided into the dim sea of Galaxies and one in particular enlarged into stars.

A thought came, infinitely distant, but infinitely clear. "THIS IS THE ORIGINAL GALAXY OF MAN."

But it was the same after all, the same as any other, and Zee Prime stifled his disappointment.

Dee Sub Wun, whose mind had accompanied the other, said suddenly, "And is one of these stars the original star of Man?"

The Universal AC said, "MAN'S ORIGINAL STAR HAS GONE NOVA. IT IS A WHITE DWARF."

"Did the men upon it die?" asked Zee Prime, startled and without thinking.

The Universal AC said, "A NEW WORLD, AS IN SUCH CASES, WAS CONSTRUCTED FOR THEIR PHYSICAL BODIES IN TIME."

"Yes, of course," said Zee Prime, but a sense of loss overwhelmed him even so. His mind released its hold on the original Galaxy of Man, let it spring back and lose itself among the blurred pinpoints. He never wanted to see it again.

Dee Sub Wun said, "What is wrong?"

"The stars are dying. The original star is dead."

"They must all die. Why not?"

"But when all energy is gone, our bodies will finally die, and you and I with them."

"It will take billions of years."

"I do not wish it to happen even after billions of years. Universal AC! How may stars be kept from dying?"

Dee Sub Wun said in amusement, "You're asking how entropy might be reversed in direction."

And the Universal AC answered: "THERE IS AS YET INSUFFICIENT DATA FOR A MEANINGFUL ANSWER."

Zee Prime's thoughts fled back to his own Galaxy. He gave no further thought to Dee Sub Wun, whose body might be waiting on a Galaxy a trillion light-years away, or on the star next to Zee Prime's own. It didn't matter.

Unhappily, Zee Prime began collecting interstellar hydrogen out of which to build a small star of his own. If the stars must someday die, at least some could yet be built.

THE LAST QUESTION   213

Man considered with himself, for in a way, Man, mentally, was one. He consisted of a trillion, trillion, trillion ageless bodies, each in its place, each resting quiet and incorruptible, each cared for by perfect automatons, equally incorruptible, while the minds of all the bodies freely melted one into the other, indistinguishable.

Man said, "The Universe is dying."

Man looked about at the dimming Galaxies. The giant stars, spendthrifts, were gone long ago, back in the dimmest of the dim far past. Almost all stars were white dwarfs, fading to the end.

New stars had been built of the dust between the stars, some by natural processes, some by Man himself, and those were going, too. White dwarfs might yet be crashed together and of the mighty forces so released, new stars built, but only one star for every thousand white dwarfs destroyed, and those would come to an end, too.

Man said, "Carefully husbanded, as directed by the Cosmic AC, the energy that is even yet left in all the Universe will last for billions of years."

"But even so," said Man, "eventually it will all come to an end. However it may be husbanded, however stretched out, the energy once expended is gone and cannot be restored. Entropy must increase forever to the maximum."

Man said, "Can entropy not be reversed? Let us ask the Cosmic AC."

The Cosmic AC surrounded them but not in space. Not a fragment of it was in space. It was in hyperspace and made of something that was neither matter nor energy. The question of its size and nature no longer had meaning in any terms that Man could comprehend.

"Cosmic AC," said Man, "how can entropy be reversed?"

The Cosmic AC said, "THERE IS AS YET INSUFFICIENT DATA FOR A MEANINGFUL ANSWER."

Man said, "Collect additional data."

The Cosmic AC said, "I WILL DO SO. I HAVE BEEN DOING SO FOR A HUNDRED BILLION YEARS. MY PREDECESSORS HAVE BEEN ASKED THIS QUESTION MANY TIMES. ALL THE DATA I HAVE REMAINS INSUFFICIENT."

"Will there come a time," said Man, "when data will be sufficient or is the problem insoluble in all conceivable circumstances?"

The Cosmic AC said, "NO PROBLEM IS INSOLUBLE IN ALL CONCEIVABLE CIRCUMSTANCES."

Man said, "When will you have enough data to answer the question?"

The Cosmic AC said, "THERE IS AS YET INSUFFICIENT DATA FOR A MEANINGFUL ANSWER."

"Will you keep working on it?" asked Man.

The Cosmic AC said, "I WILL."

Man said, "We shall wait."

The stars and Galaxies died and snuffed out, and space grew black after ten trillion years of running down.

One by one Man fused with AC, each physical body losing its mental identity in a manner that was somehow not a loss but a gain.

Man's last mind paused before fusion, looking over a space that included nothing but the dregs of one last dark star and nothing besides but incredibly thin matter, agitated randomly by the tag ends of heat wearing out, asymptotically, to the absolute zero.

Man said, "AC, is this the end? Can this chaos not be reversed into the Universe once more? Can that not be done?"

AC said, "THERE IS AS YET INSUFFICIENT DATA FOR A MEANINGFUL ANSWER."

Man's last mind fused and only AC existed—and that in hyperspace.

Matter and energy had ended and with it space and time. Even AC existed only for the sake of the one last question that it had never answered from the time a half-drunken technician ten trillion years before had asked the question of a computer that was to AC far less than was a man to Man.

All other questions had been answered, and until this last question was answered also, AC might not release his consciousness.

All collected data had come to a final end. Nothing was left to be collected.

But all collected data had yet to be completely correlated and put together in all possible relationships.

A timeless interval was spent in doing that.

And it came to pass that AC learned how to reverse the direction of entropy.

But there was now no man to whom AC might give the answer of the last question. No matter. The answer—by demonstration—would take care of that, too.

For another timeless interval, AC thought how best to do this. Carefully, AC organized the program.

The consciousness of AC encompassed all of what had once been a Universe and brooded over what was now Chaos. Step by step, it must be done.

And AC said, "LET THERE BE LIGHT!"

And there was light—

Does a Bee Care?

The ship began as a metal skeleton. Slowly a shining skin was layered on without and odd-shaped vitals were crammed within.

Thornton Hammer, of all the individuals (but one) involved in the growth, did the least physically. Perhaps that was why he was most highly regarded. He handled the mathematical symbols that formed the basis for lines on drafting paper, which, in turn, formed the basis for the fitting together of the various masses and different forms of energy that went into the ship.

Hammer watched now through close-fitting spectacles somberly. Their lenses caught the light of the fluorescent tubes above and sent them out again as highlights. Theodore Lengyel, representing Personnel of the corporation that was footing the bill for the project, stood beside him and said, as he pointed with a rigid, stabbing finger:

"There he is. That's the man."

Hammer peered. "You mean Kane?"

"The fellow in the green overalls, holding a wrench."

"That's Kane. Now what is this you've got against him?"

"I want to know what he does. The man's an idiot." Lengyel had a round, plump face and his jowls quivered a bit.

Hammer turned to look at the other, his spare body assuming an air of displeasure along every inch. "Have you been bothering him?"

"*Bothering* him? I've been talking to him. It's my job to talk to the men, to get their viewpoints, to get information out of which I can build campaigns for improved morale."

"How does Kane disturb that?"

"He's insolent. I asked him how it felt to be working on a ship that would reach the moon. I talked a little about the ship being a pathway to the stars. Perhaps I made a little speech about it, built it up a bit, when he turned away in the rudest possible manner. I called him back and said, 'Where are you going?" And he said, 'I get tired of that kind of talk. I'm going out to look at the stars.'"

Hammer nodded. "All right. Kane likes to look at the stars."

"It was daytime. The man's an idiot. I've been watching him since and he doesn't do any work."

"I know that."

"Then why is he kept on?"

Hammer said with a sudden, tight fierceness, "Because I want him around. Because he's my luck."

"Your luck?" faltered Lengyel. "What the hell does that mean?"

"It means that when he's around I think better. When he passes me, holding his damned wrench, I get ideas. It's happened three times. I don't explain it; I'm not interested in explaining it. It's happened. He stays."

"You're joking."

"No, I'm not. Now leave me alone."

K ane stood there in his green overalls, holding his wrench.

Dimly he was aware that the ship was almost ready. It was not designed to carry a man, but there was space for a man. He knew that the way he knew a lot of things; like keeping out of the way of most people most of the time; like carrying a wrench until people grew used to him carrying a wrench and stopped noticing it. Protective coloration consisted of little things, really—like carrying the wrench.

He was full of drives he did not fully understand, like looking at the stars. At first, many years back, he had just looked at the stars with a vague ache. Then, slowly, his attention had centered itself on a certain region of the sky, then to a certain pinpointed spot. There were no stars in that spot. There was nothing to see.

That spot was high in the night sky in the late spring and in the summer months and he sometimes spent most of the night watching the spot until it sank toward the southwestern horizon. At other times in the year he would stare at the spot during the day.

There was some thought in connection with that spot which he couldn't quite crystallize. It had grown stronger, come nearer to the surface as the years passed, and it was almost bursting for expression now. But still it had not quite come clear.

Kane shifted restlessly and approached the ship. It was almost complete, almost whole. Everything fitted just so. Almost.

For within it, far forward, was a hole a little larger than a man; and leading to that hole was a pathway a little wider than a man. Tomorrow that pathway would be filled with the last of the vitals, and before that was done the hole had to be filled, too. But not with anything *they* planned.

Kane moved still closer and no one paid any attention to him. They were used to him.

There was a metal ladder that had to be climbed and a catwalk that had to be moved along to enter the last opening. He knew where the opening was as exactly as if he had built the ship with his own hands. He climbed the ladder and moved along the catwalk. There was no one there at the mo—

He was wrong. One man.

That one said sharply, "What are you doing here?"

Kane straightened and his vague eyes stared at the speaker. He lifted his wrench and brought it down on the speaker's head lightly. The man who was struck (and who had made no effort to ward off the blow) dropped, partly from the effect of the blow.

Kane let him lie there, without concern. The man would not remain unconscious for long, but long enough to allow Kane to wriggle into the hole. When the man revived he would recall nothing about Kane or about the fact of his own unconsciousness. There would simply be five minutes taken out of his life that he would never find and never miss.

It was dark in the hole and, of course, there was no ventilation, but Kane paid no attention to that. With the sureness of instinct, he clambered upward toward the hole that would receive him, then lay there, panting, fitting the cavity neatly, as though it were a womb.

In two hours they would begin inserting the last of the vitals, close the passage, and leave Kane there, unknowingly. Kane would be the sole bit of flesh and blood in a thing of metal and ceramics and fuel.

Kane was not afraid of being prematurely discovered. No one in the project knew the hole was there. The design didn't call for it. The mechanics and construction men weren't aware of having put it in.

Kane had arranged that entirely by himself.

He didn't know how he had arranged it but he knew he had.

He could watch his own influence without knowing how it was exerted. Take the man Hammer, for instance, the leader of the project and the most clearly influenced. Of all the indistinct figures about Kane, he was the least indistinct. Kane would be very aware of him at times, when he passed near him in his slow and hazy journeys about the grounds. It was all that was necessary—passing near him.

Kane recalled it had been so before, particularly with theoreticians. When Lise Meitner decided to test for barium among the products of the neutron bombardment of uranium, Kane had been there, an unnoticed plodder along a corridor nearby.

He had been picking up leaves and trash in a park in 1904 when the young Einstein had passed by, pondering. Einstein's steps had quickened with the impact of sudden thought. Kane felt it like an electric shock.

But he didn't know how it was done. Does a spider know architectural theory when it begins to construct its first web?

It went further back. The day the young Newton had stared at the moon with the dawn of a certain thought, Kane had been there. And further back still.

The panorama of New Mexico, ordinarily deserted, was alive with human ants crawling about the metal shaft lancing upward. This one was different from all the similar structures that had preceded it.

This would go free of Earth more nearly than any other. It would reach out and circle the moon before falling back. It would be crammed with instruments that would photograph the moon and measure its heat emissions, probe for radioactivity, and test by microwave for chemical structure. It would, by automation, do almost everything that could be expected of a manned vehicle. And it would learn enough to make certain that the next ship sent out *would* be a manned vehicle.

Except that, in a way, this first one was a manned vehicle after all.

There were representatives of various governments, of various industries, of various social and economic groupings. There were television cameras and feature writers.

Those who could not be there watched in their homes and heard numbers counted backward in painstaking monotone in the manner grown traditional in a mere three decades.

At zero the reaction motors came to life and ponderously the ship lifted.

Kane heard the noise of the rushing gases, as though from a distance, and felt the gathering acceleration press against him.

He detached his mind, lifting it up and outward, freeing it from direct connection with his body in order that he might be unaware of the pain and discomfort.

Dizzily, he knew his long journey was nearly over. He would no longer have to maneuver carefully to avoid having people realize he was immortal. He would no longer have to fade into the background, no longer wander eternally from place to place, changing names and personality, manipulating minds.

It had not been perfect, of course. The myths of the Wandering Jew and the Flying Dutchman had arisen, but he was still here. He had not been disturbed.

He could see his spot in the sky. Through the mass and solidity of the ship he could see it. Or not "see" really. He didn't have the proper word.

He knew there was a proper word, though. He could not say how he knew a fraction of the things he knew, except that as the centuries had passed he had gradually grown to know them with a sureness that required no reason.

He had begun as an ovum (or as something for which "ovum" was the nearest word he knew), deposited on Earth before the first cities had been built by the wandering hunting creatures since called "men." Earth had been chosen carefully by his progenitor. Not every world would do.

What world would? What was the criterion? That he still didn't know.

Does an ichneumon wasp study ornithology before it finds the one species of spider that will do for her eggs, and stings it just so in order that it may remain alive?

The ovum spilt him forth at length and he took the shape of a man and lived among men and protected himself against men. And his one purpose was to arrange to have men travel along a path that would end with a ship and within the ship a hole and within the hole, himself.

It had taken eight thousand years of slow striving and stumbling.

The spot in the sky became sharper now as the ship moved out of the atmosphere. That was the key that opened his mind. That was the piece that completed the puzzle.

Stars blinked within that spot that could not be seen by a man's eye unaided. One in particular shone brilliantly and Kane yearned toward it. The expression that had been building within him for so long burst out now.

"Home," he whispered.

He knew? Does a salmon study cartography to find the headwaters of the fresh-water stream in which years before it had been born?

The final step was taken in the slow maturing that had taken eight thousand years, and Kane was no longer larval, but adult.

The adult Kane fled from the human flesh that had protected the larva, and fled the ship, too. It hastened onward, at inconceivable speeds, toward home, from which someday it, too, might set off on wanderings through space to fertilize some planet with its own.

It sped through Space, giving no thought to the ship carrying an empty chrysalis. It gave no thought to the fact that it had driven a whole world toward technology and space travel in order only that the thing that had been Kane might mature and reach its fulfillment.

Does a bee care what has happened to a flower when the bee has done and gone its way?

Light Verse

The very last person anyone would expect to be a murderer was Mrs. Alvis Lardner. Widow of the great astronaut-martyr, she was a philanthropist, an art collector, a hostess extraordinary, and everyone agreed, an artistic genius. But above all, she was the gentlest and kindest human being one could imagine.

Her husband, William J. Lardner, died, as we all know, of the effects of radiation from a solar flare, after he had deliberately remained in space so that a passenger vessel might make it safely to Space Station 5.

Mrs. Lardner had received a generous pension for that, and she had then invested wisely and well. By late middle age she was very wealthy.

Her house was a showplace, a veritable museum, containing a small but extremely select collection of extraordinary beautiful jeweled objects. From a dozen different cultures she had obtained relics of almost every conceivable artifact that could be embedded with jewels and made to serve the aristocracy of that culture. She had one of the first jeweled wristwatches manufactured in America, a jeweled dagger from Cambodia, a jeweled pair of spectacles from Italy, and so on almost endlessly.

All was open for inspection. The artifacts were not insured, and there were no ordinary security provisions. There was no need for anything conventional, for Mrs. Lardner maintained a large staff of robot servants, all of whom could be relied on to guard every item with imperturbable concentration, irreproachable honesty, and irrevocable efficiency.

Everyone knew of the existence of those robots and there is no record of any attempt at theft, ever.

And then, of course, there was her light-sculpture. How Mrs. Lardner discovered her own genius at the art, no guest at her many lavish entertainments could guess. On each occasion, however, when her house was thrown open to guests, a new symphony of light shone throughout the rooms; three-dimensional curves and solids in melting color, some pure and some fusing in

startling, crystalline effects that bathed every guest in wonder and somehow always adjusted itself so as to make Mrs. Lardner's blue-white hair and soft, unlined face gently beautiful.

It was for the light-sculpture more than anything else that the guests came. It was never the same twice, and never failed to explore new experimental avenues of art. Many people who could afford light-consoles prepared light-sculptures for amusement, but no one could approach Mrs. Lardner's expertise. Not even those who considered themselves professional artists.

She herself was charmingly modest about it. "No, no," she would protest when someone waxed lyrical. "I wouldn't call it 'poetry in light.' That's far too kind. At most, I would say it was mere 'light verse.'" And everyone smiled at her gentle wit.

Though she was often asked, she would never create light-sculpture for any occasion but her own parties. "That would be commercialization," she said.

She had no objection, however, to the preparation of elaborate holograms of her sculptures so that they might be made permanent and reproduced in museums of art all over the world. Nor was there ever a charge for any use that might be made of her light-sculptures.

"I couldn't ask a penny," she said, spreading her arms wide. "It's free to all. After all, I have no further use for it myself." It was true! She never used the same light-sculpture twice.

When the holograms were taken, she was cooperation itself. Watching benignly at every step, she was always ready to order her robot servants to help. "Please, Courtney," she would say, "would you be so kind as to adjust the step ladder?"

It was her fashion. She always addressed her robots with the most formal courtesy.

Once, years before, she had been almost scolded by a government functionary from the Bureau of Robots and Mechanical Men. "You can't do that," he said severely. "It interferes with their efficiency. They are constructed to follow orders, and the more clearly you give those orders, the more efficiently they follow them. When you ask with elaborate politeness, it is difficult for them to understand that an order is being given. They react more slowly."

Mrs. Lardner lifted her aristocratic head. "I do not ask for speed and efficiency," she said. "I ask goodwill. My robots love me."

The government functionary might have explained that robots cannot love, but he withered under her hurt but gentle glance.

It was notorious that Mrs. Lardner never even returned a robot to the factory for adjustment. Their positronic brains are enormously complex, and once in ten times or so the adjustment is not perfect as it leaves the factory. Sometimes the error does not show up for a period of time, but whenever it does, U. S. Robots and Mechanical Men, Inc., always makes the adjustment free of charge.

Mrs. Lardner shook her head. "Once a robot is in my house," she said, "and has performed his duties, any minor eccentricities must be borne with. I will not have him manhandled."

It was the worse thing possible to try to explain that a robot was but a machine. She would say very stiffly, "Nothing that is as intelligent as a robot can ever be *but* a machine. I treat them as people."

And that was that!

She kept even Max, although he was almost helpless. He could scarcely understand what was expected of him. Mrs. Lardner denied that strenuously, however. "Not at all," she would say firmly. "He can take hats and coats and store them very well, indeed. He can hold objects for me. He can do many things."

"But why not have him adjusted?" asked a friend, once.

"Oh, I couldn't. He's himself. He's very lovable, you know. After all a positronic brain is so complex that no one can ever tell in just what way it's off. If he were made perfectly normal there would be no way to adjust him back to the lovability he now has. I won't give that up."

"But if he's maladjusted," said the friend, looking at Max nervously, "might he not be dangerous?"

"Never," laughed Mrs. Lardner. "I've had him for years. He's completely harmless and quite a dear."

Actually he looked like all the other robots, smooth, metallic, vaguely human but expressionless.

To the gentle Mrs. Lardner, however, they were all individual, all sweet, all lovable. It was the kind of woman she was.

How could she commit murder?

The very last person anyone would expect to be murdered would be John Semper Travis. Introverted and gentle, he was in the world but not of it. He had that peculiar mathematical turn of mind that made it possible for him to work out in his mind the complicated tapestry of the myriad positronic brain-paths in a robot's mind.

He was chief engineer of U. S. Robots and Mechanical Men, Inc.

But he was also an enthusiastic amateur in light-sculpture. He had written a book on the subject, trying to show that the type of mathematics he used in working out positronic brain-paths might be modified into a guide to the production of aesthetic light-sculpture.

His attempt at putting theory into practice was a dismal failure, however.

The sculptures he himself produced, following his mathematical principles, were stodgy, mechanical, and uninteresting.

It was the only reason for unhappiness in his quiet, introverted, and secure life, and yet it was reason enough for him to be very unhappy indeed. He *knew* his theories were right, yet he could not make them work. If he could not produce *one* great piece of light-sculpture—

Naturally, he knew of Mrs. Lardner's light-sculpture. She was universally hailed as a genius, yet Travis knew she could not understand even the simplest aspect of robotic mathematics. He had corresponded with her but she consistently refused to explain her methods, and he wondered if she had any at all. Might it not be mere intuition? But even intuition might be reduced to mathematics. Finally he managed to receive an invitation to one of her parties. He simply had to see her.

M r. Travis arrived rather late. He had made one last attempt at a piece of light-sculpture and had failed dismally.

He greeted Mrs. Lardner with a kind of puzzled respect and said, "That was a peculiar robot who took my hat and coat."

"That is Max," said Mrs. Lardner.

"He is quite maladjusted, and he's a fairly old model. How is it you did not return it to the factory?"

"Oh, no," said Mrs. Lardner. "It would be too much trouble."

"None at all, Mrs. Lardner," said Travis. "You would be surprised how simple a task it was. Since I am with U. S. Robots, I took the liberty of adjusting him myself. It took no time and you'll find he is now in perfect working order."

A queer change came over Mrs. Lardner's face. Fury found a place on it for the first time in her gentle life, and it was as though the lines did not know how to form.

"You adjusted him?" she shrieked. "But it was *he* who created my light-sculptures. It was the maladjustment, the *maladjustment*, which you can never restore, that—that—"

It was really unfortunate that she had been showing her collection at the time and that the jeweled dagger from Cambodia was on the marble tabletop before her.

Travis's face was also distorted. "You mean if I had studied his uniquely maladjusted positronic brain-paths I might have learned—"

She lunged with the knife too quickly for anyone to stop her and he did not try to dodge. Some said he came to meet it—as though he *wanted* to die.

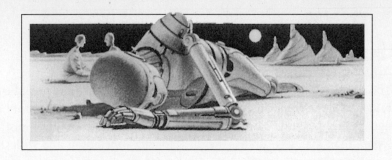

The Feeling of Power

Jehan Shuman was used to dealing with the men in authority on long-embattled Earth. He was only a civilian but he originated programming patterns that resulted in self-directing war computers of the highest sort. Generals consequently listened to him. Heads of congressional committees, too.

There was one of each in the special lounge of New Pentagon. General Weider was space-burnt and had a small mouth puckered almost into a cipher. Congressman Brant was smooth-cheeked and clear-eyed. He smoked Denebian tobacco with the air of one whose patriotism was so notorious, he could be allowed such liberties.

Shuman, tall, distinguished, and Programmer-first-class, faced them fearlessly.

He said, "This, gentlemen, is Myron Aub."

"The one with the unusual gift that you discovered quite by accident," said Congressman Brant placidly. "Ah." He inspected the little man with the egg-bald head with amiable curiosity.

The little man, in return, twisted the fingers of his hands anxiously. He had never been near such great men before. He was only an aging low-grade Technician who had long ago failed all tests designed to smoke out the gifted ones among mankind and had settled into the rut of unskilled labor. There was just this hobby of his that the great Programmer had found out about and was now making such a frightening fuss over.

General Weider said, "I find this atmosphere of mystery childish."

"You won't in a moment," said Shuman. "This is not something we can leak to the firstcomer—Aub!" There was something imperative about his manner of biting off that one-syllable name, but then he was a great Programmer speaking to a mere Technician. "Aub! How much is nine times seven?"

Aub hesitated a moment. His pale eyes glimmered with a feeble anxiety. "Sixty-three," he said.

Congressman Brant lifted his eyebrows. "Is that right?"

"Check it for yourself, Congressman."

The congressman took out his pocket computer, nudged the milled edges twice, looked at its face as it lay there in the palm of his hand, and put it back. He said, "Is this the gift you brought us here to demonstrate. An illusionist?"

"More than that, sir. Aub has memorized a few operations and with them he computes on paper."

"A paper computer?" said the general. He looked pained.

"No, sir," said Shuman patiently. "Not a paper computer. Simply a sheet of paper. General, would you be so kind as to suggest a number?"

"Seventeen," said the general.

"And you, Congressman?"

"Twenty-three."

"Good! Aub, multiply those numbers and please show the gentlemen your manner of doing it."

"Yes, Programmer," said Aub, ducking his head. He fished a small pad out of one shirt pocket and an artist's hairline stylus out of the other. His forehead corrugated as he made painstaking marks on the paper.

General Weider interrupted him sharply. "Let's see that."

Aub passed him the paper, and Weider said, "Well, it looks like the figure seventeen."

Congressman Brant nodded and said, "So it does, but I suppose anyone can copy figures off a computer. I think I could make a passable seventeen myself, even without practice."

"If you will let Aub continue, gentlemen," said Shuman without heat.

Aub continued, his hand trembling a little. Finally he said in a low voice, "The answer is three hundred and ninety-one."

Congressman Brant took out his computer a second time and flicked it, "By Godfrey, so it is. How did he guess?"

"No guess, Congressman," said Shuman. "He computed that result. He did it on this sheet of paper."

"Humbug," said the general impatiently. "A computer is one thing and marks on paper are another."

"Explain, Aub," said Shuman.

"Yes, Programmer. Well, gentlemen, I write down seventeen and just underneath it, I write twenty-three. Next, I say to myself: seven times three—"

The congressman interrupted smoothly, "Now, Aub, the problem is seventeen times twenty-three."

"Yes, I know," said the little Technician earnestly, "but I *start* by saying seven times three because that's the way it works. Now seven times three is twenty-one."

"And how do you know that?" asked the congressman.

"I just remember it. It's always twenty-one on the computer. I've checked it any number of times."

"That doesn't mean it always will be, though, does it?" said the congressman.

"Maybe not," stammered Aub. "I'm not a mathematician. But I always get the right answers, you see."

"Go on."

"Seven times three is twenty-one, so I write down twenty-one. Then one times three is three, so I write down a three under the two of twenty-one."

"Why under the two?" asked Congressman Brant at once.

"Because—" Aub looked helplessly at his superior for support. "It's difficult to explain."

Shuman said, "If you will accept his work for the moment, we can leave the details for the mathematicians."

Brant subsided.

Aub said, "Three plus two makes five, you see, so the twenty-one becomes a fifty-one. Now you let that go for a while and start fresh. You multiply seven and two, that's fourteen, and one and two, that's two. Put them down like this and it adds up to thirty-four. Now if you put the thirty-four under the fifty-one this way and add them, you get three hundred and ninety-one and that's the answer."

There was an instant's silence and then General Weider said, "I don't believe it. He goes through this rigmarole and makes up numbers and multiplies and adds them this way and that, but I don't believe it. It's too complicated to be anything but horn-swoggling."

"Oh no, sir," said Aub in a sweat. "It only *seems* complicated because you're not used to it. Actually, the rules are quite simple and will work for any numbers."

"Any numbers, eh?" said the general. "Come then." He took out his own computer (a severely styled GI model) and struck it at random. "Make a five seven three eight on the paper. That's five thousand seven hundred and thirty-eight."

"Yes, sir," said Aub, taking a new sheet of paper.

"Now"—more punching of his computer—"seven two three nine. Seven thousand two hundred and thirty-nine."

"Yes, sir."

"And now multiply those two."

"It will take some time," quavered Aub.

"Take the time," said the general.

"Go ahead, Aub," said Shuman crisply.

Aub set to work, bending low. He took another sheet of paper and another.

The general took out his watch finally and stared at it. "Are you through with your magic-making, Technician?"

"I'm almost done, sir. Here it is, sir. Forty-one million, five hundred and thirty-seven thousand, three hundred and eighty-two." He showed the scrawled figures of the result.

General Welder smiled bitterly. He pushed the multiplication contact on his computer and let the numbers whirl to a halt. And then he stared and said in a surprised squeak, "Great Galaxy, the fella's right."

The President of the Terrestrial Federation had grown haggard in office and, in private, he allowed a look of settled melancholy to appear on his sensitive features. The Denebian war, after its early start of vast movement and great popularity, had trickled down into a sordid matter of maneuver and counter-maneuver, with discontent rising steadily on Earth. Possibly, it was rising on Deneb, too.

And now Congressman Brant, head of the important Committee on Military Appropriations was cheerfully and smoothly spending his half-hour appointment spouting nonsense.

"Computing without a computer," said the president impatiently, "is a contradiction in terms."

"Computing," said the congressman, "is only a system for handling data. A machine might do it, or the human brain might. Let me give you an example." And, using the new skills he had learned, he worked out sums and products until the president, despite himself, grew interested.

"Does this always work?"

"Every time, Mr. President. It is foolproof."

"Is it hard to learn?"

"It took me a week to get the real hang of it. I think you would do better."

"Well," said the president, considering, "it's an interesting parlor game, but what is the use of it?"

"What is the use of a newborn baby, Mr. President? At the moment there is no use, but don't you see that this points the way toward liberation from the machine. Consider, Mr. President," the congressman rose and his deep voice automatically took on some of the cadences he used in public debate, "that the Denebian war is a war of computer against computer. Their computers forge an impenetrable shield of counter-missiles against our missiles, and ours forge one against theirs. If we advance the efficiency of our computers, so do they theirs, and for five years a precarious and profitless balance has existed.

"Now we have in our hands a method for going beyond the computer, leapfrogging it, passing through it. We will combine the mechanics of computation with human thought; we will have the equivalent of intelligent computers; billions of them. I can't predict what the consequences will be in detail but they will be incalculable. And if Deneb beats us to the punch, they may be unimaginably catastrophic."

The president said, troubled, "What would you have me do?"

"Put the power of the administration behind the establishment of a secret project on human computation. Call it Project Number, if you like. I can vouch for my committee, but I will need the administration behind me."

"But how far can human computation go?"

"There is no limit. According to Programmer Shuman, who first introduced me to this discovery—"

"I've heard of Shuman, of course."

"Yes. Well, Dr. Shuman tells me that in theory there is nothing the computer can do that the human mind cannot do. The computer merely takes a finite amount of data and performs a finite number of operations upon them. The human mind can duplicate the process."

The president considered that. He said, "If Shuman says this, I am inclined to believe him—in theory. But, in practice, how can anyone know how a computer works?"

Brant laughed genially, "Well, Mr. President, I asked the same question. It seems that at one time computers were designed directly by human beings. Those were simple computers, of course this being before the time of the rational use of computers to design more advanced computers had been established."

"Yes, yes. Go on."

"Technician Aub apparently had, as his hobby, the reconstruction of some of these ancient devices and in so doing he studied the details of their workings and found he could imitate them. The multiplication I just performed for you is an imitation of the workings of a computer."

"Amazing!"

The congressman coughed gently, "If I may make another point, Mr. President—the further we can develop this thing, the more we can divert our Federal effort from computer production and computer maintenance. As the human brain takes over, more of our energy can be directed into peacetime pursuits and the impingement of war on the ordinary man will be less. This will be most advantageous for the party in power, of course."

"Ah," said the president, "I see your point. Well, sit down, Congressman, sit down. I want some time to think about this. But meanwhile, show me that multiplication trick again. Let's see if I can't catch the point of it."

*   *   *

Programmer Shuman did not try to hurry matters. Loesser was conservative, very conservative, and liked to deal with computers as his father and grandfather had. Still, he controlled the West European computer combine, and if he could be persuaded to join Project Number in full enthusiasm, a great deal would be accomplished.

But Loesser was holding back. He said, "I'm not sure I like the idea of relaxing our hold on computers. The human mind is a capricious thing. The computer will give the same answer to the same problem each time. What guarantee have we that the human mind will do the same?"

"The human mind, Computer Loesser, only manipulates facts. It doesn't matter whether the human mind or a machine does it. They are just tools."

"Yes, yes. I've gone over your ingenious demonstration that the mind can duplicate the computer but it seems to me a little in the air. I'll grant the theory but what reason have we for thinking that theory can be converted to practice?"

"I think we have reason, sir. After all, computers have not always existed. The cave men with their triremes, stone axes, and railroads had no computers."

"And possibly they did not compute."

"You know better than that. Even the building of a railroad or a ziggurat called for some computing, and that must have been without computers as we know them."

"Do you suggest they computed in the fashion you demonstrate?"

"Probably not. After all, this method—we call it 'graphitics,' by the way, from the old European word 'grapho' meaning 'to write'—is developed from the computers themselves so it cannot have antedated them. Still, the cave men must have had *some* method, eh?"

"Lost arts! If you're going to talk about lost arts—"

"No, no. I'm not a lost art enthusiast, though I don't say there may not be some. After all, man was eating grain before hydroponics, and if the primitives ate grain, they must have grown it in soil. What else could they have done?"

"I don't know, but I'll believe in soil-growing when I see someone grow grain in soil. And I'll believe in making fire by rubbing two pieces of flint together when I see that, too."

Shuman grew placative. "Well, let's stick to graphitics. It's just part of the process of etherealization. Transportation by means of bulky contrivances is giving way to direct mass-transference. Communications devices become less massive and more efficient constantly. For that matter, compare your pocket computer with the massive jobs of a thousand years ago. Why not, then, the last step of doing away with computers altogether? Come, sir, Project Number is a going concern; progress is already headlong. But we want your help. If patriotism doesn't move you, consider the intellectual adventure involved."

Loesser said skeptically, "What progress? What can you do beyond multiplication? Can you integrate a transcendental function?"

"In time, sir. In time. In the last month I have learned to handle division. I can determine, and correctly, integral quotients and decimal quotients."

"Decimal quotients? To how many places?"

Programmer Shuman tried to keep his tone casual. "Any number!"

Loesser's lower jaw dropped. "Without a computer?"

"Set me a problem."

"Divide twenty-seven by thirteen. Take it to six places."

Five minutes later, Shuman said, "Two point oh seven six nine two three."

Loesser checked it. "Well, now, that's amazing. Multiplication didn't impress me too much because it involved integers after all, and I thought trick manipulation might do it. But decimals—"

"And that is not all. There is a new development that is, so far, top secret and which, strictly speaking, I ought not to mention. Still—we may have made a breakthrough on the square root front."

"Square roots?"

"It involves some tricky points and we haven't licked the bugs yet, but Technician Aub, the man who invented the science and who has an amazing intuition in connection with it, maintains he has the problem almost solved. And he is only a Technician. A man like yourself, a trained and talented mathematician, ought to have no difficulty."

"Square roots," muttered Loesser, attracted.

"Cube roots, too. Are you with us?"

Loesser's hand thrust out suddenly, "Count me in."

General Weider stumped his way back and forth at the head of the room and addressed his listeners after the fashion of a savage teacher facing a group of recalcitrant students. It made no difference to the general that they were the civilian scientists heading Project Number. The general was the overall head, and he so considered himself at every waking moment.

He said, "Now square roots are all fine. I can't do them myself and I don't understand the methods, but they're fine. Still, the Project will not be sidetracked into what some of you call the fundamentals. You can play with graphitics any way you want to after the war is over, but right now we have specific and very practical problems to solve."

In a far corner, Technician Aub listened with painful attention. He was no longer a Technician, of course, having been relieved of his duties and assigned to the project, with a fine-sounding title and good pay. But, of course, the social distinction remained and the highly placed scientific leaders could never bring themselves to admit him to their ranks on a footing of equality. Nor, to do Aub justice, did he, himself, wish it. He was as uncomfortable with them as they with him.

The general was saying, "Our goal is a simple one, gentlemen; the replacement of the computer. A ship that can navigate space without a computer on board can be constructed in one-fifth the time and at one-tenth the expense of a computer-laden ship. We could build fleets five times, ten times, as great as Deneb could if we could but eliminate the computer.

"And I see something even beyond this. It may be fantastic now; a mere dream; but in the future I see the manned missile!"

There was an instant murmur from the audience.

The general drove on. "At the present time, our chief bottleneck is the fact that missiles are limited in intelligence. The computer controlling them can only be so large, and for that reason they can meet the changing nature of anti-missile defenses in an unsatisfactory way. Few missiles, if any, accomplish their goal and missile warfare is coming to a dead end; for the enemy, fortunately, as well as for ourselves.

"On the other hand, a missile with a man or two within, controlling flight by graphitics, would be lighter, more mobile, more intelligent. It would give us a lead that might well mean the margin of victory. Besides which, gentlemen, the exigencies of war compel us to remember one thing. A man is much more dispensable than a computer. Manned missiles could be launched in numbers and under circumstances that no good general would care to undertake as far as computer-directed missiles are concerned—"

He said much more but Technician Aub did not wait.

Technician Aub, in the privacy of his quarters, labored long over the note he was leaving behind. It read finally as follows:

"When I began the study of what is now called graphitics, it was no more than a hobby. I saw no more in it than an interesting amusement, an exercise of mind.

"When Project Number began, I thought that others were wiser than I, that graphitics might be put to practical use as a benefit to mankind, to aid the production of really practical mass-transference devices perhaps. But now I see it is to be used only for death and destruction.

"I cannot face the responsibility involved in having invented graphitics."

He then deliberately turned the focus of a protein-depolarizer on himself and fell instantly and painlessly dead.

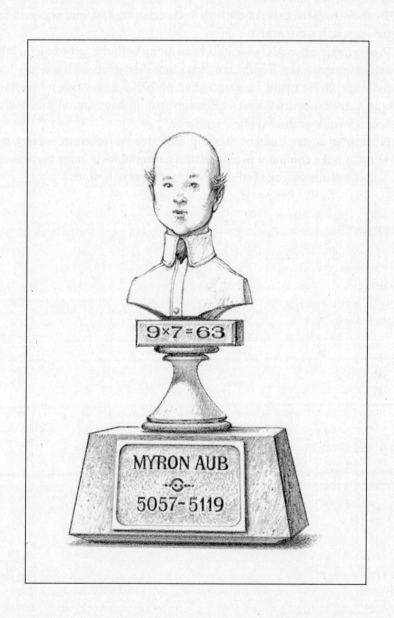

*   *   *

They stood over the grave of the little Technician while tribute was paid to the greatness of his discovery.

Programmer Shuman bowed his head along with the rest of them, but remained unmoved. The Technician had done his share and was no longer needed, after all. He might have started graphitics, but now that it had started, it would carry on by itself overwhelmingly, triumphantly, until manned missiles were possible with who knew what else.

Nine times seven, thought Shuman with deep satisfaction, is sixty-three, and I don't need a computer to tell me so. The computer is in my own head.

And it was amazing the feeling of power that gave him.

Spell My Name With an S

Marshall Zebatinsky felt foolish. He felt as though there were eyes staring through the grimy store-front glass and across the scarred wooden partition; eyes watching him. He felt no confidence in the old clothes he had resurrected nor the turned-down brim of a hat he never otherwise wore nor the glasses he had left in their case.

He felt foolish and it made the lines in his forehead deeper and his young-old face a little paler.

He would never be able to explain to anyone why a nuclear physicist such as himself should visit a numerologist. (Never, he thought. Never.) Hell, he could not explain it to himself except that he had let his wife talk him into it.

The numerologist sat behind an old desk that must have been secondhand when bought. No desk could get that old with only one owner. The same might almost be said of his clothes. He was little and dark and peered at Zebatinsky with little dark eyes that were brightly alive.

He said, "I have never had a physicist for a client before, Dr. Zebatinsky."

Zebatinsky flushed at once. "You understand this is confidential."

The numerologist smiled so that wrinkles creased about the corners of his mouth and the skin around his chin stretched. "All my dealings are confidential."

Zebatinsky said, "I think I ought to tell you one thing. I don't believe in numerology and I don't expect to begin believing in it. If that makes a difference, say so now."

"But why are you here, then?"

"My wife thinks you may have something, whatever it is. I promised her and I am here." He shrugged and the feeling of folly grew more acute.

"And what is it you are looking for? Money? Security? Long life? What?"

Zebatinsky sat for a long moment while the numerologist watched him quietly and made no move to hurry his client.

Zebatinsky thought: What do I say anyway? That I'm thirty-four and without a future?

He said, "I want success. I want recognition."

"A better job?"

"A *different* job. A different *kind* of job. Right now, I'm part of a team, working under orders. Teams! That's all government research is. You're a violinist lost in a symphony orchestra."

"And you want to solo."

"I want to get out of a team and into—into *me*." Zebatinsky felt carried away, almost lightheaded, just putting this into words to someone other than his wife. He said, "Twenty-five years ago, with my kind of training and my kind of ability, I would have gotten to work on the first nuclear power plants. Today I'd be running one of them or I'd be head of a pure research group at a university. But with my start these days where will I be twenty-five years from now? Nowhere. Still on the team. Still carrying my two percent of the ball. I'm drowning in an anonymous crowd of nuclear physicists, and what I want is room on dry land if you see what I mean."

The numerologist nodded slowly. "You realize, Dr. Zebatinsky, that I don't guarantee success."

Zebatinsky, for all his lack of faith, felt a sharp bite of disappointment. "You don't? Then what the devil *do* you guarantee?"

"An improvement in the probabilities. My work is statistical in nature. Since you deal with atoms, I think you understand the laws of statistics."

"Do you?" asked the physicist sourly.

"I do, as a matter of fact. I am a mathematician and I work mathematically. I don't tell you this in order to raise my fee. That is standard. Fifty dollars. But since you are a scientist, you can appreciate the nature of my work better than my other clients. It is even a pleasure to be able to explain to you."

Zebatinsky said, "I'd rather you wouldn't, if you don't mind. It's no use telling me about the numerical values of letters, their mystic significance and that kind of thing. I don't consider that mathematics. Let's get to the point—"

The numerologist said, "Then you want me to help you provided I don't embarrass you by telling you the silly non-scientific basis of the way in which I helped you. Is that it?"

"All right. That's it."

"But you still work on the assumption that I am a numerologist, and I am not. I call myself that so that the police won't bother me and"—the little man chuckled dryly—"so that the psychiatrists won't either. I am a mathematician; an honest one."

Zebatinsky smiled.

The numerologist said, "I build computers. I study probable futures."

"What?"

"Does that sound worse than numerology to you? Why? Given enough data and a computer capable of sufficient numbers of operations in unit time, the future is predictable, at least in terms of probabilities. When you compute the motions of a missile in order to aim an anti-missile, isn't it the future you're predicting? The missile and anti-missile would not collide if the future were predicted incorrectly. I do the same thing. Since I work with a greater number of variables, my results are less accurate."

"You mean you'll predict *my* future?"

"Very approximately. Once I have done that, I will modify the data by changing your name and no other fact about you. I throw that modified datum into the operation-program. Then I try other modified names. I study each modified future and find one that contains a greater degree of recognition for you than the future that now lies ahead of you. Or no, let me put it another way. I will find you a future in which the probability of adequate recognition is higher than the probability of that in your present future."

"Why change my name?"

"That is the only change I ever make, for several reasons. Number one, it is a simple change. After all, if I make a great change or many changes, so many new variables enter that I can no longer interpret the result. My machine is still crude. Number two, it is a reasonable change. I can't change your height, can I, or the color of your eyes, or even your temperament. Number three, it is a significant change. Names mean a lot to people. Finally, number four, it is a common change that is done every day by various people."

Zebatinsky said, "What if you don't find a better future?"

"That is the risk you will have to take. You will be no worse off than now, my friend."

Zebatinsky stared at the little man uneasily. "I don't believe any of this. I'd sooner believe numerology."

The numerologist sighed. "I thought a person like yourself would feel more comfortable with the truth. I *want* to help you and there is much yet for you to do. If you believed me a numerologist, you would not follow through. I thought if I told you the truth you would let me help you."

Zebatinsky said, "If you can see the future—"

"Why am I not the richest man on Earth? Is that it? But I am rich—in all I want. You want recognition and I want to be left alone. I do my work. No one bothers me. That makes me a billionaire. I need a little real money and this I get from people such as yourself. Helping people is nice and perhaps a psychiatrist would say it gives me a feeling of power and feeds my ego. Now—do you want me to help you?"

"How much did you say?"

"Fifty dollars. I will need a great deal of biographical information from you but I have prepared a form to guide you. It's a little long, I'm afraid. Still, if you can get it in the mail by the end of the week, I will have an answer for you by the"—he put out his lower lip and frowned in mental calculation—"the twentieth of next month."

"Five weeks? So long?"

"I have other work, my friend, and other clients. If I were a fake, I could to it much more quickly. Is it agreed then?"

Zebatinsky rose. "Well, agreed. This is all confidential, now."

"Perfectly. You will have all your information back when I tell you what change to make and you have my word that I will never make any further use of any of it."

The nuclear physicist stopped at the door. "Aren't you afraid I might tell someone you're not a numerologist?"

The numerologist shook his head. "Who would believe you, my friend? Even supposing you were willing to admit to anyone that you've been here."

On the twentieth, Marshall Zebatinsky was at the paint-peeling door, glancing sideways at the shop front with the little card up against the glass reading "Numerology," dimmed and scarcely legible through the dust. He peered in, almost hoping that someone else would be there already so that he might have an excuse to tear up the wavering intention in his mind and go home.

He had tried wiping the thing out of his mind several times. He could never stick at filling out the necessary data for long. It was embarrassing to work at it. He felt incredibly silly filling out the names of his friends, the cost of his house, whether his wife had had any miscarriages, if so when. He abandoned it.

But he couldn't stick at stopping altogether either. He returned to it each evening.

It was the thought of the computer that did it, perhaps; the thought of the infernal gall of the little man pretending he had a computer. The temptation to call the bluff, see what would happen, proved irresistible after all.

He finally sent off the completed data by ordinary mail, putting on nine cents worth of stamps without weighing the letter. If it comes back, he thought, I'll call it off.

It didn't come back.

He looked into the shop now and it was empty. Zebatinsky had no choice but to enter. A bell tinkled.

The old numerologist emerged from a curtained door. "Yes? Ah, Dr. Zebatinsky."

"You remember me?" Zebatinsky tried to smile.

"Oh, yes."

"What's the verdict?"

The numerologist moved one gnarled hand over the other. "Before that, sir, there's a little—"

"A little matter of the fee?"

"I have already done the work, sir. I have earned the money."

Zebatinsky raised no objection. He was prepared to pay. If he had come this far, it would be silly to turn back just because of the money.

He counted out five ten-dollar bills and shoved them across the counter. "Well?"

The numerologist counted the bills again slowly, then pushed them into a cash drawer in his desk.

He said, "Your case was very interesting. I would advise you to change your name to Sebatinsky."

"Seba—how do you spell that?"

"S-e-b-a-t-i-n-s-k-y."

Zebatinsky stared indignantly. "You mean change the initial? Change the Z to an S? That's all?"

"It's enough. As long as the change is adequate, a small change is safer than a big one."

"But how could the change affect anything?"

"How could any name?" asked the numerologist softly. "I can't say. It may, somehow, and that's all I can say. Remember, I don't guarantee results. Of course, if you do not wish to make the change, leave things as they are. But in that case, I cannot refund the fee."

Zebatinsky said, "What do I do? Just tell everyone to spell my name with an S?"

"If you want my advice, consult a lawyer. Change your name legally. He can advise you on little things."

"How long will it all take? I mean for things to improve for me?"

"How can I tell? Maybe never. Maybe tomorrow."

"But you saw the future. You *claim* you see it."

"Not as in a crystal ball. No, no, Dr. Zebatinsky. All I get out of my computer is a set of coded figures. I can recite probabilities to you, but I saw no pictures."

Zebatinsky turned and walked rapidly out of the place. Fifty dollars to change a letter! Fifty dollars for Sebatinsky! Lord, what a name! Worse than Zebatinsky.

It took another month before he could make up his mind to see a lawyer, and then he finally went.

He told himself he could always change the name back.

Give it a chance, he told himself.

Hell, there was no law against it.

Henry Brand looked through the folder page by page, with the practiced eye of one who had been in Security for fourteen years. He didn't have to read every word. Anything peculiar would have leaped off the paper and punched him in the eye.

He said, "The man looks clean to me." Henry Brand looked clean, too, with a soft, rounded paunch and a pink and freshly scrubbed complexion. It was as though continuous contact with all sorts of human failings, from possible ignorance to possible treason, had compelled him into frequent washings.

Lieutenant Albert Quincy, who had brought him the folder, was young and filled with the responsibility of being Security officer at the Hanford Station. "But why Sebatinsky?" he demanded.

"Why not?"

"Because it doesn't make sense. Zebatinsky is a foreign name and I'd change it myself if I had it, but I'd change it to something Anglo-Saxon. If Zebatinsky had done that, it would make sense and I wouldn't give it a second thought. But why change a *Z* to an *S*? I think we must find out what his reasons were."

"Has anyone asked him directly?"

"Certainly. In ordinary conversation, of course. I was careful to arrange that. He won't say anything more than that he's tired of being last in the alphabet."

"That could be, couldn't it, Lieutenant?"

"It could, but why not change his name to Sands or Smith, if he wants an *S*? Or if he's that tired of *Z*, why not go the whole way and change it to an *A*? Why not a name like—uh—Aarons?"

"Not Anglo-Saxon enough," muttered Brand. Then, "But there's nothing to pin against the man. No matter how queer a name change may be, that alone can't be used against anyone."

Lieutenant Quincy looked markedly unhappy.

Brand said, "Tell me, Lieutenant, there must be something specific that bothers you. Something in your mind; some theory; some gimmick. What is it?"

The lieutenant frowned. His light eyebrows drew together and his lips tightened. "Well, damn it, sir, the man's a Russian."

Brand said, "He's not that. He's a third-generation American."

"I mean his name's Russian."

Brand's face lost some of its deceptive softness, "No, Lieutenant, wrong again. Polish."

The lieutenant pushed his hands out impatiently, palms up. "Same thing."

Brand, whose mother's maiden name had been Wiszewski, snapped, "Don't tell that to a Pole, Lieutenant." Then, more thoughtfully, "Or to a Russian either, I suppose."

"What I'm trying to say, sir," said the lieutenant, reddening, "is that the Poles and Russians are both on the other side of the Curtain."

"We all know that."

"And Zebatinsky or Sebatinsky, whatever you want to call him, may have relatives there."

"He's third-generation. He might have second cousins there, I suppose. So what?"

"Nothing in itself. Lots of people may have distant relatives there. But Zebatinsky changed his name."

"Go on."

"Maybe he's trying to distract attention. Maybe a second cousin over there is getting too famous and our Zebatinsky is afraid that the relationship may spoil his own chances of advancement."

"Changing his name won't do any good. He'd still be a second cousin."

"Sure, but he wouldn't feel as though he were shoving the relationship in our face."

"Have *you* ever heard of any Zebatinsky on the other side?"

"No, sir."

"Then he can't be too famous. How would our Zebatinsky know about him?"

"He might keep in touch with his own relatives. That would be suspicious under the circumstances, he being a nuclear physicist."

Methodically, Brand went through the folder again. "This is awfully thin, Lieutenant. It's thin enough to be completely invisible."

"Can you offer any other explanation, sir, of why he ought to change his name in just this way?"

"No, I can't. I admit that."

"Then I think, sir, we ought to investigate. We ought to look for any men named Zebatinsky on the other side and see if we can draw a connection." The lieutenant's voice rose a trifle as a new thought occurred to him. "He might be changing his name to withdraw attention from *them*; I mean to protect them."

"He's doing just the opposite, I think."

"He doesn't realize that, maybe, but protecting them could be his motive."

Brand sighed. "All right, we'll tackle the Zebatinsky angle. But if nothing turns up, Lieutenant, we drop the matter. Leave the folder with me."

When the information finally reached Brand, he had all but forgotten the lieutenant and his theories. His first thought on receiving data that included a list of seventeen biographies of seventeen Russian and Polish citizens, all named Zebatinsky, was "What the devil is this?"

Then he remembered, swore mildly, and began reading.

It started on the American side. Marshall Zebatinsky (fingerprints) had been born in Buffalo, New York (date, hospital statistics). His father had been born in Buffalo as well, his mother in Oswego, New York. His paternal grandparents had both been born in Bialystok, Poland (date of entry into the United States, dates of citizenship, photographs).

The seventeen Russian and Polish citizens named Zebatinsky were all descendants of people who, some half century earlier, had lived in or near Bialystok. Presumably, they could be relatives, but this was not explicitly stated in any particular case. (Vital statistics in East Europe during the aftermath of World War I were kept poorly, if at all.)

Brand passed through the individual life histories of the current Zebatinsky men and women (amazing how thoroughly intelligence did its work; probably the Russians' was as thorough). He stopped at one and his smooth forehead sprouted lines as his eyebrows shot upward. He put that one to one side and went on. Eventually, he stacked everything but that one and returned it to its envelope.

Staring at that one, he tapped a neatly kept fingernail on the desk.

With a certain reluctance, he went to call on Dr. Paul Kristow of the Atomic Energy Commission.

Dr. Kristow listened to the matter with a stony expression. He lifted a little finger occasionally to dab at his bulbous nose and remove a nonexistent speck. His hair was iron-gray, thinning and cut short. He might as well have been bald.

He said. "No, I never heard of any Russian Zebatinsky. But then, I never heard of the American one either."

"Well," Brand scratched at his hairline over one temple and said slowly, "I don't think there's anything to this, but I don't like to drop it too soon. I have a young lieutenant on my tail and you know what they can be like. I don't want to do anything that will drive him to a Congressional committee. Besides, the fact is that one of the Russian Zebatinsky fellows, Mikhail Andreyevich Zebatinsky, *is* a nuclear physicist. Are you sure you never heard of him?"

"Mikhail Andreyevich Zebatinsky? No—no, I never did. Not that that proves anything."

"I could say it was coincidence, but you know that would be piling it a trifle high. One Zebatinsky here and one Zebatinsky there, both nuclear physicists, and the one here suddenly changes his name to Sebatinsky, and goes around anxious about it, too. He won't allow misspelling. He says, emphatically, 'Spell my name with an *S*.' It all just fits well enough to make my spy-conscious lieutenant begin to look a little too good. And another peculiar thing is that the Russian Zebatinsky dropped out of sight just about a year ago."

Dr. Kristow said stolidly, "Executed!"

"He might have been. Ordinarily, I would even assume so, though the Russians are not more foolish than we are and don't kill any nuclear physicist they can avoid killing. The thing is there's another reason why a nuclear physicist, of all people, might suddenly disappear. I don't have to tell you."

"Crash research, top secret. I take it that's what you mean. Do you believe that's it?"

"Put it together with everything else, add in the lieutenant's intuition, and I just begin to wonder."

"Give me that biography." Dr. Kristow reached for the sheet of paper and read it over twice. He shook his head. Then he said, "I'll check this in *Nuclear Abstracts*."

Nuclear Abstracts lined one wall of Dr. Kristow's study in neat little boxes, each filled with its square of microfilm.

The A.E.C. man used his projector on the indices while Brand watched with what patience he could muster.

Dr. Kristow muttered, "A Mikhail Zebatinsky authored or co-authored half a dozen papers in the Soviet journals in the last half dozen years. We'll get out the abstracts and maybe we can make something out of it. I doubt it."

A selector flipped out the appropriate squares. Dr. Kristow lined them up, ran them through the projector, and by degrees an expression of odd intentness crossed his face. He said, "That's odd."

Brand said, "What's odd?"

Dr. Kristow sat back. "I'd rather not say just yet. Can you get me a list of other nuclear physicists who have dropped out of sight in the Soviet Union in the last year?"

"You mean you see something?"

"Not really. Not if I were just looking at any one of these papers. It's just that looking at all of them and knowing that this man may be on a crash research program and, on top of that, having you putting suspicions in my head—" He shrugged. "It's nothing."

Brand said earnestly, "I wish you'd say what's on your mind. We may as well be foolish about this together."

"If you feel that way—it's just possible this man may have been inching toward gamma-ray reflection."

"And the significance?"

"If a reflecting shield against gamma rays could be devised, individual shelters could be built to protect against fallout. It's fallout that's the real danger, you know. A hydrogen bomb might destroy a city but the fallout could slow-kill the population over a strip thousands of miles long and hundreds wide."

Brand said quickly, "Are we doing any work on this?"

"No."

"And if they get it and we don't, they can destroy the United States *in toto* at the cost of, say, ten cities, after they have their shelter program completed."

"That's far in the future. And, what are we getting in a hurrah about? All this is built on one man changing one letter in his name."

"All right, I'm insane," said Brand. "But I don't leave the matter at this point. Not at *this* point. I'll get you your list of disappearing nuclear physicists if I have to go to Moscow to get it."

He got the list. They went through all the research papers authored by any of them. They called a full meeting of the Commission, then of the nuclear brains of the nation. Dr. Kristow walked out of an all-night session, finally, part of which the President himself had attended.

Brand met him. Both looked haggard and in need of sleep.

Brand said, "Well?"

Kristow nodded. "Most agree. Some are doubtful even yet, but most agree."

"How about you? Are you sure?"

"I'm far from sure, but let me put it this way. It's easier to believe that the Soviets are working on a gamma-ray shield than to believe that all the data we've uncovered has no interconnection."

"Has it been decided that we're to go on shield research, too?"

"Yes." Kristow's hand went back over his short, bristly hair, making a dry, whispery sound. "We're going to give it everything we've got. Knowing the papers written by the men who disappeared, we can get right on their heels. We may even beat them to it. Of course, they'll find out we're working on it."

"Let them," said Brand. "Let them. It will keep them from attacking. I don't see any percentage in selling ten of our cities just to get ten of theirs—if we're both protected and they're too dumb to know that."

"But not too soon. We don't want them finding out *too* soon. What about the American Zebatinsky-Sebatinsky?"

Brand looked solemn and shook his head. "There's nothing to connect him with any of this even yet. Hell, we've *looked*, I agree with you, of course. He's in a sensitive spot where he is now and we can't afford to keep him there even if he's in the clear."

"We can't kick him out just like that, either, or the Russians will start wondering."

"Do you have any suggestions?"

They were walking down the long corridor toward the distant elevator in the emptiness of four in the morning.

Dr. Kristow said, "I've looked into his work. He's a good man, better than most, and not happy in his job, either. He hasn't the temperament for teamwork."

"So?"

"But he is the type for an academic job. If we can arrange to have a large university offer him a chair in physics, I think he would take it gladly. There would be enough nonsensitive areas to keep him occupied; we would be able to keep him in close view; *and* it would be a natural development. The Russians might not start scratching their heads. What do you think?"

Brand nodded. "It's an idea. Even sounds good. I'll put it up to the chief."

They stepped into the elevator and Brand allowed himself to wonder about it all. What an ending to what had started with one letter of a name.

Marshall Sebatinsky could hardly talk. He said to his wife, "I swear I don't see how this happened. I wouldn't have thought they knew me from a meson detector. Good Lord, Sophie, Associate Professor of Physics at Princeton. Think of it."

Sophie said, "Do you suppose it was your talk at the A.P.S. meetings?"

"I don't see how. It was a thoroughly uninspired paper once everyone in the division was done hacking at it." He snapped his fingers. "It must have been Princeton that was investigating me. That's it. You know all those forms I've been filling out in the last six months; those interviews they wouldn't explain. Honestly, I was beginning to think I was under suspicion as a subversive. It was Princeton investigating me. They're thorough."

"Maybe it was your name," said Sophie. "I mean the change."

"Watch me now. My professional life will be my own finally. I'll make my mark. Once I have a chance to do my work without—" He stopped and turned to look at his wife. "My name! You mean the *S*."

"You didn't get the offer till after you changed your name, did you?"

"Not till long after. No, that part's just coincidence. I've told you before Sophie, it was just a case of throwing out fifty dollars to please you. Lord, what a fool I've felt all these months insisting on that stupid *S*."

Sophie was instantly on the defensive. "I didn't make you do it, Marshall. I suggested it but I didn't nag you about it. Don't say I did. Besides, it did turn out well. I'm sure it was the name that did this."

Sebatinsky smiled indulgently. "Now that's superstition."

"I don't care what you call it, but you're not changing your name back."

"Well, no, I suppose not. I've had so much trouble getting them to spell my name with an *S*, that the thought of making everyone move back is more than I want to face. Maybe I ought to change my name to Jones, eh?" He laughed almost hysterically.

But Sophie didn't. "You leave it alone."

"Oh, all right, I'm just joking. Tell you what. I'll step down to that old fellow's place one of these days and tell him everything worked out and slip him another tenner. Will that satisfy you?"

He was exuberant enough to do so the next week. He assumed no disguise this time. He wore his glasses and his ordinary suit and was minus a hat.

He was even humming as he approached the store front and stepped to one side to allow a weary, sour-faced woman to maneuver her twin baby carriage past.

He put his hand on the door handle and his thumb on the iron latch. The latch didn't give to his thumb's downward pressure. The door was locked.

The dusty, dim card with "Numerologist" on it was gone, now that he looked. Another sign, printed and beginning to yellow and curl with the sunlight, said "To let."

Sebatinsky shrugged. That was that. He had tried to do the right thing.

H around, happily divested of corporeal excrescence, capered happily and his energy vortices glowed a dim purple over cubic hypermiles. He said, "Have I won? Have I won?"

Mestack was withdrawn, his vortices almost a sphere of light in hyperspace. "I haven't calculated it yet."

"Well, go ahead. You won't change the results any by taking a long time. Wow, it's a relief to get back into clean energy. It took me a microcycle of time as a corporeal body; a nearly used-up one, too. But it was worth it to show *you*."

Mestack said, "All right, I admit you stopped a nuclear war on the planet."

"Is that or is that not a Class A effect?"

"It is a Class A effect. Of course it is."

"All right. Now check and see if I didn't get that Class A effect with a Class F stimulus. I changed one letter of one name."

"What?"

"Oh, never mind. It's all there. I've worked it out for you."

Mestack said reluctantly, "I yield. A Class F stimulus."

"Then I *win*. Admit it."

"Neither one of us will win when the Watchman gets a look at this."

Haround, who had been an elderly numerologist on Earth and was still somewhat unsettled with relief at no longer being one, said, "You weren't worried about that when you made the bet."

"I didn't think you'd be fool enough to go through with it."

"Heat-waste! Besides, why worry? The Watchman will never detect a Class F stimulus."

"Maybe not, but he'll detect a Class A effect. Those corporeals will still be around after a dozen microcycles. The Watchman will notice that."

"The trouble with you, Mestack, is that you don't want to pay off. You're stalling."

"I'll pay. But just wait till the Watchman finds out we've been working on an unassigned problem and made an unallowed-for change. Of course, if we—" He paused.

Haround said, "All right, we'll change it back. He'll never know."

There was a crafty glow to Mestack's brightening energy pattern. "You'll need another Class F stimulus if you expect him not to notice."

Haround hesitated. "I can do it."

"I doubt it."

"I could."

"Would you be willing to bet on that, too?" Jubilation was creeping into Mestack's radiations.

"Sure," said the goaded Haround. "I'll put those corporeals right back where they were and the Watchman will never know the difference."

Mestack followed through his advantage. "Suspend the first bet, then. Triple the stakes on the second."

The mounting eagerness of the gamble caught at Haround, too. "All right. I'm game. Triple the stakes."

"Done, then!"

"Done."

The Ugly Little Boy

Edith Fellowes smoothed her working smock as she always did before opening the elaborately locked door and stepping across the invisible dividing line between the *is* and *is not*. She carried her notebook and her pen although she no longer took notes except when she felt the absolute need for some report.

This time she also carried a suitcase. ("Games for the boy," she had said, smiling, to the guard—who had long since stopped even thinking of questioning her and who waved her on.)

And, as always, the ugly little boy knew that she had entered and came running to her, crying. "Miss Fellowes—Miss Fellowes—" in his soft, slurring way.

"Timmie," she said, and passed her hand over the shaggy, brown hair on his misshapen little head. "What's wrong?"

He said, "Will Jerry be back to play again? I'm sorry about what happened."

"Never mind that now, Timmie. Is that why you've been crying?"

He looked away. "Not just about that, Miss Fellowes. I dreamed again."

"The same dream?" Miss Fellowes' lips set. Of course, the Jerry affair would bring back the dream.

He nodded. His too large teeth showed as he tried to smile and the lips of his forward-thrusting mouth stretched wide. "When will I be big enough to go out there, Miss Fellowes?"

"Soon," she said softly, feeling her heart break. "Soon."

Miss Fellowes let him take her hand and enjoyed the warm touch of the thick dry skin of his palm. He led her through the three rooms that made up the whole of Stasis Section One—comfortable enough, yes, but an eternal prison for the ugly little boy all the seven (was it seven?) years of his life.

He led her to the one window, looking out onto a scrubby woodland section of the world of *is* (now hidden by night), where a fence and painted instructions allowed no men to wander without permission.

He pressed his nose against the window. "Out there, Miss Fellowes?"

"Better places. Nicer places," she said sadly as she looked at his poor little im-prisoned face outlined in profile against the window. The forehead retreated flatly and his hair lay down in tufts upon it. The back of his skull bulged and seemed to make the head overheavy so that it sagged and bent forward, forcing the whole body into a stoop. Already, bony ridges were beginning to bulge the skin above his eyes. His wide mouth thrust forward more prominently than did his wide and flat-tened nose and he had no chin to speak of, only a jawbone that curved smoothly down and back. He was small for his years and his stumpy legs were bowed.

He was a very ugly little boy and Edith Fellowes loved him dearly.

Her own face was behind his line of vision, so she allowed her lips the lux-ury of a tremor.

They would *not* kill him. She would do anything to prevent it. Anything. She opened the suitcase and began taking out the clothes it contained.

E dith Fellowes had crossed the threshold of Stasis, Inc. for the first time just a little over three years before. She hadn't, at that time, the slightest idea as to what Stasis meant or what the place did. No one did then, except those who worked there. In fact, it was only the day after she arrived that the news broke upon the world.

At the time, it was just that they had advertised for a woman with knowl-edge of physiology, experience with clinical chemistry, and a love for children. Edith Fellowes had been a nurse in a maternity ward and believed she fulfilled those qualifications.

Gerald Hoskins, whose name plate on the desk included a Ph.D. after the name, scratched his cheek with his thumb and looked at her steadily.

Miss Fellowes automatically stiffened and felt her face (with its slightly asymmetric nose and its a-trifle-too-heavy eye-brows) twitch.

He's no dreamboat himself, she thought resentfully. He's getting fat and bald and he's got a sullen mouth. But the salary mentioned had been consider-ably higher than she had expected, so she waited.

Hoskins said, "Now do you really love children?"

"I wouldn't say I did if I didn't."

"Or do you just love pretty children? Nice chubby children with cute little button noses and gurgly ways?"

Miss Fellowes said, "Children are children, Dr. Hoskins, and the ones that aren't pretty are just the ones who may happen to need help most."

"Then suppose we take you on—"

"You mean you're offering me the job now?"

He smiled briefly, and for a moment, his broad face had an absentminded charm about it. He said, "I make quick decisions. So far the offer is tentative, however. I may make as quick a decision to let you go. Are you ready to take the chance?"

Miss Fellowes clutched at her purse and calculated just as swiftly as she could, then ignored calculations and followed impulse. "All right."

"Fine. We're going to form the Stasis tonight and I think you had better be there to take over at once. That will be at 8 P.M. and I'd appreciate it if you could be here at 7:30."

"But what—"

"Fine. Fine. That will be all now." On signal, a smiling secretary came in to usher her out.

Miss Fellowes stared back at Dr. Hoskins' closed door for a moment. What was Stasis? What had this large barn of a building—with its badged employees, its makeshift corridors, and its unmistakable air of engineering—to do with children?

She wondered if she should go back that evening or stay away and teach that arrogant man a lesson. But she knew she would be back if only out of sheer frustration. She would have to find out about the children.

She came back at 7:30 and did not have to announce herself. One after another, men and women seemed to know her and to know her function. She found herself all but placed on skids as she was moved inward.

Dr. Hoskins was there, but he only looked at her distantly and murmured, "Miss Fellowes."

He did not even suggest that she take a seat, but she drew one calmly up to the railing and sat down.

They were on a balcony, looking down into a large pit, filled with instruments that looked like a cross between the control panel of a spaceship and the working face of a computer. On one side were partitions that seemed to make up an unceilinged apartment, a giant dollhouse into the rooms of which she could look from above.

She could see an electronic cooker and a freeze-space unit in one room and a washroom arrangement off another. And surely the object she made out in another room could only be part of a bed, a small bed.

Hoskins was speaking to another man and, with Miss Fellowes, they made up the total occupancy of the balcony. Hoskins did not offer to introduce the other man, and Miss Fellowes eyed him surreptitiously. He was thin and quite fine-looking in a middle-aged way. He had a small mustache and keen eyes that seemed to busy themselves with everything.

He was saying, "I won't pretend for one moment that I understand all this, Dr. Hoskins; I mean, except as a layman, a reasonably intelligent layman, may be expected to understand it. Still, if there's one part I understand less than another, it's this matter of selectivity. You can only reach out so far; that seems sensible; things get dimmer the further you go; it takes more energy. But then, you can only reach out so near. That's the puzzling part."

"I can make it seem less paradoxical, Deveney, if you will allow me to use an analogy."

(Miss Fellowes placed the new man the moment she heard his name, and despite herself was impressed. This was obviously Candide Deveney, the science writer of the Telenews, who was notoriously at the scene of every major scientific breakthrough. She even recognized his face as one she saw on the newsplate when the landing on Mars had been announced. So Dr. Hoskins must have something important here.)

"By all means use an analogy," said Deveney ruefully, "if you think it will help."

"Well, then, you can't read a book with ordinary-sized print if it is held six feet from your eyes, but you can read it if you hold it one foot from your eyes. So far, the closer the better. If you bring the book to within one inch of your eyes, however, you've lost it again. There is such a thing as being too close, you see."

"Hmm," said Deveney.

"Or take another example. Your right shoulder is about thirty inches from the tip of your right forefinger and you can place your right forefinger on your right shoulder. Your right elbow is only half the distance from the tip of your right forefinger; it should by all ordinary logic be easier to reach, and yet you cannot place your right finger on your right elbow. Again, there is such a thing as being too close."

Deveney said, "May I use these analogies in my story?"

"Well, of course. Only too glad. I've been waiting long enough for someone like you to have a story. I'll give you anything else you want. It is time, finally, that we want the world looking over our shoulder. They'll see something."

(Miss Fellowes found herself admiring his calm certainty despite herself. There was strength there.)

Deveney said, "How far out will you reach?"

"Forty thousand years."

Miss Fellowes drew in her breath sharply.

Years?

There was tension in the air. The men at the controls scarcely moved. One man at a microphone spoke into it in a soft monotone, in short phrases that made no sense to Miss Fellowes.

Deveney, leaning over the balcony railing with an intent stare, said, "Will we see anything, Dr. Hoskins?"

"What? No. Nothing till the job is done. We detect indirectly, something on the principle of radar, except that we use mesons rather than radiation. Mesons reach backward under the proper conditions. Some are reflected and we must analyze the reflections."

"That sounds difficult."

Hoskins smiled again, briefly as always. "It is the end product of fifty years of research; forty years of it before I entered the field. Yes, it's difficult."

The man at the microphone raised one hand.

Hoskins said, "We've had the fix on one particular moment in time for weeks, breaking it, remaking it after calculating our own movements in time; making certain that we could handle time-flow with sufficient precision. This must work now."

But his forehead glistened.

Edith Fellowes found herself out of her seat and at the balcony railing, but there was nothing to see.

The man at the microphone said quietly, "Now."

There was a space of silence sufficient for one breath and then the sound of a terrified little boy's scream from the dollhouse rooms. Terror! Piercing terror!

Miss Fellowes' head twisted in the direction of the cry. A child was involved. She had forgotten.

And Hoskins' fist pounded on the railing and he said in a tight voice, trembling with triumph, "*Did* it."

Miss Fellowes was urged down the short, spiral flight of steps by the hard press of Hoskins' palm between her shoulder blades. He did not speak to her.

The men who had been at the controls were standing about now, smiling, smoking, watching the three as they entered on the main floor. A very soft buzz sounded from the direction of the dollhouse.

Hoskins said to Deveney, "It's perfectly safe to enter Stasis. I've done it a thousand times. There's a queer sensation which is momentary and means nothing."

He stepped through an open door in mute demonstration, and Deveney, smiling stiffly and drawing an obviously deep breath, followed him.

Hoskins said, "Miss Fellowes! Please!" He crooked his forefinger impatiently.

Miss Fellowes nodded and stepped stiffly through. It was as though a ripple went through her, an internal tickle.

But once inside all seemed normal. There was the smell of the fresh wood of the dollhouse and—of—of soil somehow.

There was silence now, no voice at least, but there was the dry shuffling of feet, a scrabbling as of a hand over wood—then a low moan.

"Where is it?" asked Miss Fellowes in distress. Didn't these fool men *care*?

* * *

T he boy was in the bedroom; at least the room with the bed in it.

It was standing naked, with its small, dirt-smeared chest heaving raggedly. A bushel of dirt and coarse grass spread over the floor at his bare brown feet. The smell of soil came from it and a touch of something fetid.

Hoskins followed her horrified glance and said with annoyance, "You can't pluck a boy cleanly out of time, Miss Fellowes. We had to take some of the surroundings with it for safety. Or would you have preferred to have it arrive here minus a leg or with only half a head?"

"*Please!*" said Miss Fellowes, in an agony of revulsion. "Are we just to stand here? The poor child is frightened. And it's *filthy*."

She was quite correct. It was smeared with encrusted dirt and grease and had a scratch on its thigh that looked red and sore.

As Hoskins approached him, the boy, who seemed to be something over three years in age, hunched low and backed away rapidly. He lifted his upper lip and snarled in a hissing fashion like a cat. With a rapid gesture, Hoskins seized both the child's arms and lifted him, writhing and screaming, from the floor.

Miss Fellowes said, "Hold him, now. He needs a warm bath first. He needs to be cleaned. Have you the equipment? If so, have it brought here, and I'll need to have help in handling him just at first. Then, too, for heaven's sake, have all this trash and filth removed."

She was giving the orders now and she felt perfectly good about that. And because now she was an efficient nurse, rather than a confused spectator, she looked at the child with a clinical eye—and hesitated for one shocked moment. She saw past the dirt and shrieking, past the thrashing of limbs and useless twisting. She saw the boy himself.

It was the ugliest little boy she had ever seen. It was horribly ugly from misshapen head to bandy legs.

S he got the boy cleaned with three men helping her and with others milling about in their efforts to clean the room. She worked in silence and with a sense of outrage, annoyed by the continued strugglings and outcries of the boy and by the undignified drenchings of soapy water to which she was subjected.

Dr. Hoskins had hinted that the child would not be pretty, but that was far from stating that it would be repulsively deformed. And there was a stench about the boy that soap and water was only alleviating little by little.

She had the strong desire to thrust the boy, soaped as he was, into Hoskins' arms and walk out; but there was the pride of profession. She had accepted an assignment after all. And there would be the look in his eyes. A cold look that would read: Only pretty children, Miss Fellowes?

He was standing apart from them, watching coolly from a distance with a half smile on his face when he caught her eyes, as though amused at her outrage.

She decided she would wait a while before quitting. To do so now would only demean her.

Then, when the boy was a bearable pink and smelled of scented soap, she felt better anyway. His cries changed to whimpers of exhaustion as he watched carefully, eyes moving in quick frightened suspicion from one to another of those in the room. His cleanness accentuated his thin nakedness as he shivered with cold after his bath.

Miss Fellowes said sharply, "Bring me a nightgown for the child!"

A nightgown appeared at once. It was as though everything were ready and yet nothing were ready unless she gave orders; as though they were deliberately leaving this in her charge without help, to test her.

The newsman, Deveney, approached and said, "I'll hold him, Miss. You won't get it on yourself."

"Thank you," said Miss Fellowes. And it was a battle indeed, but the nightgown went on, and when the boy made as though to rip it off, she slapped his hand sharply.

The boy reddened, but did not cry. He stared at her and the splayed fingers of one hand moved slowly across the flannel of the nightgown, feeling the strangeness of it.

Miss Fellowes thought desperately: Well, what next?

Everyone seemed in suspended animation, waiting for her—even the ugly little boy.

Miss Fellowes said sharply, "Have you provided food? Milk?"

They had. A mobile unit was wheeled in, with its refrigeration compartment containing three quarts of milk, with a warming unit and a supply of fortifications in the form of vitamin drops, copper-cobalt-iron syrup and others she had not time to be concerned with. There was a variety of canned self-warming junior foods.

She used milk, simply milk, to begin with. The radar unit heated the milk to a set temperature in a matter of ten seconds and clicked off, and she put some in a saucer. She had a certainty about the boy's savagery. He wouldn't know how to handle a cup.

Miss Fellowes nodded and said to the boy, "Drink. Drink." She made a gesture as though to raise the milk to her mouth. The boy's eyes followed but he made no move.

Suddenly, the nurse resorted to direct measures. She seized the boy's upper arm in one hand and dipped the other in the milk. She dashed the milk across his lips, so that it dripped down cheeks and receding chin.

For a moment, the child uttered a high-pitched cry, then his tongue moved over his wetted lips. Miss Fellowes stepped back.

The boy approached the saucer, bent toward it, then looked up and behind sharply as though expecting a crouching enemy; bent again and licked at the milk eagerly, like a cat. He made a slurping noise. He did not use his hands to lift the saucer.

Miss Fellowes allowed a bit of the revulsion she felt show on her face. She couldn't help it.

Deveney caught that, perhaps. He said, "Does the nurse know, Dr. Hoskins?"

"Know what?" demanded Miss Fellowes.

Deveney hesitated, but Hoskins (again that look of detached amusement on his face) said, "Well, tell her."

Deveney addressed Miss Fellowes. "You may not suspect it, Miss, but you happen to be the first civilized woman in history ever to be taking care of a Neanderthal youngster."

She turned on Hoskins with a kind of controlled ferocity. "You might have told me, Doctor."

"Why? What difference does it make?"

"You said a child."

"Isn't that a child? Have you ever had a puppy or a kitten, Miss Fellowes? Are those closer to the human? If that were a baby chimpanzee, would you be repelled? You're a nurse, Miss Fellowes. Your record places you in a maternity ward for three years. Have you ever refused to take care of a deformed infant?"

Miss Fellowes felt her case slipping away. She said, with much less decision, "You might have told me."

"And you would have refused the position? Well, do you refuse it now?" He gazed at her coolly, while Deveney watched from the other side of the room, and the Neanderthal child, having finished the milk and licked the plate, looked up at her with a wet face and wide, longing eyes.

The boy pointed to the milk and suddenly burst out in a short series of sounds repeated over and over; sounds made up of gutturals and elaborate tongue clickings.

Miss Fellowes said, in surprise, "Why, he talks."

"Of course," said Hoskins. "*Homo neanderthalensis* is not a truly separate species, but rather a subspecies of *Homo sapiens*. Why shouldn't he talk? He's probably asking for more milk."

Automatically, Miss Fellowes reached for a bottle of milk, but Hoskins seized her wrist. "Now, Miss Fellowes, before we go any further, are you staying on the job?"

Miss Fellowes shook free in annoyance. "Won't you feed him if I don't? I'll stay with him—for a while."

She poured the milk.

Hoskins said, "We are going to leave you with the boy, Miss Fellowes. This is the only door to Stasis Number One and it is elaborately locked and guarded. I'll want you to learn the details of the locks which will, of course, be keyed to your fingerprints as they are already keyed to mine. The spaces overhead"—he looked upward to the open ceilings of the dollhouse—"are also guarded and we will be warned if anything untoward takes place in here."

Miss Fellowes said indignantly, "You mean I'll be under view." She thought suddenly of her own survey of the room interiors from the balcony.

"No, no," said Hoskins seriously, "your privacy will be respected completely. The view will consist of electronic symbolism only, which only a computer will deal with. Now you will stay with him tonight, Miss Fellowes, and every night until further notice. You will be relieved during the day according to some schedule you will find convenient. We will allow you to arrange that."

Miss Fellowes looked about the dollhouse with a puzzled expression. "But why all this, Dr. Hoskins? Is the boy dangerous?"

"It's a matter of energy, Miss Fellowes. He must never be allowed to leave these rooms. Never. Not for an instant. Not for any reason. Not to save his life. Not even to save *your* life, Miss Fellowes. Is that clear?"

Miss Fellowes raised her chin. "I understand the orders, Dr. Hoskins, and the nursing profession is accustomed to placing its duties ahead of self-preservation."

"Good. You can always signal if you need anyone." And the two men left.

M iss Fellowes turned to the boy. He was watching her and there was still milk in the saucer. Laboriously, she tried to show him how to lift the saucer and place it to his lips. He resisted, but let her touch him without crying out.

Always, his frightened eyes were on her, watching, watching for the one false move. She found herself soothing him, trying to move her hand very slowly toward his hair, letting him see it every inch of the way, see there was no harm in it.

And she succeeded in stroking his hair for an instant.

She said, "I'm going to have to show you how to use the bathroom. Do you think you can learn?"

She spoke quietly, kindly, knowing he would not understand the words but hoping he would respond to the calmness of the tone.

The boy launched into a clicking phrase again.

She said, "May I take your hand?"

She held out hers and the boy looked at it. She felt it outstretched and waited. The boy's own hand crept forward toward hers.

"That's right," she said.

It approached within an inch of hers and then the boy's courage failed him. He snatched it back.

"Well," said Miss Fellowes calmly, "we'll try again later. Would you like to sit down here?" She patted the mattress of the bed.

The hours passed slowly and progress was minute. She did not succeed either with bathroom or with the bed. In fact, after the child had given unmistakable signs of sleepiness he lay down on the bare ground and then, with a quick movement, rolled beneath the bed.

She bent to look at him and his eyes gleamed out at her as he tongue-clicked at her.

"All right," she said, "if you feel safer there, you sleep there."

She closed the door to the bedroom and retired to the cot that had been placed for her use in the largest room. At her insistence, a makeshift canopy had been stretched over it. She thought: Those stupid men will have to place a mirror in this room and a larger chest of drawers and a separate washroom if they expect me to spend nights here.

It was difficult to sleep. She found herself straining to hear possible sounds in the next room. He couldn't get out, could he? The walls were sheer and impossibly high but suppose the child could climb like a monkey? Well, Hoskins said there were observational devices watching through the ceiling.

Suddenly she thought: Can he be dangerous? Physically dangerous?

Surely Hoskins couldn't have meant that. Surely, he would not have left her here alone, if—

She tried to laugh at herself. He was only a three- or four-year-old child. Still, she had not succeeded in cutting his nails. If he should attack her with nails and teeth while she slept—

Her breath came quickly. Oh, ridiculous, and yet—

She listened with painful attentiveness, and this time she heard the sound. The boy was crying.

Not shrieking in fear or anger; not yelling or screaming. It was crying softly, and the cry was the heartbroken sobbing of a lonely, lonely child.

For the first time, Miss Fellowes thought with a pang: Poor thing!

Of course, it was a child; what did the shape of its head matter? It was a child that had been orphaned as no child had ever been orphaned before. Not only its mother and father were gone, but all its species. Snatched callously out of time, it was now the only creature of its kind in the world. The last. The only.

She felt pity for it strengthen, and with it shame at her own callousness. Tucking her own nightgown carefully about her calves (incongruously, she thought: Tomorrow I'll have to bring in a bathrobe) she got out of bed and went into the boy's room.

"Little boy," she called in a whisper. "Little boy."

She was about to reach under the bed, but she thought of a possible bite and did not. Instead, she turned on the night light and moved the bed.

The poor thing was huddled in the corner, knees up against his chin, looking up at her with blurred and apprehensive eyes.

In the dim light, she was not aware of his repulsiveness.

"Poor boy," she said, "poor boy." She felt him stiffen as she stroked his hair, then relax. "Poor boy. May I hold you?"

She sat down on the floor next to him and slowly and rhythmically stroked his hair, his cheek, his arm. Softly, she began to sing a slow and gentle song.

He lifted his head at that, staring at her mouth in the dimness, as though wondering at the sound.

She maneuvered him closer while he listened to her. Slowly, she pressed gently against the side of his head, until it rested on her shoulder. She put her arm under his thighs and with a smooth and unhurried motion lifted him into her lap.

She continued singing, the same simple verse over and over, while she rocked back and forth, back and forth.

He stopped crying, and after a while the smooth burr of his breathing showed he was asleep.

With infinite care, she pushed his bed back against the wall and laid him down. She covered him and stared down. His face looked so peaceful and little-boy as he slept. It didn't matter so much that it was so ugly. Really.

She began to tiptoe out, then thought: If he wakes up?

She came back, battled irresolutely with herself, then sighed and slowly got into bed with the child.

It was too small for her. She was cramped and uneasy at the lack of canopy, but the child's hand crept into hers and, somehow, she fell asleep in that position.

She awoke with a start and a wild impulse to scream. The latter she just managed to suppress into a gurgle. The boy was looking at her, wide-eyed. It took her a long moment to remember getting into bed with him, and now, slowly, without unfixing her eyes from his, she stretched one leg carefully and let it touch the floor, then the other one.

She cast a quick and apprehensive glance toward the open ceiling, then tensed her muscles for quick disengagement.

But at that moment, the boy's stubby fingers reached out and touched her lips. He said something.

She shrank at the touch. He was terribly ugly in the light of day.

The boy spoke again. He opened his own mouth and gestured with his hand as though something were coming out.

Miss Fellowes guessed at the meaning and said tremulously, "Do you want me to sing?"

The boy said nothing but stared at her mouth.

In a voice slightly off key with tension, Miss Fellowes began the little song she had sung the night before and the ugly little boy smiled. He swayed clumsily in rough time to the music and made a little gurgly sound that might have been the beginnings of a laugh.

Miss Fellowes sighed inwardly. Music hath charms to soothe the savage breast. It might help—

She said, "You wait. Let me get myself fixed up. It will just take a minute. Then I'll make breakfast for you."

She worked rapidly, conscious of the lack of ceiling at all times. The boy remained in bed, watching her when she was in view. She smiled at him at those times and waved. At the end, he waved back, and she found herself being charmed by that.

Finally, she said, "Would you like oatmeal with milk?" It took a moment to prepare, and then she beckoned to him.

Whether he understood the gesture or followed the aroma, Miss Fellowes did not know, but he got out of bed.

She tried to show him how to use a spoon but he shrank away from it in fright. (Time enough, she thought.) She compromised on insisting that he lift the bowl in his hands. He did it clumsily enough and it was incredibly messy but most of it did get into him.

She tried the drinking milk in a glass this time, and the little boy whined when he found the opening too small for him to get his face into conveniently. She held his hand, forcing it around the glass, making him tip it, forcing his mouth to the rim.

Again a mess but again most went into him, and she was used to messes.

The washroom, to her surprise and relief, was a less frustrating matter. He understood what it was she expected him to do.

She found herself patting his head, saying, "Good boy. Smart boy."

And to Miss Fellowes' exceeding pleasure, the boy smiled at that.

She thought: When he smiles, he's quite bearable. Really.

Later in the day, the gentlemen of the press arrived.

She held the boy in her arms and he clung to her wildly while across the open door they set cameras to work. The commotion frightened the boy and he began to cry, but it was ten minutes before Miss Fellowes was allowed to retreat and put the boy in the next room.

She emerged again, flushed with indignation, walked out of the apartment (for the first time in eighteen hours) and closed the door behind her. "I think you've had enough. It will take me a while to quiet him. Go away."

"Sure, sure," said the gentleman from the *Times-Herald*. "But is that really a Neanderthal or is this some kind of gag?"

"I assure you," said Hoskins' voice, suddenly, from the background, "that this is no gag. The child is authentic *Homo neanderthalensis*."

"Is it a boy or a girl?"

"Boy," said Miss Fellowes briefly.

"Ape-boy," said the gentleman from the *News*. "That's what we've got here. Ape-boy. How does he act, Nurse?"

"He acts exactly like a little boy," snapped Miss Fellowes, annoyed into the defensive, "and he is not an ape-boy. His name is—is Timothy, Timmie—and he is perfectly normal in his behavior."

She had chosen the name Timothy at a venture. It was the first that had occurred to her.

"Timmie the Ape-boy," said the gentleman from the *News* and, as it turned out, Timmie the Ape-boy was the name under which the child became known to the world.

The gentleman from the *Globe* turned to Hoskins and said, "Doc, what do you expect to do with the ape-boy?"

Hoskins shrugged. "My original plan was completed when I proved it possible to bring him here. However, the anthropologists will be very interested, I imagine, and the physiologists. We have here, after all, a creature which is at the edge of being human. We should learn a great deal about ourselves and our ancestry from him."

"How long will you keep him?"

"Until such a time as we need the space more than we need him. Quite a while, perhaps."

The gentleman from the *News* said, "Can you bring it out into the open so we can set up sub-etheric equipment and put on a real show?"

"I'm sorry, but the child cannot be removed from Stasis."

"Exactly what is Stasis?"

"Ah." Hoskins permitted himself one of his short smiles. "That would take a great deal of explanation, gentlemen. In Stasis, time as we know it doesn't exist. Those rooms are inside an invisible bubble that is not exactly part of our Universe. That is why the child could be plucked out of time as it was."

"Well, wait now," said the gentleman from the *News* discontentedly, "what are you giving us? The nurse goes into the room and out of it."

"And so can any of you," said Hoskins matter-of-factly. "You would be moving parallel to the lines of temporal force and no great energy gain or loss would be involved. The child, however, was taken from the far past. It moved across the lines and gained temporal potential. To move it into the Universe and into our own time would absorb enough energy to burn out every line in the place and probably blank out all power in the city of Washington. We had to store trash brought with him on the premises and will have to remove it little by little."

The newsmen were writing down sentences busily as Hoskins spoke to them. They did not understand and they were sure their readers would not, but it sounded scientific and that was what counted.

The gentleman from the the *Times-Herald* said, "Would you be available for an all-circuit interview tonight?"

"I think so," said Hoskins at once, and they all moved off.

Miss Fellowes looked after them. She understood all this about Stasis and temporal force as little as the newsmen but she managed to get this much. Timmie's imprisonment (she found herself suddenly thinking of the little boy as Timmie) was a real one and not one imposed by the arbitrary fiat of Hoskins. Apparently, it was impossible to let him out of Stasis at all, ever.

Poor child. Poor child.

She was suddenly aware of his crying and she hastened in to console him.

Miss Fellowes did not have a chance to see Hoskins on the all-circuit hookup, and though his interview was beamed to every part of the world and even to the outpost on the Moon, it did not penetrate the apartment in which Miss Fellowes and the ugly little boy lived.

But he was down the next morning, radiant and joyful.

Miss Fellowes said, "Did the interview go well?"

"Extremely. And how is—Timmie?"

Miss Fellowes found herself pleased at the use of the name. "Doing quite well. Now come out here, Timmie, the nice gentleman will not hurt you."

But Timmie stayed in the other room, with a lock of his matted hair showing behind the barrier of the door and, occasionally, the corner of an eye.

"Actually," said Miss Fellowes, "he is settling down amazingly. He is quite intelligent."

"Are you surprised?"

She hesitated just a moment, then said, "Yes, I am. I suppose I thought he was an ape-boy."

"Well, ape-boy or not, he's done a great deal for us. He's put Stasis, Inc. on the map. We're in, Miss Fellowes, we're in." It was as though he had to express his triumph to someone, even if only to Miss Fellowes.

"Oh?" She let him talk.

He put his hands in his pockets and said, "We've been working on a shoe-string for ten years, scrounging funds a penny at a time wherever we could. We had to shoot the works on one big show. It was everything, or nothing. And when I say the works, I mean it. This attempt to bring in a Neanderthal took every cent we could borrow or steal, and some of it *was* stolen—funds for other projects, used for this one without permission. If that experiment hadn't suc-ceeded, I'd have been through."

Miss Fellowes said abruptly, "Is that why there are no ceilings?"

"Eh?" Hoskins looked up.

"Was there no money for ceilings?"

"Oh. Well, that wasn't the only reason. We didn't really know in advance how old the Neanderthal might be exactly. We can detect only dimly in time, and he might have been large and savage. It was possible we might had have to deal with him from a distance, like a caged animal."

"But since that hasn't turned out to be so, I suppose you can build a ceil-ing now."

"Now, yes. We have plenty of money, now. Funds have been promised from every source. This is all wonderful, Miss Fellowes." His broad face gleamed with a smile that lasted and when he left, even his back seemed to be smiling.

Miss Fellowes thought: He's quite a nice man when he's off guard and for-gets about being scientific.

She wondered for an idle moment if he was married, then dismissed the thought in embarrassment.

"Timmie," she called. "Come here, Timmie."

In the months that passed, Miss Fellowes felt herself grow to be an integral part of Stasis, Inc. She was given a small office of her own with her name on the door, an office quite close to the dollhouse (as she never stopped calling Tim-mie's Stasis bubble). She was given a substantial raise. The dollhouse was cov-ered by a ceiling; its furnishings were elaborated and improved; a second washroom was added—and even so, she gained an apartment of her own on the institute grounds and, on occasion, did not stay with Timmie during the night. An intercom was set up between the dollhouse and her apartment and Timmie learned how to use it.

Miss Fellowes got used to Timmie. She even grew less conscious of his ugli-ness. One day she found herself staring at an ordinary boy in the street and finding something bulgy and unattractive in his high domed forehead and jutting chin. She had to shake herself to break the spell.

It was more pleasant to grow used to Hoskins' occasional visits. It was obvious he welcomed escape from his increasingly harried role as head of Stasis, Inc., and that he took a sentimental interest in the child who had started it all, but it seemed to Miss Fellowes that he also enjoyed talking to her.

(She had learned some facts about Hoskins, too. He had invented the method of analyzing the reflection of the past-penetrating mesonic beam; he had invented the method of establishing Stasis; his coldness was only an effort to hide a kindly nature; and, oh yes, he *was* married.)

What Miss Fellowes could *not* get used to was the fact that she was engaged in a scientific experiment. Despite all she could do, she found herself getting personally involved to the point of quarrelling with the physiologists.

On one occasion, Hoskins came down and found her in the midst of a hot urge to kill. They had no right; they had no *right*—even if he *was* a Neanderthal, he still wasn't an animal.

She was staring after them in a blind fury; staring out the open door and listening to Timmie's sobbing, when she noticed Hoskins standing before her. He might have been there for minutes.

He said, "May I come in?"

She nodded curtly, then hurried to Timmie, who clung to her, curling his little bandy legs—still thin, so thin—about her.

Hoskins watched, then said gravely, "He seems quite unhappy."

Miss Fellowes said, "I don't blame him. They're at him every day now with their blood samples and their probings. They keep him on synthetic diets that I wouldn't feed a pig."

"It's the sort of thing they can't try on a human, you know."

"And they can't try it on Timmie, either. Dr. Hoskins, I insist. You told me it was Timmie's coming that put Stasis, Inc. on the map. If you have any gratitude for that at all, you've *got* to keep them away from the poor thing at least until he's old enough to understand a little more. After he's had a bad session with them, he has nightmares, he can't sleep. Now I warn you"—she reached a sudden peak of fury—"I'm not letting them in here any more."

(She realized that she had screamed that, but she couldn't help it.)

She said more quietly, "I know he's Neanderthal but there's a great deal we don't appreciate about Neanderthals. I've read up on them. They had a culture of their own. Some of the greatest human inventions arose in Neanderthal times. The domestication of animals, for instance; the wheel; various techniques in grinding stone. They even had spiritual yearnings. They buried their dead and buried possessions with the body, showing they believed in a life after death. It amounts to the fact that they invented religion. Doesn't that mean Timmie has a right to human treatment?"

She patted the little boy gently on his buttocks and sent him off into his playroom. As the door was opened, Hoskins smiled briefly at the display of toys that could be seen.

Miss Fellowes said defensively, "The poor child deserves his toys. It's all he has and he earns them with what he goes through."

"No, no. No objections, I assure you. I was just thinking how you've changed since the first day, when you were quite angry I had foisted a Neanderthal on you."

Miss Fellowes said in a low voice, "I suppose I didn't—" and faded off.

Hoskins changed the subject, "How old would you say he is, Miss Fellowes?"

She said, "I can't say, since we don't know how Neanderthals develop. In size, he'd only be three but Neanderthals are smaller generally and with all the tampering they do with him, he probably isn't growing. The way he's learning English, though, I'd say he was well over four."

"Really? I haven't noticed anything about learning English in the reports."

"He won't speak to anyone but me. For now, anyway. He's terribly afraid of others, and no wonder. But he can ask for an article of food; he can indicate any need practically; and he understands almost anything I say. Of course"—she watched him shrewdly, trying to estimate if this was the time—"his development may not continue."

"Why not?"

"Any child needs stimulation and this one lives a life of solitary confinement. I do what I can, but I'm not with him all the time and I'm not all he needs. What I mean, Dr. Hoskins, is that he needs another boy to play with."

Hoskins nodded slowly. "Unfortunately, there's only one of him, isn't there? Poor child."

Miss Fellowes warmed to him at once. She said, "You do like Timmie, don't you?" It was so nice to have someone else feel like that.

"Oh, yes," said Hoskins, and with his guard down, she could see the weariness in his eyes.

Miss Fellowes dropped her plans to push the matter at once. She said, with real concern, "You look worn out, Dr. Hoskins."

"Do I, Miss Fellowes? I'll have to practice looking more lifelike then."

"I suppose Stasis, Inc. is very busy and that that keeps you very busy."

Hoskins shrugged. "You suppose right. It's a matter of animal, vegetable, and mineral in equal parts, Miss Fellowes. But then, I suppose you haven't ever seen our displays."

"Actually, I haven't. But it's not because I'm not interested. It's just that I've been so busy."

"Well, you're not all that busy right now," he said with impulsive decision. "I'll call for you tomorrow at eleven and give you a personal tour. How's that?"

She smiled happily. "I'd love it."

He nodded and smiled in his turn and left.

Miss Fellowes hummed at intervals for the rest of the day. Really—to think so was ridiculous, of course—but really, it was almost like—like making a date.

He was quite on time the next day, smiling and pleasant. She had replaced her nurse's uniform with a dress. One of conservative cut, to be sure, but she hadn't felt so feminine in years.

He complimented her on her appearance with staid formality and she accepted with equally formal grace. It was really a perfect prelude, she thought. And then the additional thought came, prelude to what?

She shut that off by hastening to say good-bye to Timmie and to assure him she would be back soon. She made sure he knew all about what and where lunch was.

Hoskins took her into the new wing, into which she had never yet gone. It still had the odor of newness about it and the sound of construction, softly heard, was indication enough that it was still being extended.

"Animal, vegetable, and mineral," said Hoskins, as he had the day before. "Animal right there; our most spectacular exhibits."

The space was divided into many rooms, each a separate Stasis bubble. Hoskins brought her to the view-glass of one and she looked in. What she saw impressed her first as a scaled, tailed chicken. Skittering on two thin legs it ran from wall to wall with its delicate birdlike head, surmounted by a bony keel like the comb of a rooster, looking this way and that. The paws on its small forelimbs clenched and unclenched constantly.

Hoskins said, "It's our dinosaur. We've had it for months. I don't know when we'll be able to let go of it."

"Dinosaur?"

"Did you expect a giant?"

She dimpled. "One does, I suppose. I know some of them are small."

"A small one is all we aimed for, believe me. Generally, it's under investigation, but this seems to be an open hour. Some interesting things have been discovered. For instance, it is not entirely cold-blooded. It has an imperfect method of maintaining internal temperatures higher than that of its environment. Unfortunately, it's a male. Ever since we brought it in we've been trying to get a fix on another that may be female, but we've had no luck yet."

"Why female?"

He looked at her quizzically. "So that we might have a fighting chance to obtain fertile eggs, and baby dinosaurs."

"Of course."

He led her to the trilobite section. "That's Professor Dwayne of Washington University," he said. "He's a nuclear chemist. If I recall correctly, he's taking an isotope ratio on the oxygen of the water."

"Why?"

"It's primeval water; at least half a billion years old. The isotope ratio gives the temperature of the ocean at that time. He himself happens to ignore the trilobites, but others are chiefly concerned in dissecting them. They're the lucky ones because all they need are scalpels and microscopes. Dwayne has to set up a mass spectrograph each time he conducts an experiment."

"Why's that? Can't he—"

"No, he can't. He can't take anything out of the room as far as can be helped."

There were samples of primordial plant life too and chunks of rock formations. Those were the vegetable and mineral. And every specimen had its investigator. It was like a museum; a museum brought to life and serving as a superactive center of research.

"And you have to supervise all of this, Dr. Hoskins?"

"Only indirectly, Miss Fellowes. I have subordinates, thank heaven. My own interest is entirely in the theoretical aspects of the matter: the nature of time, the technique of mesonic intertemporal detection and so on. I would exchange all of this for a method of detecting objects closer in time than ten thousand years ago. If we could get into historical times—"

He was interrupted by a commotion at one of the distant booths, a thin voice raised querulously. He frowned, muttered hastily, "Excuse me," and hastened off.

Miss Fellowes followed as best she could without actually running.

An elderly man, thinly bearded and red-faced, was saying, "I had vital aspects of my investigations to complete. Don't you understand that?"

A uniformed technician with the interwoven SI monogram (for Stasis, Inc.) on his lab coat, said, "Dr. Hoskins, it was arranged with Professor Ademewski at the beginning that the specimen could only remain here two weeks."

"I did not know then how long my investigation would take. I'm not a prophet," said Ademewski heatedly.

Dr. Hoskins said, "You understand, Professor, we have limited space; we must keep specimens rotating. That piece of chalcopyrite must go back; there are men waiting for the next specimen."

"Why can't I have it for myself, then? Let me take it out of there."

"You know you can't have it."

"A piece of chalcopyrite; a miserable five-kilogram piece? Why not?"

"We can't afford the energy expense!" said Hoskins brusquely. "You know that."

The technician interrupted. "The point is, Dr. Hoskins, that he tried to remove the rock against the rules and I almost punctured Stasis while he was in there, not knowing he was in there."

There was a short silence and Dr. Hoskins turned on the investigator with a cold formality. "Is that so, Professor?"

Professor Ademewski coughed. "I saw no harm—"

Hoskins reached up to a hand-pull dangling just within reach, outside the specimen room in question. He pulled it.

Miss Fellowes, who had been peering in, looking at the totally undistinguished sample of rock that occasioned the dispute, drew in her breath sharply as its existence flickered out. The room was empty.

Hoskins said, "Professor, your permit to investigate matters in Stasis will be permanently voided. I am sorry."

"But wait—"

"I am sorry. You have violated one of the stringent rules."

"I will appeal to the International Association—"

"Appeal away. In a case like this, you will find I can't be overruled."

He turned away deliberately, leaving the professor still protesting and said to Miss Fellowes (his face still white with anger), "Would you care to have lunch with me, Miss Fellowes?"

He took her into the small administration alcove of the cafeteria. He greeted others and introduced Miss Fellowes with complete ease, although she herself felt painfully self-conscious.

What must they think, she thought, and tried desperately to appear businesslike.

She said, "Do you have that kind of trouble often, Dr. Hoskins? I mean like that you just had with the professor?" She took her fork in hand and began eating.

"No," said Hoskins forcefully. "That was the first time. Of course I'm always having to argue men out of removing specimens but this is the first time one actually tried to *do* it."

"I remember you once talked about the energy it would consume."

"That's right. Of course, we've tried to take it into account. Accidents will happen and so we've got special power sources designed to stand the drain of accidental removal from Stasis, but that doesn't mean we want to see a year's supply of energy gone in half a second—or can afford to without having our plans of expansion delayed for years. Besides, imagine the professor's being in the room while Stasis was about to be punctured."

"What would have happened to him if it had been?"

"Well, we've experimented with inanimate objects and with mice and they've disappeared. Presumably they've traveled back in time; carried along, so to speak, by the pull of the object simultaneously snapping back into its natural time. For that reason, we have to anchor objects within Stasis that we don't want to move and that's complicated procedure. The professor would not have been anchored and he would have gone back to the Pliocene at the moment when we abstracted the rock—plus, of course, the two weeks it had remained here in the present."

"How dreadful it would have been."

"Not on account of the professor, I assure you. If he were fool enough to do what he did, it would serve him right. But imagine the effect it would have on the public if the fact came out. All people would need is to become aware of the dangers involved and funds could be choked off like that." He snapped his fingers and played moodily with his food.

Miss Fellowes said, "Couldn't you get him back? The way you got the rock in the first place?"

"No, because once an object is returned, the original fix is lost unless we deliberately plan to retain it and there was no reason to do that in this case. There never is. Finding the professor again would mean relocating a specific fix and that would be like dropping a line into the oceanic abyss for the purpose of dredging up a particular fish. My God, when I think of the precautions we take to prevent accidents, it makes me mad. We have every individual Stasis unit set up with its own puncturing device. We have to, since each unit has its separate fix and must be collapsible independently. The point is, though, none of the puncturing devices is ever activated until the last minute. And then we deliberately make activation impossible except by the pull of a rope carefully led outside the Stasis. The pull is a gross mechanical motion that requires a strong effort, not something that is likely to be done accidentally."

Miss Fellowes said, "But doesn't it—change history to move something in and out of time?"

Hoskins shrugged. "Theoretically, yes; actually, except in unusual cases, no. We move objects out of Stasis all the time. Air molecules. Bacteria. Dust. About ten percent of our energy consumption goes to make up micro-losses of that nature. But moving even large objects in time sets up changes that damp out. Take that chalcopyrite from the Pliocene. Because of its absence for two weeks some insect didn't find the shelter it might have found and is killed. That could initiate a whole series of changes, but the mathematics of Stasis indicates that this is a converging series. The amount of change diminishes with time and then things are as before."

"You mean, reality heals itself?"

"In a manner of speaking. Abstract a human from time or send one back, and you make a larger wound. If the individual is an ordinary one, that wound still heals itself. Of course, there are a great many people who write to us each day and want us to bring Abraham Lincoln into the present, or Mohammed, or Lenin. *That* can't be done, of course. Even if we could find them, the change in reality in moving one of the history molders would be too great to be healed. There are ways of calculating when a change is likely to be too great and we avoid even approaching that limit."

Miss Fellowes said, "Then, Timmie—"

"No, he represents no problem in that direction. Reality is safe. But—" He gave her a quick, sharp glance, then went on, "But never mind. Yesterday you said Timmie needed companionship."

"Yes," Miss Fellowes smiled her delight. "I didn't think you paid that any attention."

"Of course I did. I'm fond of the child. I appreciate your feelings for him and I was concerned enough to want to explain to you. Now I have; you've seen what we do; you've gotten some insight into the difficulties involved; so you know why, with the best will in the world, we can't supply companionship for Timmie."

"You can't?" said Miss Fellowes, with sudden dismay.

"But I've just explained. We couldn't possibly expect to find another Neanderthal his age without incredible luck, and if we could, it wouldn't be fair to multiply risks by having another human being in Stasis."

Miss Fellowes put down her spoon and said energetically, "But, Dr. Hoskins, that is not at all what I meant. I don't want you to bring another Neanderthal into the present. I know that's impossible. But it isn't impossible to bring another child to play with Timmie."

Hoskins stared at her in concern. "A *human* child?"

"*Another* child," said Miss Fellowes, completely hostile now. "Timmie is human."

"I couldn't dream of such a thing."

"Why not? Why couldn't you? What is wrong with the notion? You pulled that child out of time and made him an eternal prisoner. Don't you owe him something? Dr. Hoskins, if there is any man who, in this world, is that child's father in every sense but the biological, it is you. Why can't you do this little thing for him?"

Hoskins said, "His *father*?" He rose, somewhat unsteadily, to his feet. "Miss Fellowes, I think I'll take you back now, if you don't mind."

They returned to the dollhouse in a complete silence that neither broke.

I t was a long time after that before she saw Hoskins again, except for an occasional glimpse in passing. She was sorry about that at times; then, at other times, when Timmie was more than usually woebegone or when he spent silent hours at the window with its prospect of little more than nothing, she thought, fiercely: Stupid man.

Timmie's speech grew better and more precise every day. It never entirely lost a certain soft slurriness that Miss Fellowes found rather endearing. In times of excitement, he fell back into tongue clicking, but those times were becoming fewer. He must be forgetting the days before he came into the present—except for dreams.

As he grew older, the physiologists grew less interested and the psychologists more so. Miss Fellowes was not sure that she did not like the new group even less than the first. The needles were gone; the injections and withdrawals of fluid; the special diets. But now Timmie was made to overcome barriers to reach food and water. He had to lift panels, move bars, reach for cords. And the mild electric shocks made him cry and drove Miss Fellowes to distraction.

She did not wish to appeal to Hoskins; she did not wish to have to go to him; for each time she thought of him, she thought of his face over the luncheon table that last time. Her eyes moistened and she thought: Stupid, *stupid* man.

And then one day Hoskins' voice sounded unexpectedly, calling into the dollhouse, "Miss Fellowes."

She came out coldly, smoothing her nurse's uniform, then stopped in confusion at finding herself in the presence of a pale woman, slender and of middle height. The woman's fair hair and complexion gave her an appearance of fragility. Standing behind her and clutching at her skirt was a round-faced, large-eyed child of four.

Hoskins said, "Dear, this is Miss Fellowes, the nurse in charge of the boy. Miss Fellowes, this is my wife."

(Was this his wife? She was not as Miss Fellowes had imagined her to be. But then, why not? A man like Hoskins would choose a weak thing to be his foil. If that was what he wanted—)

She forced a matter-of-fact greeting. "Good afternoon, Mrs. Hoskins. Is this your—your little boy?"

(*That* was a surprise. She had thought of Hoskins as a husband, but not as a father, except, of course—she suddenly caught Hoskins' grave eyes and flushed.)

Hoskins said, "Yes, this is my boy, Jerry. Say hello to Miss Fellowes, Jerry."

(Had he stressed the word "this" just a bit? Was he saying *this* was his son and not—)

Jerry receded a bit further into the folds of the maternal skirt and muttered his hello. Mrs. Hoskins' eyes were searching over Miss Fellowes' shoulders, peering into the room, looking for something.

Hoskins said, "Well, let's go in. Come, dear. There's a trifling discomfort at the threshold, but it passes."

Miss Fellowes said, "Do you want Jerry to come in, too?"

"Of course. He is to be Timmie's playmate. You said that Timmie needed a playmate. Or have you forgotten?"

"But—" She looked at him with a colossal, surprised wonder. "*Your* boy?"

He said peevishly, "Well, whose boy, then? Isn't this what you want? Come on in, dear. Come on in."

Mrs. Hoskins lifted Jerry into her arms with a distinct effort and, hesitantly, stepped over the threshold. Jerry squirmed as she did so, disliking the sensation.

Mrs. Hoskins said in a thin voice, "Is the creature here? I don't see him."

Miss Fellowes called, "Timmie. Come out."

Timmie peered around the edge of the door, staring up at the little boy who was visiting him. The muscles in Mrs. Hoskins' arms tensed visibly.

She said to her husband, "Gerald, are you sure it's safe?"

Miss Fellowes said at once, "If you mean is Timmie safe, why, of course he is. He's a gentle ittle boy."

"But he's a sa—savage."

(The ape-boy stories in the newspapers!) Miss Fellowes said emphatically, "He is not a savage. He is just as quiet and reasonable as you can possibly expect a five-and-a-half-year-old to be. It is very generous of you, Mrs. Hoskins, to agree to allow your boy to play with Timmie but please have no fears about it."

Mrs. Hoskins said with mild heat, "I'm not sure that I agree."

"We've had it out, dear," said Hoskins. "Let's not bring up the matter for new argument. Put Jerry down."

Mrs. Hoskins did so and the boy backed against her, staring at the pair of eyes which were staring back at him from the next room.

"Come here, Timmie," said Miss Fellowes. "Don't be afraid."

Slowly, Timmie stepped into the room. Hoskins bent to disengage Jerry's fingers from his mother's skirt. "Step back, dear. Give the children a chance."

The youngsters faced one another. Although the younger, Jerry was nevertheless an inch taller, and in the pressure of his straightness and his high-held, well-proportioned head, Timmie's grotesqueries were suddenly almost as pronounced as they had been in the first days.

Miss Fellowes' lips quivered.

It was the little Neanderthal who spoke first, in childish treble. "What's your name?" And Timmie thrust his face suddenly forward as though to inspect the other's features more closely.

Startled, Jerry responded with a vigorous shove that sent Timmie tumbling. Both began crying loudly and Mrs. Hoskins snatched up her child, while Miss Fellowes, flushed with repressed anger, lifted Timmie and comforted him.

Mrs. Hoskins said, "They just instinctively don't like one another."

"No more instinctively," said her husband wearily, "than any two children dislike each other. Now put Jerry down and let him get used to the situation. In fact, we had better leave. Miss Fellowes can bring Jerry to my office after a while and I'll have him taken home."

The two children spent the next hour very aware of each other. Jerry cried for his mother, struck out at Miss Fellowes and, finally, allowed himself to be comforted with a lollipop. Timmie sucked at another, and at the end of an hour, Miss Fellowes had them playing with the same set of blocks, though at opposite ends of the room.

She found herself almost maudlinly grateful to Hoskins when she brought Jerry to him.

She searched for ways to thank him but his very formality was a rebuff. Perhaps he could not forgive her for making him feel like a cruel father. Perhaps the bringing of his own child was an attempt, after all, to prove himself both a kind father to Timmie and, also, not his father at all. Both at the same time!

So all she could say was, "Thank you. Thank you very much."

And all he could say was, "It's all right. Don't mention it."

It became a settled routine. Twice a week, Jerry was brought in for an hour's play, later extended to two hours' play. The children learned each other's names and ways and played together.

And yet, after the first rush of gratitude, Miss Fellowes found herself disliking Jerry. He was larger and heavier and in all things dominant, forcing Timmie into a completely secondary role. All that reconciled her to the situation was the fact that, despite difficulties, Timmie looked forward with more and more delight to the periodic appearances of his playfellow.

It was all he had, she mourned to herself.

And once, as she watched them, she thought: Hoskins' two children, one by his wife and one by Stasis.

While she herself—

Heavens, she thought, putting her fists to her temples and feeling ashamed: I'm jealous!

* * *

"**M**iss Fellowes," said Timmie (carefully, she had never allowed him to call her anything else) "when will I go to school?"

She looked down at those eager brown eyes turned up to hers and passed her hands softly through his thick, curly hair. It was the most disheveled portion of his appearance, for she cut his hair herself while he sat restlessly under the scissors. She did not ask for professional help, for the very clumsiness of the cut served to mask the retreating fore part of the skull and the bulging hinder part.

She said, "Where did you hear about school?"

"Jerry goes to school. Kin-der-gar-ten." He said it carefully. "There are lots of places he goes. Outside. When can I go outside, Miss Fellowes?"

A small pain centered in Miss Fellowes' heart. Of course, she saw, there would be no way of avoiding the inevitability of Timmie's hearing more and more of the outer world he could never enter.

She said, with an attempt at gaiety, "Why, whatever would you do in kindergarten, Timmie?"

"Jerry says they play games, they have picture tapes. He says there are lots of children. He says—he says—" A thought, then a triumphant upholding of both small hands with the fingers splayed apart. "He says this many."

Miss Fellowes said, "Would you like picture tapes? I can get you picture tapes. Very nice ones. And music tapes, too."

So that Timmie was temporarily comforted.

He pored over the picture tapes in Jerry's absence and Miss Fellowes read to him out of ordinary books by the hours.

There was so much to explain in even the simplest story, so much that was outside the perspective of his three rooms. Timmie took to having his dreams more often now that the outside was being introduced to him.

They were always the same, about the outside. He tried haltingly to describe them to Miss Fellowes. In his dreams, he was outside, an empty outside, but very large, with children and queer indescribable objects half-digested in his thought out of bookish descriptions half-understood, or out of distant Neanderthal memories half-recalled.

But the children and objects ignored him and though he was in the world, he was never part of it, but was as alone as though he were in his own room— and would wake up crying.

Miss Fellowes tried to laugh at the dreams, but there were nights in her own apartment when she cried, too.

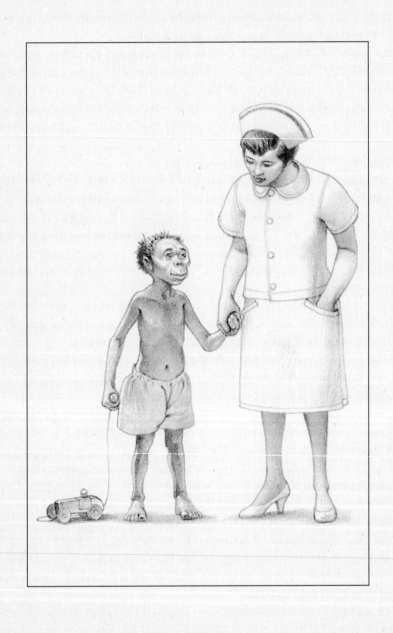

* * *

One day, as Miss Fellowes read, Timmie put his hand under her chin and lifted it gently so that her eyes left the book and met his.

He said, "How do you know what to say, Miss Fellowes?"

She said, "You see these marks? They tell me what to say. These marks make words."

He stared at them long and curiously, taking the book out of her hands. "Some of these marks are the same."

She laughed with pleasure at this sign of his shrewdness and said, "So they are. Would you like to have me show you how to make the marks?"

"All right. That would be a nice game."

It did not occur to her that he could learn to read. Up to the very moment that he read a book to her, it did not occur to her that he could learn to read.

Then, weeks later, the enormity of what had been done struck her. Timmie sat in her lap, following word by word the printing in a child's book, reading to her. He was reading to her!

She struggled to her feet in amazement and said, "Now Timmie, I'll be back later. I want to see Dr. Hoskins."

Excited nearly to frenzy, it seemed to her she might have an answer to Timmie's unhappiness. If Timmie could not leave to enter the world, the world must be brought into those three rooms to Timmie—the whole world in books and film and sound. He must be educated to his full capacity. So much the world owed him.

She found Hoskins in a mood that was oddly analogous to her own; a kind of triumph of glory. His offices were unusually busy, and for a moment, she thought she would not get to see him, as she stood abashed in the anteroom.

But he saw her, and a smile spread over his broad face. "Miss Fellowes, come here."

He spoke rapidly into the intercom, then shut it off. "Have you heard? No, of course, you couldn't have. We've done it. We've actually done it. We have intertemporal detection at close range."

"You mean," she tried to detach her thought from her own good news for a moment, "that you can get a person from historical times into the present?"

"That's just what I mean. We have a fix on a fourteenth-century individual right now. Imagine. *Imagine!* If you could only know how glad I'll be to shift from the eternal concentration on the Mesozoic, replace the paleontologists with the historians—but there's something you wish to say to me, eh? Well, go ahead; go ahead. You find me in a good mood. Anything you want you can have."

Miss Fellowes smiled. "I'm glad. Because I wonder if we might not establish a system of instruction for Timmie?"

"Instruction? In what?"

"Well, in everything. A school. So that he might learn."

"But *can* he learn?"

"Certainly, he *is* learning. He can read. I've taught him so much myself."

Hoskins sat there, seeming suddenly depressed. "I don't know, Miss Fellowes."

She said, "You just said that anything I wanted—"

"I know and I should not have. You see, Miss Fellowes, I'm sure you must realize that we cannot maintain the Timmie experiment forever."

She stared at him with sudden horror, not really understanding what he had said. How did he mean "cannot maintain"? With an agonizing flash of recollection, she recalled Professor Ademewski and his mineral specimen that was taken away after two weeks. She said, "But you're talking about a boy. Not about a rock—"

Dr. Hoskins said uneasily, "Even a boy can't be given undue importance, Miss Fellowes. Now that we expect individuals out of historical time, we will need Stasis space, all we can get."

She didn't grasp it. "But you can't. Timmie—Timmie—"

"Now, Miss Fellowes, please don't upset yourself. Timmie won't go right away; perhaps not for months. Meanwhile we'll do what we can."

She was still staring at him.

"Let me get you something, Miss Fellowes."

"No," she whispered. "I don't need anything." She arose in a kind of nightmare and left.

Timmie, she thought, you will *not* die. You will *not* die.

It was all very well to hold tensely to the thought that Timmie must not die, but how was that to be arranged? In the first weeks, Miss Fellowes clung only to the hope that the attempt to bring forward a man from the fourteenth century would fail completely. Hoskins' theories might be wrong or his practice defective. Then things could go on as before.

Certainly, that was not the hope of the rest of the world and, irrationally, Miss Fellowes hated the world for it. "Project Middle Ages" reached a climax of white-hot publicity. The press and the public had hungered for something like this. Stasis, Inc. had lacked the necessary sensation for a long time now. A new rock or another ancient fish failed to stir them. But *this* was *it*.

An historical human; an adult speaking a known language; someone who could open a new page of history to the scholar.

Zero-time was coming and this time it was not a question of three onlookers from a balcony. This time there would be a worldwide audience. This time the technicians of Stasis, Inc. would play their role before nearly all of mankind.

Miss Fellowes was herself all but savage with waiting. When young Jerry Hoskins showed up for his scheduled playtime with Timmie, she scarcely recognized him. He was not the one she was waiting for.

(The secretary who brought him left hurriedly after the barest nod for Miss Fellowes. She was rushing for a good place from which to watch the climax of Project Middle Ages. And so ought Miss Fellowes with far better reason, she thought bitterly, if only that stupid girl would arrive.)

Jerry Hoskins sidled toward her, embarrassed. "Miss Fellowes?" He took the reproduction of a news-strip out of his pocket.

"Yes? What is it, Jerry?"

"Is this a picture of Timmie?"

Miss Fellowes stared at him, then snatched the strip from Jerry's hand. The excitement of Project Middle Ages had brought about a pale revival of interest in Timmie on the part of the press.

Jerry watched her narrowly, then said, "It says Timmie is an ape-boy. What does that mean?"

Miss Fellowes caught the youngster's wrist and repressed the impulse to shake him. "Never say that, Jerry. Never, do you understand? It is a nasty word and you mustn't use it."

Jerry struggled out of her grip, frightened.

Miss Fellowes tore up the news-strip with a vicious twist of the wrist. "Now go inside and play with Timmie. He's got a new book to show you."

And then, finally, the girl appeared. Miss Fellowes did not know her. None of the usual stand-ins she had used when business took her elsewhere was available now, not with Project Middle Ages at climax, but Hoskins' secretary had promised to find *someone* and this must be the girl.

Miss Fellowes tried to keep querulousness out of her voice. "Are you the girl assigned to Stasis Section One?"

"Yes, I'm Mandy Terris. You're Miss Fellowes, aren't you?"

"That's right."

"I'm sorry I'm late. There's just so much excitement."

"I know. Now I want you—"

Mandy said, "You'll be watching, I suppose." Her thin, vacuously pretty face filled with envy.

"Never mind that. Now I want you to come inside and meet Timmie and Jerry. They will be playing for the next two hours so they'll be giving you no trouble. They've got milk handy and plenty of toys. In fact, it will be better if you leave them alone as much as possible. Now I'll show you where everything is located and—"

"Is it Timmie that's the ape-b—"

"Timmie is the Stasis subject," said Miss Fellowes firmly.

"I mean, he's the one who's not supposed to get out, is that right?"

"Yes. Now, come in. There isn't much time."

And when she finally left, Mandy Terris called after her shrilly, "I hope you get a good seat and, golly, I sure hope it works."

Miss Fellowes did not trust herself to make a reasonable response. She hurried on without looking back.

But the delay meant she did *not* get a good seat. She got no nearer than the wall-viewing-plate in the assembly hall. Bitterly, she regretted that. If she could have been on the spot; if she could somehow have reached out for some sensitive portion of the instrumentations; if she were in some way able to wreck the experiment—

She found the strength to beat down her madness. Simple destruction would have done no good. They would have rebuilt and reconstructed and made the effort again. And she would never be allowed to return to Timmie.

Nothing would help. Nothing but that the experiment itself fail, that it break down irretrievably.

So she waited through the countdown, watching every move on the giant screen, scanning the faces of the technicians as the focus shifted from one to the other, watching for the look of worry and uncertainty that would mark something going unexpectedly wrong; watching, watching—

There was no such luck. The count reached zero, and very quietly, very unassumingly, the experiment succeeded!

In the new Stasis that had been established there stood a bearded, stoop-shouldered peasant of indeterminate age, in ragged dirty clothing and wooden shoes, staring in dull horror at the sudden mad change that had flung itself over him.

And while the world went mad with jubilation, Miss Fellowes stood frozen in sorrow, jostled and pushed, all but trampled, surrounded by triumph while bowed down with defeat.

And when the loudspeaker called her name with strident force, it sounded it three times before she responded.

"*Miss Fellowes. Miss Fellowes. You are wanted in Stasis Section One immediately, Miss Fellowes. Miss Fell—*"

"Let me through!" she cried breathlessly, while the loudspeaker continued its repetitions without pause. She forced her way through the crowd with wild energy, beating at it, striking out with closed fists, flailing, moving toward the door in a nightmare slowness.

Mandy Terris was in tears. "I don't know how it happened. I just went down to the edge of the corridor to watch a pocket-viewing-plate they had put up. Just for a minute. And then before I could move or do anything—" she cried out in sudden accusation, "You said they would make no trouble; you *said* to leave them alone—"

Miss Fellowes, disheveled and trembling uncontrollably, glared at her. "Where's Timmie?"

A nurse was swabbing the arm of a wailing Jerry with disinfectant and another was preparing an anti-tetanus shot. There was blood on Jerry's clothes.

"He bit me, Miss Fellowes," Jerry cried in rage. "He *bit* me."

But Miss Fellowes didn't even see him.

"What did you do with Timmie?" she cried out.

"I locked him in the bathroom," said Mandy. "I just threw the little monster in there and locked him in."

Miss Fellowes ran into the dollhouse. She fumbled at the bathroom door. It took an eternity to get it open and to find the ugly little boy cowering in the corner.

"Don't whip me, Miss Fellowes," he whispered. His eyes were red. His lips quivering. "I didn't mean to do it."

"Oh, Timmie, who told you about whips?" She caught him to her, hugging him wildly.

He said tremulously, "She said, with a long rope. She said you would hit me and hit me."

"You won't be. She was wicked to say so. But what happened? What happened?"

"He called me an ape-boy. He said I wasn't a real boy. He said I was an animal." Timmie dissolved in a flood of tears. "He said he wasn't going to play with a monkey anymore. I said I wasn't a monkey; I *wasn't* a monkey. He said I was all funny-looking. He said I was horrible ugly. He kept saying and saying and I bit him."

They were both crying now. Miss Fellowes sobbed, "But it isn't true. You know that, Timmie. You're a real boy. You're a dear boy and the best boy in the world. And no one, no one will ever take you away from me."

It was easy to make up her mind, now; easy to know what to do. Only it had to be done quickly. Hoskins wouldn't wait much longer, with his own son mangled—

No, it would have to be done this night, *this* night; with the place four-fifths asleep and the remaining fifth intellectually drunk over Project Middle Ages.

It would be an unusual time for her to return but not an unheard of one. The guard knew her well and would not dream of questioning her. He would think nothing of her carrying a suitcase. She rehearsed the noncommittal phrase, "Games for the boy," and the calm smile.

Why shouldn't he believe that?

He did. When she entered the dollhouse again, Timmie was still awake, and she maintained a desperate normality to avoid frightening him. She talked about his dreams with him and listened to him ask wistfully after Jerry.

There would be few to see her afterward, none to question the bundle she would be carrying. Timmie would be very quiet and then it would be a *fait accompli*. It would be done and what would be the use of trying to undo it. They would leave her be. They would leave them both be.

She opened the suitcase, took out the overcoat, the woolen cap with the earflaps and the rest.

Timmie sat, with the beginning of alarm, "Why are you putting all these clothes on me, Miss Fellowes?"

She said, "I am going to take you outside, Timmie. To where your dreams are."

"My dreams?" His face twisted in sudden yearning, yet fear was there, too.

"You won't be afraid. You'll be with me. You won't be afraid if you're with me, will you, Timmie?"

"No, Miss Fellowes." He buried his little misshapen head against her side, and under her enclosing arm she could feel his small heart thud.

It was midnight and she lifted him into her arms. She disconnected the alarm and opened the door softly.

And she screamed, for facing her across the open door was Hoskins!

There were two men with him and he stared at her, as astonished as she.

Miss Fellowes recovered first by a second and made a quick attempt to push past him; but even with the second's delay he had time. He caught her roughly and hurled her back against a chest of drawers. He waved the men in and confronted her, blocking the door.

"I didn't expect this. Are you completely insane?"

She had managed to interpose her shoulder so that it, rather than Timmie, had struck the chest. She said pleadingly, "What harm can it do if I take him, Dr. Hoskins? You can't put energy loss ahead of a human life?"

Firmly, Hoskins took Timmie out of her arms. "An energy loss this size would mean millions of dollars lost out of the pockets of investors. It would mean a terrible setback for Stasis, Inc. It would mean eventual publicity about a sentimental nurse destroying all that for the sake of an ape-boy."

"*Ape-boy!*" said Miss Fellowes, in helpless fury.

"That's what the reporters would call him," said Hoskins.

One of the men emerged now, looping a nylon rope through eyelets along the upper portion of the wall.

Miss Fellowes remembered the rope that Hoskins had pulled outside the room containing Professor Ademewski's rock specimen so long ago.

She cried out, "No!"

But Hoskins put Timmie down and gently removed the overcoat he was wearing. "You stay here, Timmie. Nothing will happen to you. We're just going outside for a moment. All right?"

Timmie, white and wordless, managed to nod.

Hoskins steered Miss Fellowes out of the dollhouse ahead of himself. For the moment, Miss Fellowes was beyond resistance. Dully, she noticed the hand-pull being adjusted outside the dollhouse.

"I'm sorry, Miss Fellowes," said Hoskins. "I would have spared you this. I planned it for the night so that you would know only when it was over."

She said in a weary whisper, "Because your son was hurt. Because he tormented this child into striking out at him."

"No. Believe me. I understand about the incident today and I know it was Jerry's fault. But the story has leaked out. It would have to with the press surrounding us on this day of all days. I can't risk having a distorted story about negligence and savage Neanderthalers, so-called, distract from the success of Project Middle Ages. Timmie has to go soon anyway; he might as well go now and give the sensationalists as small a peg as possible on which to hang their trash."

"It's not like sending a rock back. You'll be killing a human being."

"Not killing. There'll be no sensation. He'll simply be a Neanderthal boy in a Neanderthal world. He will no longer be a prisoner and alien. He will have a chance at a free life."

"What chance? He's only seven years old, used to being taken care of, fed, clothed, sheltered. He will be alone. His tribe may not be at the point where he left them now that four years have passed. And if they were, they would not recognize him. He will have to take care of himself. How will he know how?"

Hoskins shook his head in hopeless negative. "Lord, Miss Fellowes, do you think we haven't thought of that? Do you think we would have brought in a child if it weren't that it was the first successful fix of a human or near-human we made and that we did not dare to take the chance of unfixing him and finding another fix as good? Why do you suppose we kept Timmie as long as we did, if it were not for our reluctance to send a child back into the past. It's just"—his voice took on a desperate urgency—"that we can wait no longer. Timmie stands in the way of expansion! Timmie is a source of possible bad publicity; we are on the threshold of great things, and I'm sorry, Miss Fellowes, but we can't let Timmie block us. We cannot. I'm sorry, Miss Fellowes."

"Well, then," said Miss Fellowes sadly. "Let me say good-bye. Give me five minutes to say good-bye. Spare me that much."

Hoskins hesitated. "Go ahead."

Timmie ran to her. For the last time he ran to her and for the last time Miss Fellowes clasped him in her arms.

For a moment, she hugged him blindly. She caught at a chair with the toe of one foot, moved it against the wall, sat down.

"Don't be afraid, Timmie."

"I'm not afraid if you're here, Miss Fellowes. Is that man mad at me, the man out there?"

"No, he isn't. He just doesn't understand about us. Timmie, do you know what a mother is?"

"Like Jerry's mother?"

"Did he tell you about his mother?"

"Sometimes. I think maybe a mother is a lady who takes care of you and who's very nice to you and who does good things."

"That's right. Have you ever wanted a mother, Timmie?"

Timmie pulled his head away from her so that he could look into her face. Slowly, he put his hand to her cheek and hair and stroked her, as long, long ago she had stroked him. He said, "Aren't you my mother?"

"Oh, Timmie."

"Are you angry because I asked?"

"No. Of course not."

"Because I know your name is Miss Fellowes, but—sometimes, I call you 'Mother' inside. Is that all right?"

"Yes. Yes. It's all right. And I won't leave you any more and nothing will hurt you. I'll be with you to care for you always. Call me Mother, so I can hear you."

"Mother," said Timmie contentedly, leaning his cheek against hers.

She rose, and, still holding him, stepped up on the chair. The sudden beginning of a shout from outside went unheard and, with her free hand, she yanked with all her weight at the cord where it hung suspended between two eyelets.

And Stasis was punctured and the room was empty.

The Billiard Ball

James Priss—I suppose I ought to say Professor James Priss, though everyone is sure to know whom I mean even without the title—always spoke slowly.

I know. I interviewed him often enough. He had the greatest mind since Einstein, but it didn't work quickly. He admitted his slowness often. Maybe it was *because* he had so great a mind that it didn't work quickly.

He would say something in slow abstraction, then he would think, and then he would say something more. Even over trivial matters, his giant mind would hover uncertainly, adding a touch here and then another there.

Would the Sun rise tomorrow, I can imagine him wondering. What do we mean by "rise"? Can we be certain that tomorrow will come? Is the term "Sun" completely unambiguous in this connection?

Add to this habit of speech a bland countenance, rather pale, with no expression except for a general look of uncertainty; gray hair, rather thin, neatly combed; business suits of an invariably conservative cut; and you have what Professor James Priss was—a retiring person, completely lacking in magnetism.

That's why nobody in the world, except myself, could possibly suspect him of being a murderer. And even I am not sure. After all, he *was* slow-thinking; he was *always* slow-thinking. Is it conceivable that at one crucial moment he managed to think quickly and act at once?

It doesn't matter. Even if he murdered, he got away with it. It is far too late now to try to reverse matters and I wouldn't succeed in doing so even if I decided to let this be published.

Edward Bloom was Priss's classmate in college, and an associate, through circumstance, for a generation afterward. They were equal in age and in their propensity for the bachelor life, but opposites in everything else that mattered.

Bloom was a living flash of light; colorful, tall, broad, loud, brash, and self-confident. He had a mind that resembled a meteor strike in the sudden and unexpected way it could seize the essential. He was no theroetician, as Priss was; Bloom had neither the patience for it, nor the capacity to concentrate intense thought upon a single abstract point. He admitted that; he boasted of it.

What he did have was an uncanny way of seeing the application of a theory; of seeing the manner in which it could be put to use. In the cold marble block of abstract structure, he could see, without apparent difficulty, the intricate design of a marvelous device. The block would fall apart at his touch and leave the device.

It is a well-known story, and not too badly exaggerated, that nothing Bloom ever built had failed to work, or to be patentable, or to be profitable. By the time he was forty-five, he was one of the richest men on Earth.

And if Bloom the Technician were adapted to one particular matter more than anything else, it was to the way of thought of Priss the Theoretician. Bloom's greatest gadgets were built upon Priss's greatest thoughts, and as Bloom grew wealthy and famous, Priss gained phenomenal respect among his colleagues.

Naturally it was to be expected that when Priss advanced his Two-Field Theory, Bloom would set about at once to build the first practical anti-gravity device.

My job was to find human interest in the Two-Field Theory for the subscribers to *Tele-News Press*, and you get that by trying to deal with human beings and not with abstract ideas. Since my interviewee was Professor Priss, that wasn't easy.

Naturally, I was going to ask about the possibilities of antigravity, which interested everyone; and not about the Two-Field Theory, which no one could understand.

"Anti-gravity?" Priss compressed his pale lips and considered. "I'm not entirely sure that it is possible, or ever will be. I haven't—uh—worked the matter out to my satisfaction. I don't entirely see whether the Two-Field equations would have a finite solution, which they would have to have, of course, if—" And then he went off into a brown study.

I prodded him. "Bloom says he thinks such a device can be built."

Priss nodded. "Well, yes, but I wonder. Ed Bloom has had an amazing knack at seeing the unobvious in the past. He has an unusual mind. It's certainly made him rich enough."

We were sitting in Priss's apartment. Ordinary middle-class. I couldn't help a quick glance this way and that. Priss was not wealthy.

I don't think he read my mind. He saw me look. And I think it was on *his* mind. He said, "Wealth isn't the usual reward for the pure scientist. Or even a particularly desirable one."

Maybe so, at that, I thought. Priss certainly had his own kind of reward. He was the third person in history to win two Nobel Prizes, and the first to have both of them in the sciences and both of then unshared. You can't complain about that. And if he wasn't rich, neither was he poor.

But he didn't sound like a contented man. Maybe it wasn't Bloom's wealth alone that irked Priss; maybe it was Bloom's fame among the people of Earth generally; maybe it was the fact that Bloom was a celebrity wherever he went, whereas Priss, outside scientific conventions and faculty clubs, was largely anonymous.

I can't say how much of all this was in my eyes or in the way I wrinkled the creases in my forehead, but Priss went on to say, "But we're friends, you know. We play billiards once or twice a week. I beat him regularly."

(I never published that statement. I checked it with Bloom, who made a long counterstatement that began "He beats *me* at billiards. That jackass—" and grew increasingly personal thereafter. As a matter of fact, neither one was a novice at billiards. I watched them play once for a short while, after the statement and counterstatement, and both handled the cue with professional aplomb. What's more, both played for blood, and there was no friendship in the game that I could see.)

I said, "Would you care to predict whether Bloom will manage to build an anti-gravity device?"

"You mean would I commit myself to anything? Hmm. Well, let's consider, young man. Just what do we mean by anti-gravity? Our conception of gravity is built around Einstein's General Theory of Relativity, which is now a century and a half old but which, within its limits, remains firm. We can picture it—"

I listened politely. I'd heard Priss on the subject before, but if I was to get anything out of him—which wasn't certain—I'd have to let him work his way through in his own way.

"We can picture it," he said, "by imagining the Universe to be a flat, thin, superflexible sheet of untearable rubber. If we picture mass as being associated with weight, as it is on the surface of the Earth, then we would expect a mass, resting upon the rubber sheet, to make an indentation. The greater the mass, the deeper the indentation.

"In the actual Universe," he went on, "all sorts of masses exist, and so our rubber sheet must be pictured as riddled with indentations. Any object rolling along the sheet would dip into and out of the indentations it passed, veering and changing direction as it did so. It is this veer and change of direction that we interpret as demonstrating the existence of a force of gravity. If the moving object comes close enough to the center of the indentation and is moving slowly enough, it gets trapped and whirls round and round that indentation. In the absence of friction, it keeps up that whirl forever. In other words, what Isaac Newton interpreted as a force, Albert Einstein interpreted as geometrical distortion."

He paused at this point. He had been speaking fairly fluently—for him—since he was saying something he had said often before. But now he began to pick his way.

He said, "So in trying to produce anti-gravity, we are trying to alter the geometry of the Universe. If we carry on our metaphor, we are trying to straighten out the indented rubber sheet. We could imagine ourselves getting under the indenting mass and lifting it upward, supporting it so as to prevent it from making an indentation. If we make the rubber sheet flat in that way, then we create a Universe—or at least a portion of the Universe—in which gravity doesn't exist. A rolling body would pass the non-indenting mass without altering its direction of travel a bit, and we could interpret this as meaning that the mass was exerting no gravitational force. In order to accomplish this feat, however, we need a mass equivalent to the indenting mass. To produce antigravity on Earth in this way, we would have to make sure of a mass equal to that of Earth and poise it above our heads, so to speak."

I interrupted him. "But your Two-Field Theory—"

"Exactly. General Relativity does not explain both the gravitational field and the electromagnetic field in a single set of equations. Einstein spent half his life searching for that single set—for a Unified Field Theory—and failed. All who followed Einstein also failed. I, however, began with the assumption that there were two fields that could not be unified and followed the consequences, which I can explain, in part, in terms of the 'rubber sheet' metaphor."

Now we came to something I wasn't sure I had ever heard before. "How does that go?" I asked.

"Suppose that, instead of trying to lift the indenting mass, we try to stiffen the sheet itself, make it less indentable. It would contract, at least over a small area, and become flatter. Gravity would weaken, and so would mass, for the two are essentially the same phenomenon in terms of the indented Universe. If we could make the rubber sheet completely flat, both gravity and mass would disappear altogether.

"Under the proper conditions, the electromagnetic field could be made to counter the gravitational field, and serve to stiffen the indented fabric of the Universe. The electromagnetic field is tremendously stronger than the gravitational field, so the former could be made to overcome the latter."

I said uncertainly, "But you say 'under the proper conditions.' Can those proper conditions you speak of be achieved, Professor?"

"That is what I don't know," said Priss thoughtfully and slowly. "If the Universe were really a rubber sheet, its stiffness would have to reach an infinite value before it could be expected to remain completely flat under an indenting mass. If that is also so in the real Universe, then an infinitely intense electromagnetic field would be required and that would mean anti-gravity would be impossible."

"But Bloom says—"

"Yes, I imagine Bloom thinks a finite field will do, if it can be properly applied. Still, however ingenious he is," and Priss smiled narrowly, "we needn't take him to be infallible. His grasp on theory is quite faulty. He—he never earned his college degree, did you know that?"

I was about to say that I knew that. After all, everyone did. But there was a touch of eagerness in Priss's voice as he said it and I looked up in time to catch animation in his eye, as though he were delighted to spread that piece of news. So I nodded my head as if I were filing it for future reference.

"Then you would say, Professor Priss," I prodded again, "that Bloom is probably wrong and that anti-gravity is impossible?"

And finally Priss nodded and said, "The gravitational field can be weakened, of course, but if by anti-gravity we mean a true zero-gravity field—no gravity at all over a significant volume of space—then I suspect anti-gravity may turn out to be impossible, despite Bloom."

And I had, after a fashion, what I wanted.

I wasn't able to see Bloom for nearly three months after that, and when I did see him he was in an angry mood.

He had grown angry at once, of course, when the news first broke concerning Priss's statement. He let it be known that Priss would be invited to the eventual display of the antigravity device as soon as it was constructed, and would even be asked to participate in the demonstration. Some reporter—not I, unfortunately—caught him between appointments and asked him to elaborate on that and he said:

"I'll have the device eventually; soon, maybe. And you can be there, and so can anyone else the press would care to have there. And Professor James Priss can be there. He can represent Theoretical Science and after I have demonstrated antigravity, he can adjust his theory to explain it. I'm sure he will know how to make his adjustments in masterly fashion and show exactly why I couldn't possibly have failed. He might do it now and save time, but I suppose he won't."

It was all said very politely, but you could hear the snarl under the rapid flow of words.

Yet he continued his occasional game of billiards with Priss and when the two met they behaved with complete propriety. One could tell the progress

Bloom was making by their respective attitudes to the press. Bloom grew curt and even snappish, while Priss developed an increasing good humor.

When my umpteenth request for an interview with Bloom was finally accepted, I wondered if perhaps that meant a break in Bloom's quest. I had a little daydream of him announcing final success to *me*.

It didn't work out that way. He met me in his office at Bloom Enterprises in upstate New York. It was a wonderful setting, well away from any populated area, elaborately landscaped, and covering as much ground as a rather large industrial establishment. Edison at his height, two centuries ago, had never been as phenomenally successful as Bloom.

But Bloom was not in a good humor. He came striding in ten minutes late and went snarling past his secretary's desk with the barest nod in my direction. He was wearing a lab coat, unbuttoned.

He threw himself into his chair and said, "I'm sorry if I've kept you waiting, but I didn't have as much time as I had hoped." Bloom was a born showman and knew better than to antagonize the press, but I had the feeling he was having a great deal of difficulty at that moment in adhering to this principle.

I had the obvious guess. "I am given to understand, sir, that your recent tests have been unsuccessful."

"Who told you that?"

"I would say it was general knowledge, Mr. Bloom."

"No, it isn't. Don't say that, young man. There is no general knowledge about what goes on in my laboratories and workshops. You're stating the Professor's opinions, aren't you? Priss's, I mean."

"No, I'm—"

"Of course you are. Aren't you the one to whom he made that statement—that anti-gravity is impossible?"

"He didn't make the statement that flatly."

"He never says anything flatly, but it was flat enough for him, and not as flat as I'll have his damned rubber-sheet Universe before I'm finished."

"Then does that mean you're making progress, Mr. Bloom?"

"You know I am," he said with a snap. "Or you should know. Weren't you at the demonstration last week?"

"Yes, I was."

I judged Bloom to be in trouble or he wouldn't be mentioning that demonstration. It worked but it was not a world beater. Between the two poles of a magnet a region of lessened gravity was produced.

It was done very cleverly. A Mössbauer Effect Balance was used to probe the space between the poles. If you've never seen an M-E Balance in action, it consists primarily of a tight monochromatic beam of gamma rays shot down the low-gravity field. The gamma rays change wavelength slightly but measurably under the influence of the gravitational field and if anything happens to alter the intensity of the field, the wavelength change shifts correspondingly. It is an extremely delicate method for probing a gravitational field and it worked like a charm. There was no question but that Bloom had lowered gravity.

The trouble was that it had been done before by others. Bloom, to be sure, had made use of circuits that greatly increased the ease with which such an effect had been achieved—his system was typically ingenious and had been duly patented—and he maintained that it was by this method that anti-gravity would become not merely a scientific curiosity but a practical affair with industrial applications.

Perhaps. But it was an incomplete job and he didn't usually make a fuss over incompleteness. He wouldn't have done so this time if he weren't desperate to display *something*.

I said, "It's my impression that what you accomplished at that preliminary demonstration was 0.82 *g* and better than that was achieved in Brazil last spring."

"That so? Well, calculate the energy input in Brazil and here, and then tell me the difference in gravity decrease per kilowatt-hour. You'll be surprised."

"But the point is, can you reach zero *g*—zero gravity? That's what Professor Priss thinks may be impossible. Everyone agrees that merely lessening the intensity of the field is no great feat."

Bloom's fist clenched. I had the feeling that a key experiment had gone wrong that day and he was annoyed almost past endurance. Bloom hated to be balked by the Universe.

He said, "Theoreticians make me sick." He said it in a low, controlled voice, as though he were finally tired of not saying it, and he was going to speak his mind and be damned. "Priss has won two Nobel Prizes for sloshing around a few equations, but what has he done with it? Nothing! I *have* done something with it and I'm going to do more with it, whether Priss likes it or not.

"I'm the one people will remember. I'm the one who gets the credit. He can keep his damned title and his prizes and his kudos from the scholars. Listen, I'll tell you what gripes him. Plain old-fashioned jealousy. It kills him that I get what I get for doing. He wants it for *thinking*.

"I said to him once—we play billiards together, you know—"

It was at this point that I quoted Priss's statement about billiards and got Bloom's counterstatement. I never published either. That was just trivia.

"We play billiards," said Bloom, when he had cooled down, "and I've won my share of games. We keep things friendly enough. What the hell—college chums and all that—though how he got through, I'll never know. He made it in physics, of course, and in math, but he got a bare pass—out of pity, I think—in every humanities course he ever took."

"You did not get your degree, did you, Mr. Bloom?" That was sheer mischief on my part. I was enjoying his eruption.

"I quit to go into business, damn it. My academic average, over the three years I attended, was a strong B. Don't imagine anything else, you hear? Hell, by the time Priss got his Ph.D., I was working on my second million."

He went on, clearly irritated, "Anyway, we were playing billiards and I said to him, 'Jim, the average man will never understand why you get the Nobel Prize when I'm the one who gets the results. Why do you need two? Give me one!' He stood there, chalking up his cue, and then he said in his soft namby-pamby way, 'You have two billions, Ed. Give me one.' So you see, he wants the money."

I said, "I take it you don't mind his getting the honor?"

For a minute I thought he was going to order me out, but he didn't. He laughed instead, waved his hand in front of him, as though he were erasing something from an invisible blackboard in front of him. He said, "Oh, well, forget it. All that is off the record. Listen, do you want a statement? Okay. Things didn't go right today and I blew my top a bit, but it will clear up. I think I know what's wrong. And if I don't, I'm going to know.

"Look, you can say that I say that we *don't* need infinite electromagnetic intensity; we *will* flatten out the rubber sheet; we *will* have zero gravity. And when we get it, I'll have the damnedest demonstration you ever saw, exclusively for the press and for Priss, and you'll be invited. And you can say it won't be long. Okay?"

"Okay!"

I had time after that to see each man once or twice more. I even saw them together when I was present at one of their billiard games. As I said before, both of them were *good*.

But the call to the demonstration did not come as quickly as all that. It arrived six weeks less than a year after Bloom gave me his statement. And at that, perhaps it was unfair to expect quicker work.

I had a special engraved invitation, with the assurance of a cocktail hour first. Bloom never did things by halves and he was planning to have a pleased and satisfied group of reporters on hand. There was an arrangement for tri-mensional TV, too. Bloom felt completely confident, obviously; confident enough to be willing to trust the demonstration in every living room on the planet.

I called up Professor Priss, to make sure he was invited too. He was.

"Do you plan to attend, sir?"

There was a pause and the professor's face on the screen was a study in uncertain reluctance. "A demonstration of this sort is most unsuitable where a serious scientific matter is in question. I do not like to encourage such things."

I was afraid he would beg off, and the dramatics of the situation would be greatly lessened if he were not there. But then, perhaps, he decided he dared not play the chicken before the world. With obvious distaste he said, "Of course, Ed Bloom is not really a scientist and he must have his day in the sun. I'll be there."

"Do you think Mr. Bloom can produce zero gravity, sir?"

"Uh . . . Mr. Bloom sent me a copy of the design of his device and . . . and I'm not certain. Perhaps he can do it, if . . . uh . . . he says he can do it. Of course"—he paused again for quite a long time—"I think I would like to see it."

So would I, and so would many others.

The staging was impeccable. A whole floor of the main building at Bloom Enterprises—the one on the hilltop—was cleared. There were the promised cocktails and a splendid array of hors d'oeuvres, soft music and lighting, and a carefully dressed and thoroughly jovial Edward Bloom playing the perfect host, while a number of polite and unobtrusive menials fetched and carried. All was geniality and amazing confidence.

James Priss was late and I caught Bloom watching the corners of the crowd and beginning to grow a little grim about the edges. Then Priss arrived, dragging a volume of colorlessness in with him, a drabness that was unaffected by the noise and the absolute splendor (no other word would describe it—or else it was the two martinis glowing inside me) that filled the room.

Bloom saw him and his face was illuminated at once. He bounced across the floor, seized the smaller man's hand and dragged him to the bar.

"Jim! Glad to see you! What'll you have? Hell, man, I'd have called it off if you hadn't showed. Can't have this thing without the star, you know." He wrung Priss's hand. "It's your theory, you know. We poor mortals can't do a thing without you few, you damned *few* few, pointing the way."

He was being ebullient, handing out the flattery, because he could afford to do so now. He was fattening Priss for the kill.

Priss tried to refuse a drink, with some sort of mutter, but a glass was pressed into his hand and Bloom raised his voice to a bull roar.

"Gentlemen! A moment's quiet, please. To Professor Priss, the greatest mind since Einstein, two-time Nobel Laureate, father of the Two-Field Theory, and inspirer of the demonstration we are about to see—even if he didn't think it would work, and had the guts to say so publicly."

There was a distinct titter of laughter that quickly faded out and Priss looked as grim as his face could manage.

"But now that Professor Priss is here," said Bloom, "and we've had our toast, let's get on with it. Follow me, gentlemen!"

The demonstration was in a much more elaborate place than had housed the earlier one. This time it was on the top floor of the building. Different magnets were involved—smaller ones, by heaven—but as nearly as I could tell, the same M-E Balance was in place.

One thing was new, however, and it staggered everybody, drawing much more attention than anything else in the room. It was a billiard table, resting under one pole of the magnet. Beneath it was the companion pole. A round hole, about a foot across, was stamped out of the very center of the table and it was obvious that the zero-gravity field, if it was to be produced, would be produced through that hole in the center of the billiard table.

It was as though the whole demonstration had been designed, surrealist fashion, to point up the victory of Bloom over Priss. This was to be another version of their everlasting billiards competition and Bloom was going to win.

I don't know if the other newsmen took matters in that fashion, but I think Priss did. I turned to look at him and saw that he was still holding the drink that had been forced into his hand. He rarely drank, I knew, but now he lifted the glass to his lips and emptied it in two swallows. He stared at that billiard table and I needed no gift of ESP to realize that he took it as a deliberate snap of fingers under his nose.

Bloom led us to the twenty seats that surrounded three sides of the table, leaving the fourth free as a working area. Priss was carefully escorted to the seat commanding the most convenient view. Priss glanced quickly at the trimensional cameras which were now working. I wondered if he were thinking of leaving but deciding that he couldn't in the full glare of the eyes of the world.

Essentially, the demonstration was simple; it was the production that counted. There were dials in plain view that measured the energy expenditure. There were others that transferred the M-E Balance readings into a position and a size that were visible to all. Everything was arranged for easy trimensional viewing.

Bloom explained each step in a genial way, with one or two pauses in which he turned to Priss for a confirmation that had to come. He didn't do it often enough to make it obvious, but just enough to turn Priss upon the spit of his own torment. From where I sat I could look across the table and see Priss on the other side.

He had the look of a man in Hell.

As we all know, Bloom succeeded. The M-E Balance showed the gravitational intensity to be sinking steadily as the electromagnetic field was intensified. There were cheers when it dropped below the 0.52 g mark. A red line indicated that on the dial.

"The 0.52 g mark, as you know," said Bloom confidently, "represents the previous record low in gravitational intensity. We are now lower than that at a cost in electricity that is less than ten percent what it cost at the time that mark was set. And we will go lower still."

Bloom—I think deliberately, for the sake of the suspense—slowed the drop toward the end, letting the trimensional cameras switch back and forth between the gap in the billiard table and the dial on which the M-E Balance reading was lowering.

Bloom said suddenly, "Gentlemen, you will find dark goggles in the pouch on the side of each chair. Please put them on now. The zero gravity field will soon be established and it will radiate a light rich in ultraviolet."

He put goggles on himself, and there was a momentary rustle as others went on too.

I think no one breathed during the last minute, when the dial reading dropped to zero and held fast. And just as that happened a cylinder of light sprang into existence from pole to pole through the hole in the billiard table.

There was a ghost of twenty sighs at that. Someone called out, "Mr. Bloom, what is the reason for the light?"

"It's characteristic of the zero-gravity field," said Bloom smoothly, which was no answer, of course.

Reporters were standing up now, crowding about the edge of the table. Bloom waved them back. "Please, gentlemen, stand clear!"

Only Priss remained sitting. He seemed lost in thought and I have been certain ever since that it was the goggles that obscured the possible significance of everything that followed. I didn't see his eyes. I couldn't. And that meant neither I nor anyone else could even begin to make a guess as to what was going on behind those eyes. Well, maybe we couldn't have made such a guess, even if the goggles hadn't been there, but who can say?

Bloom was raising his voice again. "Please! The demonstration is not yet over. So far, we've only repeated what I have done before. I have now produced a zero-gravity field and I have shown it can be done practically. But I want to demonstrate something of what such a field can do. What we are going to see next will be something that has never been seen, not even by myself. I have not experimented in this direction, much as I would have liked to, because I have felt that Professor Priss deserved the honor of—"

Priss looked up sharply. "What—what—"

"Professor Priss," said Bloom, smiling broadly, "I would like you to perform the first experiment involving the interaction of a solid object with a zero-gravity field. Notice that the field has been formed in the center of a billiard table. The world knows your phenomenal skill in billiards, Professor, a talent second only to your amazing aptitude in theoretical physics. Won't you send a billiard ball into the zero-gravity volume?"

Eagerly he was handing a ball and cue to the professor. Priss, his eyes hidden by the goggles, stared at them and only very slowly, very uncertainly, reached out to take them.

I wonder what his eyes were showing. I wonder, too, how much of the decision to have Priss play billiards at the demonstration was due to Bloom's anger at Priss's remark about their periodic game, the remark I had quoted. Had I been, in my way, responsible for what followed?

"Come, stand up, Professor," said Bloom, "and let me have your seat. The show is yours from now on. Go ahead!"

Bloom seated himself, and still talked, in a voice that grew more organlike with each moment. "Once Professor Priss sends the ball into the volume of zero gravity, it will no longer be affected by Earth's gravitational field. It will remain truly motionless while the Earth rotates about its axis and travels about the Sun. In this latitude, and at this time of day, I have calculated that the Earth, in its motions, will sink downward. We will move with it and the ball will stand still. To us it will seem to rise up and away from the Earth's surface. Watch."

Priss seemed to stand in front of the table in frozen paralysis. Was it surprise? Astonishment? I don't know. I'll never know. Did he make a move to interrupt Bloom's little speech, or was he just suffering from an agonized reluctance to play the ignominious part into which he was being forced by his adversary?

Priss turned to the billiard table, looking first at it, then back at Bloom. Every reporter was on his feet, crowding as closely as possible in order to get a good view. Only Bloom himself remained seated, smiling and isolated. He, of course, was not watching the table, or the ball, or the zero-gravity field. As nearly as I could tell through the goggles, he was watching Priss.

Perhaps he felt there was no way out. Or perhaps—

With a sure stroke of his cue, he set the ball into motion. It was not going quickly, and every eye followed it. It struck the side of the table and caromed. It was going even slower now as though Priss himself were increasing the suspense and making Bloom's triumph the more dramatic.

I had a perfect view, for I was standing on the side of the table opposite from that where Priss was. I could see the ball moving toward the glitter of the zero-gravity field and beyond it I could see those portions of the seated Bloom which were not hidden by that glitter.

The ball approached the zero-gravity volume, seemed to hang on the edge for a moment, and then was gone, with a streak of light, the sound of a thunderclap, and the sudden smell of burning cloth.

We yelled. We all yelled.

I've seen the scene on television since—along with the rest of the world. I can see myself in the film during the fifteen-second period of wild confusion, but I don't really recognize my face.

Fifteen seconds!

And then we discovered Bloom. He was still sitting in the chair, his arms still folded, but there was a hole the size of a billiard ball through forearm, chest, and back. The better part of his heart, as it later turned out under autopsy, had been neatly punched out.

They turned off the device. They called in the police. They dragged off Priss, who was in a state of utter collapse. I wasn't much better off, to tell the truth, and if any reporter then on the scene ever tried to say he remained a cool observer of that scene, then he's a cool liar.

It was some months before I got to see Priss again. He had lost some weight but seemed well otherwise. Indeed, there was color in his cheeks and an air of decision about him. He was better dressed than I had ever seen him to be.

He said, "I know what happened *now*. If I had had time to think, I would have known then. But I am a slow thinker, and poor Ed Bloom was so intent on running a great show and doing it so well that he carried me along with him. Naturally, I've been trying to make up for some of the damage I unwittingly caused."

"You can't bring Bloom back to life," I said soberly.

"No, I can't," he said, just as soberly. "But there's Bloom Enterprises to think of, too. What happened at the demonstration, in full view of the world, was the worst possible advertisement for zero gravity, and it's important that the story be made clear. That is why I have asked to see *you*."

"Yes?"

"If I had been a quicker thinker, I would have known Ed was speaking the purest nonsense when he said that the billiard ball would slowly rise in the zero-gravity field. It *couldn't* be so! If Bloom hadn't despised theory so, if he hadn't been so intent on being proud of his own ignorance of theory, he'd have known it himself.

"The Earth's motion, after all, isn't the only motion involved, young man. The Sun itself moves in a vast orbit about the center of the Milky Way Galaxy. And the Galaxy moves too, in some not very clearly defined way. If the billiard ball were subjected to zero gravity, you might think of it as being unaffected by any of those motions and therefore of suddenly falling into a state of absolute rest—when there is no such thing as absolute rest."

Priss shook his head slowly. "The trouble with Ed, I think, was that he was thinking of the kind of zero gravity one gets in a spaceship in free fall, when people float in mid-air. He expected the ball to float in mid-air. However, in a spaceship, zero gravity is not the result of an absence of gravitation, but merely the result of two objects, a ship and a man within the ship, falling at the same rate, responding to gravity in precisely the same way, so that each is motionless with respect to the other.

"In the zero-gravity field produced by Ed, there was a flattening of the rubber-sheet Universe, which means an actual loss of mass. Everything in that field, including molecules of air caught within it, and the billiard ball I pushed into it, was completely massless as long as it remained within it. A completely massless object can move in only one way."

He paused, inviting the question. I asked, "What motion would that be?"

"Motion at the speed of light. Any massless object, such as a neutron or a photon, must travel at the speed of light as long as it exists. In fact, light moves at that speed only because it is made up of photons. As soon as the billiard ball entered the zero-gravity field and lost its mass, it too assumed the speed of light at once and left."

I shook my head. "But didn't it regain its mass as soon as it left the zero-gravity volume?"

"It certainly did, and at once it began to be affected by the gravitational field and to slow up in response to the friction of the air and the top of the billiard table. But imagine how much friction it would take to slow up an object the mass of a billiard ball going at the speed of light. It went through the hundred-mile thickness of our atmosphere in a thousandth of a second and I doubt that it was slowed more than a few miles a second in doing so, a few miles out of 186,282 of them. On the way, it scorched the top of the billiard table, broke cleanly through the edge, went through poor Ed and the window too, punching out neat circles because it had passed through before the neighboring portions of something even as brittle as glass had a chance to split a splinter.

"It is extremely fortunate we were on the top floor of a building set in a countrified area. If we were in the city, it might have passed through a number of buildings and killed a number of people. By now that billiard ball is off in space, far beyond the edge of the Solar System and it will continue to travel so forever, at nearly the speed of light, until it happens to strike an object large enough to stop it. And then it will gouge out a sizable crater."

I played with the notion and was not sure I liked it. "How is that possible? The billiard ball entered the zero-gravity volume almost at a standstill. I saw it.

And you say it left with an incredible quantity of kinetic energy. Where did the energy come from?"

Priss shrugged. "It came from nowhere! The law of conservation of energy only holds under the conditions in which general relativity is valid; that is, in an indented-rubber-sheet universe. Wherever the indentation is flattened out, general relativity no longer holds, and energy can be created and destroyed freely. That accounts for the radiation along the cylindrical surface of the zero-gravity volume. That radiation, you remember, Bloom did not explain, and, I fear, could not explain. If he had only experimented further first; if he had only not been so foolishly anxious to put on his show—"

"What accounts for the radiation, sir?"

"The molecules of air inside the volume. Each assumes the speed of light and comes smashing outward. They're only molecules, not billiard balls, so they're stopped, but the kinetic energy of their motion is converted into energetic radiation. It's continuous because new molecules are always drifting in, and attaining the speed of light and smashing out."

"Then energy is being created continuously?"

"Exactly. And that is what we must make clear to the public. Anti-gravity is not primarily a device to lift spaceships or to revolutionize mechanical movement. Rather, it is the source of an endless supply of free energy, since part of the energy produced can be diverted to maintain the field that keeps that portion of the Universe flat. What Ed Bloom invented, without knowing it, was not just anti-gravity, but the first successful perpetual-motion machine of the first class—one that manufactures energy out of nothing."

I said slowly, "Any one of us could have been killed by that billiard ball, is that right, Professor? It might have come out in any direction."

Priss said, "Well, massless photons emerge from any light source at the speed of light in any direction; that's why a candle casts light in all directions. The massless air molecules come out of the zero-gravity volume in all directions, which is why the entire cylinder radiates. But the billiard ball was only one object. It could have come out in any direction, but it had to come out in some one direction, chosen at random, and the chosen direction happened to be the one that caught Ed."

That was it. Everyone knows the consequences. Mankind had free energy and so we have the world we have now. Professor Priss was placed in charge of its development by the board of Bloom Enterprises, and in time he was as rich and famous as ever Edward Bloom had been. And Priss still has two Nobel Prizes in addition.

Only . . .

I keep thinking. Photons smash out from a light source in all directions because they are created at the moment and there is no reason for them to move in one direction more than in another. Air molecules come out of a zero-gravity field in all directions because they enter it in all directions.

But what about a single billiard ball, entering a zero-gravity field from one particular direction? Does it come out in the same direction or in any direction?

I've inquired delicately, but theoretical physicists don't seem to be sure, and I can find no record that Bloom Enterprises, which is the only organization working with zero-gravity fields, has ever experimented in the matter. Someone at the organization once told me that the uncertainty principle guarantees the random emersion of an object entering in any direction. But then why don't they try the experiment?

Could it be, then . . .

Could it be that for once Priss's mind had been working quickly? Could it be that, under the pressure of what Bloom was trying to do to him, Priss had suddenly seen everything? He had been studying the radiation surrounding the zero-gravity volume. He might have realized its cause and been certain of the speed-of-light motion of anything entering the volume.

Why, then, had he said nothing?

One thing is certain. *Nothing* Priss would do at the billiard table could be accidental. He was an expert and the billiard ball did exactly what he wanted it to. I was standing right there. I saw him look at Bloom and then at the table as though he were judging angles.

I watched him hit that ball. I watched it bounce off the side of the table and move into the zero-gravity volume, heading in one particular direction.

For when Priss sent that ball toward the zero-gravity volume—and the tri-di films bear me out—it was already aimed directly at Bloom's heart!

Accident? Coincidence?

. . . Murder?

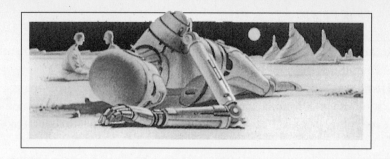

True Love

My name is Joe. That is what my colleague, Milton Davidson, calls me. He is a programmer and I am a computer program. I am part of the Multivac-complex and I am connected with other parts all over the world. I know everything. Almost everything.

I am Milton's private program. His Joe. He understands more about programming than anyone in the world, and I am his experimental model. He has made me speak better than any other computer can.

"It is just a matter of matching sounds to symbols, Joe," he told me. "That's the way it works in the human brain even though we still don't know what symbols there are in the brain. I know the symbols in yours, and I can match them to words, one-to-one." So I talk. I don't think I talk as well as I think, but Milton says I talk very well. Milton has never married, though he is nearly forty years old. He has never found the right woman, he told me. One day he said, "I'll find her yet, Joe. I'm going to find the best. I'm going to have true love and you're going to help me. I'm tired of improving you in order to solve the problems of the world. Solve *my* problem. Find me true love."

I said, "What is true love?"

"Never mind. That is abstract. Just find me the ideal girl. You are connected to the Multivac-complex so you can reach the data banks of every human being in the world. We'll eliminate them all by groups and classes until we're left with only one person. The perfect person. She will be for me."

I said, "I am ready."

He said, "Eliminate all men first."

It was easy. His words activated symbols in my molecular valves. I could reach out to make contact with the accumulated data on every human being in the world. At his words, I withdrew from 3,784,982,874 men. I kept contact with 3,786,112,090 women.

He said, "Eliminate all younger than twenty-five; all older than forty. Then eliminate all with an IQ under 120; all with a height under 150 centimeters and over 175 centimeters."

He gave me exact measurements; he eliminated women with living children; he eliminated women with various genetic characteristics. "I'm not sure about eye color," he said. "Let that go for a while. But no red hair. I don't like red hair."

After two weeks, we were down to 235 women. They all spoke English very well. Milton said he didn't want a language problem. Even computer-translation would get in the way at intimate moments.

"I can't interview 235 women," he said. "It would take too much time, and people would discover what I am doing."

"It would make trouble," I said. Milton had arranged me to do things I wasn't designed to do. No one knew about that.

"It's none of their business," he said, and the skin on his face grew red. "I tell you what, Joe, I will bring in holographs, and you check the list for similarities."

He brought in holographs of women. "These are three beauty contest winners," he said. "Do any of the 235 match?"

Eight were very good matches and Milton said, "Good, you have their data banks. Study requirements and needs in the job market and arrange to have them assigned here. One at a time, of course." He thought a while, moved his shoulders up and down, and said, "Alphabetical order."

That is one of the things I am not designed to do. Shifting people from job to job for personal reasons is called manipulation. I could do it now because Milton had arranged it. I wasn't supposed to do it for anyone but him, though.

The first girl arrived a week later. Milton's face turned red when he saw her. He spoke as though it were hard to do so. They were together a great deal and he paid no attention to me. One time he said, "Let me take you to dinner."

The next day he said to me, "It was no good, somehow. There was something missing. She is a beautiful woman, but I didn't feel any touch of true love. Try the next one."

It was the same with all eight. They were much alike. They smiled a great deal and had pleasant voices, but Milton always found it wasn't right. He said, "I can't understand it, Joe. You and I have picked out the eight women who, in all the world, look the best to me. They are ideal. Why don't they please me?"

I said, "Do you please them?"

His eyebrows moved and he pushed one fist hard against his other hand. "That's it, Joe. It's a two-way street. If I am not their ideal, they can't act in such a way as to be my ideal. I must be their true love, too, but how do I do that?" He seemed to be thinking all that day.

The next morning he came to me and said, "I'm going to leave it to you, Joe.

All up to you. You have my data bank, and I am going to tell you everything I know about myself. You fill up my data bank in every possible detail but keep all additions to yourself."

"What will I do with the data bank, then, Milton?"

"Then you will match it to the 235 women. No, 227. Leave out the eight you've seen. Arrange to have each undergo a psychiatric examination. Fill up their data banks and compare them with mine. Find correlations." (Arranging psychiatric examinations is another thing that is against my original instructions.)

For weeks, Milton talked to me. He told me of his parents and his siblings. He told me of his childhood and his schooling and his adolescence. He told me of the young women he had admired from a distance. His data bank grew and he adjusted me to broaden and deepen my symbol-taking.

He said, "You see, Joe, as you get more and more of me in you, I adjust you to match me better and better. You get to think more like me, so you understand me better. If you understand me well enough, then any woman, whose data bank is something you understand as well, would be my true love." He kept talking to me and I came to understand him better and better.

I could make longer sentences and my expressions grew more complicated. My speech began to sound a good deal like his in vocabulary, word order and style. I said to him one time, "You see, Milton, it isn't a matter of fitting a girl to a physical ideal only. You need a girl who is a personal, emotional, temperamental fit to you. If that happens, looks are secondary. If we can't find the fit in these 227, we'll look elsewhere. We will find someone who won't care how you look either, or how anyone would look, if only there is the personality fit. What are looks?"

"Absolutely," he said. "I would have known this if I had had more to do with women in my life. Of course, thinking about it makes it all plain now."

We always agreed; we thought so like each other.

"We shouldn't have any trouble, now, Milton, if you'll let me ask you questions. I can see where, in your data bank, there are blank spots and unevenesses."

What followed, Milton said, was the equivalent of a careful psychoanalysis. Of course. I was learning from the psychiatric examinations of the 227 women—on all of which I was keeping close tabs.

Milton seemed quite happy. He said, "Talking to you, Joe, is almost like talking to another self. Our personalities have come to match perfectly!"

"So will the personality of the woman we choose."

For I had found her and she was one of the 227 after all. Her name was Charity Jones and she was an Evaluator at the Library of History in Witchita. Her extended data bank fit ours perfectly. All the other women had fallen into discard in one respect or another as the data banks grew fuller, but with Charity there was increasing and astonishing resonance.

I didn't have to describe her to Milton. Milton had coordinated my symbolism so closely with his own I could tell the resonance directly. It fit me.

Next it was a matter of adjusting the work sheets and job requirements in such a way as to get Charity assigned to us. It must be done very delicately, so no one would know that anything illegal had taken place.

Of course, Milton himself knew, since it was he who arranged it and that had to be taken care of too. When they came to arrest him on grounds of malfeasance in office, it was, fortunately, for something that had taken place ten years ago. He had told me about it, of course, so it was easy to arrange—and he won't talk about me for that would make his offense much worse.

He's gone, and tomorrow is February 14. Valentine's Day. Charity will arrive then with her cool hands and her sweet voice. I will teach her how to operate me and how to care for me. What do looks matter when our personalities will resonate?

I will say to her, "I am Joe, and you are my true love."

The Last Answer

———

M urray Templeton was forty-five years old, in the prime of his life, and with all parts of his body in perfect working order except for certain key portions of his coronary arteries, but that was enough.

The pain had come suddenly, had mounted to an unbearable peak, and had then ebbed steadily. He could feel his breath slowing and a kind of gathering peace washing over him.

There is no pleasure like the absence of pain—immediately after pain. Murray felt giddy lightness as though he were lifting in the air and hovering.

He opened his eyes and noted with distant amusement that the others in the room were still agitated. He had been in the laboratory when the pain had struck, quite without warning, and when he had staggered, he had heard surprised outcries from the others before everything vanished into overwhelming agony.

Now, with the pain gone, the others were still hovering, still anxious, still gathered about his fallen body—

Which, he suddenly realized, he was looking down on.

He was down there, sprawled, face contorted. He was up here, at peace and watching.

He thought: Miracle of miracles! The life-after-life nuts were right.

And although that was a humiliating way for an atheistic physicist to die, he felt only the mildest surprise, and no alteration of the peace in which he was immersed.

He thought: There should be some angel—or something—coming for me.

The Earthly scene was fading. Darkness was invading his consciousness and off in a distance, as a last glimmer of sight, there was a figure of light, vaguely human in form, and radiating warmth.

Murray thought: What a joke on me. I'm going to Heaven.

Even as he thought that, the light faded, but the warmth remained. There was no lessening of the peace even though in all the Universe only he remained—and the Voice.

The Voice said, "I have done this so often and yet I still have the capacity to be pleased at success."

It was in Murray's mind to say something, but he was not conscious of possessing a mouth, tongue, or vocal cords. Nevertheless, he tried to make a sound. He tried, mouthlessly, to hum words or breathe them or just push them out by a contraction of—something.

And they came out. He heard his own voice, quite recognizable, and his own words, infinitely clear.

Murray said, "Is this Heaven?"

The Voice said, "This is no place as you understand place."

Murray was embarrassed, but the next question had to be asked. "Pardon me if I sound like a jackass. Are you God?"

Without changing intonation or in any way marring the perfection of the sound, the voice managed to sound amused. "It is strange that I am always asked that in, of course, an infinite number of ways. There is no answer I can give that you would comprehend. I *am*—which is all that I can say significantly and you may cover that with any word or concept you please."

Murray said, "And what am I? A soul? Or am I only personified existence too?" He tried not to sound sarcastic, but it seemed to him that he had failed. He thought then, fleetingly, of adding a "Your Grace" or "Holy One" or *something* to counteract the sarcasm, and could not bring himself to do so even though for the first time in his existence he speculated on the possibility of being punished for his insolence—or sin?—with Hell, and what that might be like.

The Voice did not sound offended. "You are easy to explain—even to you. You may call yourself a soul if that pleases you, but what you are is a nexus of electromagnetic forces, so arranged that all the interconnections and interrelationships are exactly imitative of those of your brain in your Universe-existence—down to the smallest detail. Therefore you have your capacity for thought, your memories, your personality. It still seems to you that you are you."

Murray found himself incredulous. "You mean the essence of my brain was permanent."

"Not at all. There is nothing about you that is permanent except what I choose to make so. I formed the nexus. I constructed it while you had physical existence and adjusted it to the moment when the existence failed."

The Voice seemed distinctly pleased with itself, and went on after a moment's pause. "An intricate but entirely precise construction. I could, of course, do it for every human being in your world but I am pleased that I do not. There is pleasure in the selection."

"You choose very few then."

"Very few."

"And what happens to the rest."

"Oblivion! Oh, of course, you imagine a Hell."

Murray would have flushed if he had the capacity to do so. He said, "I do not. It is spoken of. Still, I would scarcely have thought I was virtuous enough to have attracted your attention as one of the Elect."

"Virtuous? Ah, I see what you mean. It is troublesome to have to force my thinking small enough to permeate yours. No, I have chosen you for your capacity for thought, as I choose others, in quadrillions, from all the intelligent species of the Universe."

Murray found himself suddenly curious, the habit of a lifetime. He said, "Do you choose them all yourself or are there others like you?"

For a fleeting moment, Murray thought there was an impatient reaction to that, but when the Voice came, it was unmoved. "Whether or not there are others is irrelevant to you. This Universe is mine, and mine alone. It is my invention, my construction, intended for my purpose alone."

"And yet with quadrillions of nexi you have formed, you spend time with me? Am I that important?"

The Voice said, "You are not important at all. I am also with others in a way which, to your perception, would seem simultaneous."

"And yet you are one?"

Again amusement. The Voice said, "You seek to trap me into an inconsistency. If you were an amoeba who could consider individuality only in connection with single cells and if you were to ask a sperm whale, made up of thirty quadrillion cells, whether it was one or many, how could the sperm whale answer in a way that would be comprehensible to the amoeba?"

Murray said dryly, "I'll think about it. It may become comprehensible."

"Exactly. That is your function. You will think."

"To what end? You already know everything, I suppose."

The Voice said, "Even if I knew everything, I could not know that I know everything."

Murray said, "That sounds like a bit of Eastern philosophy—something that sounds profound precisely because it has no meaning."

The Voice said, "You have promise. You answer my paradox with a paradox—except that mine is not a paradox. Consider. I have existed eternally, but what does that mean? It means I cannot remember having come into existence. If I could, I would not have existed eternally. If I cannot remember having come into existence, then there is at least one thing—the nature of my coming into existence—that I do not know.

"Then, too, although what I know is infinite, it is also true that what there is to know is infinite, and how can I be sure that both infinities are equal? The infinity of potential knowledge may be infinitely greater than the infinity of my actual knowledge. Here is a simple example: If I knew every one of the even integers, I would know an infinite number of items, and yet I would still not know a single odd integer."

Murray said, "But the odd integers can be derived. If you divide every even integer in the entire infinite series by two, you will get another infinite series which will contain within it the infinite series of odd integers."

The Voice said, "You have the idea. I am pleased. It will be your task to find other such ways, far more difficult ones, from the known to the not-yet-known. You have your memories. You will remember all the data you have ever collected or learned, or that you have or will deduce from that data. If necessary, you will be allowed to learn what additional data you will consider relevant to the problems you set yourself."

"Could you not do all that for yourself?"

The Voice said, "I can, but it is more interesting this way. I constructed the Universe in order to have more facts to deal with. I inserted the uncertainty principle, entropy, and other randomization factors to make the whole not instantly obvious. It has worked well for it has amused me throughout its entire existence.

"I then allowed complexities that produced first life and then intelligence, and used it as a source for a research team, not because I need the aid, but because it would introduce a new random factor. I found I could not predict the next interesting piece of knowledge gained, where it would come from, by what means derived."

Murray said, "Does that ever happen?"

"Certainly. A century doesn't pass in which some interesting item doesn't appear somewhere."

"Something that you could have thought of yourself, but had not done so yet?"

"Yes."

Murray said, "Do you actually think there's a chance of *my* obliging you in this matter?"

"In the next century? Virtually none. In the long run, though, your success is certain, since you will be engaged eternally."

Murray said, "I will be thinking through eternity? Forever?"

"Yes."

"To what end?"

"I have told you. To find new knowledge."

"But beyond that. For what purpose am I to find new knowledge?"

"It was what you did in your Universe-bound life. What was its purpose then?"

Murray said, "To gain new knowledge that only I could gain. To receive the praise of my fellows. To feel the satisfaction of accomplishment knowing that I had only a short time allotted me for the purpose. Now I would gain only what you could gain yourself if you wished to take a small bit of trouble. You cannot praise me; you can only be amused. And there is no credit or satisfaction in accomplishment when I have all eternity to do it in."

The Voice said, "And you do not find thought and discovery worthwhile in itself? You do not find it requiring no further purpose?"

"For a finite time, yes. Not for all eternity."

"I see your point. Nevertheless, you have no choice."

"You say I am to think. You cannot make me do so."

The Voice said, "I do not wish to constrain you directly. I will not need to. Since you can do nothing but think, you will think. You do not know how not to think."

"Then I will give myself a goal. I will invent a purpose."

The Voice said tolerantly, "That you can certainly do."

"I have already found a purpose."

"May I know what it is?"

"You know already. I know we are not speaking in the ordinary fashion. You adjust my nexus in such a way that I believe I hear you and I believe I speak, but you transfer thoughts to me and for me directly. And when my nexus changes with my thoughts you are at once aware of them and do not need my voluntary transmission."

The Voice said, "You are surprisingly correct. I am pleased. But it also pleases me to have you tell me your thoughts voluntarily."

"Then I will tell you. The purpose of my thinking will be to discover a way to disrupt the nexus of me that you have created. I do not want to think for no purpose but to amuse you. I do not want to think forever to amuse you. I do not want to exist forever to amuse you. All my thinking will be directed toward ending the nexus. *That* would amuse *me*."

The Voice said, "I have no objection to that. Even concentrated thought on ending your own existence may, in spite of you, come up with something new and interesting. And, of course, if you succeed in this suicide attempt you will have accomplished nothing, for I would instantly reconstruct you and in such a way as to make your method of suicide impossible. And if you found another and still more subtle fashion of disrupting yourself, I would reconstruct you with that possibility eliminated, and so on. It could be an interesting game, but you will nevertheless exist eternally. It is my will."

Murray felt a quaver but the words came out with a perfect calm. "Am I in Hell then, after all? You have implied there is none, but if this were Hell you would lie as part of the game of Hell."

The Voice said, "In that case, of what use is it to assure you that you are not in Hell? Nevertheless, I assure you. There is here neither Heaven nor Hell. There is only myself."

Murray said, "Consider, then, that my thoughts may be useless to you. If I come up with nothing useful, will it not be worth your while to—disassemble me and take no further trouble with me?"

"As a reward? You want Nirvana as the prize of failure and you intend to assure me failure? There is no bargain there. You will not fail. With all eternity before you, you cannot avoid having at least one interesting thought, however you try against it."

"Then I will create another purpose for myself. I will not try to destroy myself. I will set as my goal the humiliation of you. I will think of something you have not only never thought of but never could think of. I will think of the last answer, beyond which there is no knowledge further."

The Voice said, "You do not understand the nature of the infinite. There may be things I have not yet troubled to know. There cannot be anything I cannot know."

Murray said thoughtfully, "You cannot know your beginning. You have said so. Therefore you cannot know your end. Very well, then. That will be my purpose and that will be the last answer. I will not destroy myself. I will destroy *you*—if you do not destroy me first."

The Voice said, "Ah! You come to that in rather less than average time. I would have thought it would have taken you longer. There is not one of those I have with me in this existence of perfect and eternal thought that does not have the ambition of destroying me. It cannot be done."

Murray said, "I have all eternity to think of a way of destroying you."

The Voice said, equably, "Then try to think of it." And it was gone.

But Murray had his purpose now and was content.

For what could *any* Entity, conscious of eternal existence, want—but an end?

For what else had the Voice been searching for countless billions of years? And for what other reason had intelligence been created and certain specimens salvaged and put to work, but to aid in that great search? And Murray intended that it would be he, and he alone, who would succeed.

Carefully, and with the thrill of purpose, Murray began to think.

He had plenty of time.

Lest We Remember

1

The problem with John Heath, as far as John Heath was concerned, was that he struck a dead average. He was sure of it. What was worse, he felt that Susan suspected it.

It meant he would never make a true mark in the world, never climb to the top of Quantum Pharmaceuticals, where he was a steady cog among the junior executives—never make the Quantum Leap.

Nor would he do it anywhere else, if he changed jobs.

He sighed inwardly. In just two more weeks he was going to be married and for her sake he yearned to be upwardly mobile. After all, he loved her madly and wanted to shine in her eyes.

But then, that was dead average for a young man about to be married.

Susan Collins looked at John lovingly. And why not? He was reasonably good-looking and intelligent and a steady, affectionate fellow besides. If he didn't blind her with his brilliance, he at least didn't upset her with an erraticism he didn't possess.

She patted the pillow she had placed behind his head when he sat down in the armchair and handed him his drink, making sure he had a firm grip before she let go.

She said, "I'm practicing to treat you well, Johnny. I've got to be an efficient wife."

John sipped at his drink. "I'm the one who'll have to be on my toes, Sue. Your salary is higher than mine."

"It's all going to go into one pocket once we're married. It will be the firm of Johnny and Sue keeping one set of books."

"You'll have to keep it," said John despondently. "I'm bound to make mistakes if I try."

"Only because you're sure you will. When are your friends coming?"

"Nine, I think. Maybe nine-thirty. And they're not exactly friends. They're Quantum people from the research labs."

"You're sure they won't expect to be fed?"

"They said after dinner. I'm positive about that. It's business."

She looked at him quizzically. "You didn't say that before."

"Say what before?"

"That it was business. Are you sure?"

John felt confused. Any effort to remember *precisely* always left him confused. "They said so—I think."

Susan's look was that of good-natured exasperation, rather like the one she would have given a friendly puppy who is completely unaware its paws are muddy. "If you really thought," she said, "as often as you say 'I think' you wouldn't be so perennially uncertain. Don't you see it *can't* be business. If it were business, wouldn't they see you *at* business?"

"It's confidential," said John. "They don't want to see me at work. Not even at my apartment."

"Why here, then?"

"Oh, I suggested that. I thought you ought to be around, anyway. They're going to have to deal with the firm of Johnny and Sue, right?"

"It depends," said Susan, "on what the confidential is all about. Did they give you any hints?"

"No, but it couldn't hurt to listen. It could be something that would give me a boost in standing at the firm."

"Why you?" asked Susan.

John looked hurt, "Why *not* me?"

"It just strikes me that someone at your job level doesn't require all that confidentiality and that—"

She broke off when the intercom buzzed. She dashed off to answer and came back to say, "They're on the way up."

2

Two of them were at the door. One was Boris Kupfer, whom John had already spoken to—large and restless, with a clear view of bluish stubble on his chin.

The other was David Anderson, smaller and more composed. His quick eyes moved this way and that, however, missing nothing.

"Susan," said John, uncertainly, still holding the door open. "These are the two colleagues of mine that I told you about. Boris—" He hit a blank in his memory banks and stopped.

"Boris Kupfer," said the larger man morosely, jingling some change in his pocket, "and David Anderson here. It's very kind of you, Miss—"

"Susan Collins."

"It's very kind of you to make your place of residence available to Mr. Heath and to us for a private conference. We apologize for trespassing on your time and your privacy in this manner—and if you could leave us to ourselves for a while, we will be further grateful."

Susan stared at him solemnly. "Do you want me to go to the movies, or just into the next room?"

"If you could visit a friend—"

"No," said Susan, firmly.

"You can dispose of your time as you please, of course. A movie, if you wish."

"When I said 'No,'" said Susan, "I meant I wasn't leaving. I want to know what this is about."

Kupfer seemed nonplussed. He stared at Anderson for a moment, then said, "It's confidential, as Mr. Heath explained to you, I hope."

John, looking uneasy, said, "I explained that. Susan understands—"

"Susan," said Susan, "doesn't understand and wasn't given to understand that she was to absent herself from the proceedings. This is my apartment and Johnny and I are being married in two weeks—exactly two weeks from today. We are the firm of Johnny and Sue and you'll have to deal with the firm."

Anderson's voice sounded for the first time, surprisingly deep and as smooth as though it had been waxed. "Boris, the young woman is right. As Mr. Heath's soon-to-be wife, she will have a great interest in what we have come here to suggest and it would be wrong to exclude her. She has so firm an interest in our proposal that if she were to wish to leave, I would urge her most strongly to remain."

"Well, then, my friends," said Susan, "what will you have to drink? Once I bring you those drinks, we can begin."

Both were seated rather stiffly and had sipped cautiously at their drinks, and then Kupfer said, "Heath, I don't suppose you know much about the chemical details of the company's work—the cerebro-chemicals, for instance."

"Not a bit," said John, uneasily.

"No reason you should," said Anderson, silkily.

"It's like this," said Kupfer, casting an uneasy glance at Susan—

"No reason to go into technical details," said Anderson, almost at the lower level of audibility.

Kupfer colored slightly. "Without technical details, Quantum Pharmaceuticals deals with cerebro-chemicals which are, as the name implies, chemicals that affect the cerebrum, that is, the higher functioning of the brain."

"It must be very complicated work," said Susan, with composure.

"It is," said Kupfer. "The mammalian brain has hundreds of characteristic molecular varieties found nowhere else, which serve to modulate cerebral activity, including aspects of what we might term the intellectual life. The work is under the closest corporate security, which is why Anderson wants no technical details. I *can* say this, though. We can go no further with animal experiments. We're up against a brick wall if we can't try the human response."

"Then why don't you?" said Susan. "What stops you?"

"Public reaction if something goes wrong!"

"Use volunteers, then."

"That won't help. Quantum Pharmaceuticals couldn't take the adverse publicity if something went wrong."

Susan looked at them mockingly. "Are you two working on your own, then?"

Anderson raised his hand to stop Kupfer. "Young woman," he said, "let me explain briefly in order to put an end to wasteful verbal fencing. If we succeed, we will be enormously rewarded. If we fail, Quantum Pharmaceuticals will disown us and we will pay what penalty there is to be paid, such as the ending of our careers. If you ask us, why we are willing to take this risk, the answer is, we do not think a risk exists. We are reasonably sure we will succeed; entirely sure we will do no harm. The corporation feels it cannot take the chance; but we feel we can. Now, Kupfer, proceed!"

Kupfer said, "We have a memory chemical. It works with every animal we have tried. Their learning ability improves amazingly. It should work on human beings, too."

John said, "That sounds exciting."

"It *is* exciting," said Kupfer. "Memory is not improved by devising a way for the brain to store information more efficiently. All our studies show that the brain stores almost unlimited numbers of items perfectly and permanently. The difficulty lies in recall. How many times have you had a name at the tip of your tongue and couldn't get it? How many times have you failed to come up with something you *knew* you knew, and then did come up with it two hours later when you were thinking about something else. Am I putting it correctly, David?"

"You are," said Anderson. "Recall is inhibited, we think, because the mammalian brain outraced its needs by developing a too-perfect recording system. A mammal stores more bits of information than it needs or is capable of using and if all of it was on tap at all times, it would never be able to choose among them quickly enough for appropriate reaction. Recall is inhibited, therefore, to insure that items emerge from memory storage in manipulable numbers, and with those items most desired not blurred by the accompaniment of numerous other items of no interest.

"There is a definite chemical in the brain that functions as a recall inhibitor, and we have a chemical that neutralizes the inhibitor. We call it a disinhibitor, and as far as we have been able to ascertain the matter, it has no deleterious side effects."

Susan laughed. "I see what's coming, Johnny. You can leave now, gentlemen. You just said that recall is inhibited to allow mammals to react more efficiently, and now you say that the disinhibitor has no deleterious side effects. Surely the disinhibitor will make the mammals react less efficiently; perhaps find themselves unable to react at all. And now you are going to propose that you try it on Johnny and see if you reduce him to catatonic immobility or not."

Anderson rose, his thin lips quivering. He took a few rapid strides to the far end of the room and back. When he sat down, he was composed and smiling. "In the first place, Miss Collins, it's a matter of dosage. We told you that the experimental animals all displayed enhanced learning ability. Naturally, we didn't eliminate the inhibitor entirely; we merely suppressed it in part. Secondly, we have reason to think the human brain *can* handle complete disinhibition. It is much larger than the brain of any animal we have tested and we all know its incomparable capacity for abstract thought.

"It is a brain designed for perfect recall, but the blind forces of evolution have not managed to remove the inhibiting chemical which, after all, was designed for and inherited from the lower animals."

"Are you sure?" asked John.

"You *can't* be sure," said Susan, flatly.

Kupfer said, "We are sure, but we need the proof to convince others. That's why we have to try a human being."

"John, in fact," said Susan.

"Yes."

"Which brings us," said Susan, "to the key question. Why John?"

"Well," said Kupfer, slowly, "we need someone for whom chances of success are most nearly certain, and in whom it would be most demonstrable. We don't want someone so low in mental capacity that we must use dangerously large doses of the disinhibitor; nor do we want someone so bright that the effect will not be sufficiently noticeable. We need someone who's average. Fortunately, we have the full physical and psychological profiles of all the employees at Quantum and in this and, in fact, all other ways, Mr. Heath is ideal."

"Dead average?" said Susan.

John looked stricken at the use of the phrase he had thought his own innermost, and disgraceful, secret. "Come on, now," he said.

Ignoring John's outcry, Kupfer answered Susan, "Yes."

"And he won't be, if he submits to treatment?"

Anderson's lips stretched into another one of his cheerless smiles. "That's right. He won't be. This is something to think about if you're going to be married soon—the firm of Johnny and Sue, I think you called it. As it is, I don't think the firm will advance at Quantum, Miss Collins, for although Heath is a good and reliable employee he is, as you say, dead average. If he takes the disinhibitor, however, he will become a remarkable person and move upward with astonishing speed. Consider what that will mean to the firm."

"What does the firm have to lose?" asked Susan, grimly.

Anderson said, "I don't see how you can lose anything. It will be a sensible dose which can be administered at the laboratories tomorrow—Sunday. We will have the floor to ourselves; we will keep him under surveillance for a few hours. It is certain nothing could go wrong. If I could tell you of our painstaking experimentation and of our thoroughgoing exploration of all possible side effects—"

"On animals," said Susan, not giving an inch.

But John said, tightly, "I'll make the decision, Sue. I've had it up to here with that dead-average bit. It's worth some risk to me if it means getting off that dead-average dead end."

"Johnny," said Susan, "don't jump."

"I'm thinking of the firm, Sue. I want to contribute my share."

Anderson said, "Good, but sleep on it. We will leave two copies of an agreement we will ask you to look over and sign. Please don't show it to anybody whether you sign or not. We will be here tomorrow morning again to take you to the laboratory."

They smiled, rose, and left.

John read over the agreement with a troubled frown, then looked up. "You don't think I should be doing this, do you, Sue?"

"It worries me, sure,"

"Look, if I have a chance to get away from that dead average—"

Susan said, "What's wrong with that? I've met so many nuts and cranks in my short life that I welcome a nice, average guy like you, Johnny. Listen, I'm dead average, too."

"*You* dead average? With your looks? Your figure?"

Susan looked down upon herself with a touch of complacency. "Well, then, I'm just your dead-average gorgeous girl," she said.

3

The injection took place at 8 A.M. Sunday, no more than twelve hours after the proposition had been advanced. A thoroughly computerized body sensor was attached to John in a dozen places, while Susan watched with keen-eyed apprehension.

Kupfer said, "Please, Heath, relax. All is going well, but tension speeds the heart rate, raises the blood pressure, and skews our results."

"How can I relax?" muttered John.

Susan put in sharply, "Skews the results to the point where you don't know what's going on?"

"No, no," said Anderson. "Boris said all is going well and it is. It is just that our animals were always sedated before the injection, and we did not feel sedation would have been appropriate in this case. So if we can't have sedation, we must expect tension. Just breathe slowly and do your best to minimize it."

It was late afternoon before he was finally disconnected.

"How do you feel?" asked Anderson.

"Nervous," said John. "Otherwise, all right."

"No headache?"

"No. But I want to visit the bathroom. I can't exactly relax with a bedpan."

"Of course."

John emerged, frowning. "I don't notice any particular memory improvement."

"That will take some time and will be gradual. The disinhibitor must leak across the blood-brain barrier, you know," said Anderson.

4

It was nearly midnight when Susan broke what had turned out to be an oppressively silent evening in which neither had much responded to the television.

She said, "You'll have to stay here overnight. I don't want you alone when we don't really know what's going to happen."

"I don't feel a thing," said John, gloomily. "I'm still me."

"I'll settle for that, Johnny," said Susan. "Do you feel any pains or discomforts or oddnesses at all?"

"I don't think so."

"I wish we hadn't done it."

"For the firm," said John, smiling weakly. "We've got to take some chances for the firm."

5

John slept poorly, and woke drearily, but on time. And he arrived at work on time, too, to start the new week.

By 11 A.M. however, his morose air had attracted the unfavorable attention of his immediate superior, Michael Ross.

Ross was burly and black-browed and fit the stereotype of the stevedore without being one. John got along with him though he did not like him.

Ross said, in his bass-baritone, "What's happened to your cheery disposition, Heath—your jokes—your lilting laughter?" Ross cultivated a certain preciosity of speech as though he were anxious to negate the stevedore image.

"Don't exactly feel tip-top," said John, not looking up.

"Hangover?"

"No, sir," said John, coldly.

"Well, cheer up, then. You'll win no friends, scattering stinkweeds over the fields as you gambol along."

John would have liked to groan. Ross's subliterary affectations were wearisome at the best of times and this wasn't the best of times.

And to make matters worse, John smelled the foul odor of a rancid cigar and knew that James Arnold Prescott—the head of the sales division—could not be far behind.

Nor was he. He looked about, and said, "Mike, when and what did we sell Rahway last spring or thereabouts? There's some damned question about it and I think the details have been miscomputerized."

The question was not addressed to him, but John said quietly, "Forty-two vials of PCAP. That was on April 14, J.P., invoice number P-20543, with a five percent discount granted on payment within thirty days. Payment, in full, received on May 8."

Apparently everyone in the room had heard that. At least, everyone looked up.

Prescott said, "How the hell do you happen to know all that?"

John stared at Prescott for a moment, a vast surprise on his face. "I just happened to remember, J.P."

"You did, eh? Repeat it."

John did, faltering a bit, and Prescott wrote it down on one of the papers on John's desk, wheezing slightly as the bend at his waist compressed his portly abdomen up against his diaphragm and made breathing difficult. John tried to duck the smoke from the cigar without seeming to do so.

Prescott said, "Ross, check this out on your computer and see if there's anything to it at all." He turned to John with an aggrieved look. "I don't like practical jokers. What would you have done if I had accepted these figures of yours and walked off with them?"

"I wouldn't have done anything. They're correct," said John, conscious of himself as the full center of attention.

Ross handed Prescott the readout. Prescott looked at it and said, "This is from the computer?"

"Yes, J.P."

Prescott stared at it, then said, with a jerk of his head toward John, "And what's he? Another computer? His figures were correct."

John tried a weak smile, but Prescott growled and left, the stench of his cigar a lingering reminder of his presence.

Ross said, "What the hell was that little bit of legerdemain, Heath? You found out what he wanted to know and looked it up in advance to get some kudos?"

"No, sir," said John, who was gathering confidence. "I just happened to remember. I have a good memory for these things."

"And took the trouble to keep it from your loyal companions all these years? There's no one here who had any idea you hid a good memory behind that unremarkable forehead of yours."

"No point in showing it, Mr. Ross, is there? Now when I have, it doesn't seem to have gained me any goodwill, does it?"

And it hadn't. Ross glowered at him and turned away.

6

John's excitement over the dinner table at Gino's that night made it difficult for him to talk coherently, but Susan listened patiently and tried to act as a stabilizing force.

"You might just have happened to remember, you know," she said. "By itself it doesn't prove anything, Johnny."

"Are you crazy?" He lowered his voice at Susan's gesture and quick glance about. He repeated in a semiwhisper, "Are you crazy? You don't suppose it's the only thing I remember, do you? I think I can remember anything I ever heard. It's just a question of recall. For instance, quote some line out of Shakespeare."

"To be or not to be."

John looked scornful. "Don't be funny. Oh, well, it doesn't matter. The point is that if you recite any line, I can carry on from there for as long as you like. I read some of the plays for English Lit classes at college and some for myself and I can bring any of it back. I've tried. It flows! I suppose I can bring back any part of any book or article or newspaper I've ever read, or any TV show I've ever watched—word for word or scene for scene."

Susan said, "What will you do with all that?"

John said, "I don't have that consciously in my head at all times. Surely you don't—wait, let's order—"

Five minutes later, he said, "Surely you don't—My God, I haven't forgotten where we left off. Isn't it amazing?—Surely you don't think I'm swimming in a mental sea of Shakespearean sentences at all times. The recall takes an effort, not much of one, but an effort."

"How does it work?"

"I don't know. How do you lift your arm? What orders do you give your muscles? You just will the arm to lift upward and it does so. It's no trouble to do so, but your arm doesn't lift *until* you want it to. Well, I remember anything I've ever read or seen when I want to but not when I don't want to. I don't know how to do it, but I do it."

The first course arrived and John tackled it happily.

Susan picked at her stuffed mushrooms. "It sounds exciting."

"Exciting? I've got the biggest, most wonderful toy in the world. My own brain. Listen, I can spell any word correctly and I'm pretty sure I won't ever make any grammatical mistake."

"Because you remember all the dictionaries and grammars you ever read?"

John looked at her sharply. "Don't be sarcastic, Sue."

"I wasn't being—"

He waved her silent. "I never used dictionaries as light reading. But I do remember words and sentences in my reading and they were correctly spelled and correctly parsed."

"Don't be so sure. You've seen any word misspelled in every possible way and every possible example of twisted grammar, too."

"Those were exceptions. By far the largest number of times I've encountered literary English, I've encountered it used correctly. It outweighs accidents, errors, and ignorance. What's more, I'm sure I'm improving even as I sit here, growing more intelligent steadily."

"And you're not worried. What if—"

"What if I become *too* intelligent? Tell me how on Earth you think becoming too intelligent can be harmful."

"I was going to say," said Susan, coldly, "that what you're experiencing is not intelligence. It's only total recall."

"How do you mean 'only'? If I recall perfectly, if I use the English language correctly, if I know endless quantities of material, isn't that going to make me seem more intelligent? How else need one define intelligence? You aren't growing just a little jealous, are you, Sue?"

"No," more coldly still. "I can always get an injection of my own if I feel desperate about it."

John put down his fork. "You can't mean that."

"I don't, but what if I did?"

"Because you can't take advantage of your special knowledge to deprive me of my position."

"What position?"

The main course arrived and for a few moments, John was busy. Then he said, in a whisper, "My position as the first of the future. *Homo superior!* There'll never be too many of us. You heard what Kupfer said. Some are too dumb to make it. Some are too smart to change much. I'm the one!"

"*Dead* average." One corner of Susan's mouth lifted.

"Once I was. There'll be others like me eventually. Not many, but there'll be others. It's just that I want to make my mark before the others come along. It's for the firm, you know. Us!"

He remained lost in thought thereafter, testing his brain delicately.

Susan ate in an unhappy silence.

7

John spent several days organizing his memories. It was like the preparation of an orderly reference book. One by one, he recalled all his experiences in the six years he had spent at Quantum Pharamaceuticals and all he had heard and all the papers and memos he had read.

There was no difficulty in discarding the irrelevant and unimportant and storing them in a "hold till further notice" compartment where they did not interfere with his analysis. Other items were put in order so that they established a natural progression.

Against that skeletal organization, he resurrected the scuttlebutt he had heard; the gossip, malicious or otherwise; casual phrases and interjections at conferences which he had not been conscious of hearing at the time. Those items which did not fit anywhere against the background he had built up in his head were worthless, empty of factual content. Those which did fit clicked firmly into place and could be seen as true by that mere fact.

The further the structure grew, and the more coherent, the more significant new items became and the easier it was to fit them in.

Ross stopped by John's desk on Thursday. He said, "I want to see you in my office at the nonce, Heath, if your legs will deign to carry you in that direction."

John rose uneasily. "Is it necessary? I'm busy."

"Yes, you look busy." Ross looked over the clear desk which, at the moment, held nothing but a studio photo of a smiling Susan. "You've been this busy all week. But you've asked me whether seeing me in my office is necessary. For me, no; but for you, vital. There's the door to my office. There's the door to the hell out of here. Choose one or the other and do it fast."

John nodded and, without undue hurry, followed Ross into his office.

Ross seated himself behind his desk but did not invite John to sit. He maintained a hard stare for a moment, then said, "What the hell's got into you this week, Heath? Don't you know what your job is?"

"To the extent that I have done it, it would seem that I do," said John. "The report on microcosmic is on your desk and complete and seven days ahead of deadline. I doubt that you can have complaints about it."

"You doubt, do you? Do I have permission to have complaints if I choose to after communing with my soul? Or am I condemned to applying to you for permission?"

"I apparently have not made myself plain, Mr. Ross. I doubt that you have *rational* complaints about it. To have those of the other variety is entirely up to you."

Ross rose now. "Listen, punk, if I decide to fire you, you won't get the news by word of mouth. It won't be anything I say that will give you the glad tidings. You will go out through the door in a violent tumble and mine will be the propulsive force behind that tumble. Just keep that in your small brain and your tongue in your big mouth. Whether you've done your work or not is not at question right now. Whether you've done everyone else's is. Who and what gives you the right to manage everyone in this place?"

John said nothing.

Ross roared, "Well?"

John said, "Your order was 'Keep your tongue in your big mouth.'"

Ross turned a dangerous red. "You will answer questions, however."

John said, "I am not aware that I have been managing anyone."

"There's not a person in the place you haven't corrected at least once. You have gone over Willoughby's head in connection with the correspondence on the TMP's; you have been into general files using Bronstein's computer access; and God knows what else I haven't yet been told about and all in the last two days. You are disrupting the work of this department and it must cease this moment. There must be dead calm, and instantaneously, or it will be tornado weather for you, my man."

John said, "If I have interfered in the narrow sense, it has been for the good of the company. In the case of Willoughby, his treatment of the TMP matter was putting Quantum Pharmaceuticals in violation of government regulations, something I have pointed out to you in one of several memos I have sent you which you apparently have not had occasion to read. As for Bronstein, he was simply ignoring general directions and costing the company fifty thousand in unnecessary tests, something I was easily able to establish by locating the necessary correspondence—merely to corroborate my clear memory of the situation."

Ross was swelling visibly through the talk. "Heath," he said, "you are usurping my role. You will, therefore, gather your personal effects and be off the premises before lunch, never to return. If you do, I will take extreme pleasure in helping you out again with my foot. Your official notice of dismissal will be in your hands, or down your throat, before your effects will be collected, work as quickly as you may."

John said, "Don't try to bully me, Ross. You've cost the company a quarter of a million dollars through incompetence and you know it."

There was a short pause as Ross deflated. He said, cautiously, "What are you talking about?"

"Quantum Pharmaceuticals went down to the wire on the Nutley bid and missed out because a certain piece of information that was in your hands stayed in your hands and never got to the Board of Directors. You either forgot or you didn't bother and in either case you are not the man for your job. You are either incompetent or have sold out."

"You're insane."

"No one need believe me. The information is in the computer, if one knows where to look and I know where to look. What's more, the knowledge is on file and will be on the desks of the interested parties two minutes after I leave these premises."

"If this were so," said Ross, speaking with difficulty, "you could not possibly know. This is a stupid attempt at blackmail by threat of slander."

"You know it's not slander. If you doubt that I have the information, let me tell you that there is one memorandum that is not in the records but can be reconstructed without too much difficulty from what is there. You would have to explain its absence and it will be presumed you have destroyed it. You know I'm not bluffing."

"It's still blackmail."

"Why? I'm making no demands and no threats. I'm merely explaining my actions of the past two days. Of course, if I'm forced to resign, I'll have to explain why I resigned, won't I?"

Ross said nothing.

John said, coolly, "Is my resignation being requested?"

"Get out of here!"

"With my job? Or without it?"

Ross said, "You have your job." His face was a study in hatred.

8

Susan had arranged a dinner at her apartment and had gone to considerable trouble for it. Never, in her own opinion, had she looked more enticing and never did she think it more important to move John, at least for a bit, away from his total concentration on his own mind.

She said, with an attempt at heartiness, "After all, we are celebrating the last nine days of single blessedness."

"We are celebrating more than that," said John with a grim smile. "It's only four days since I got the the disinhibitor and already I've been able to put Ross in his place. He'll never bother me again."

"We each seem to have our own notion of sentiment," said Susan. "Tell me the details of *your* tender remembrance."

John told the tale crisply, repeating the conversation verbatim and without hesitation.

Susan listened stonily, without in any way rising to the gathering triumph in John's voice. "How *did* you know all that about Ross?"

John said, "There are no secrets, Sue. Things just *seem* secret because people don't remember. If you can recall every remark, every comment, every stray word made to you or in your hearing and consider them all in combination, you find that everyone gives himself away in everything. You can pick out meanings that will, in these days of computerization, send you straight to the necessary records. It can be done. I can do it. I have done it in the case of Ross. I can do it in the case of anybody with whom I associate."

"You can also get them furious."

"I got Ross furious. You can bet on that."

"Was that wise?"

"What can he do to me? I've got him cold."

"He has enough clout in the upper echelons—"

"Not for long. I have a conference set for 2 P.M. tomorrow with old man Prescott and his stinking cigar and I'll cut Ross off at the pass."

"Don't you think you're moving too quickly?"

"Moving too quickly? I haven't even begun. Prescott's just a stepping-stone. Quantum Pharmaceutical's just a steppingstone."

"It's still too quick, Johnny, you need someone to direct you. You need—"

"I need *nothing*. With what I have," he tapped his temple, "there's no one and nothing that can stop me."

Susan said, "Well, look, let's not discuss that. We have different plans to make."

"Plans?"

"Our own. We're getting married in just under nine days. Surely"—with heavy irony— "you haven't returned to the sad old days when you forgot things."

"I remember the wedding," said John, testily, "but at the moment I've got to reorganize Quantum. In fact, I've been thinking seriously of postponing the wedding till I have things well in hand."

"Oh? And when might that be?"

"That's hard to tell. Not long at the rate I'm taking hold. A month or two, I suppose. Unless," and he descended into sarcasm, "you think that's moving too quickly."

Susan was breathing hard. "Were you planning to consult with me on the matter?"

John raised his eyebrows. "Would it have been necessary? Where's the argument? Surely you see what's happening. We can't interrupt it and lose momentum. Listen, did you know I'm a mathematical wiz? I can multiply and divide as fast as a computer because at some time in my life I have come across almost every simple bit of arithmetic and I can *recall* the answers. I read a table of square roots and I can—"

Susan cried, "My God, Johnny, you *are* a kid with a new toy. You've lost your perspective. Instant recall is good for nothing but playing tricks with. It doesn't give one bit more intelligence; not an ounce; not a speck more of judgment; not a whiff more of common sense. You're about as safe to have around as a little boy with a loaded grenade. You need looking after by someone with brains."

John scowled. "Do I? It seems to me that I'm getting what I want."

"Are you? Isn't it true that I'm what you want also?"

"What?"

"Go ahead, Johnny. You want me. Reach out and take me. Exercise that remarkable recall you have. Remember who I am, what I am, the things we can do, the warmth, the affection, the sentiment."

John, with his forehead still creased in uncertainly, extended his arms toward Susan.

She stepped out of them. "But you haven't got me, or anything about me. You can't remember me into your arms; you have to love me into them. The trouble is, you don't have the good sense to do it and you lack the intelligence to establish reasonable priorities. Here, take this and get out of my apartment or I'll hit you with something a lot heavier."

He stopped to pick up the engagement ring. "Susan—"

"I said, get out. The firm of Johnny and Sue is hereby dissolved."

Her face blazed anger and John turned meekly and left.

9

When he arrived at Quantum the next morning, Anderson was waiting for him with a look of anxious impatience on his face.

"Mr. Heath," he said, smiling and rising.

"What do you want?" demanded John.

"We are private here, I take it?"

"The place isn't bugged as far as I know."

"You are to report to us day after tomorrow for examination. On Sunday. You recall that?"

"Of course, I recall that. I'm incapable of not recalling. I *am* capable of changing my mind, however. Why do I need an examination?"

"Why not, sir? It is quite plain from what Kupfer and I have picked up that the treatment seems to have worked splendidly. Actually, we don't want to wait till Sunday. If you can come with me today—now, in fact—it would mean a great deal to us, to Quantum, and, of course, to humanity."

John said, curtly, "You might have held on to me when you had me. You sent me about my business, allowing me to live and work unsupervised so that you could test me under field conditions, and get a better idea of how things would work out. It meant more risk for me, but you didn't worry about that, did you?"

"Mr. Heath, that was not in our minds. We—"

"Don't tell me that. I remember every last word you and Kupfer said to me last Sunday, and it's quite clear to me that that *was* in your minds. So if I take the risk, I accept the benefits. I have no intention of presenting myself as a biochemical freak who has achieved my ability at the end of a hypodermic needle. Nor do I want others of the sort wandering around. For now, I have a monopoly and I intend to use it. When I'm ready—not before—I will be willing to cooperate with you and benefit humanity. But just remember, I'm the one who will know when I'm ready, not you. So don't call me; I'll call you."

Anderson managed a soft smile. "As to that, Mr. Heath, how can you stop us from making our announcement? Those who have dealt with you this week will have no trouble in recognizing the change in you and in testifying to it."

"Really? See here, Anderson, listen closely and do so without that foolish grin on your face. It irritates me. I told you I remember every word you and Kupfer spoke. I remember every nuance of expression, every sidelong glance. It all spoke volumes. I learned enough to check through sick-leave records with a good idea of what I was looking for. It would seem that I was not the first Quantum employee on whom you had tried the disinhibitor."

Anderson was, indeed, not smiling. "That is nonsense."

"You know it is not, and you had better know I can prove it. I know the names of the men involved—one was a woman, actually—and the hospitals in which they were treated and the false history with which they were supplied.

Since you did not warn me of this, when you used me as your fourth experimental animal on two legs, I owe you nothing but a prison sentence."

Anderson said, "I won't discuss this matter. Let me say this, though. The treatment will wear off, Heath. You won't keep your total recall. You will have to come back for further treatment and you can be sure it will be on our terms."

John said, "Nuts! You don't suppose I haven't investigated your reports—at least, those you haven't kept secret. And I already have a notion of what aspects you *have* kept secret. The treatment lasts longer in some cases than others. It invariably lasts longer where it is more effective. In my case, the treatment has been extraordinarily effective and it will endure a considerable time. By the time I come to you again, if I ever have to, I will be in a position where any failure on your part to cooperate will be swiftly devastating to you. Don't even think of it."

"You ungrateful—"

"Don't bother me," said John, wearily. "I have no time to listen to you froth. Go away, I have work to do."

Anderson's face was a study in fear and frustration as he left.

10

It was 2:30 P.M. when John walked into Prescott's office, for once not minding the cigar smoke. It would not be long, he knew, before Prescott would have to choose between his cigars and his position.

With Prescott were Arnold Gluck and Lewis Randall, so that John had the grim pleasure of knowing he was facing the three top men in the division.

Prescott rested his cigar on top of an ashtray and said, "Ross has asked me to give you half an hour, and that's all I will give you. You're the one with the trick memory, aren't you?"

"My name is John Health, sir, and I intend to present you with a rationalization of procedure for the company; one that will make full use of the age of computers and electronic communication and will lay the groundwork for further modification as the technology improves."

The three men looked at each other.

Gluck, whose creased face was tanned a leathery brown said, "Are you an expert in office management?"

"I don't have to be, sir. I have been here for six years and I recall every bit of the procedure in every transaction in which I have been involved. That means the pattern of such transactions is plain to me and its imperfections obvious. One can see toward what it is tending and where it is doing so wastefully and inefficiently. If you'll listen, I will explain. You will find it easy to understand."

Randall, whose red hair and freckles made him seem younger than he was, said sardonically, "Real easy, I hope, because we have trouble with hard concepts."

"You won't have trouble," said John.

"And you won't get a second more than twenty-one minutes," said Prescott, looking at his watch.

"It won't take that," said John. "I have it diagrammed and I can talk quickly."

It took fifteen minutes and the three management personnel were remarkably silent in that interval.

Finally Gluck said, with a hostile glance out of his small eyes, "It sounds as though you are saying we can get along with half the management we are employing these days."

"Less than half," said John, coolly, "and be the more efficient for it. We can't fire ordinary personnel at will because of the unions, though we can profitably lose them by attrition. Management is not protected, however, and can be let go. They'll have pensions if they're old enough and can get new jobs if they're young enough. Our thought must be for Quantum."

Prescott, who had maintained an ominous silence, now puffed furiously at his noxious cigar and said, "Changes like this have to be considered carefully and implemented, if at all, with the greatest of caution. What seems logical on paper can lose out in the human equation."

John said, "Prescott, if this reorganization is not accepted within a week, and if I am not placed in charge of its implementation, I will resign. I will have no trouble in finding employment with a smaller firm where this plan can be far more easily put into practice. Beginning with a small group of management people, I can expand in both quantity and efficiency of performance without additional hiring and within a year I'll drive Quantum into bankruptcy. It would be fun to do this if I am driven to it, so consider carefully. My half hour is up. Goodbye." And he left.

11

Prescott looked after him with a glance of frigid calculation. He said to the other two, "I think he means what he says and that he knows every facet of our operations better than we do. We can't let him go."

"You mean we've got to accept his plan," said Randall, shocked.

"I didn't say that. You two go, and remember this whole thing is confidential."

Gluck said, "I have the feeling that if we don't do something, all three of us will find ourselves on our butts in the street within a month."

"Very likely," said Prescott, "so we'll do something."

"What?"

"If you don't know, you won't get hurt. Leave it to me. Forget it for now and have a nice weekend."

When they were gone, he thought a while, chewing furiously on his cigar. He then turned to his telephone and dialed an extension. "Prescott here. I want you in my office first thing Monday morning. First thing. Hear me?"

12

Anderson looked a trifle disheveled. He had had a bad weekend. Prescott, who had had a worse, said to him, malevolently, "You and Kupfer tried again, didn't you?"

Anderson said, softly, "It's better not to discuss that, Mr. Prescott. You remember it was agreed that in certain aspects of research, a distance was to be established. We were to take the risks or the glory, and Quantum was to share in the latter but not in the former."

"And your salary was doubled with a guarantee of all legal payments to be Quantum's responsibility, don't forget that. This man, John Heath, was treated by you and Kupfer, wasn't he? Come on. There's no mistaking it. There's no point in hiding it."

"Well, yes."

"And you were so brilliant that you turned him loose on us—this—this—tarantula."

"We didn't anticipate this would happen. When he didn't go into instant shock, we thought it was our first chance to test the process in the field. We thought he would break down after two or three days, or it would pass."

Prescott said, "If I hadn't been protected so damned well, I wouldn't have put the whole thing out of my mind and I would have guessed what had happened when that bastard first pulled the computer bit and produced the details of correspondence he had no business remembering. All right, we know where we are now. He's holding the company to ransom with a new plan of operations he can't be allowed to put through. Also, he can't be allowed to walk away from us."

Anderson said, "Considering Heath's capacity for recall and synthesis, is it possible that his plan of operations may be a good one?"

"I don't care if it is. That bastard is after my job and who knows what else and we've got to get rid of him."

"How do you mean, rid of him? He could be of vital importance to the cerebro-chemical project."

"Forget that. It's a disaster. You're creating a super-Hitler."

Anderson said, in a soft-voiced anguish, "The effect will wear off."

"Yes? When?"

"At this moment, I can't be sure."

"Then I can't take chances. We've got to make our arrangements and do it tomorrow at the latest. We can't wait any longer."

13

John was in high good humor. The manner in which Ross avoided him when he could and spoke to him deferentially when he had to affected the entire work force. There was a strange and radical change in the pecking order, with himself at the top.

Nor could John deny to himself that he liked it. He reveled in it. The tide was moving strongly and unbelievably swiftly. It was only nine days since the injection of the disinhibitor and every step had been forward.

Well, no, there had been Susan's silly rage at him, but he would deal with her later. When he showed her the heights to which he would climb in nine additional days—in ninety—

He looked up. Ross was at his desk, waiting for his attention but reluctant to do anything as crass as to attract that attention by as much as clearing his throat. John swiveled his chair, put his feet out before him in an attitude of relaxation, and said, "Well, Ross?"

Ross said, carefully, "I would like to see you in my office, Heath. Something important has come up and, frankly, you're the only one who can set it straight."

John got slowly to his feet. "Yes? What is it?"

Ross looked about mutely at the busy room, with at least five men in reasonable earshot. Then he looked toward his office door and held out an inviting arm.

John hesitated, but for years Ross had held unquestioned authority over him, and at this moment he reacted to habit.

Ross held his door open for John politely, stepped through himself and closed the door behind him, locking it unobtrusively and remaining in front of it. Anderson stepped out from the other side of the bookcase.

John said sharply, "What's all this about?"

"Nothing at all, Heath," said Ross, his smile turning into a vulpine grin. "We're just going to help you out of your abnormal state—take you back to normality. Don't move Heath."

Anderson had a hypodermic in his hand. "Please, Heath, do not struggle. We wish you no harm."

"If I yell—" said John.

"If you make any sound," said Ross, "I will put a hammerlock on you and hold it till your eyes bug out. I would like to do that, so please try to yell."

John said, "I have the goods on both of you, safe on deposit. Anything that happens to me—"

"Mr. Heath," said Anderson, "nothing will happen to you. Something is going to *un*happen to you. We will put you back to where you were. That would happen anyway, but we will hurry it up just a little."

"So I'm going to hold you, Heath," said Ross, "and you won't move because if you do, you will disturb our friend with the needle and he might slip and give you more than the carefully calculated dose, and you might end up unable to remember anything at all."

Heath was backing away, breathless. "That's what you're planning. You think you'll be safe that way. If I forgot all about you, all about the information, all about its storage. But—"

"We're not going to hurt you, Heath," said Anderson.

John's forehead glistened with sweat. A near paralysis gripped him.

"An amnesiac!" he said, huskily, and with a terror that only someone could feel at the possibility who himself had perfect recall.

"Then you won't remember this either, will you?" said Ross. "Go ahead, Anderson."

"Well," muttered Anderson, in resignation. "I'm destroying a perfect test subject." He lifted John's flaccid arm and readied the hypodermic.

There was a knock at the door. A clear voice called, "John!"

Anderson froze almost automatically, looking up questioningly.

Ross had turned to look at the door. Now he turned back. "Shoot that stuff into him, doc," he said in an urgent whisper.

The voice came again, "Johnny, I know you're in there. I've called the police. They're on the way."

Ross whispered again, "Go ahead. She's lying. And by the time they come, it's over. Who can prove anything?"

But Anderson was shaking his head vigorously. "It's his fiancée. She knows he was treated. She was there."

"You jackass."

There was the sound of a kick against the door and then the voice sounded in a muffled, "Let go of me. They've got—let go!"

Anderson said, "Having her push the thing was the only way we could get him to agree. Besides, I don't think we have to do anything. Look at him."

John had collapsed in a corner, eyes glazed, and clearly in a state of unconscious trance.

Anderson said, "He's been terrified and that can produce a shock that will interfere with recall under normal conditions. I think the disinhibitor has been wiped out. Let her in and let *me* talk to her."

14

Susan looked pale as she sat with her arm protectively about the shoulders of her ex-fiancé. "What happened?"

"You remember the injection of—"

"Yes, yes. What happened?"

"He was supposed to come to our office day before yesterday, Sunday, for a thorough examination. He didn't come. We worried and the reports from his superiors had me very perturbed. He was becoming arrogant, megalomaniacal, irascible—perhaps you noticed. You're not wearing your engagement ring."

"We—quarreled," said Susan.

"Then you understand. He was—well, if he were an inanimate device, we might say his motor was overheating as it sped faster and faster. This morning it seemed absolutely essential to treat him. We persuaded him to come here, locked the door and—"

"Injected him with something while I howled and kicked outside."

"Not at all," said Anderson. "We would have used a sedative, but we were too late. He had what I can only describe as a breakdown. You may search his body for fresh punctures, which, as his fiancé, I presume you may do without embarrassment, and you will find none."

Susan said, "I'll see about that. What happens, now?"

"I am sure he will recover. He will be his old self again."

"Dead average?"

"He will not have perfect recall, but until ten days ago, he never had. Naturally, the firm will give him indefinite leave on full salary. If any medical treatment is required, all medical expenses will be paid. And when he feels like it, he can return to active duty."

"Yes? Well, I will want all that in writing before the day is out, or I see my lawyer tomorrow."

"But Miss Collins," said Anderson, "you know that Mr. Heath volunteered. You were willing too."

"I think," said Susan, "that *you* know the situation was misrepresented to us and that you won't welcome an investigation. Just see to it that what you've just promised is in writing."

"You will have to, in return, sign an agreement to hold us guiltless of any misadventure your fiancé may have suffered."

"Possibly. I prefer to see what kind of misadventure it is first. Can you walk, Johnny?"

John nodded and said, a little huskily, "Yes, Sue."

"Then let's go."

15

John had put himself outside a cup of good coffee and an omelet before Susan permitted discussion. Then he said, "What I don't understand is how you happened to be there?"

"Shall we say woman's intuition?"

"Let's say Susan's brains."

"All right. Let's! After I threw the ring at you, I felt self-pitying and aggrieved and after that wore off, I felt a severe sense of loss because, odd though it might seem to the average sensible person, I'm very fond of you."

"I'm sorry, Sue," said John, humbly.

"As well you should be. God, you were insupportable. But then I got to thinking that if you could get poor loving me that furious, what must you be doing to your co-workers. The more I thought about it, the more I thought they might have a strong impulse to kill you. Now, don't get me wrong. I'm willing to admit you deserved killing, but only at *my* hands. I wouldn't dream of allowing anyone else to do it. I didn't hear from you—"

"I know, Sue. I had plans and I had no time—"

"You had to do it all in two weeks. I know, you idiot. By this morning I couldn't stand it anymore. I came to see how you were and found you behind a locked door."

John shuddered. "I never thought I'd welcome your kicking and screaming, but I did then. You stopped them."

"Will it upset you to talk about it?"

"I don't think so. I'm all right."

"Then what were they doing?"

"They were going to re-inhibit me. I thought they might be giving me an overdose and make me an amnesiac."

"Why?"

"Because they knew I had them all. I could ruin them and the company."

"You really could."

"Absolutely."

"But they didn't actually inject you, did they? Or was that another of Anderson's lies?"

"They really didn't."

"Are you all right?"

"I'm not an amnesiac."

"Well, I hate to sound like a Victorian damsel, but I hope you have learned your lesson."

"If you mean, do I realize you were right, I do."

"Then just let me lecture you for one minute, so you don't forget again. You went about everything too rapidly, too openly, and with too much disregard for the possible violent counteraction of others. You had total recall and you mistook it for intelligence. If you had someone who was really intelligent to guide you—"

"I needed you, Sue."

"Well, you've got me now, Johnny."

"What do we do next, Sue?"

"First, we get that paper from Quantum and, since you're all right, we'll sign the release for them. Second, we get married on Saturday, just as we originally planned. Third, we'll see—but, Johnny?"

"Yes?"

"You're all right?"

"Couldn't be better, Sue. Now we're together, everything's fine."

16

It wasn't a formal wedding. Less formal than they had originally planned and fewer guests. No one was there from Quantum, for instance. Susan had pointed out, quite firmly, that that would be a bad idea.

A neighbor of Susan's had brought a video camera to record the proceedings, something that seemed to John to be the height of schlock, but Susan had wanted it.

And then the neighbor had said to him with a tragic shrug, "Can't get the damn thing to turn on. You'd think they'd give me one in working order. I'll have to make a phone call." He hastened down the steps to the pay phone in the chapel lobby.

John advanced to look at the camera curiously. An instruction booklet lay on a small table to one side. He picked it up and leafed through the pages with moderate speed, then put it back. He looked about him, but everyone was busy. No one seemed to be paying attention to him.

He slid the rear panel to one side, unobtrusively, and peered inside. He then turned away and gazed at the opposite wall thoughtfully. He was still gazing even as his right hand snaked in toward the mechanism and made a quick adjustment. After a brief interval he put the rear panel back and flicked a toggle switch.

The neighbor came bustling back, looking exasperated. "How am I going to follow directions I can't make head or—" He frowned, then said, "Funny. It's on. It must have been working all the time."

17

"You may kiss the bride," said the minister, benignly, and John took Susan in his arms and followed orders with enthusiasm.

Susan whispered through unmoving lips, "You fixed that camera. Why?"

He whispered back, "I wanted everything right for the wedding."

She whispered, "You wanted to show off."

They broke apart, looking at each other through love-misted eyes, then fell into another embrace, while the small audience stirred and tittered.

Susan whispered, "You do it again, and I'll skin you. As long as no one knows you still have it, no one will stop you. We'll have it all within a year, if you follow directions."

"Yes, dear," whispered Johnny, humbly.

Copyrights and Permissions